Advance ...
Wande...

"From the first page, I was all in for th... ...ul, thrilling, and romantic trip around the world. Everhart's writing is both light and cinematic, tying the reader's heartbeat to every moment of Dylan and Jack's love story."

—Annabel Monaghan, author of
Nora Goes Off Script and *Same Time Next Summer*

"*Wanderlust* is an absolutely stunning rom-com debut! Elle Everhart masterfully crafts a heartfelt and adorable love story while also delving into complex family relationships and seriously relatable real-life issues. On top of characters I immediately fell in love with, the book takes us on a gorgeous trip around the world—I was left with major travel envy! This romance had me smiling the entire time, even through my tears. Elle Everhart is a writer to watch!"

—Falon Ballard, author of *Lease on Love*
and *Just My Type*

"Elle Everhart more than delivers with a sparkling voice, mastery of craft, and character chemistry that sizzles off the page, all while unpacking the timely and critical topic of reproductive justice. Carefree yet complex Dylan and adorably uptight cinnamon roll Jack stole my heart and swept me around the world in this cinematic, immersive, steamy dream of a ride!"

—Courtney Kae, author of *In the Event of Love*

"Elle Everhart's debut is laugh-out-loud funny, sizzling hot, and full of heart. Jack and Dylan are undeniable proof that opposites do attract, and following them around the world is the great escape we all need right now!"

—Jenny L. Howe, author of *The Make-Up Test*

"*Wanderlust* is perfect for anyone who's longed to travel the globe seeking love, adventure, and even themselves. This is a soaring escapist romance that unpacks timely real-life issues and reminds us that trusting your own heart can lead to destinations unknown and unforgettable, that going away means coming back, and that the best journeys are in memories, not miles. *Wanderlust* is a book to be whisked away and enjoyed in a sun-drenched somewhere."

—Lillie Vale, author of *The Shaadi Set-Up* and *The Decoy Girlfriend*

Wanderlust

Wanderlust

A NOVEL

Elle Everhart

G. P. Putnam's Sons · New York

PUTNAM
— EST. 1838 —
G. P. PUTNAM'S SONS
Publishers Since 1838
An imprint of Penguin Random House LLC
penguinrandomhouse.com

Trade paperback ISBN: 9780593545089

Printed in the United States of America
1st Printing

Book design by Elke Sigal
Title page art: Suitcases © Tomacco / Shutterstock.com

This is a work of fiction. Names, characters, places, and
incidents either are the product of the author's imagination or are used
fictitiously, and any resemblance to actual persons, living or dead,
businesses, companies, events, or locales is entirely coincidental.

To Emmet, who makes the whole world brighter,
and to everyone who needs a reminder to be brave x

Travel isn't always pretty. It isn't always comfortable. Sometimes it hurts, it even breaks your heart. But that's okay. The journey changes you; it should change you. It leaves marks on your memory, on your consciousness, on your heart, and on your body. You take something with you. Hopefully, you leave something good behind.

—ANTHONY BOURDAIN

CHAPTER 1

Dylan Coughlan was having an absolutely shit day.

The Northern line was delayed fourteen minutes (just long enough to piss her off and one minute less than she needed to get the journey refunded), and when it finally arrived, every carriage was completely packed, so she spent the duration of her commute tucked into a stranger's armpit, which, while less offensive than it would have been on a blistering-hot day, was still not the ideal way to spend the first twenty-five minutes of her morning. That would've been bad enough—*should've* been bad enough—but some arsehole in a suit slammed into her the moment she walked out of the station and sent her £5 emergency splurge coffee flying into the window of the Hard Rock Cafe. Then, of course, Chantel, her editor, had shouted at her in no fewer than six separate emails before nine thirty, and now, she was sitting at her desk, dangerously under-caffeinated, drafting another pointless quiz.

A task that was next to impossible because, on top of everything else that had gone wrong today, her parents were now blowing up her WhatsApp. And, worse, they showed no signs of stopping.

Even her brother, Sean, though well-intentioned, was starting to grate on her nerves. He was using every bit of his training as a therapist to keep them all from going nuclear on one another (again), but it was making Dylan wish she could go home and crawl under her duvet for the next month and a half.

A solution that wouldn't be effective anyway, because—apparently—hiding from your problems didn't do anything in the way of solving them.

Dylan wouldn't say she planned on getting into rows with her parents, but if she even so much as breathed in their direction these days, they ended up arguing. Today's fight had started with the annual *so what are we doing for Christmas* conversation, which, in an impressive seven messages, devolved into her parents berating Dylan for having the audacity to make decisions they disagreed with.

Though she supposed "disagreed with" was putting it lightly.

Dylan locked her phone and flipped it over with a bit more force than was probably necessary. At the hard clack of the screen against her desktop, her deskmate, Afua, looked up, eyes wide with surprise.

"Everything alright?"

"Yeah, sorry." Dylan was lying through her teeth, and judging by the way Afua's eyes narrowed ever so slightly, Afua knew it. "Just need a cuppa. 'D you like one?"

Afua's expression immediately brightened. "Yeah, cheers."

Dylan dragged her phone off her desk and, in a show of surprising self-control, dropped it into her pocket rather than checking her messages. She was almost positive that there was at least one from her brother that was probably bearable, but Dylan didn't think she could keep reading the family chat if she wanted to retain her (basically) positive reputation in the office.

Buxom's office was like every other trendy, millennial-dominated workplace in London, although the magazine covers adorning the walls and the endless stashes of makeup, sex toys, face products, and clothes likely differentiated it from the others. She liked the open space and the feeling of being around everyone all day—having someone else to stare at, cry to, or talk things through with was instrumental when she was writing. Not that she was doing much of that these days.

Their small kitchen was tucked away in a corner behind the fire exit stairs, down a short, dark, brick-lined corridor that played a sharp contrast to the bright, open office. It had taken Dylan six months to realize this kitchen was here.

Dylan grabbed a pair of mugs off the mug tree in the corner and, after refilling the kettle, leaned back up against the cupboards.

She shouldn't check WhatsApp.

She knew she shouldn't.

The first few times Dylan's mam had spouted off, Dylan had been reduced to tears (in this very kitchen, in fact), but now, after nine months of this, she knew what to expect. It was the same line of argument, the same "points," and as much as Dylan wanted to say it didn't faze her anymore, the hard knots in her gut begged to differ.

She clicked out of the family chat without reading the most recent wall of texts and popped into her private conversation with Sean.

Dylan: nothing like a bit of family drama to spice up the morning

Typing appeared almost immediately underneath Sean's name at the top of her screen.

Sean: mam literally needs to get herself together I'm sick
   of this

Dylan exhaled, the knots in her stomach pulling tighter. It was
easy to hope that it really could be that simple. That her mother
could just . . . decide not to care about something that really wasn't
worth all this emotional turmoil.

Dylan: couldn't have put it better myself
Sean: funny, seeing as your the writer

Dylan snorted.

Dylan: *you're
Sean: asksdf piss off you know I dont care about grammar
Sean: its a social construct, etc etc
Dylan: I mean yes, but I think we can also agree you only
   think so because you were rubbish at English
Sean: I can't be good at everything dill
Sean: it'd be massively unfair
Dylan: alsjdhdiskahdka
Sean: it would be
Sean: im an adonis
Dylan: omg
Sean: god at maths
Dylan: do people LIKE people who are good at
   maths???
Sean: im basically a comedian
Sean: [replying to: do people LIKE . . .] yes. Yes they do

Dylan: right. That makes sense given how many friends
   you had at school
Sean: THAT WAS OUT OF ORDER

Dylan laughed, a deep, genuine laugh, for the first time that day.

For as long as she could remember, Sean had been the main constant in her life. They were only eleven months apart, but as children they'd moved as a duo, inseparable, as though they were actually twins. Most of her school friends hated their younger brothers, but (barring the Attempted Drowning of 1993) Dylan and Sean had always been as thick as thieves.

Dylan: somehow I think your ego will survive it
Sean: you're cruel
Dylan: that's what they tell me

Afua smiled up at Dylan as she approached, five minutes later, with their tea.

"Ah, cheers, Dylan."

Afua accepted the mug and took a sip, and Dylan tried not to drop too pathetically back into her chair.

She loved her job—really, she did—but she also knew that the people who told you they loved their job (that they *really did*) were also the same people who spent at least thirty-six of the unnecessary forty hours a week staring up at the ceiling tiles wishing everything about said job was completely different. But Dylan did love her job.

Really.

It was just that her editor was fucking sadistic.

"How's it coming along?"

Afua was eyeing her over the edge of her mug. Dylan groaned and leaned back in her chair, barely stopping herself from going full teenage angst and throwing her head back against the headrest.

"I don't know anything about astrology. Chantel just gave me this assignment to torture me."

Afua laughed softly, her box braids sliding over one shoulder as she leaned forward and set her mug down. Afua had a small coaster in front of her pen cup, a neat resting place so she didn't end up with rings and tea stains all over her desk. (The same could not be said for Dylan, whose desk looked, most days, like the recycling bin had thrown up on it.)

"I doubt she wanted to *torture* you."

"This is my payback for asking about a column again."

"Well, that might not be entirely off the mark," Afua said, "but I still think calling it torture is a bit extreme."

"You know I deal only in extremes."

Afua snorted. "Fair enough."

Dylan had thought that after writing something as popular and contentious as her March feature, she'd finally be able to have a conversation with Chantel about getting her own column without getting laughed out of the room. Dylan hadn't made it a secret that she was angling for her own column—she'd been talking about it since she joined *Buxom* three years ago after a long stint writing freelance—but she'd only brought it up three times, once for each year she'd spent languishing behind a desk here, her name scattered across the lesser pages of the magazine. The last time she'd asked had been in March, right before The Article™ had gone live, and she'd thought, finally, that she and Chantel had been getting somewhere.

"We'll see how the feature does," Chantel had said, barely even looking up at Dylan as she speed-walked—yes, she actually did this—at her treadmill desk and furiously typed on her laptop. "We'll revisit it next week."

Next week never came. Or, well, it came, but instead of rich, fulfilling conversations about her future, it was Dylan buried under her duvet at home writing harmless things about *Real Housewives* and *Made in Chelsea* without her byline in hopes the trolls would stop flooding the comments with threats.

Apparently putting her mental health, safety, and relationships on the line wasn't enough for Chantel to believe that Dylan deserved her own dedicated column in the magazine.

"You know she's going to be breathing down your neck even more if you don't get the quiz in on time." Afua paused for a second, thinking. "When's she expecting it?"

"Today."

"Fucking hell."

"Tell me about it."

Afua traced her index finger along the edge of her mug. "Is this *the* moment?"

A simple question, but Dylan knew what she meant. They'd been talking about it in hushed whispers in the kitchen, the loo, the lifts, everywhere possible for the last three years. Every time one of them got even vaguely close to snapping, it always came down to this exact same question.

Was this the moment you valued yourself more than the promise of a paycheck?

"I don't know." Dylan frowned at her computer screen, the bright white blank document blinking sharply against her retinas. "If I go in now, she'll think it's about having to write the quiz."

If Dylan was being honest, it was partially about the quiz. She knew she was a complete disappointment to the queer community because she didn't know the first thing about astrology, and this assignment wasn't going to change that. But she couldn't let Chantel think it came down to the quiz alone. They'd only leave that meeting with Chantel thinking Dylan was "not a team player." Because apparently the only way you could be a team player was by lying down on the tracks and letting Chantel drive the train over you.

"Maybe casually mention it when you send the quiz in," Afua suggested.

"Yeah." Dylan smiled gratefully. "Thank you."

"Anytime, babe."

Before she could let herself get too distracted (again), she plugged in her noise-canceling headphones and opened Radio 1's website. She didn't listen to the radio often, but there was something about letting go of control of what was playing that helped ease her mind into concentration.

Apparently, though, her bad luck wasn't finished, because the song (one of her favorites) was fading and the announcer was speaking when the site finally loaded.

"That was the latest smashing single from Little Mix off their new album. Stay tuned because we'll be back with Maisie Peters next. But before that, I know you're probably most excited about this, we're finally opening up phone lines for the Around the World contest we've been teasing all week. We're giving away a holiday around the world, and I don't know about you, but I can't think of a better way to kick off the new year. This is the biggest giveaway we've ever done, and it's all thanks to Plum Tree Hotels, whose gorgeous hotels will greet you at every destination. Get ready because we're opening up those lines now and we're looking for caller number ten!"

Dylan wondered how the host managed to talk so quickly without drawing breath.

She lined up Post-it notes on her desk and started drafting her quiz questions, half listening to the announcer telling people they hadn't won and half wondering what the hell kind of sex a Sagittarius was supposed to have.

The more she tried to rack her brain for questions, though, the more her thoughts started drifting to the vacation giveaway caller number seven had just missed out on. It would be glorious to be sitting on a beach somewhere, far away from Wi-Fi and even farther away from her family (excluding, exclusively, Sean). It was the kind of thing she'd dreamed about—fantasized about—but even her most serious thoughts had only featured a weekend away. Going around the world felt like a radical wiping clean of the slate, the perfect opportunity to finally take a deep breath and start moving forward from the hell her life had become.

Because, yes, today was particularly bad as far as her luck was concerned, but she'd had to deal with far worse over the last nine months from both the internet and her incredibly insistent parents.

The announcer clicked off the line he'd been on and said, "The next one is going to be the big one! Caller ten, what's your name?"

The person on the line screamed and Dylan frowned as she tapped the volume down a few notches.

"Susan!" The caller damn near shouted it down the line. "Susan Meyers!"

"Congratulations!" The host sounded like he was trying to beat Susan Meyers in a volume contest. "Are you ready for your holiday?"

"Absolutely!"

"Now, Susan." The host's voice became suddenly grave, and in spite of herself, Dylan tapped the volume up again. "I have to let you know there's a catch."

Susan gasped. "Oh, no. Really?"

"Yes. Do you want to hear it?"

Susan sighed heavily, and Dylan breathed a laugh. You didn't normally get this kind of overacting outside of *Emmerdale*. "Yeah, go on."

"The catch . . ."—the host sounded like he was biting back laughter now—"is you have to go on this holiday with one other person that we get to pick out of your phone." He paused for a moment to let it sink in before he said, "What do you think?"

"Oh, uh—I don't know, I—"

"Is that something you'd be open to?"

Susan was quiet for a long, painful moment before exhaling shakily. "No. There're too many risky people in my contacts."

"So you're turning down a free, around-the-world holiday?" The host sounded flabbergasted. Dylan herself had barely managed to keep her jaw from hitting the desk.

Susan's anguish was palpable as she replied. "Sounds like it."

She turned down a free holiday. A free bloody holiday. Who in their right mind . . .

"Alright, well, thanks for playing then, Susan, but it looks like we're going to have to open up those phone lines again, caller number ten, the prize is yours."

Without thinking, Dylan snatched up her phone and unlocked it, fingers fumbling as she dialed the station's number. Afua looked up, concerned at Dylan's sudden jolt into action, and Dylan smiled in a way that she hoped was more reassuring and less completely unhinged as she half slid her headphones off and pressed her phone to her ear.

She wasn't expecting anything—she wanted a free holiday, sure, and there were probably a few risky people in her contacts who should make her think twice about this whole thing, but honestly.

It wasn't like she was going to win.

The people who won these things had some sort of strategy, a plan, whereas Dylan had just picked up her bloody phone.

The phone, which had just stopped ringing.

"Thank you for calling Radio 1, we're going to whack you on hold, when Scott picks up, you'll be live on the air."

Dylan cleared her throat and grabbed her pen again, twirling it between her fingers. "Uh, okay."

"Great." The person on the line didn't even wait for Dylan to finish speaking before they clicked off.

Dylan resumed writing her quiz questions while she waited, though typing one-handed made progress slow going. She was almost in the zone when Scott came back and started picking up lines, and then Dylan's entire body went rigid.

Especially because she wasn't caller one. Wasn't caller three or six or nine.

The line went live, and suddenly, she heard Scott's voice in her ear, followed by a slight delay over her headphones. "Caller ten! What's your name?"

Dylan hastily moved her trembling fingers to mute the computer. "Hi, uh, I'm Dylan Coughlan."

Holy shit. Holy shit, holy shit, holy *shit*.

"Well, congratulations, Dylan! Did you hear about the catch with our last caller?"

Dylan nodded, though she knew they couldn't see her. "Yes. And you can pick whoever you like out of my phone," she said, breathing a laugh so shaky it was probably a solid seven on the Richter scale.

"Brilliant! So, Dylan, you're going around the world! How do you feel?"

"A— Well, a little shocked, actually."

The announcer laughed. "Naturally. Okay, well, Dylan, congratulations again. I'm going to put you on hold so you can chat with our producer about what's going to happen next, alright?"

Dylan opened up WhatsApp on her computer, clicked on her conversation with her best friend, Gwen, and typed out a quick message.

I.......won a radio contest???????

CHAPTER 2

"Congratulations again, Ms. Coughlan."

An hour later Alan, the producer she'd spoken to on the phone, was leading Dylan through the Radio 1 office in Portland Place. It was a bright, open-plan space not unlike her own, and the similarity helped her pulse settle from the rapid staccato it'd been beating against her throat.

After she had hung up her phone, she'd more or less run in to Chantel's office and said, voice very much trembling, that she was taking an early lunch. Whether Chantel had thought Dylan was in the midst of yet another crisis or what, Dylan didn't know, but Chantel hadn't questioned it, which was the best possible outcome where her boss was concerned. Dylan'd been hoping for a long chat with her best friend, Gwen, on the walk over, but Dylan had barely gotten the full story out before Gwen needed to run back onto the ward because one of her kids was "super tachy today" and his monitor was, once again, throwing off alarm bells.

It put Dylan's life into very harsh perspective, Gwen's job.

"You can call me Dylan."

Alan smiled absently. "Of course."

They walked the rest of the way in silence before pausing in front of a door with a large, red **On Air** sign illuminated overhead.

There was a viewing window cut into the wall, and Alan waved to someone behind the glass before he opened the door.

Despite the window and the bright overhead lights, the studio was much darker than the main office. The walls were slate gray, but the space was saved from looking like a tomb by the neon posters lining the walls featuring musicians who'd appeared at the station. A redheaded man was sitting behind a massive desk that spanned nearly the whole width of the room. There were five computer monitors in a semicircle facing him, and even from the doorway, Dylan could see a number of keyboards and sound-mixing machines. She had no idea how anyone worked at that desk and knew what they were doing.

"Scott," Alan said, stepping inside, "this is Dylan. Your contest winner."

Scott removed his headphones and stood, hand extended over the computers. "Dylan, nice to meet you. I'd walk around, but . . ." He gestured down at the clutter.

Dylan grinned as she shook his hand. "No problem. Nice to meet you, too."

Alan rapped on the doorframe. "I'll let you two get on with it. Oh, and . . ." He held out a packet of papers to Scott, who took them, briefly skimming the top sheet. "These are for her to sign before she leaves."

Her. As though Dylan weren't standing literally a foot from him.

Scott nodded. "Of course."

Dylan raised her hand in halfhearted farewell as Alan pulled the door shut behind him.

"This is your contract," Scott said, holding up the packet.

"We'll go over it before you leave. It's standard stuff. I'll have Mina, our intern, make a copy for you and grab you a pair of— Ah, thanks, Mina."

Mina had slid out from behind a door Dylan hadn't seen and handed her a pair of headphones. Mina was small, at least half a foot shorter than Dylan, and looked as though she couldn't have been a day older than eighteen. Her dark brown eyes were lined in electric-blue eyeliner and her jagged black bob nearly faded into the perfectly worn leather jacket she had draped over her shoulders. Dylan had never looked even half as cool.

Dylan smiled in thanks, but Mina's lips only twitched and threatened a return smile that never materialized.

"You'll plug in there"—Scott pointed at a headphone jack underneath Dylan's massive microphone—"and we can get started. Have you ever been on radio before?"

"Nope. First time."

Scott clapped his hands together before he adjusted his headphones so one ear was covered again. "Well, this'll be great, I swear. We'll start by talking a bit about who you are, then we'll give Mina your contacts and jump into some more music." Scott raised his eyebrows. "You ready?"

Dylan pulled her headphones on. "Ready."

Scott began talking before the song finished fading over the airwaves. It was disconcerting, hearing his voice playing over her headphones at a rate that was slightly behind Scott in real time.

"Welcome back to Radio 1. We'll have some more hits in a few minutes, but now, we've got a treat for you." Scott met Dylan's gaze between the monitors. "I'm in the studio with Dylan, our Radio 1 Around the World contest winner. How are ya, Dylan?"

"I'm alright." If it was strange hearing Scott's voice over her headphones, it was even weirder hearing her own.

Scott tipped his head to the side with concern. She must have had some kind of expression on her face.

"Bit shaken?"

"No." Dylan consciously relaxed her features. "Surprised. Didn't expect this this morning."

"Didn't expect to win?"

"Didn't even expect to call in."

"What changed your mind?"

"Well, when the first winner decided not to play contact roulette I thought"—she shrugged—"ah, well. Might as well give it a go. I could use the holiday."

Scott laughed. "It's a bloody good holiday, so I can't fault you. Why don't you tell us a bit about you, Dylan?"

She hated these questions. She never knew what to say.

"I live in London, but I'm from Liverpool—"

Scott laughed again. "Didn't have to tell us that, love." He accented "love" especially hard like it was some kind of in-joke between them, and Dylan suppressed the urge to roll her eyes.

"Once a Scouser, always a Scouser. But yeah, I live in London now, and I write for *Buxom*."

"Oh, *Buxom*." Scott's voice had that same slyly interested tone everyone got when she said she worked there, but Dylan ignored the invitation to start talking about every remotely sexual piece she'd penned in the last three years.

"I love it. It's really interesting work."

"I'll bet it is. But down to business." Scott held his hand out. "You ready to let us choose your travel companion?"

Dylan swallowed and tried her best to smother her nerves with a joke. "As long as you promise not to choose someone horrible."

She passed her phone between the monitors and tried not to show the anxiety pitching in her gut as Scott scrolled through her contacts.

"You've got loads of contacts here." Scott eyed her. "You swear you didn't sneakily delete any on the way over?"

"I never erase contacts." Honestly, she hadn't even considered it. Maybe that was foolish, but she'd been far too distracted talking with Gwen and then obsessing over where they might send her. "You never know when you might need someone's details."

"I hear that." Scott handed her phone to Mina. "Alright, so, Dylan, Mina, our intern, will enter your contacts into a list so we can put them in the randomizer and pick out your travel buddy."

Dylan nodded and, remembering she was on radio, leaned forward to speak. "Alright."

Scott raised an eyebrow. "Feeling nervous?"

Dylan shook her head. "Not really. I think we would make a good time of it, me and whoever I end up traveling with."

As soon as she said it, she had a nightmare vision of having to travel with her mother—or, god, *worse*, Chantel—and she wished she could take back the words in case she'd just fantastically jinxed herself.

"Well, that's exciting to hear, Dylan, almost as exciting"—Dylan heard a bit of music start in the background—"as 'Funky Friday' from Dave, on the airwaves for you now, then we've got a bit of Ava Max. We'll be back before the ten." The "on air" light overhead switched off as Scott leaned back in his seat. "Mina's quick. We should have the list before break's out. Did Alan explain how this'll go?"

Alan had said about five words to her their entire walk through the office, and most of them had been in this room.

"Not really."

Scott hummed, the sound tight. "So we have the randomizer. If they say no, we'll pull another name. You're not going to lose out because someone isn't willing to go with you."

"Good to know."

At that moment, Mina walked back in, laptop in one hand and Dylan's phone in the other. She handed Dylan her phone, muttering, "I like your phone case," before she sat the laptop on Scott's left.

"Here's the list," Mina said, scrolling her fingers over the trackpad. "Tap that button and you've got your name."

Scott grinned. "Brilliant, thank you. You want to work the board?"

Mina's eyes lit up. "Yeah, that'd be mint."

Scott and Mina spent the next minute going over the board—which buttons did what, how to bleep things out ("We probably won't need to use that," Scott said, "but just in case"), and how to end the call without making the line ring over the airwaves.

Mina's fingers moved lightly over the board in front of her, an almost reverential look on her face, as the song they were playing started to come to an end. That seemed to act as a signal because Mina's back went rigid, and she looked down at the controls with laser focus.

Scott turned back to Dylan. "You ready?"

And even though she hadn't been lying when Scott had asked

her if she was okay, his question tapped into that peak of energy that had pitched in her stomach before. She wasn't sure—and her uncertainty made her feel all sorts of ways—if this feeling was genuine nervousness or, maybe, if it was just excitement.

"Absolutely."

Scott nodded once, and Dylan watched as his expression became all business, his tone sliding back into his radio voice as he leaned closer to the microphone. "Welcome back to Radio 1, I'm here with Dylan, our Around the World contest winner. We're about to choose Dylan's traveling partner. How're you feeling, Dylan?"

"Excited to see who I'm going with."

"Anyone you're hoping for?"

"Well, my best friend told me I better pick her." Dylan smiled at the memory, Gwen shouting it down the phone an hour before as she rushed along the ward. "She's an NHS nurse, so she could use the break."

Scott grinned. "I hope we manage to select her, then. Let's go ahead and run this, eh?"

"Seal my fate."

Suspenseful music whispered down the line, and Dylan fought the wave of emotion building in her chest. She felt like she was balancing on a knife's edge, and the adrenaline was making her a bit light-headed.

"Okay." Scott looked up at her, his eyes bright. "We've got your name."

The music swelled and Dylan nearly swallowed her tongue.

"You're going on your trip with—and this is the name Dylan entered into her contacts, before anyone tries to start—'Jack the Posho'!" Scott let that sink in for a beat. "Any idea if he'll say yes?"

"I—" Dylan shook her head. Despite the immediate relief that Scott hadn't said someone horrible, the anxiety was rapidly building again. "I have no idea who that is."

"Oh, really?"

She shrugged, a pathetic attempt at seeming calm. "No clue. It's possible we met at a work thing, but I don't think I've spoken to a Jack recently."

She probably wouldn't have remembered even if she had. Her work events were always a rush of meeting people she never thought about again. Much like her early twenties.

"Could it be an old contact?"

"It'd have to be."

"Well, let's see if we can get this posho on the line, eh?"

Scott was looking at her, but Dylan wasn't sure what she was supposed to say to that. She cleared her throat and nodded, her fingers fumbling with her phone so she could get his contact info up. "Yeah, alright."

Dylan handed the phone back to Mina, and after a beat, the soft sound of the dial tone started on the airwaves. The volume knocked up a few notches as the line began to ring.

It rang once, twice, and was about to ring a third time when someone picked up.

"Jack Hunton." The moment she heard his voice, Dylan knew it sounded familiar. She couldn't place it, but the smooth, posh accent, the mid-tone sound . . .

Where the hell did she know him from?

Scott grinned. "Is this Jack the Posho?"

There was a heavy, protracted silence. "This is Jack Hunton."

"Well, are you posh, Jack?"

Dylan wasn't sure why Scott even needed to ask. Jack's accent alone was proof enough he'd probably gone to the Royal Ascot this year.

Jack was quiet for another beat before he cleared his throat, the sound the audio equivalent of haughtily straightening a tie and turning up your nose.

"I've been told I'm posh, yes."

"Great." Scott beamed at Dylan, and Dylan fought the urge to give him the world's most sarcastic thumbs-up. "This must be you, then. I'm Scott from Radio 1—"

"Ah." Jack sounded slightly more relaxed now. "I thought I recognized your voice."

"Regular listener, Jack?"

"Not if I can help it." Jack's tone was devastatingly dry. Audible grit paper. Dylan smiled in spite of herself and quickly bit her lip so Scott didn't see.

Scott sucked in a breath through his teeth, but Dylan didn't miss the flush of amusement on his face. "Harsh."

Jack hummed noncommittally. Scott paused to give him space to say something, but Jack, apparently, didn't feel the need to fill the silence.

Scott cleared his throat. "Anyway, Jack, you might be wondering why we've called. I've got Dylan here—"

"Dylan?"

There was a note of recognition in his voice, and Dylan's brow furrowed. How the fuck could he remember her when she didn't have the slightest idea who he was?

Scott caught her eye. "So, *you* know Dylan."

Scott's emphasis made it completely clear that Dylan had no idea who Jack was prior to ringing him up a few minutes ago. And Jack, wonderfully, didn't miss the subtext.

"We met at a club a few months back," Jack said. Though his tone was bored, there was an obvious tension there. "Classic boy meets girl."

Despite the fact that "classic boy meets girl" had never described anything in Dylan's life that she could remember, she did feel something start tugging at the very back of her memory. The last few people she'd met out, though, had been women, and even then, they hadn't met in a club. The last time she'd been in a club—

Scott's eyes brightened. "So, she's an old flame?"

Dylan opened her mouth to say something, she didn't know what, but Jack beat her to it. She was about to be thankful she didn't have to attempt to cobble a sentence together when she heard Jack's reply.

"Nope. She never called. I had the restaurant picked out and everything."

I had the restaurant picked out.

As he said it, a vivid memory flooded in. Sweaty bodies vibrating on the dance floor, the thrum of music tickling her skin, the flash of neon lights in her eyes.

She knew who he was now.

Bright blue eyes. Dark, ruffled hair. A shade of stubble along his sharp jaw, and a too-gorgeous smile as she ribbed him for daring to talk to her with that boarding school accent.

The man she'd met the night her life had gone to absolute hell.

"Yikes, mate. Well, she's called now, hasn't she?"

"And with a bit more than a restaurant, I presume."

Dylan thought, or maybe she hoped, that Jack sounded slightly amused now.

"You presume correctly." Scott's voice was all business again. "Dylan's won a holiday around the world, courtesy of our generous sponsors over at Plum Tree Hotels. Together, you'll be traveling to nine cities around the world, complete with hotel accommodations and local guides and activities to make your experience once-in-a-lifetime."

Scott paused, waiting for Jack to fill the silence with excitement or awe.

After a long, tense beat, Jack cleared his throat. "Okay."

"This could be your second chance to sweep her off her feet," Scott said. He was grinning now, and Dylan wanted to tear off her headphones and run out of the room. "Skip those awkward first dates and jump right into the romantic getaway."

The silence rang heavily over the line for a beat, two, Jack apparently not intrigued enough by the premise to reply, and Dylan too busy gulping air like a flounder to attempt a response.

"So what do you think, Jack?" Scott continued. "You interested in a trip around the world with our Dylan here?"

Jack was quiet for a second before he sighed heavily into the phone. "Fuck it. Why not?"

He barely got the "F—" out before Mina, her fingers rapping hard against the board, blanked out the rest for the broadcast.

CHAPTER 3

"Jack Hunton? Who is that?" Gwen swirled her chip through a healthy amount of ketchup before tipping her head back to drop it into her mouth.

Slightly questionable table manners aside, Gwen Pierce was a real-life Cinderella. She already had it locked down with her stunning turquoise eyes, flowing blond hair, and bright shining laugh, but then her parents, because they'd either had a moment of impressive foresight or had somehow altered the future, went and named her Gwendolen and her fate was sealed. She was doomed— "doomed"—to a life of everyone assuming cartoon birds dressed her every morning.

Gwen insisted that her parents had actually named her after that character in *Daniel Deronda*, but Dylan knew, one, they probably hadn't read *Daniel Deronda* because no one, outside of people foolish enough to do a literature course at university (e.g., Dylan), had read it, and two, if they *had* somehow read it, they definitely wouldn't have named her after Gwendolen Harleth because, as Dylan had said, *If they were going to name you after a tragic Victorian, there are way more interesting options than Gwendolen Harleth*.

"Well, you wouldn't have known his full name. He was 'Jack the Posho' in my phone." Dylan speared a bit of chicken and put it into her mouth, groaning at the absolute triumph that was Nando's Extra Hot Peri-Peri Sauce. The heat of the chilies made her tongue feel like it was vibrating and the sharp lemon juice brought a touch of brightness to the flavor. She would literally eat a boot if it was slathered in this sauce.

"Oh my god." Gwen covered her mouth with the back of her hand. "Is that how they addressed him when he answered?"

"Yup. He was thrilled."

Gwen grabbed another chip, amusement clear on her face. "I'll bet."

In the aftermath of her sudden stint on the BBC, Dylan had texted Gwen and begged—I know you "cook at home" because you're "on your savings grind" but please god can I order us a Nando's I'm in need and also I'll buy

Gwen, thankfully, sent back a string of laugh/crying emojis and one short message.

Lemon and herb pls xx

Gwen didn't get off work until seven, and while the last thing Dylan wanted to do was go back to her desk and pretend nothing had changed, she still had a long list of things to do and five hours she was contractually obligated to attempt them. She was uncharacteristically focused through the rest of the afternoon—to the point where Afua even asked her if she was alright a few times—so, by the time she was slinging her coat on a few minutes after five, she'd managed to finish her quiz and write several terrible clues for the crossword. She'd even forced herself to write a Very Professional Email to Chantel informing her of her upcoming travel and requesting a meeting to *discuss how it might fit in with her writing work over the next few months.*

Dylan had swiftly busied herself when she got home, if only to keep from staring at her inbox. She put through their Deliveroo order, fed Gwen's very annoying (read: very lovable) cat, Cat Stevens, and made herself so many cups of tea that, by the time Gwen walked through the door at half seven, Dylan was nearly vibrating out of her skin.

"It was so awkward," Dylan said, popping another bite of chicken into her mouth. "Scott was all, 'So, *you* know Dylan,' and it could not have been plainer that I didn't have the slightest clue who he was, which, by the way, I'd confirmed on air before they rang him, and then this fucking arsehole—" She took a quick drink of her water. "On the radio, this arsehole tells everyone that he'd asked me out and then he goes, 'She never called. I had the restaurant picked out and everything.'"

Gwen snorted but quickly covered her smile when Dylan glared at her.

"That's not funny."

"Right. Not funny."

Dylan's glare intensified.

Gwen ignored her. "Where did you meet this guy anyway?"

"Remember last March when we went to Veil?" As it always did whenever the subject of conversation ventured close to The Day, Dylan's voice went ultracasual in a way that perfectly conveyed the exact opposite.

"Mm-hmm."

"Well, he was the bloke you found me wrapped around before

we left." She wished "wrapped around" was an overstatement, but it was, devastatingly, the most accurate description she could think of.

They'd gone out that night to celebrate the publication of Dylan's article—a bright-eyed decision that had the twofold intention of congratulating Dylan for writing (in her humble opinion) the best piece of her career and keeping Dylan from staring at the article's stats and comments for the entire evening. She'd been leaning up against the bar, nursing a gin and tonic while Gwen danced circles around some guy on the dance floor, when she realized that someone—Jack—was standing next to her.

She hadn't meant to end their brief interaction with their mouths pressed together like she was trying to breathe life into him, but he'd made her laugh and he'd run with her "posho" joke when he'd entered his name into her phone, giving himself the title after she'd refused to stop teasing him about it and, well . . .

Gwen thought for a moment before her lips widened with a smile. "He was fucking fit."

"I know." Dylan hadn't meant to sound so tragic, but there it was.

"Look . . ." Gwen sighed, and her softer, gentler tone was clearly supposed to bring Dylan back from the cliff she was on. "I'm sure he wasn't as offended as he sounded. You met in a club. You knew him for five minutes."

"He didn't sound *not* offended."

"Maybe he was playing it up for the radio?"

"By making me look like a complete dick?" She grabbed one of Gwen's chips and swiped it through ketchup. "That's worse."

"I doubt you sounded like a dick." Gwen slid her plate closer as

Dylan reached for another chip. "And if people think you're a dick because you didn't call some random man you met in a club, then they can go fuck themselves."

Dylan laughed, covering her mouth just in time to avoid spraying Gwen with ketchup.

When they'd finished eating, Dylan gathered up their mostly empty containers and Gwen reached out and put her hand on Dylan's forearm. "Wait, let me help you."

She tried to take her container out of Dylan's hand, but Dylan just moved farther out of Gwen's reach. "No, I'll clean up. You've had a long day."

"So did you."

Dylan rolled her eyes. "Please, you were gone before I even woke up this morning. Just go get a shower."

Dylan walked into the kitchen, and Cat Stevens slunk in behind her, meowing and weaving between Dylan's legs. She laughed, setting the takeaway containers on the island. "Hi, Stevie."

He meowed again, louder this time, and Dylan rolled her eyes before scratching one of his ears.

"You can't have this. It'll hurt your tummy."

He continued weaving in and out of her legs as she packed away the leftover chicken, his meows getting louder the more she ignored him.

Cat Stevens nudged his nose against her calf, and Dylan sighed, running her hand over his back and shaking the fur on her hand off onto the floor. "You already ate. I'm not feeding you again."

She would swear on her life this cat understood English, because, at her words, he finally skated out from between her legs and, tail swishing angrily, stalked off into the lounge and planted himself in front of one of the windows to watch the pigeons.

Those windows were a big part of why Cat Stevens had adjusted to the flat so easily when they'd moved over the summer. It hadn't been a, uh, *planned* move, but one necessitated by the fact that some arsehole had doxxed Dylan (and, thus, Gwen) across every single corner of the internet. She'd hoped, foolishly, that they could have stayed in their old flat, but it'd become almost immediately clear that people had, in fact, seen her address and taken it upon themselves to make her life absolute hell.

Dylan had urged Gwen to move out, to at least get herself away from the chaos, but Gwen had made it clear that she wasn't going anywhere.

"If you think I'm abandoning you now," Gwen'd said, the pair of them huddled on the sofa, Dylan sobbing into her neck, "you're an idiot."

It had taken a bit of searching, but, in a stroke of what Dylan liked to jokingly think of as divine intervention, they'd managed to find a flat even more gorgeous than the one they'd been forced out of.

It was open plan, something uncommon in older buildings. Their landlord and her wife had been on something of a *Grand Designs* binge and ended up knocking down most of the interior walls when they'd first bought the place. The front door opened right onto the kitchen—there was a wall of cabinets, the oven, the refrigerator, and their washing machine to the right as you walked in—and there was a massive kitchen island that they used instead of attempting to squeeze in a proper kitchen table. The rest of the space looked a bit sparse—other than a set of stools at the island, they only had a small sofa, a winged armchair, and a bookshelf in the lounge. Their bedrooms were off to the left with their shared bathroom in the center, and there were massive windows along all the exterior walls, so during the day, the flat was flooded with light.

Not that Dylan was ever home often enough to properly enjoy it (or that London was ever that sunny), but the view was nice.

Dylan switched off the lights in the kitchen before making her way to her bedroom. There was just the barest glow from the streetlamp arching across the desk she had shoved in the corner between the wall and her chest of drawers, but rather than switch on the overhead, she walked across her room, careful to avoid the scatter of shoes across her rug, to switch on her bedside lamp.

Her room wasn't a *disaster*, at least, not if you asked Dylan. Sure, she still hadn't picked up her socks from the day before and her desk was covered in balls of crumpled paper, but it made her room feel more lived-in than Gwen's borderline sterile room across the hall.

Secretly, Dylan aspired to the level of cleanliness Gwen managed naturally, but she figured there was no sense fighting this part of herself after twenty-eight years.

Dylan tossed her mobile onto her duvet and kicked off her slippers, frowning as one flew underneath her bed. She should probably ring her brother (she'd promised she would on the way home that afternoon), but she needed a minute to breathe and a nice long shower before she could even think about that again.

She'd just thrown her jumper in the vague direction of her desk chair when her mobile lit up. She glanced down, half expecting it to be Sean (he had an uncanny ability to call her just as she was thinking about him) and, instead, felt her heart claw its way into her throat.

Chantel was ringing her.

Chantel had only ever called her twice—once to offer her the job three years ago and once in March to let her know that the comments had been disabled on all her articles and she should seriously consider not coming in to work for a few weeks because of the "disturbing number of anonymous threats we've received."

Dylan was pretty sure it was none of those things—they hadn't received a threat to the office in months, though, of course, Dylan was still getting them every once in a while in her DMs—but it didn't stop her heart from hammering and her throat from tightening as she accepted the call.

CHAPTER 4

"Hi, Chantel. How are you?"

Chantel ignored her question.

"Listen, Dylan, I got your email. Do you have a few minutes to chat?"

Fucking hell.

Dylan hummed, the sound a little more high-pitched than normal, as she started pacing back and forth across the limited space in her room. "Yeah, of course."

"I have a few notes about the quiz questions, those are in your inbox, and then I've also suggested you reach out to Thom about the quiz mechanics because I think some of the responses aren't coded correctly."

It was hilarious how swiftly Dylan swung from terrified to totally annoyed.

"Mm-hmm."

"But the main reason I'm calling is because I wanted to talk to you about this trip. I wasn't even aware radio contests were a thing anymore."

She sounded skeptical, like she thought Dylan'd planned a two-month holiday and then needed a last-minute lie to get the time off work.

"I wasn't, either," Dylan said. "But yeah, it's that contest Radio 1 was running."

"Right, I had Steph send me the details. They posted on their Instagram that you're going with a 'Jack'? How do you two know each other?"

If there was an easy way to talk to your boss about someone you'd once drunkenly snogged, Dylan didn't know it.

"We, uh, met on a night out a few months ago. I don't know him really."

Her embarrassment was so thick, Dylan's words kept getting stuck in it.

"'A night out.'" The spark of intrigue in Chantel's voice made Dylan immediately nervous. "So this is a second-chance romance, then?"

Dylan nearly choked on her tongue.

"I don't know about *romance*—"

"This is a brilliant opportunity. Might finally lead to your column."

Dylan felt her entire body go still.

"My column?"

"There's an opportunity here," Chantel said, her tone the lofty, imperious one she used in meetings when she was trying to make it seem like she was gracing them all with her presence and opinions. "Readers love stories about people finding their way back to each other. I know you've been hoping to have your own column for a while, and until now, I haven't thought you were ready for the responsibility."

Dylan gritted her teeth to keep from snapping out a retort she'd absolutely regret.

"But this could be a chance to get your feet wet. Test the waters and see what kind of readership you get. With something this hot, it shouldn't be difficult. A surprise reunion on a romantic holiday? This is gold."

Dylan physically cringed. As much as she wanted to argue with Chantel's framing, there was something a little more pressing Dylan needed to understand first.

"This sounds like it wouldn't be a permanent column then. Just something for the duration of my trip?" It took all Dylan's effort to keep her voice even, curious instead of outright accusatory.

"Whether or not you kept your column—and whether or not we add it to the magazine—would be dependent on how well your travel stories do on the dot com."

Dylan hummed in acknowledgment but, otherwise, didn't say anything as she let that sink in.

On the one hand, it was absolutely outrageous that Chantel was expecting Dylan to prove herself even further. That Chantel couldn't find the evidence over the last year—hell, even over the last month alone—to prove that Dylan was consistently getting engagement. Dylan could probably demonstrate it right now if she had five minutes.

But this was how Chantel worked. For better or worse (and it was mostly worse), you needed to prove yourself ten thousand times before you got even the slightest bit of praise out of her. It was frustrating and made it feel impossible to keep coming to work sometimes, but Dylan also knew her boss was somehow still producing a thriving magazine in a market that was barely interested in print media anymore.

There were still nicer ways to go about running things, and Dylan would absolutely argue that to the ends of the earth, but at least there were results. At least they still had jobs.

The same could definitely not be said for some of Dylan's friends at other magazines.

As annoyed as she was at having to clear this last hurdle, Dylan couldn't deny that this seemed like . . . well, not a perfect solution, but a decent one. If Chantel was going to ask her to write the series, then Chantel must be agreeing to her time spent out of the office, and if Dylan managed to pull numbers (which, not to toot her own horn, she knew she definitely would), she'd end this holiday with the one thing that she'd been working toward for the last three years.

It would be a bit awkward pretending it was some kind of couple's holiday, but maybe she could just . . . ease her way around that until it became clear she and Jack had zero chemistry and Chantel dropped it altogether.

"I think that sounds reasonable," Dylan said, somehow managing to keep the sarcasm out of her voice. "We haven't gotten our itinerary yet, but I think an article about each location makes sense. Maybe a few preparation articles—winning the contest, packing, and then a conclusion article, you know, wrapping up the experience. . . ."

"Okay, great, just make sure you include all the sexy details. That's what people will really be after."

Before Dylan could say that she didn't think there would be any *sexy details*, Chantel barreled on.

"You'll have to talk with HR tomorrow about organizing the

time out of the office, but I'll send Denice an email to let her know you're coming and we've already talked."

"Alright. But, quickly, in terms of the numbers . . ." She needed to word this delicately. "What kind of engagement would it take for me to get a permanent column? I have pretty steady numbers now and have done for a while."

So much for delicate.

"Well, to be honest, Dylan"—ah, Chantel's *I'm making this bollocks up right on the spot* tone—"an uptick in your numbers would be great. The engagement we had on the dot com after your big article was excellent, but there was definitely a downward trend in the months after that."

"Well, people stopped coming to the website to tell me to kill myself," Dylan said. She hadn't really meant to say it like that, but it was true. Still, she should probably salvage the point. "My clicks were down, but I think if you compared the engagement ratios, it's not a significant difference—"

"Either way. We obviously don't want you receiving a lot of negative attention, that was really hard on us."

Harder on Dylan, she'd wager, but she supposed it wasn't a competition.

"But to your question, I think if we could get a twenty percent increase in traffic by the end of the series, the column is yours."

Twenty percent.

It was a lot—she was already doing well—but it wasn't impossible.

And, actually, coupled with some of the things the station was asking her to do . . .

"That sounds doable," Dylan said. "And it would be a column in the magazine, right? With a companion column on the dot com?"

She might as well ask for the fucking stars now.

Chantel was quiet for so long that Dylan actually checked to make sure the line hadn't dropped.

"If you can manage twenty percent, then, yes."

Oh my god.

Dylan's heart throbbed in the back of her throat. She had rings of energy zinging around her body and she shook her free hand in an effort to release some of it so she didn't dance right out of her skin.

She'd have to summarize all this into an email back to Chantel so she actually had everything in writing, but holy fucking shit, this. *This.*

This was everything she'd ever wanted.

Minus the *having to pretend she was in a rom-com* part, but she could write her way through that.

"Excellent." She sat down slowly on her bed, tucking her right foot underneath her. "Thank you, Chantel."

Dylan didn't think she needed to be thanking her, seeing as Dylan would be the one putting all the work in, but she knew Chantel was expecting it.

"Oh, Dylan, it's really no trouble." They were quiet for a beat, though Dylan couldn't work out what it was Chantel wanted her to say. Finally, Chantel cleared her throat. "Well, I'll let you get on with your evening. See you tomorrow."

And, without any further preamble, Chantel rang off.

In something of a haze, Dylan let her mobile fall back down onto the duvet.

"Holy fucking shit."

If she'd made a prediction about how this day would've gone, she never, in a million years, would've guessed this. Well, she would have guessed the part about a hellish commute and having another row with her parents, that was standard by now, but a column? Or the chance at a column? Because she'd won a fucking holiday?

Part of her was irritated that this trip was what it had taken for Chantel to finally put a bit of faith in her—a freak opportunity that literally no one could have predicted—but it didn't annoy her enough to push back. It was going to take an immense amount of work, but Dylan was confident in what she wrote and she didn't have to grow twenty percent on one article alone.

As resistant as she was to masquerade this as some kind of sexy reunion trip, Dylan had to admit that it was a good pitch. She didn't even have to lean into it too hard: She was genuinely nervous about leaving, and could play that up, and it was easy enough to take advantage of her saying, on air, she hadn't the slightest clue who he was. She'd keep it confined to her own awkwardness as much as possible, though, and she was definitely going to have to get a vibe off Jack to figure out how to play it once they were traveling together. He hadn't seemed that enthusiastic on the phone, but based on the way he'd been talking to Scott, he probably would've said if he didn't really want to go. He'd just sounded so . . . out of sorts, especially when he was talking about how she hadn't called him. Like he was still bothered by it, even months later.

Dylan didn't owe him anything—and, good thing, because he

wasn't going to get anything from her—but it still made her nervous, going into this trip with literally no way to predict how it would go. In normal circumstances, she might have thought that was a bit of added fun, but she needed this break from her life, and even more, she needed this column.

She clicked into WhatsApp before she could talk herself out of it and scrolled down to Jack the Posho in her contacts. When the chat screen appeared, her fingers hovered over the keys for a few seconds before she finally tapped something out and hit SEND.

so...... You excited for our holiday?

The double ticks turned blue almost as soon as she sent the message, but Jack didn't start typing right away. After a full minute of staring, a little too intensely, at her screen, she locked her phone and tossed it to the end of her bed.

She wasn't going to wait for him to text her back. That was pathetic to the highest degree.

Still, her phone was within her direct line of sight, so she noticed the moment it lit up with a notification.

And she *might* have scrambled to snatch it up again.

I don't know if "excited" is the right word.

Well, that's not the response she was expecting. She had half a mind to close out WhatsApp, leave him on read, and forget about it.

But she was going to have to sit next to this man in a three-by-three-millimeter airplane seat in, like, less than a month, so she should probably try and establish some kind of relationship with him.

Teasing him within an inch of his life had worked the first time they met, so maybe it would work again this time.

> Dylan: wow I'm thrilled to be travelling with you, you're so good at building excitement 😃
>
> Jack: I have too many things going on at the moment to be excited about something that has actually made things quite a bit more difficult for me.

Dylan's brow furrowed. How could a holiday make anyone's life more difficult, let alone a free holiday? Sure, sometimes things were a bit wild when you came back to them, but not before. The whole point of going on a holiday was to escape the difficult things, not multiply them.

> Dylan: you didn't have to accept the invitation if you didn't want to come
>
> Jack: I don't need the reminder that I've gone and screwed up my own life, thanks.

What. The. Hell.

She hadn't meant it rudely, just as a reminder that he was the one who'd signed up for this. Yes, she'd rung him up, but he'd been completely within his rights to say no. And, honestly, if he was going to be this doom and gloom about it, she wished he *had* said no. There was no way that he was going to be any fun to travel around with if even the idea of leaving was sending him into anxious spirals.

She frowned down at her screen for another long moment before she huffed a sigh and typed out one final message.

well on that happy note, I'll leave you to your evening.

Any satisfaction she felt about that *very* passive-aggressive full stop at the end went completely out the window when he left her on read.

CHAPTER 5

Despite Dylan's best attempts, things between her and Jack didn't exactly improve as they crept closer toward the new year.

She reached out a few times, just about simple things, but every "conversation" was so terse and difficult and one-sided that Dylan gave up by the time they hit the five-text mark.

23 DECEMBER—18.47

Dylan: roughly how big of a bag are you bringing so I can plan accordingly and not look completely unhinged

Jack: https://www.britishairways.com/en-gb/information/ baggage-essentials/checked-baggage-allowances

Dylan: ....

Dylan: I could have done that

Jack: And yet.

28 DECEMBER—13.09

Dylan: did you get the itinerary Mina sent over

Jack: Yes.

Dylan: .....what did you think? Seems cool, though, tbh, I don't know how closely I'll want to follow an itinerary

Jack: There's no point in us having an itinerary if you're not going to stick to it, Dylan.

Dylan: you really like to live life on the edge don't you?

✓✓ [Read]

She could just imagine Jack sitting in his very posh West London flat, surrounded by half-empty bottles of *champers* and laughing manically about how he was driving her completely mad. In her mind, he looked like the demonic love child of Jacob Rees-Mogg and the Monopoly man, all twirling mustache and infuriating accent and deeply ingrained sense of entitlement.

It seemed impossible that *this* was someone she'd connected with, however fleetingly, on a night out. That she'd seen him and gone *yeah, he'll do* and borderline kissed the life out of him up against the bar. It must have been the evening, the combination of *I absolutely cannot check my notifications, but I really want to check my notifications* stress and utter euphoria at having done something she was deeply proud of and, alright, a drink or two. But no amount of alcohol seemed like enough to convince her that kissing someone this aggravating was a good idea. At least, not now that she was approaching her thirties. She'd rather not think about some of the people she'd kissed when she was at uni.

Dylan knew that she should be rational, that they should meet up and get to know each other before they were stuck together for the better part of two months. But, honestly, if he was going to act like he'd rather chew glass and then go lay in the middle of the M25 than text her, Dylan didn't feel even the least bit inclined to spend any more time with him than she was already going to have to. The full stops on his messages *alone* had sent Dylan into more than one ranting fit, but it was his complete lack of excitement, his lack of any emotion really, that had Dylan deeply dreading their upcoming trip.

Which pissed her off because this trip was the first thing she'd been excited about in a while.

Still, she tried to rally some positive spirit as December bled into January. She went up to Birmingham to see her brother after Christmas, went radio silent in the family group chat in hopes of drowning out her mother's complaints that, for the first time ever, Dylan hadn't gone to Liverpool for the family celebration despite *clearly needing the time in confession*, and wrote a brief series of introductory articles for the travel series that, okay, hadn't quite created the initial stir she'd been hoping for, but a few people were excited, so she still counted it as a win.

Sure, all their comments had been about how deliciously awkward it would be to be sent around the world with a one-night stand—Jack wasn't even technically a one-night stand, but Dylan could forgive the mistake after the first tagline Chantel insisted on, "From one-night stand to travel companion"—but Dylan was sure she could bring the focus of the articles around before long. She knew she could make readers care more about the cities she was visiting than whether or not she and Jack had "reconciled."

Something that, at this point, was going to happen over Dylan's dead body.

On the third of January, she and Gwen made an early journey to the Breakfast Club near London Bridge for a final send-off, her last hours in London passing so swiftly Dylan would've sworn they hadn't gone at all. They'd sat there, pots of tea between them, and laughed for three full hours. By the time they were walking out of the restaurant around eleven, though, Gwen was near tears.

Tears that started falling in earnest as they said goodbye inside London Bridge station.

"It's okay," Dylan said, pulling Gwen into her arms and rocking them from side to side. "I'll be back in six weeks. And I'm going to talk to you constantly. Every time I get the slightest bit of Wi-Fi, I'm going to text you."

Gwen laughed, but it was watery. "You better."

"You know I will. I know better than to ignore you."

Gwen gave Dylan another deep squeeze.

"Be good," Gwen said into her hair. "Have fun."

"Having fun and being good don't seem like compatible goals."

Gwen huffed. "Don't start."

"Alright, *Mum*, I'll be good." Dylan's eyes caught the clock on the far wall and she swore. "I've got to go, babe. My train leaves in five."

"Alright, alright. Have fun." Gwen kissed Dylan's cheek. "Have a safe flight."

Dylan took a few steps backward toward the ticket queues. "I'll text you as soon as I land."

"Good. Have a safe trip. Love you."

"Love you, too!"

Dylan had to move at double time through the station, but she arrived on the platform one minute before her train was due to leave. She threw herself into the nearest carriage and, after heaving her case into the luggage rack, sat down in the only remaining window seat.

She was just getting settled when her mobile buzzed, and she looked down to find a message from Sean.

on your way???

She grinned.

Dylan: headed to meet his royal highness rn
Sean: askldjf stop
Sean: what if he's nice

That made Dylan actually laugh out loud.

Dylan: right and what if the devil is just misunderstood
Sean: he might be you know
Dylan: the devil or this arsehole?
Sean: both
Dylan: I might have actually believed you if you were only
    talking about satan

Dylan started gathering her things as the train pulled out of Horley, careful to check around her to make sure she had everything. She hadn't gotten much out, but it would've been perfectly like her to somehow leave her charger on this train and spend the next two months having to beg one off Jack.

Dylan slid her suitcase out of the luggage rack when the train pulled into Gatwick, stumbling a little as she adjusted to the weight. She checked in at one of the self-service kiosks inside the airport and dropped her case with one of the desk agents before she glanced down at her ticket. *North Terminal. Gate 338.*

Jesus Christ, she was going to have to walk for ages.

She trudged through security, and after a bit of fighting to get her laptop back into her too-full backpack, she walked over to the airport map and skimmed it. She should probably head to her gate—the boarding time on her ticket was twenty minutes from now—but she was craving a coffee, and she didn't really feel like sitting outside the gate if she could avoid it.

She'd be sitting on the plane for the next, like, eight hours until their layover. She could stretch her legs a bit longer.

Though, as Dylan started toward the upstairs departure lounge, she was starting to think she was delaying the inevitable.

They were announcing boarding for families with small children by the time Dylan arrived at the gate. She was scanning anxiously for Jack as she approached, though her foggy memories didn't give her a good idea of what to look for. She didn't know what he'd be wearing or what his bag would look like, and if his back was to her, he was likely going to look just like any other bloke. But then she spotted him standing near the customer service desk, and there was no doubt in her mind. He had a backpack similar to her own, and his hands were in his coat pockets as he shifted his weight back and forth across his heels. He looked far too formal for someone about to board a long-haul flight—who wore proper fucking trousers on a plane apart from insufferable capitalists?—but even Dylan had to admit, they looked good on him, especially paired with his brown longline wool coat.

Jack was taller than she remembered, and his hair looked a

mess in the best way. And, yes, his face was already in something of a scowl, especially once his eyes found hers, but god damn it, he was still as sexy as he was that first night. As much as she wanted to, even she couldn't deny it.

Dylan exhaled softly and really hated her own self-awareness just then.

She raised her coffee in acknowledgment, a jaunty little smile on her lips, before she stepped into the waiting area close to the boarding queue. She couldn't exactly see him from this angle, but if he really wanted to talk to her about why he was already seemingly in a mood, he could come to her.

She'd only been standing there for a minute when, sure enough, she felt him move beside her.

"You're late."

Those were *really* going to be his first words to her?

She took a sip of her coffee to smother her most homicidal impulses. When she lowered her cup, her expression was clear. Neutral.

"Nice to see you, too!" She injected an extra bit of happiness into her tone and tried not to grin triumphantly when his lips twitched with what had to be annoyance. "And I'm not late. They're still boarding the kids."

She pointed toward the queue full of babies in front of the gate agent.

Jack's frown intensified. "What if you'd missed boarding? And the plane? For a coffee?"

"I wasn't going to miss boarding. They would've announced it, and I would've come running."

"Still—"

"Jack." Her voice sharpened, and Jack fell silent. "I'm here. Let it go."

Jack sighed, pulled his mobile out of his pocket, and immediately became immersed in whatever was happening on his screen.

Dylan would have happily followed suit, but she knew if she got her phone out, she was going to text Gwen about what a shit Jack was being, and as Jack was standing right next to her and he was definitely tall enough to see over her shoulder and read her texts, she decided not to risk it.

They'd been standing around for a few minutes when she remembered they were meant to be getting content for the radio station. It had been a clause buried on page three of the contract, the one she'd spent an hour going over in Alan's lunch-meat-smelling office after Scott and Mina hadn't been able to answer all her questions.

It was simple enough really, a reasonable request that hadn't surprised her—they just needed to send photos from each city featuring their officially organized activities—but it was yet another thing she'd been avoiding thinking about, the fact that she and Jack were now going to be running around the world acting like influencers. Even with the hotel sponsorship, Dylan was sure the station was spending an absurd amount of money on this trip, so she supposed a few pictures weren't the end of the world.

She pulled her mobile out of her jacket pocket and turned it around in her hands. "We should get a shot of us leaving London," she said, turning to Jack. "For the station."

Jack sighed and reached up to run a hand through his hair, knocking some of the strands at the back out of place so they stood up a bit. "I forgot we were doing that."

From his tone, you would have thought Radio 1 had asked for a kidney.

"Did you send Mina your Instagram?"

Jack laughed derisively. "I don't have Instagram."

She frowned. "Why's that funny?"

"Instagram's trivial." His blue eyes were boring into her, as cold and unmovable as a sheet of ice. "My sister keeps trying to convince me to get one, but I don't have time to be scrolling through other people's pictures all day."

Secretly, Dylan was a little jealous that he hadn't sold his soul to Mark Zuckerberg and lived his life without being glued to the endless scroll, but on the surface, she had a very different reaction.

"Right, I forgot you were incredibly important."

Jack's cheeks tinged pink, so lightly that Dylan wouldn't've noticed if she hadn't watched the color paint itself across his skin.

"I didn't mean it like that."

Dylan rolled her eyes. So, he was rude *and* a coward who backed down from his beliefs at the first sign of conflict.

"Whatever. Let's just get this picture over with."

Dylan scanned the gate for someone who might be willing to grab a picture of them, especially this close to boarding. There was a woman seated next to an older kid, watching as he played some sort of game on his tablet, and though she wasn't sure, Dylan thought she'd be a safe bet.

Dylan walked over, her mobile visibly in her hands, and cleared her throat.

"Excuse me. Uh, hi," she said as the woman looked up. "I'm wondering if you'd be able to take our picture." She nodded her head back toward Jack, who she hoped was looking less irritated than when she'd left him.

The woman's smile blossomed. "Oh, of course! Under the departure board? So you can get the destination in?"

Dylan hadn't thought of that. "That's a great idea."

Dylan and Jack walked over to the screen with their flight information and, after a few seconds of awkwardly trying to ensure they were centered, turned to smile.

The woman grinned and tipped her head to the side. "Budge up!"

Dylan turned her head to look at Jack, but Jack was rigid, his gaze trained forward on the woman taking their picture. He raised his arm tentatively and swallowed, his head turning very slightly toward Dylan before he changed course and looked down at his shoes.

"Arm around you alright?"

She nodded and Jack slid his arm into place around her shoulders. She moved her own arm automatically, wrapping it around his waist instead of leaving it sandwiched between them, and then looked up to check that Jack was alright with it.

She thought he'd be looking at the camera, but he was looking at her. His expression was blank and his dark blue eyes were emotionless, but she felt the slightest pressure of his fingers against her shoulder as their eyes caught.

"Very nice!"

Dylan's attention snapped back and she turned to look at their photographer. She smiled at Dylan, a warm, lovesick sort of smile, and Dylan's stomach rolled. The fact that anyone could look at her and Jack and see something that made them look that gooey was absurd.

"Nice big smiles and I think we've got it."

This was what Dylan got for asking a mum to take their picture.

Still, she smiled as bright and as brilliant a smile as she could muster, and the woman captured a few angles before she stepped forward to return Dylan's phone.

"Hold on to that one," she said, dropping her voice low as Dylan took her phone. "He looks at you like you hung the moon."

The woman winked and then walked back to her son, and Dylan suppressed the urge to laugh. He had only looked at her once, and even then, there had been absolutely nothing positive on his face. How this woman had mistaken very obvious disgust for attraction she would never know. Honestly, it was a little alarming. Something to write about in a future article.

The gate agent's voice crackled on over the speakers. "Boarding will now begin for flight sixteen, service to Dubai, first-class and business-class passengers, you're welcome to board. All general boarding customers please remain seated until the general boarding call is made."

Jack raised an eyebrow at her. "Ready?"

She flicked her gaze up at him before scrolling through their pictures. "Ready enough."

He made a sound somewhere between a laugh and a scoff. "You sound thrilled."

She liked the photos of them grinning at the camera, their arms around each other, happy smiles that belied the tension between them. She'd scrolled back through a few more before she fell onto one that made everything go still.

They were looking at each other. Right after they'd first moved closer, after she'd wrapped her arm around Jack's waist. They were just looking at each other, but there was something about the picture that made Dylan pause, something that caught her attention and made her feel short of breath. It was the way their gazes held, but more than that, there was an unmistakable energy between them.

One that, shockingly, wasn't homicidal.

She hadn't known this picture had been snapped, but she remembered now—*Very nice!* the woman said—and she had to agree.

They looked . . .

Very nice.

She met his eyes again.

"Just excited at the prospect of spending so much uninterrupted time with you," she said.

She thought he might frown, scowl, turn away, but he tipped his head in acknowledgment. "Things are better when uninterrupted."

She smirked. "Isn't that a Spotify advert?"

Jack shrugged, his expression imperious. "I wouldn't know. I'm on premium."

Dylan scoffed. "Prick."

Jack turned so he was properly facing her, his mouth open like he was going to say something before he was interrupted by another announcement.

"General boarding will now begin for flight sixteen, service to Dubai. Passengers should please have their boarding passes and passports ready for presentation before entering the aircraft."

The moment the boarding call was over, she turned her phone

round. She'd flicked away from the photo of them staring at each other to a more innocent one of them smiling at the camera. It was bland, generically happy, but it captured the excitement she wanted to pretend she was feeling.

"Does this picture work for you?"

Jack's expression flattened. She wouldn't have thought he'd *had* an expression on the moment before, but seeing this shift in his face now was like watching him deflate.

"Yeah." He stuffed his hands into his pockets. "That photo's fine."

"Cool." Dylan opened her sharing panel and attached the photo to an email. "Oh, and do you mind if I send this to my editor, too?"

Jack's entire face pinched. "Your editor?"

Dylan nodded. "I'm writing a series about our travel for my magazine. She's going to want pictures and if we're already sending them off to the station—"

"Fine." Jack bit the word out and Dylan was three-quarters of the way to arguing with him when, without another word, Jack walked off to stand at the back of the boarding queue.

CHAPTER 6

By the time they stepped off the airplane in Sydney late the next night, Dylan was so exhausted she could've fallen asleep on her feet.

Literally on her feet. No wall to support her or anything.

As tempted as she was to grab a coffee from one of the airport cafés, she knew she'd regret it. She reminded herself of that as she saw a Starbucks and Hudson's Coffee *and* Coast Café—*we'll regret it, we'll regret it, we'll regret it*. She was proud of herself for resisting, but once they got to immigration and Dylan had to stand still?

She was sure her head lolled off to the side at least a few times.

"You should've slept on the plane," Jack said.

She turned and found him looking at her, an annoyingly superior expression on his face. Everything about him was irritating in that moment—his attractively untidy hair, the shadow of stubble along his jaw, the incredibly pompous way he'd draped his wool coat over his arm the minute they'd stepped off the plane. He looked the picture of perfectly prim professionalism.

"Shut up. You're so annoying."

"But I'm right."

And he was right, she should've slept, but Dylan had never

figured out how to relax enough on an airplane to actually fall asleep.

She opened her mouth to reply and ended up yawning instead. Jack's eyebrow arched, all stupid and cocky and knowing.

"Stop looking at me like that."

"Looking at you like what?" There was the slightest hint of amusement on Jack's face, and it made Dylan scowl.

"You know exactly how you're looking at me."

"How exactly am I looking at you?" There was a smoky quality to Jack's voice, and horrifically, it curled tight in Dylan's stomach.

She frowned harder and valiantly changed the subject. "I can't sleep on planes."

"Anxious flyer?"

"No." She did sometimes imagine they were going to plummet to the earth when they hit a spot of particularly bad turbulence, but she was fairly sure that was normal. "Planes are small and stupid and I can't get comfortable."

"Small and stupid. Got it."

She crossed her arms. "Now you're just mocking me."

"I'm not trying to mock you," Jack said. "I'm just saying that 'small and stupid' is hardly a reason not to sleep on a fourteen-hour flight."

"I want to sleep tonight. Adjust to local time."

"I didn't say sleep the whole time." Jack pulled his mobile out of his trouser pocket. "I'm still tired, but at least I'm not collapsing in public."

"Well, I'm sorry the sight of me offends your delicate sensibilities. And put away your mobile, they're not allowed."

She pointed to the sign a few feet away from them, and Jack scowled as he stuffed his phone back into his pocket.

After getting through immigration, Jack ordered a rideshare while they waited for her bag at the baggage claim—his checked bag, annoyingly, had been the first off the bloody conveyor—and they stood a few meters back from the belt in stiff silence, watching all the bags that weren't hers roll past.

Jack checked his phone, a slight tip of the screen out of his pocket like he was trying to check it without getting caught.

"The car should be here soon."

Dylan very nearly stomped her foot. She had something of a temper at the best of times but add in the fact that she hadn't slept in thirty-six hours and she was basically a tall toddler.

"I can't do anything about when my bag will get here, Jack."

"No, I was just—" Jack actually looked a little horrified, though whether at Dylan's anger or at his having caused her anger, Dylan wasn't sure. She knew which she would wager on, though. "I just meant you won't have to keep standing much longer."

Dylan nearly cracked a smile, but then, luckily, her bag rolled out of the back onto the conveyor belt, and she took the excuse to step away.

Jack raised his eyebrows at her bag as she dragged it over to where he was waiting. "Did you pack your entire flat into that bag?"

In fairness, her bag *was* the largest one she could find, a massive, purple hard-shell case she'd borrowed off Gwen that was so tall it was even with her hips and Dylan could use the hand loop to push it. She hadn't planned on bringing something this large, but when she'd looked through the list of places they'd be traveling (and the weather she could expect), there was no way around the fact that she needed to bring half her closet if she was going to be comfortable.

She looked at Jack's sensible green case, a compact thing that could have been carried on if he'd wanted to bother with it.

"Did *you* bring the right amount of clothes to handle, like, fifteen different climates?"

"We're actually only going through nine climates."

Rather than reply, she gave Jack the finger and, for dramatic effect, yanked the handle up with a snap before rolling her bag toward the door.

Their rideshare was idling outside as they walked out of baggage claim, and the driver opened the boot so they could drop their bags inside. Jack frowned as Dylan walked back behind the car and held his hand out.

"Give me that. Get in, close your eyes." Jack reached for the handle of her suitcase and she scowled at him.

"I can put it in."

"I know you can. But I'm offering."

"You're not offering." She slid the handle down and Jack pulled his hand away before his fingers got pinched. "You're demanding."

She slung her case into the boot beside his and shut the door.

If he'd asked, she would have happily handed over her bag because she was about three seconds away from collapsing and the last thing she needed was to rupture a disc because she couldn't be arsed to lift properly, but he hadn't asked, and damn it, it was the principle.

Even thinking it reminded Dylan forcefully of Gwen—*you need to pick better hills to die on, Dylan*—and Dylan used the last of her feeble connection to the airport Wi-Fi to send Gwen a quick text.

> no idea what time it is there but we just landed in syd.
> It's 2300 here and I'm fucking knackered
> losing wifi so this better send. I love you and I'll talk to
> you tomorrow (your today???) xx

If you'd asked Dylan what happened on their drive to the hotel, she wouldn't have been able to recall any of the details. She thought that Jack and the driver had chatted for a while though she couldn't tell you what about. Jack had, probably for the express purpose of annoying her, sat in the front, and Dylan took the opportunity to stretch out along the back seat.

Their hotel was a nondescript brick building with an iron awning over the pavement that made it look more like an old theater. Inside, though, the hotel had a cool, intentionally rustic feel. The reception desk was made of a series of modular yellow and orange squares with a sleek matte-black top, and the lobby was softly lit by curved track lighting set into the ceiling. There was a small seating area with a lamp that looked more like an art piece than a lighting fixture directly opposite the desk, and Jack immediately nodded at one of the armchairs.

"Would you like to sit down? I can check us in."

Dylan shook her head. "If I sit down, I won't get back up."

Jack looked like he had half a mind to argue with her, but thankfully decided to drop it.

Their hotel room was split into two sections, a tiled entry and bathroom and a bedroom with forest-green carpet. There were two queen beds in the space, though just barely so—there was a narrow aisle on the far side of each bed and little more than a foot between the beds themselves, not even enough room that a bedside table could be crammed in between. There were small shelves in the corner at the head of each bed that could serve as makeshift side tables and individual wall lamps over each of them, but the idea of sleeping that close to Jack for the next week was . . . well, unsettling to say the least.

Dylan dropped her room key onto the chest of drawers opposite the beds and dragged her bag over to the bed nearest her. She was about to sling her bag up when Jack cleared his throat.

"I want the bed nearest the door."

She paused, half bent in the process of lifting her bag. "What?"

He nodded toward the bed. "I want that bed."

"Why?"

"I—I just do."

Dylan huffed angrily, but rather than fight with him about it, she dragged her bag over toward the other bed and swung it none too gently into the narrow space between the bed and the window.

Jack didn't move for a second, just watched her stripping off her things—his eyes followed the arc of her jacket as she tossed it onto the chair in the corner, the sharp lines of her shoes as she kicked them off, one of them bouncing off the window and the other bouncing off the chair leg. His features pinched tighter with each item she flung until, when she dropped her backpack heavily onto the floor, her water bottle falling out of the side and rolling under the bed, he exhaled.

"Do you come into every room like a bull in a china shop?"

"'Bull in a china shop'? You sound like my nan."

"Nan or not, you don't need to fling everything around."

Dylan ignored him and grabbed her mobile charger out of her backpack. After a bit of fumbling with the USB, she managed to plug her phone in. She chucked the brick in the general direction of her backpack, the loud smack of the plastic telling her she'd hit her mark, before she unbuttoned her jeans. She was just conscious enough to strip them off—paying no mind to the fact that Jack was behind her and now probably mildly traumatized—and climb into bed.

She was asleep before Jack even turned off the light.

CHAPTER 7

When Dylan woke the next morning, the sun was properly up, the light slicing through the curtains and directly into her eyes. She groped on the side table for her mobile, and *fuck*, it was half bloody ten.

Dylan did a quick bit of mental maths. She'd slept for nine hours? Nine and a half? No wonder she was feeling . . . Was this what well-rested felt like? She hadn't slept that many hours since uni at least.

She lay there for a second, phone on her chest, just staring at the ceiling. The room had that stiff, almost tense silence, and though she hadn't been bothered about the close quarters last night, she was definitely feeling awkward now. She hadn't heard a single sound from Jack's side of the room, and there was something deeply unsettling about being awake in the same room as someone who was fast asleep. Especially someone you didn't know very well. Or at all.

It was possible he was sitting there, full plate of breakfast on his lap, quietly judging her for her sleeping position, but he was incredibly quiet, even for someone judging.

She drew in a soft breath, bracing herself, and turned her head.

And bloody hell, he had no business looking like he did just then.

Jack was dead asleep. His head was turned toward her on the pillow and his limbs were starfished across the mattress, his left hand dangling off the edge of the bed so that his fingertips were inches from her bed. He'd kicked off the duvet at some point in the night, and it was now tangled around his legs. Only his right forearm had managed to stay covered through whatever gymnastics he must have done while he'd been sleeping last night.

And while that was adorable—sort of adorable—the thing that was really getting to her was the rest of it.

The way his hair was flopped back off his forehead. The way his T-shirt had ridden up around his chest so that half his stomach was bared.

It wasn't that he had some sick washboard abs sort of setup. He wasn't someone, from the look of him, who spent every free minute in the gym, but that hadn't ever been Dylan's scene anyway (except for Sioned, the trainer she'd hooked up with briefly last summer who had more muscles than Dylan realized humans even had). Still, Dylan could tell that, if she was pressing herself against him, his body would feel hard against hers. Firm. And the way the sleeve of his T-shirt curved, tight, against his biceps . . .

Dylan took a deep breath and turned over so she was facing the window again.

Attractive or not, he was still a complete arsehole. And, okay, she couldn't control who she found attractive, but she could control whether or not she acted on it. And Jack was very firmly on the *do not act on it* list.

She connected her mobile to the Wi-Fi—it was unnecessarily difficult and she had to practically promise the hotel her nonexistent firstborn—and watched as the notifications started to ping in.

The most stressful of those numbers, her email inbox, started going up almost immediately.

She'd put a delayed response notification on her email so people didn't think she was ignoring them—especially since her time zones were going to be all over the place for the next few weeks—but delayed response notification or not, she knew Chantel was still expecting replies to her messages more or less the moment she sent them.

Dylan cleared out the lower-level work emails until, finally, only the ones from Chantel were left. She had two to choose from: Pitch Meeting Assignments and the ominously titled Updates. Dylan was half tempted to stick with the easier of the two, but she figured it was best to get it over with.

From: Chantel Stainton (c.stainton@buxom.co.uk)
To: Dylan Coughlan (d.coughlan@buxom.co.uk)
Subject: Updates

You've had a small uptick in your numbers, but only 4.5%—as agreed, you'll need 20% growth before you return in February.

There does, however, seem to be some excitement in the comments. Once you start writing about your ex, I bet numbers will skyrocket.

Send articles in at least 96hr, rather than 48hr, in advance with the time changes to ensure edits are in on time. Also include images from each location—posts have been lacklustre without them (include alt-text in proof sub).

Enjoy.

CS

There was nothing like a brusque email from Chantel to get your spirits up.

The schedule change wasn't surprising, though Dylan wished Chantel had mentioned it before she, you know, left the country. The image ask, too, wasn't even unexpected, but the implication that Dylan had photos she just wasn't sending before was outrageous. She'd only been sitting at her desk or packing while she wrote all of the introductory posts, it wasn't like she was missing grand photo opportunities.

The one interesting photo moment she did have—her and Jack at the airport—had seemed like a good first one to include, and it was being shared with the station anyway, but after Jack's bizarre (and not even remotely sincere) agreement at the airport, she decided not to send it to Chantel. She'd taken loads of herself on the plane, so she could easily thumb through and find something that matched the article she ended up writing.

Something she should get started on now if she was going to meet Chantel's absurd deadline.

After checking that Jack was still asleep, Dylan sat up, cringing at the creak in the mattress. She thought she'd dropped her backpack at the foot of the bed the night before, but after a quick glance, she didn't see it sitting there.

She checked all around the edges of the bed and was three-quarters of the way to panicking when she spotted it sitting on the chair beside the window.

Her eyebrows pinched together. How had it—

Jack.

Jack had moved her bag.

Why he'd thought that he could just move her stuff without asking—

She huffed, frustration thick in her tone as she muttered, "Jesus fucking Christ," and slid out from under the duvet.

The carpet was soft under her feet, and Dylan felt a chill rush down her spine as the air hit her bare legs. With a few quiet steps, she grabbed her backpack off the chair before scrambling back to bed.

Only to open her laptop and see a big flashing battery on the screen.

"Fuck."

She said it a bit louder than she'd intended, and Jack stirred. Dylan froze, her heart in her throat, her pulse hammering against her skin. She sat stock-still for a few beats before she turned to look at him again.

His left leg had slid across the bed, his foot nearly dangling off the end, and his left arm had come up so his fingers were now hidden underneath the pillow, but otherwise, he was fast asleep.

And thank Christ, because she still wasn't ready to deal with him this morning.

She opened Google Docs on her phone, and after letting her mind wander over the last day and a half, her fingers started moving.

Who invented fourteen-hour flights? Tell me.
Seriously.
I just want to talk.

There wasn't much to tell at this stage, but she was still left staring at a thousand words after half an hour's effort. Which was only five hundred words short of the total count she needed for the full article.

Dylan sighed and dropped her mobile onto her lap, flexing her fingers so they weren't so stiff.

Most of what she'd written would have to be scrapped—it lacked the *sexy details that make* Buxom *articles* Buxom *articles*, as Chantel always said—but she didn't hate a lot of what she had to say here. She liked the way she'd described being trapped in a metal tube, forced to breathe recycled air, and her genuine amazement at traveling so far in, really, such a short amount of time. She liked working through the experience of getting here, thinking through the travel itself as opposed to seeing it as a necessary burden to reach their destination.

Chantel would never let these details into the final article, but it seemed a shame to waste them.

And then, the thought struck her.

She could post this on Instagram.

She was going to post pictures anyway, and the captions would be an outlet to share the things she wouldn't have space for in the articles. It would be a nice way to promote the series, too—she'd point her (granted, small) audience toward the articles, and the images, especially if tagged well, would find new people who might be interested in her writing.

It was more work, but it was worth it if it helped her get her column.

Her hands felt like they were shaking with energy as she grabbed her mobile off her lap and navigated to her camera roll. She wasn't going to use the pictures of her and Jack at Gatwick, but she had several photos she'd taken on the plane. There were standard shots out the window, some of the multiple episodes of *Grey's Anatomy* she watched, and several absurd selfies. She had posed with her dinner (a surprisingly good mushroom risotto), posed while wearing all her British Airways in-flight accessories (the blanket scarf and eye mask really made the look), and had, eventually, captured a few of her smiling gently at the camera.

Dylan had been careful to avoid getting Jack in the photos, especially when he'd been sleeping because she felt like that crossed some *You*-style line, but there were a few flashes of him that she found amusing.

The shell of his ear in the background of her and the BA merch. The edge of his laptop in the *Grey's Anatomy* pic. He wasn't *there*, but he was there enough to satisfy the people following her "romantic getaway." Loathe though she was to give into Chantel's angle, she hoped that painting Jack very firmly along the edges like this would make it clear that there was nothing going on between the pair of them.

She selected a mix of aesthetically pleasing window shots and ridiculous selfies, and copied a block of text from the draft article. She had to fuss with it to get the character count down, but after a few minutes, she was able to get in the last bit she wanted. She had just enough room for a hashtag, so after a few attempts, she tacked on the best one she could think of.

♥Over the next few weeks, prepare to call me Ms Worldwide #dylangoesglobal

She tapped POST, and after adding a dozen more hashtags for increased visibility in the comments, dropped her phone onto the bed. Even if this didn't grow traffic, she liked the idea of sharing these outtakes. It was an extra bit of content, a sneak peek, but it was also one more record of the things she'd felt as she skipped across the world.

Satisfied, she decided to distract herself with Twitter when Jack pulled in a slow, deep breath, loud enough that it caught Dylan's attention. Dylan saw him shift out of the corner of her eye, his scattered limbs retracting as he curled up. He pulled the duvet over himself and rolled onto his side.

She couldn't tell from her periphery, but she thought his eyes were closed.

Until she checked and found him looking at her.

She barely managed not to swear out loud.

"Good morning," she said instead.

Jack's lips hitched the slightest bit at the corner, and when he went to reply, it immediately turned into a yawn. He covered his mouth with the back of his hand, and when he finished, he smiled sleepily.

"Good morning."

Dylan turned back to Twitter. "Sleep alright?"

"Mm-hmm. It took me a while to fall asleep, but I managed it in the end."

"Guess you shouldn't've slept on the plane."

Jack narrowed his eyes. "Yeah, yeah."

She grinned down at her screen. She posted a quick tweet about her Instagram series and then jumped onto her timeline and started scrolling.

After a long moment, Jack groaned softly and sat up.

"What's on the agenda today?"

She shrugged but didn't look up from her phone. "I don't know, I barely read the itinerary emails."

Jack sighed heavily. "Why are you so averse to itineraries?"

He already sounded aggravated, and Dylan was not proud that part of her was deeply amused by that fact.

"I'm not." She was. "I just think holidays should be less, like, structured. More fun."

"Structure can be fun."

Dylan snorted. "No, it can't."

Jack just stared at her. "Can you please just check?"

"You can check."

"You're already on your phone."

"I'm on Twitter." She retweeted a tweet *hard*, like she was proving a point.

"Dylan—"

She groaned. "*Fine.* Jesus."

Despite not having properly read them, Dylan had saved all the itinerary emails in her inbox. They'd gotten a bit buried in the days since but were still near enough to the top that it wasn't hard to find the message headed ITINERARY: SYDNEY.

She skimmed over the attachment, absorbing just enough to report the barest details. "Free day today. All we've got to do is pick up the hire car."

Jack hummed. "When are we due to get it?"

Dylan glanced up at the clock at the top of her screen as she clicked back into Twitter. "Half an hour."

Jack swore and immediately scrambled out of bed, his legs fighting furiously to free themselves from the duvet. "Okay, let's—"

He took one step toward the chest of drawers before turning back around, flustered. "Do you need a shower? I need a shower."

For someone who had been half asleep a minute ago, he was suddenly wide awake.

"Why are you panicking?"

Jack gaped at her. "We have to be across town in thirty minutes. Neither of us is dressed."

He was speaking to her like she was a toddler refusing to put on her shoes.

"It's not 'across town.' Mina's email said it's five minutes from here."

He waved a dismissive hand. "We can't be late. Now, do you need a shower or not, because I'm going if you don't need one."

She'd assumed that he was uptight, but if it was going to be like this for the entire trip, Dylan might kill him. She would have understood if they genuinely had to go across town or it was, like, peak hours, but it was the middle of the morning and a five-minute drive away.

They'd have to be seriously dragging their feet if they were going to be late. Even with only thirty minutes.

Dylan exhaled, frustration thick in the sound. "Yeah, I need a shower. I've got plane all over me from yesterday."

Jack waved his hand swiftly toward the bathroom, urging her on. "Alright, go ahead, then."

That hand—all commanding and *hurry up*—made her want to go as slowly as she possibly could. And if she wasn't grossed out by the thick layer of grease in her hair, she would've done.

Dylan was about to peel off the duvet when she became

viscerally aware—helped along by the realization that her jeans were still on the floor where she'd thrown them the night before—that she wasn't wearing anything on her lower half.

"Can you close your eyes?"

Jack frowned. "What?"

God, he sounded exasperated. Well, that made two of them.

"Close your eyes. I'm not wearing any trousers."

Jack dropped his gaze and shook his head, almost to himself. "I saw everything when you stripped off last night, but fine. Just hurry up."

He covered his eyes, and Dylan grabbed her bag from the foot of the bed before dashing off to the bathroom.

Dylan was still wrapped in a towel when she stepped out of the bathroom a few minutes later, her toiletries bag in one hand and her luggage dragging along behind her. She was careful not to knock off her towel and dropped her toiletries heavily onto the counter beside the sink before she stuck her head around the wall.

"I'm out of the shower."

She heard Jack start down the corridor and she began digging through her bag to find her travel container of face serum. She was rubbing the serum through her hands when Jack rounded the corner and he jumped, literally jumped, his eyes flicking down to the towel before he looked at her face and then, just as quickly, the ground.

"Sorry." He still wasn't looking at her. "I'll—" He held up the clothes he had in his hand and she glanced at him in the mirror as she began smoothing the serum across her cheeks.

"It's alright," she said. She tried to catch his eye, but he stepped into the bathroom, muttered, "Sorry," again, and shut the door.

CHAPTER 8

Their rideshare pulled up outside the rental office with three minutes to spare. Jack barreled out of the car, slamming the door shut behind him, and Dylan exhaled sharply before plastering on a smile for the driver.

"Thanks for the lift."

The driver turned round and smiled. "No problem. Enjoy your time in Sydney."

Dylan snorted. "If I make it through without murdering him, I'll consider it a success."

Jack had opted to demean himself and sit next to her in the back this time, though he'd been tense and silent the whole ride. Dylan had been more than able to fill the silence, but every minute grated against her nerves. Jack clearly didn't like to be late, but it wasn't like they were going to lose their reservation over five minutes. And even if they *did*, it wasn't going to be the end of the fucking world.

The driver laughed heartily, and Dylan flashed him another, now genuine, smile before turning to open her door. She'd barely gotten her fingers onto the handle, though, when the door opened from the outside.

Jack was standing there, a blank look on his face, one hand on her door and the other hand, laughably, extended to help her out of the car. Dylan stepped out, ignoring his hand.

She heard Jack sigh behind her, and she immediately rounded on him.

"Oh, I'm sorry." She dropped into a mock curtsy. "Would you like to rehearse that scene again, Your Highness? Allow you to assist me with the incredibly heavy door?"

A splash of pink cropped up across Jack's cheeks, though Dylan wasn't sure if it was anger or embarrassment that had put it there. He opened his mouth to say something but, maybe in response to the challenge in Dylan's expression, simply sighed again.

"I didn't mean it like that."

Dylan crossed her arms.

"It's less your intent that I care about and more the impact. And the impact is that you've well and truly pissed me off."

She expected him to snap back at her, to stand his ground, demand that they walk inside and get their stupid car, but as she watched, Jack almost curled in on himself. His head dipped forward and he swung his hands loosely.

"I'm sorry."

Watching the fight drain out of him so quickly almost made her want to back off.

Almost.

"I'm glad you didn't mean to irritate me, but this plays into this idea of benevolent sexism that—"

Jack glanced up. "Benevolent sexism?"

"Where society basically trains you to be nice to women," Dylan said, waving her hand through the air. "Though, really, just white straight cis women, because then they can weaponize it against women of color and queer and trans women. It's, like, opening doors and putting on coats and shit because we're *fragile*, as opposed to the main type of sexism that's driven by incels on Twitter."

The kind she was intimately familiar with.

Jack frowned. "I don't think you're fragile."

"Good."

Despite the queue in front of the single occupied agent's desk, it only took a few minutes to get to the front. Mina, in all her brilliance, had sent a credit authorization ahead, so the agent had only needed Dylan's driving license to prove she was, indeed, the Dylan Coughlan on the reservation. Though Dylan thought there should be a bit more checking involved before someone behind a desk handed you a set of keys, she also wasn't going to complain if it got them out of the rental office without any issues.

Their car for the next few days wasn't anything flashy, just a beige sedan with beige-er fabric seats. Dylan popped around to the driver's side and Jack made his way to the passenger's automatically . . . before nearly throwing himself out of the car again when Dylan made the mistake of mentioning that she hadn't driven a car in, well, probably close to a decade.

Jack turned so quickly she was worried he'd snapped a vertebra.

"You haven't driven in ten years?!"

"Nope," Dylan said as she adjusted her mirrors. The last person to have driven this car must have been, like, Greg fucking Davies because these mirrors were set miles above her head.

"Why don't you let me drive? I drive all the time."

Dylan scoffed. "Of course you do, Mr. I Can Afford to Live in Zone 1 and Have a Car." She shot him a stern look, one that usually withered even the most resilient. "She handed me the keys. I'm driving."

"She handed you the keys because your name happened to be on the reservation."

"So that means this is my car." Dylan plugged her phone into the charging port and busied herself with connecting to the portable Wi-Fi the station had, thankfully, thought to include in their reservation.

Jack frowned. "That isn't what that means."

Dylan shrugged and said, "Whatever," before she dropped her mobile into the cupholder and started the engine.

She expected Jack to push back a bit more, but he seemed to realize arguing was basically moot because he just sighed heavily, crossed his arms, and leaned back in his seat.

That is, until she was approaching a stop and Dylan hit the brakes a little harder than she intended. He turned and shot her a harsh look, one hand braced against the door, but Dylan smiled easily as she turned out into traffic.

"Brakes are a bit sensitive. You've got to have a really light touch."

Jack huffed and pulled his seat belt tighter.

They were both quiet while she drove. She'd thought, when she first got behind the wheel, that they'd just drive back to the hotel, but once she'd settled in . . .

Well, she was keen to drive a bit, actually.

Despite the fact that they were near the Pacific Ocean, Dylan would never have guessed they were so close to the water as they drove down Park Street. You could have told her she was in any city in the world and she probably would have believed it, though the short palm trees lining the side streets at least meant they definitely weren't in England anymore.

Though she could have been forgiven for thinking they hadn't left London. Everything they passed seemed connected to home. There was a bar called Kings Cross, an enormous park called Hyde Park—she knew why everything here was named after sites thousands of miles away, but seeing it and still viscerally feeling the distance between home and Sydney made it all sit uncomfortably in her stomach.

She was about to comment on it when Jack turned to look at her.

"This isn't the way back to the hotel."

She shook her head. "I thought we'd drive around. See the city."

"What?"

"Drive around?" She mimed driving, her hands ghosting over the wheel in a way that made Jack's face pinch. "Why do you look so annoyed?"

"You didn't want to clue me in first?"

"I clearly wasn't taking the route back to the hotel. You didn't mention anything, so I didn't think you had a problem with it."

"And this is clearly the tone someone who doesn't have 'a problem with it' would be using."

Dylan had to suppress the urge to roll her eyes. "Well, what else were we going to do? Sit in the hotel and twiddle our thumbs?"

"So, you have a destination in mind, then."

"No."

Jack ran his fingers along the lines now etched across his forehead.

"Are you serious?"

Dylan grabbed her phone out of the cupholder and unlocked it. "Would you rather me google someplace nearby?"

"I'd rather"—Jack leaned over and plucked the phone out of her hand—"you not kill us."

Dylan rolled her eyes. "I won't kill us."

"I'm glad that you're confident in your abilities, but I'll google it, thanks."

Dylan sighed and reached over to switch radio stations. The one they'd been listening to had been playing adverts for, like, five minutes, and if she had to hear that Nestlé jingle one more time she was going to run the car off the road.

"Read out everything so we have options. Except for, like, polo grounds." She glanced at him out of the corner of her eye. "I don't care about that."

Jack held two fingers up at her, and Dylan barked a laugh.

Barely a minute passed before Jack said, "Ooh," and got her attention.

"We can go to the Three Sisters." Jack tilted the phone to show her the screen, but then immediately snatched it back as though a stray glance would send them careening into the barrier. "It's a lookout point, but you can see the Three Sisters rock formation and the Blue Mountains. I think you can hike there, too, but obviously we're not doing that."

A fair statement since neither of them had proper hiking shoes on, but she still didn't like the assumption.

"What if I want to go hiking?"

He raised an eyebrow. "*You* want to go hiking?"

She scoffed. "What do you mean, '*You* want to go hiking'?" She couldn't do a posh accent to save her life, but bless her, she'd given it a go. All she'd wanted to do was irritate Jack, and judging by the look on his face, it was mission very much accomplished.

"Do you have to pick apart *everything* I say?"

"When it's wrong."

And when she thought he'd have a funny reaction. But she was definitely going to keep that part to herself.

Jack's frown intensified. "That's not even what I sound like."

"Fairly sure it's a brilliant impression," she said. She slapped the accent on again, really playing it up. "Ring the Queen, I'm ready for a title."

She waited expectantly, but annoyingly, Jack didn't take the bait. He just pressed his lips together and kept scrolling.

"Anyway," Dylan said, "I like the outdoors. So *I'd* want to go hiking if it's possible."

It wasn't entirely true—the last time she'd been hiking had been when Sean dragged her up some mountain in the Lake District like he was William fucking Wordsworth, and she'd hated at least seventy-five percent of the daylong experience—but what Jack didn't know, et cetera, et cetera. It wasn't that she didn't like being outside, it was just that she didn't relish the idea of dragging herself up cliffs unless there was something really impressive to see at the top.

"Okay, well, if *you* want to go hiking then," Jack said, twirling his hand dismissively in front of him, "by all means. But I don't feel like getting my leg bitten off by a snake one day into our trip."

It was actually a decent point, but rather than admit that, she said nothing.

The silence lingered, thick and uncomfortable, as the miles

passed beneath their tires. It wasn't unbearable, but it was awkward enough that Dylan knew she couldn't survive six whole weeks of it. She could put up with almost anything, she could ignore Jack if she absolutely had to, but the whole point of this holiday was to relax, escape, and she didn't know how she was going to do any of that if every tiny conversation drove them to the edge.

But rather than obsess over it, Dylan forced herself to ease into the feeling of just driving.

She loved living in London, but she missed driving. She loved relaxing back into her seat, music in her ears, and her mind empty of everything but the road. She missed the hum of the engine, the smooth slide of her hands over the wheel every time she had to turn or change lanes, the feeling of the miles sliding away without even having to think about them.

It made her feel like she was back in school. Stealing her da's old Peugeot, driving in circles around Liverpool until the restlessness in her finally settled.

She'd also enjoyed snogging half the girls' football team in the back of that car, but really, it was mostly the driving.

Soon enough, the tall grass lining the edges of the motorway gave way to eucalyptus-lined suburbs, the distant mountains inching closer as they drove toward the horizon. It wasn't much, but Dylan found her attention endlessly drawn to the landscape. The jewel-toned river, the rough face of the rock they'd blasted through to lay the road. The tall, dark brown trees, their bark peeling so the orange interior was baking in the sun. The road twisted as they climbed into the mountains, and with each turn, Dylan felt the weight of the silence lift off her shoulders.

CHAPTER 9

They'd just entered a small town when Jack coughed lightly and turned to her.

"So you mentioned you're writing articles about our trip? Are you—are you a writer?"

If Jack felt as awkward as he sounded, he must be boiling in his skin.

"Yes, I am," she said, easing into a turn. "I was freelance, but I've been full-time with *Buxom* for the last few years."

Jack's eyebrows shot up. "That's amazing."

Dylan shrugged. "I like it."

Three years ago, she would have licked the bottom of Chantel's shoes to be working at *Buxom*. It was almost funny how little the expectation matched the reality.

Jack turned in his seat so he was almost properly facing her. "What's your favorite part of working there?"

He sounded actually curious, not just politely so, and it took her aback.

"Oh, um . . ."

Back when she'd been writing fashion or beauty content, her favorite bit had been the free products. Her bottom desk drawer had become a veritable treasure trove of the season's most antici-pated beauty releases, and she'd loved digging through and finding new products to test. It wasn't long, though, before the products she was sent far outnumbered the amount she could conceivably fit into a desk drawer. Now, a lot of those samples had dried up.

"I love the writing," she said. "It's the best way to process the things that I'm thinking about or struggling with. The comments can be really dicey, but when you see someone connect with it, say that a piece really spoke to them—I mean, there's nothing better."

Jack hummed thoughtfully. "What's your favorite piece you've ever written?"

Truth be told, there were a million pieces she loved. Even pieces that she would write differently now were special to her because they represented a specific moment in her development as a writer. Deep down, though, she knew which one was her top, the one she wouldn't change for anything.

"In the lead-up to the abortion referendum in Ireland last year, we spent the few months before the vote posting a number of think pieces and interviews and that sort of thing, across the magazine and the dot com. For part of that effort, I wrote about the abortion I had in uni."

She paused to see if Jack was going to say anything, but he just nodded. Not slowly, not judgmentally—which, believe it or not, you could definitely distinguish—but just . . .

Normally.

Almost encouragingly. Like, *go on*.

"My parents are *very* Catholic, so our discussions about it growing up were one-sided. I didn't tell them at the time, for reasons I'm sure you can guess, but the weight of that secret was . . . a lot." Dylan was quiet for a minute, her gaze glued to the road.

"In a lot of ways, it was easier coming out to them." She tucked her hair behind her ear and laughed awkwardly. "To them, being bi meant I could still marry a man and have a straight-looking life. My parents were fine when I dated women, but I think that was always in the back of their mind. Which is horrible, but was eons better than my mates whose parents kicked them out when they were, like, barely sixteen. But abortion . . . that was a whole new level for them. When that article went up in March—it posted the night we first met, actually—it was just . . . It was bedlam."

Now, months removed, she felt like she could finally observe the events of the evening without reliving everything all over again. Things had gone from *alright* to *hell on earth* so quickly—all it had taken was for her to check her notifications and (and she'd blamed herself for this for a long time) send some cheeky responses to some arseholes on Twitter, and her entire world had imploded.

She didn't regret standing up for herself. If anything, she was angry that she lived in a world where she had to defend herself in the first place. Where defending herself only seemed to make people that much more determined to tear her down.

"I wasn't, you know— I've had some sketchy sexual experiences, but that time, it was fully consensual and with a guy I'd been seeing and—the condom just broke and I assumed we were fine and we were *not.*"

Even now, Dylan remembered how terrified she'd been. How she'd sprinted to Ty's uni house and, stumbling over the footballs and trainers and empty cider cans, thrown herself into his room, already in tears.

She'd never debated getting an abortion—she would have been a shit mum then, and as the two lines on that pregnancy test very swiftly confirmed, she never wanted to have kids anyway—but she'd been desperately sad at the realization that this was one more wedge she was going to have to drive between herself and her parents. It was an echo of the way she'd felt coming out just two years before, except this time, she knew for certain that their reaction would be far more negative.

Dylan hated that she'd been right about that.

"The piece I wrote was about that experience." Dylan drew in a soft breath to ease the tremble in her voice. "About telling my parents, about how I'd made that choice because it was the best choice, the only choice. So many of the stories I'd read were sad and negative and full of regret, and I wanted to tell a different story. Because it's healthcare. Abortions are healthcare, and it's so fucking unfair because people are literally fucking dying all the time because they can't get access to safe, free abortion care."

Dylan's voice was thick with emotion, and even though she could feel Jack's eyes on her, she didn't meet his gaze. Instead, she drew in a deep inhale, tracing the breath down to her gut, and once she felt a little steadier, she flashed Jack a small, slightly cheeky smile.

"That probably shouldn't be my favorite piece, because I then spent, like, four months getting death threats on Twitter, but I'm proud of telling that story. Of making it through the hell it became online. Though I guess I still have a few things left to get through, because my parents still aren't really talking to me."

Her voice trailed away at the end like the last bit of air being let out of a tire. Her gaze flicked over to Jack's for a beat before she quickly stared back out the windscreen. She felt unbearably vulnerable and it was making her itchy in her own skin.

She'd probably shared too much, given too much of herself away, but once she'd started talking, she hadn't been able to stop. She rarely talked about it, and never had to explain the story to anyone from the very beginning. Gwen and Sean had been with her through it all, and with others, she only had to fill in bits and pieces. Telling it all in one go like this was surprisingly cathartic. Even if it was a bit scary now that she'd finished.

Jack exhaled and there was something different to the way he was looking at her now. She didn't necessarily expect that he would have a negative reaction; the vast majority of British people supported abortion access, so odds were in her favor. But Dylan had quickly learned that even when people supported abortion in concept, they still sometimes struggled when they were faced with someone who'd made the decision, when the reality of it became tangible to them in a way it wasn't (at least to their knowledge) before.

But now, for the first time, every single one of his features was relaxed, and there was a warmth in his eyes that was impossible to mistake, especially now that she was so used to the chill in them.

It was the last thing she would have predicted from him, especially after the last few days, but it was the thing she needed most of all.

"I'm going to have to google that article," Jack said softly. "It sounds brilliant."

Rather than let herself dwell on the softness in his voice, she eased the pressure in her chest with a laugh. "Just don't read the comments."

Jack frowned. "Are they bad?"

"My Twitter mentions were worse."

Jack exhaled. "I'm sorry."

"Why? You didn't threaten to do unspeakable things to me for 'mangling a helpless baby.'"

Jack made a disgusted sound. "God."

"I knew it was going to be like that when I published it." Dylan wasn't excusing the response she got, it was still vile, but it definitely hadn't been a surprise. "And you're never ready for those things, but I was prepared. At least as much as I could be. The team spent hours giving me a full brief on, like, every possible outcome, so I knew what I was getting into."

"Yeah, but you still shouldn't have to do that. People should leave you alone." His volume ticked up a notch, and she did her best to contain the smile now tugging at her lips.

She'd seen him angry—god, he'd spent most of this trip already angry with her—but this was a different kind of anger. A righteous frustration that, honestly, looked good on him.

"It was your choice," he said, lowering his voice a bit. "Why would anyone think they get to tell you otherwise?"

She gripped the steering wheel harder. "Lots of people have opinions about my body. And I'm courting them, in the words of one of my all-time favorite trolls, by having the audacity to be online."

"Well, fuck that guy," Jack said, and though he was quieter this time, his tone was no less fierce. "You're allowed to be online and you're allowed to do whatever the hell you want with your body."

"I'm glad we're on the same page about that."

And she was glad, but she was also feeling far too exposed.

"Anyway, what do you do for work?" She smiled in a way that she hoped conveyed *isn't life hilarious* and not *I'm barely keeping it together*. "Hopefully something that inspires less Twitter outrage."

Despite her valiant attempt, Jack didn't even crack a smile. Instead, he looked down at his fingers twisting together in his lap.

Guided by Jack's phone's navigation, they turned down a small residential street, the one that, according to the map, would dead-end at the lookout point in a few minutes. There was a small, slightly crumbling brick house on the corner and a block of white concrete apartments next door, and as they crested the hill, she saw the mountains come into view through the windscreen.

Finally, Jack said, "I'm a solicitor."

He said it with such a heavy sigh that Dylan was surprised he didn't completely deflate. "Seems like you love it."

"No, no, it's . . . it's fine. It's work." He tried to smile, but he looked like Wallace while he was being chased on that motorbike. "It pays the bills."

Dylan laughed. "I'm sure it more than pays the bills."

Jack grimaced again, but she could tell he was really making an effort, so she decided to take pity on him.

"How'd you get into law?"

"My parents thought it would be a good idea." He turned his phone absently in his hands. "My siblings are something of a mixed bag—my older brother, William, is in finance, but my younger sister, Charlotte, is . . . a bit of a loose cannon. She's into design and sells things on her Instagram somehow and was not interested in *anything* our parents were trying to push her into. So they were very keen to have two out of three of us on the 'right path.'"

Dylan frowned. "What the hell is the 'right path'?"

"According to Ian and Jacqueline Hunton, the right path is the most respectable path. And 'law, Jack, is far more respectable than any other childish notions you might have about your future. Just look at your sister, she barely makes a living and is always covered in paint.'" There was a forced poshness about his accent then, and in any other circumstance, Dylan would have immediately taken the piss out of him, but she was caught up in how outrageous the idea sounded to her.

"You don't seem like the type to have childish notions about anything." Jack's childish notions were probably, like, *become prime minister one day*.

"Well." Jack laughed, the sound hollow and humorless. "That's because I made the right decision and went into law."

"*Was* it the right decision?"

Jack's gaze slid toward the mountains. "It was easier than putting up with my parents' disappointment."

"You can't always avoid disappointing your parents. Sometimes it's even fun."

And even when it wasn't fun, it was at least better doing what you thought was right.

Jack laughed, but it was harsh. The furthest thing from genuine amusement. "Ian and Jacqueline are not even remotely fun when they're disappointed. They borderline disowned my sister because she didn't go to uni and decided to paint murals for the rest of her life."

Dylan obviously didn't have a perfect relationship with her parents, but at least she was always encouraged to explore her own interests and forge her own path.

That turned out to have its limits, but she couldn't imagine having her whole life set out before her like that and then being told to just toe the line. She would've lost her mind.

"It seems like your parents' loss, then. Your sister sounds really cool."

Jack nodded slowly, a bit of warmth creeping back into his eyes. "She is."

He paused for a long moment, his expression contemplative, like he was thinking about what to say next. Dylan waited for his follow-up, but the silence stretched between them for one minute and then two. It eventually became clear he wasn't going to say anything when he leaned over and turned up the radio.

CHAPTER 10

When they arrived at the overlook, they found a criminally small number of parking spaces, all of which were full. Dylan drove up and down the surrounding roads, and after a few minutes (and a few sharp inhales from Jack every time Dylan stopped short to gauge if a space was large enough for their car), she eventually found a spot.

"Are we allowed to park here?" Jack asked, glancing around as they unbuckled.

Dylan shrugged and hopped out onto the pavement. "It doesn't say we can't."

Neither of them said anything as they walked along the winding pavement toward the visitors' center, the silence tense after the vulnerability in the car. Dylan hadn't expected they'd suddenly be friends after one conversation about her receiving a few hundred death threats, but she had expected, well, a little less awkwardness. After all, nothing broke the ice like a frank discussion of her many traumas.

They made their way past the visitors' center, weaving around a large group filing out of one of the tour buses on Echo Point Road. They stood there for a beat before Jack cleared his throat.

"Mind if I pop to the toilet?"

Dylan lingered outside the center, trying to find something to stare at so she didn't look like she was actively adding up the minutes since he'd left. There was a small sign outside the bathroom that listed a few "walks" they could take, with an arrow pointing off to the right. Dylan turned, her eyes traveling along the paved path before curiosity dragged her forward.

Maybe they weren't proper hikes, what Jack had seen online. Maybe they'd meant these walks.

There were a few trails to choose from—Spooners Lookout, Three Sisters walk, Giant Stairway—and after a few seconds tracing the paths on the map, she realized that the Three Sisters lookout wasn't really that far down the way. Maybe a kilometer at most.

She was half tempted to try the Giant Stairway, too, but the idea of climbing eight hundred steps—

"Dylan?"

Dylan wouldn't have been surprised if she'd just jumped three whole meters.

She pressed her palm to her chest. Her heart was beating so hard it was on its way to cracking her ribs. "You scared the shit out of me."

"So did you when you up and disappeared." Jack didn't look or sound the least bit sorry. "I thought you were waiting outside the toilets."

"I was." Dylan was trying her best to keep the irritation out of her voice. "But then I saw a sign for these trails and I thought this might be the hiking you saw online."

Jack surveyed the path around them.

"It's paved."

"Well spotted." Dylan took a few steps up the trail. "Apparently there's a nice view of the Three Sisters from a lookout point down this way."

She assumed Jack would follow her, but she had to take a few more steps before he so much as dragged himself an inch.

Dylan dropped her hands onto her hips, annoyed. "Are you coming or not?"

Jack mimicked her posture. "I told you I don't want my leg bitten off."

Dylan rolled her eyes. "I doubt they have snakes. It's *paved*."

"Pretty sure pavement doesn't have some kind of anti-snake coating."

"I *meant*"—she ground the word out through her teeth—"that there are people here all day long. I bet it's too active for snakes to bother coming here."

"Wasn't aware you were a snake expert." Despite the thick sarcasm, he took a step forward.

"I got a postgraduate degree in snake science," she said. "Now come on."

There were no railings, just a stretch of pavement with a steep, sloping cliff on the right and jagged rock to the left where they'd cut the trail in. There were some spots where the thick, gnarled tree roots curled over one another on the rock, desperately clinging to the cliff face despite someone having removed half their anchor. The hill was thick with trees, so there was no hint of the wide expanse that lay off to their right—the only glimpses of it were the bright spots between the trees, the sun shining golden off the soft gray bark.

All along the rock face, people had carved their names, little hearts, tallies, and dates. Some of the carvings made her laugh, like VINNY, which reminded her of *Jersey Shore*, and the collection of pi symbols someone had drawn clustered around a heart. She pointed at one of the carvings as they curved down the path. It was a sharp, jagged J+D carved near the bottom of the rock, the edges weather-worn from years in the elements.

"Do you think someone predicted we'd be here?"

Jack looked at the carving before briefly meeting Dylan's eyes.

"I've never understood what people get from doing that."

Dylan stepped on a twig and it snapped under her shoe.

"I think it's a human impulse thing." She shifted her hair off her neck, relishing the cool breeze against her heated skin. "Like we have to leave our mark on things, you know. Say we've been there."

"I think the world knows we've been here," Jack said. "It's not like we've been subtle about it." He had his phone resting in his palm, and when Dylan looked, she saw that his camera app was open. She hadn't noticed him taking pictures, but then again, he'd been walking a pace or two behind her. She'd thought that he was dragging his feet in an attempt to make his frustration known, but maybe he'd been slow because he'd been pausing to take pictures.

She nodded toward his phone. "Get any good ones?"

Jack's thumb moved automatically to lock his phone, and the screen went dark. "What?"

"Pictures." Judging by how quickly he'd locked his phone, he knew exactly what she was talking about. "You were taking some, weren't you?"

Jack half shrugged, though a splotch of pink appeared on the very apples of his cheeks, almost like he was embarrassed.

"I was taking pictures of the trees." He said it quietly, like he was admitting to some deep dark secret. "The light coming through."

He drew the smallest circle in the air with his index finger, and Dylan tipped her head back to look.

The early afternoon light dappled through the trees, making the leaves almost translucent against the sun. There were some larger gaps in the foliage where the sun warmed the ground, and the shadows of the trees against the bright streams of light were gorgeous.

She wondered what his pictures looked like. If he'd captured the warmth of the light, the silence interrupted only by the breeze and the far-off chatter of people at the distant observation decks.

She had no idea if he was actually a decent photographer, but she wanted to find out.

"I know you think it's *trivial*,"—try though she might, she couldn't quite keep the dismissal out of her voice—"but have you ever thought about getting an Instagram?"

He frowned so hard his entire face wrinkled. "Why would I get an Instagram?"

"It seems like you like taking pictures."

"There's not really a point to sharing them," Jack said. Dylan noted that he didn't deny the fact that he liked taking photos, though.

"There totally is!" As she said it, Dylan heard the LA influencer in her and barely resisted a full-body cringe. "Especially if you're into, like, proper photography, there's definitely space for that. People love those accounts. If you're good, you could get a decent following."

Jack laughed, although it seemed less to do with Dylan and more to himself. "You sound like Charlie."

Dylan frowned. "Charlie?"

Jack started slightly, like he was surprised she'd heard him.

"Oh, uh. My sister. Charlotte. She prefers Charlie, but at home she's— Well, she's always Charlotte to my parents."

Jack kicked a pebble absently, the stone bouncing down the hill and over onto Dylan's side of the path. When she reached it, she kicked it back, watching as it rolled and came to a stop a few feet in front of Jack.

She expected him to step over it, but he tapped it with the inside of his right foot and sent it flying back toward Dylan. They walked like that for a few minutes, passing the pebble back and forth until Dylan kicked it with a little too much enthusiasm and it went bouncing over the edge of the path and down into the shrubs along the edge of the cliff.

Jack sighed, the sound so deep it conveyed far more than just a lost game of pebble football.

"It's not that I think it's trivial, really," Jack said, picking up their conversation from moments before. "My sister makes a living off what she posts online and she seems to really love it. There's nothing trivial about that."

Where his words had come slowly before, there was a sense of finality in his voice, like he knew exactly what he wanted to say.

"I just don't think people would care about anything I have to post. And I don't know if I *want* them to. I like keeping my life separate from"—he drew a circle in the air with his hand, a cyclone of imaginative things swirling around his fingers—"everything happening online."

"No, yeah, I—" Dylan laughed humorlessly. "I'd obviously be the first to tell you that a whole lot of terrible shit can kick off online if you give it the chance. But there are ways to keep your personal life separate. And there are a lot of great things about being online. I couldn't have grown my freelance writing and gotten a job at *Buxom* without sharing my work for years. Your sister wouldn't have her work."

"If I'm not going to use it like that, though, for work or something, then I don't see the point."

"You don't just have to use it for work," Dylan said, her words coming out like a sigh. "You can simply make things because you like to. Because they make you happy."

Jack hummed quietly, his gaze sliding to the forest around them. The previously flat path was now sloping down, and if Dylan really looked, she could see the horizon in the distance. Dylan waited for Jack to say something else, but he stayed silent. There was a slight pinch in between his eyebrows that made Dylan obscenely curious about what was going on in his head.

After a few minutes, Dylan noticed Jack pull his phone out of his pocket again.

They passed a tree with cream-colored bark streaked with rusted orange, trees with pointed foliage that looked like crowns at the end of each branch, sections of rock that looked like sand because the cuts in the face were so smooth and swooping. At each one, Jack stopped and took some photos, and though Dylan wanted to ask to see them, she didn't want to startle him out of it again.

She could beg the photos off him later.

The decline increased as they walked, so Dylan felt like she was half attempting a backflip as they carried on toward the observation decks. It evened out as they approached the lookout, a wide, flat area covered in weathered decking, and she was grateful for the relief for her quads. There were a few people clustered along the edge of the observation deck, and Dylan and Jack waited patiently as people took in the sights and then shuffled away.

"We should probably get photos of us down here. You know, for the station?" Dylan said.

Jack nodded absently, his eyes on the horizon, and Dylan pursed her lips. She was almost annoyed with him for ignoring her when she followed his gaze and felt the frustration die in her chest.

It had been beautiful from up above, but being in the middle of it made everything look different. Brought that much closer to the thick canopy of trees and the jagged lines of the Three Sisters, Dylan was overwhelmed by the immensity and the beauty of the landscape.

Whenever she thought of Australia, she always imagined the extremes. Endless stretches of deep red sand, red rock platforms, azure beaches, but she never imagined a series of rolling tree-covered hills, never once thought about sharp, jagged rocks cutting through trees and sky all at once.

It made her realize how little she knew about the world, really. How even this place she'd thought she could imagine was completely different from the place in her mind.

Dylan'd always gravitated toward cities—she craved the energy and the action and the feeling of being one in literally millions—but there was something to this. The way that every single atom in her body settled. There weren't millions of people here, but there were millions of years in front of her, a landscape twisted and etched by time and erosion and tectonic plates. She was staring at a living record of the ways this land had changed, at the evidence of a power unlike anything she'd ever made herself think about before.

"Ready?"

Dylan jumped and she whirled round to find Jack standing there. He was looking at her, a slight smile on his face.

She crossed her arms. "Arsehole."

Jack looked down at his mobile, his grin twitching at the corner of his lips. "Have you got your AirDrop on?"

Dylan raised an eyebrow. "What for?"

Jack just stared at her. "Have you?"

Dylan pulled her mobile out of her pocket. "Yeah, should be."

"These are for you." And then he turned and started walking back toward the path. He was a few steps away when the notification came through on her phone.

Jack the Posho would like to share five photos
with you.

She accepted and watched the download progress as she followed Jack up the hill. When the download completed, Dylan had to physically hold back her surprise.

The photos were all of her. At the railing. Some were shot from the side, her hair burnt umber in the sunlight, but many of them were from the back, the mountains stretched out in front of her so she looked inconsequential in comparison.

For her, he'd said.

It was such a small thing, him taking pictures for her, but there was something about seeing herself in these pictures. It was seeing herself as he saw her. Her features were relaxed and her pale skin almost glowed in the bright, shining light of the sun, her hair blowing, ever so slightly, in the soft, ever-present breeze.

The shots were framed beautifully, the perfect balance of her against the immense landscape—he clearly had a photographer's eye. She could see the way she felt in that moment written all over her.

Dylan looked up at him as they crested the hill. Jack was already looking at her and she had the distinct impression he'd been watching her look at the photos as they walked.

"These are beautiful," she said. Her voice was softer than she'd intended and she swallowed in an attempt to revive her normal speaking voice. "Thank you."

Jack smiled at her, a gentle, warm sort of thing. "You're welcome."

Her heart was hammering. Dylan wasn't certain if it was the strain from the incline or the way Jack was looking at her.

"You're going to regret it, because now I'm going to be badgering you for pictures every five minutes."

Jack laughed. It was a big, full, resonant sound, one she hadn't yet heard from him, and she wanted a million more of them.

"I consider myself warned."

CHAPTER 11

The next morning, they were up before dawn.

Dylan and Jack didn't talk, just gulped down weak tea (made, to Jack's horror, in the room's coffeepot) as they rubbed the sleep out of their eyes. They traded turns in the bathroom, awkwardly sidestepping each other with their clothes pressed to their chests, Jack mumbling apologies as he slid into the bathroom behind her while Dylan washed her face at the sink.

Dylan attempted to read through her work email while she waited for Jack to change, but it wasn't long before she gave up and switched to Instagram. She'd written another post on the drive home from the Three Sisters (after finally consenting to let Jack drive them back to Sydney) and posted it the minute they'd hit the hotel Wi-Fi. A few people interacted with the post almost right away, but late evening her time was still early morning back in London, so she hadn't seen the kind of engagement she'd been hoping for before bed.

Now, though, there were hundreds of likes and a few dozen comments.

♥ @angelberry: I love this

♥ @lassitude: livingggg

♥**@onion_moon_child:** what you said here is!!!!

There were a few grumpy comments (like no one cares from, aptly, @dreamkiller) but they were easy to overlook. She'd developed quite the thick skin over the last few months—people were going to have to try a lot harder if they wanted to hurt her feelings.

"Ready?"

Dylan started, fumbling her mobile in her fingers.

"If you scare me again," Dylan said, "I'm going to start making you wear a little bell."

Jack stared at her. "I'd rather you just kill me."

"That can definitely be arranged."

Knowing she wouldn't be able to make a fresh cuppa in the lobby on their way out, Dylan brought her mug from the room down to the hire car so she could at least finish her tea while they drove to BridgeClimb, their destination for the morning.

"I don't think you're supposed to bring the mugs out of the room," Jack hissed, shooting the mug in her hand a significant look as they walked through the lobby.

Dylan tipped her head toward the half-conscious concierge at reception plainly thumbing through her phone. "She doesn't seem bothered."

"She probably hasn't seen."

Dylan raised the mug to her lips and Jack's eyes went wide. He waved her down as subtly as he could before reaching out to take her elbow. "Dylan!"

Dylan laughed and walked through the doors into the balmy morning air.

BridgeClimb was in the Rocks, a neighborhood on the northern tip of Sydney off Sydney Harbour. The group organized climbing expeditions up Sydney Harbour Bridge, and though there were climbing trips throughout the day, the station had signed them up for the first slot that morning because *the sunrise over the skyline would be unmissable*. It was only about fifteen minutes before they turned onto Harrington Street, both of them scanning (Jack frantically) for the car park the website had promised. Even Dylan started to think they'd passed it when they spotted the bright red parking sign on the side of a nondescript beige building.

The air was almost chilly when they stepped outside, especially with the breeze off the harbor. The parking structure smelled like oil mixed with sea salt, and Dylan crinkled her nose.

"How're you feeling?"

Jack had been remarkably quiet this morning, even considering the hour at which they'd woken. He had a slightly wild look in his eyes. He likely just wasn't a morning person, but he was also looking a little too stiff, his breathing a little too ragged.

He shrugged noncommittally, but said, "Freaking out, if I'm honest."

"Why're you freaking out?"

"I'm not great with heights." His voice was tight, a sharp contrast to his casual phrasing.

"It'll be alright." The platitude rolled out before she could stop it. "They're going to have all sorts of safety stuff."

"It's not the logical side of my brain that's struggling," Jack said. He pushed open the heavy metal door and the hinges creaked with the effort.

Dylan wasn't sure what to say to that, so she opted to say nothing.

Their climbing group—the adorably titled "Dawn Club"—was a dozen strong including their guide, Arna, who passed out climbing harnesses before walking around to check that everyone was strapping themselves in properly.

The metal pieces of Jack's harness clinked together and Dylan looked over, her gaze lingering as she tried to match her own harness to his (because he was exactly the sort of person who would attentively listen to and follow safety instructions).

"Are you alright?"

"No." Jack clicked the buckle together and pulled the strap to tighten the waist. It looked, if Dylan had to guess, a little too tight, but she also didn't have the slightest idea what was actually correct or not.

"You don't have to do this."

She also didn't want him there if he was going to be worked up the entire time, but didn't think mentioning that would help.

"The station paid for it. I'm going to do it," Jack said. He was still fussing with his harness and Dylan realized his fingers were shaking.

Dylan scoffed. "Who cares? If you're scared—"

Jack's head snapped up. He didn't look angry, but he didn't exactly look pleased, either. "I'll be fine."

Dylan opened her mouth to reply when Arna made her way over to them. And immediately pointed at Dylan's harness.

"Make sure you leave the hook on the front." Arna grabbed the hook on her own harness, showing Dylan what she meant. "This is how we're going to hook to the central tether, so make sure it's not wrapped up."

Sure enough, when Dylan looked down, the hook was incredibly tangled.

"Thanks, Arna."

Arna just smiled, and after a quick "That's perfect" to Jack, she floated away to check the next group.

Dylan was singularly focused on Jack as they approached the bridge. She kept catching sight of him fidgeting and drawing in deep breaths as if they were being marched down the gangplank. It made it hard for her to lean into her own excitement. This activity was what Dylan was looking forward to most during their time in Sydney, but every few moments, Jack did something to remind her that this was the last thing he wanted to be doing.

"You can go back," Dylan said, turning to him as Arna started hooking them to the central line. She tried to be reassuring as Jack's face was so pale his white skin glowed in the predawn light.

Jack just shook his head, and Dylan exhaled, her irritation plain in the sound.

"Well, you're doing this to yourself, then."

Dylan'd known the trip was going to take them two and a half hours, but she hadn't been prepared for the climb up to the summit. She'd thought there wouldn't be anything particularly challenging about it, but her calves were burning about five minutes in and her arse started aching not long after that. It was odd, too, climbing the bridge in the dark. She could feel the tether pulling against her waist as the people in front of her moved, could feel the weight of the people at her back, and even the lights lining the walkway up to the top of the bridge didn't make it bright enough that she could properly see her feet.

She felt like the only way she was seeing anything was due to the lights from the cars driving over the bridge below them.

It was a quarter of an hour before dawn by the time they reached the summit of the bridge. They paused, lining up neatly against the railing, and Arna granted them half an hour reprieve to watch the sun rise. Dylan wished it had been like the films, where all the pain in your body flooded away as you traced your eyes over the horizon, but unfortunately the lactic acid eating away at her muscles was there to stay. It didn't make the view any less stunning, though.

Arna was a few people ahead of them, but Dylan could just catch the sound of her talking them through the Sydney skyline. She kept pointing out over the edge of the bridge as she named various buildings, and while Dylan kept one ear on what Arna was saying, she mostly traced her gaze over the city, let her eyes draw the long, sharp lines of the buildings and the soft, uneven lines across the water.

Dylan could hear Jack consciously regulating his breathing beside her, drawing in slow, even breaths through his nose and exhaling in soft puffs, and her heart twisted with guilt. As annoyed as she'd been that he'd been kicking up such a fuss, she felt bad about it now.

She looked at him and moved her hand into the space between them, tugging lightly on the rope that tethered them together. Jack started, his gaze shooting down to the bridge. He exhaled sharply when he spotted her hand, the relief evident in the way his shoulders inched, barely, down from his ears.

"Sorry," Dylan said. "I wanted to check that you were okay."

"Well, we haven't died yet, so I suppose that's something." His voice was as tight as his grip on the railing.

Dylan laughed and said, "Definitely something," as her eyes flicked back to the horizon.

There were a few ferries coming into Sydney Harbour now, their wakes trailing through the dark water. The sun had started to come up over the hills in the distance, and it shot a bright streak down the center of the harbor, bathing the whole city in soft pink light. The sharp white sails of the Opera House, in particular, glowed a warm rose. She could just hear the sounds of the ferries in the water below, and the air smelled faintly of salt. It surprised her how much she'd missed the smell.

She couldn't even remember the last time she'd been to the seaside.

The rope tugged on her waist again, so lightly she almost didn't feel it, and she looked down. Jack's hand was on the tether, a few inches away from her waist.

She stared at his hand for a beat before she flicked her gaze up to his.

"Yeah?"

"Do you, uh—" He took a deep breath. "Can I hold your hand?"

Her stomach flipped. It was foolish, nonsensical—he was *annoying*—but it flipped all the same.

"Yeah." She let go of the railing, and immediately, Jack took her hand. His fingers were still shaking as they slid in between hers, and Dylan's hand squeezed reflexively.

"I hope I'm not ruining this for you," Jack said. His voice was so soft she could barely hear him over the breeze.

"You're not. I just wish you didn't feel like you had to torture yourself because the station bought these tickets. You don't have to do shit like that, you know?"

"I don't want to waste their money."

Dylan had never, in her entire life, met a posh person who actually thought about how much something cost. Who *cared* about throwing money away.

She squeezed his hand again, more intentionally this time, making sure he could really feel it. "Your mental health and happiness are more important than whether or not someone spent money on something."

Jack made a sound that was half agreement, half dismissal, and she gave his arm a little shake.

"Really, they are. Besides, I bet you could reimburse them if you really cared about the money bit."

He breathed a laugh as he turned and looked at her. He held her gaze for a beat, two, before he looked down at the railing and then, slowly, off toward the horizon.

It wasn't as odd as she'd thought it would be, holding Jack's hand. They'd been there before, certainly, though they hadn't been this close, in a skin-on-skin way, in an incredibly long time. And it wasn't that, standing there, she remembered what it had been like back in March, when she'd been sliding her hand up over his forearm, when she'd been stepping into him and feeling the ghost of him along the whole length of her body.

It was that this, standing there and holding his hand at what felt like the top of the world, was an entirely different thing than that night in the club. Dylan wasn't sure what it was, but she knew that it was different.

The sun was coming up properly now. The light lost its soft pink texture and started to shift into the stark white that signaled the beginnings of a perfect sky-blue morning.

"Alright, everyone!" Arna shouted from the front of the queue, and Dylan started. Her hand jerked, and Jack's arm moved forward as she pulled at him.

"We're going to get a few photos," Arna said, holding up a camera in her hand, "and then we're going to climb back down! The first one'll be a group shot, so look right here." She pointed at a camera on the pillar that Dylan hadn't seen, placed up high enough that it would be able to get everyone at once.

They bunched together and smiled before Arna started calling them up one at a time for individual photographs. Dylan kept her eyes trained on the horizon as they slowly marched forward, her gaze moving hungrily over the skyline like she was in danger of missing something if she didn't take this moment to absorb every little bit that she could.

When they reached the front, Arna smiled the same bright smile she'd been smiling all morning. Dylan didn't know how she managed it.

"Together?" Arna looked down at their clasped hands, and Dylan was positive her palm had started to sweat. She loosened her grasp, but Jack tightened his hold, like he was begging her not to let go.

"Together," he said.

Arna disappeared behind the viewfinder and, after a few waves of her hand to put them into the proper position, gave them a thumbs-up.

"Alright. Let's get a smile!"

They both grinned—Jack's smile a little wild—and Arna snapped a few photos. "Perfect. Go join the others"—she pointed behind her—"and we'll be climbing back down shortly."

Dylan'd thought Jack's fear of heights had been at its absolute worst when they'd been looking down over Sydney Harbour, but that, apparently, was nothing to his fear when they started walking over the morning traffic.

"Fucking hell." Jack had her hand in a vise grip. "We're going to die."

"We're not going to die." Dylan tried to sound soothing, but she was laughing too much to pull it off. "We're fine."

"We're walking over the *traffic*." He sounded like a trapped animal.

"They do this multiple times a day, all week," Dylan said. "I doubt anyone has ever died."

"You don't know that."

Dylan glanced back over her shoulder at him, a smile tugging at the corner of her lips. "I can ask."

"Dylan—fuck." Jack's hand tightened. "Look forward!"

The climb down was another long, muscle-burning hour, though it at least had the decency to work a different set of muscles than those from the way up. She was sore, but it was worth it for what they'd seen that morning.

She'd never seen a city like that before. Not London, not Liverpool, places she'd lived her entire life. There was something to be said for getting to know a city on the granular level, knowing the texture of the streets and the signs in the shop windows, but she'd been missing this macro picture, this view of the city on a grand scale.

She made a mental note to look up a similar experience when they got back to London in a few weeks.

Jack started undoing the harness the minute they walked back into the lobby, like he couldn't get it off fast enough.

Dylan dug into her pocket for their locker key. "Did you have fun?"

"Absolutely not." He slid his harness down over his hips, the metal clips thudding heavily against the carpeted floor. "If we've got any other tall things on the agenda for the next two months, you're going to have to do them alone."

Dylan would never have admitted it, but she was a little proud of him then. He could have used that energy about three hours ago, but it was better late than never. She undid the clips on her own harness and stepped out of it. "I'll take pictures for you."

Jack's relief was palpable. "Perfect."

CHAPTER 12

By the time they were leaving for Tokyo, their skin was a little too pink and Dylan's camera roll was more than a little too full, to the point where she finally cracked and agreed to pay Apple seventy-nine pence a month to stop the endless storage notifications. They spent their last night at a too-fancy restaurant that, according to Jack, "unfortunately doesn't have a Michelin star, but only because Australia doesn't participate in the system," and while she'd teased Jack all night, even Dylan had to admit that the grilled squid she'd had (served alongside some truly outrageous charred corn and tomato) had been worth the absurd amount of money they'd paid for it.

The moment Dylan figured out how to connect to the in-flight Wi-Fi, she finished drafting her piece on Sydney. She had a bare-bones outline and had even written a few decent sentences here and there, so it was more like filling in the gaps and finding clear through lines than writing from scratch. It only took an hour to get the article off to Chantel, and though Dylan had been certain she wouldn't hear back for ages, Chantel must have been on her computer because Dylan got feedback only a few hours into the flight.

> You need to play up the romance—it's boring without it.
> Travelling with a ONS is the interest factor.

And here Dylan thought it was the captivating way she told stories that people were after.

She knew Chantel had a point—most of the reader comments she'd received so far mentioned how excited they were for the "cringeworthy trip"—but now that she was actually *on* this trip, Dylan couldn't write articles that suggested romance was blossoming. She and Jack were still learning how not to be openly antagonistic, for god's sake; this wasn't, and wouldn't be, the second-chance romance Chantel wanted to make it out to be.

Dylan could take the suggestion, though, that she needed to talk about Jack a bit more. It didn't have to be a lot, just slight mentions of him, so it was clear that he was, in fact, still traveling with her and hadn't abandoned her at Gatwick. In all fairness, anyone who could be bothered to look it up would know they were traveling together—they'd been posted on Radio 1's website and featured a few times on their Instagram—but she'd still want to be careful, make sure she didn't accidentally slide too deep while she was meant to just be testing the waters.

> Jack took the most beautiful pictures of me at the Three Sisters (I know you want to see them—they're on my Instagram babes 😉)

> Jack chose our dinner spot, and yes, it was the most expensive restaurant I've ever been to, but I'm absolutely

devastated to report that it was also one of the best meals I've ever had.

It wasn't a lot of detail, but it was enough (hopefully) to satisfy Chantel.

She spent the rest of the flight working on corrections and was still making adjustments when they reached the hotel a few hours later. She'd been fussing with it for a while, writing and rewriting the same sentences, when Jack stepped out of the hotel bathroom, a cloud of steam following him into the corridor. He was wearing his pajamas and rubbing a towel through his hair, but he'd apparently missed a spot because Dylan could see a large drop of water tracing the side of his neck. She stared at it for a moment, watching the water's smooth progress along his throat, before she swallowed and quickly dropped her gaze back to her computer.

There was something so intimate about sharing a space like this. They weren't prancing around in the nude, but there was more to intimacy than the things you did without your clothes on. This fell into that category—the first thing you did in the morning, the way you looked fresh out of the shower, the way you slept. Jack was such a closed book it almost felt like a violation, getting to know some of these things about him. These were things he probably didn't share with people until he'd known them for weeks, months, and here she was, a few drunken hours and a radio contest later, getting to see him like this.

Jack dropped heavily onto his bed. He groaned as his arms stretched overhead, and she glanced at him before turning back to her computer.

"Tired?"

He hummed, his hands sliding along the duvet. "Exhausted."

He didn't say anything for a long minute and Dylan didn't prompt him. She kept looking at her screen, though she wasn't reading anymore. She was too busy watching him out of the corner of her eye. He was stretched out like he was trying to take up as much of the bed as possible, and she found herself subconsciously tracing him, measuring him against the space.

It was fascinating to her that someone as tall as he was didn't look this large when he was out in the world. It was like he contracted into himself, hyperaware of his own body, only to expand and relax when he was on his own. It reminded her, too, of how wild Jack looked while he slept, limbs thrown wide. It was all so at odds with his stiff, buttoned-up posture in everyday life, and it made her heart hurt, thinking that this soft, carefree Jack was cramming himself into a box from the moment he got up every morning.

Jack groaned again and pushed up to sitting. He sat there quietly for a second, watching her edit, before he tugged down the duvet.

"Do you mind if we go to bed?"

"Do you want me to turn off my laptop?"

"I mean, kind of, yeah. Or at least turn the brightness down."

Dylan shook her head. "I can't work when it's dim like that." She wasn't getting anywhere anyway, so she sent Chantel the final revisions and then shut the laptop a bit harder than she intended.

Jack exhaled. "I—"

She cringed. "No, I'm sorry, I didn't mean to slam it."

Jack nodded slowly, but he didn't say anything as he climbed under the blankets. Dylan stowed her laptop on the desk beside her bed and then slipped underneath her duvet.

She turned onto her side toward Jack's bed and reached out to the lamp on the bedside table between them.

"Ready for me to turn the light out?"

Jack was lying on his back, his hands folded neatly on his stomach, but when she spoke, he turned his head to look at her. He held her gaze for a moment, and even though they were lying in separate beds a few feet apart, Dylan felt a distinct pull in her gut as their eyes held. It wasn't electricity crackling or heart-stopping volts, but it was a hum, an undercurrent. It was something, even if she couldn't yet name it.

"Yeah," he said, swallowing before turning to look back at the ceiling. "Go on."

Dylan flicked off the lamp, and the room was immediately plunged into darkness.

It was odd lying there, listening to their breathing in the dark. She was staring straight up at the ceiling, trying to breathe silently, and all she could see was the blue power indicator light on the television. Dylan tried to close her eyes, to ease herself into the mattress, but all she could think about was the soft sound of Jack's breathing in the other bed.

Which, fucking hell, made her sound like an absolute serial killer, didn't it?

She couldn't help it. The dark crowded out everything in the room until it was just her and Jack. Even the distance between them felt like it had been erased, because she heard every rustle of the sheets like they were moving right up against her eardrum.

Jack sighed heavily, and Dylan thought she saw him, now that her eyes had adjusted, roll onto his side so that he was facing her. She lay there and listened as Jack's breathing steadied and then, after a few minutes, deepened and slowed.

Dylan's phone lit up from the bedside table, because, *shit*, she'd forgotten to put on DO NOT DISTURB. Before Jack grumbled about the light, she snatched her phone off the table and, whacking the blanket over her head, looked at her screen.

It was a WhatsApp notification from Gwen.

Dylan had never clicked into her phone faster.

snogged him again yet x

Dylan bit back a laugh.

Dylan: HAHAHA no x
Dylan: he doesn't seem that interested in snogging me tbh
Gwen: well he's deluded then
Dylan: I keep telling him as much but surprisingly he
    disagrees???
Gwen: fool

Dylan bit the inside of her lip. She knew she and Gwen were joking—Jack might be a little deluded, but who, in all honesty, wasn't at least a little deluded?—but they were just starting to edge toward this weird, amorphous thing Dylan had been feeling. If it had been anyone else, Dylan wouldn't have dared move closer to this thought than she already was, but it was Gwen, and Gwen was the exception to every rule Dylan had ever made.

Dylan: lol honestly

Dylan: though I actually like...genuinely don't think he likes me that way? Like maybe the club was a one-off

Gwen: ok. What's your evidence?

Oh, Gwen.

Dylan: a feeling I have about it?

Gwen: while I'll be the first to admit you have v good feelings, I think we both know you need more than that

Dylan: ughhh

Dylan typed out a few messages—we've literally done nothing but annoy each other and he's so closed off and frustrating and it's just very awkward all the time—but she deleted each one. There were still a few awkward moments between them, most of them having to do with the shower because Jack was apparently going to blush every single time he saw her in a towel, but they had improved since the trip first started. She wasn't, well, she wasn't annoyed with him anymore.

At least, not all the time.

Dylan: we've been travelling for like almost a week now and all that's happened is I've told him off about a thousand times

Dylan: and tbh I don't think this man would know an emotion if it literally hit him in the face

Gwen: well that's posh people for you, what do you expect

Gwen: also 🫠 🫠 🫠

Gwen: what have you told him off about I need details!

Dylan: opening doors for me

Gwen: OMFG SOMEONE SHOULD HAVE WARNED HIM

Dylan: please he's fine

Gwen: tell him there's an "I survived a Dylan Coughlan telling off" support group every Monday night at the Red Lion off High Street

Gwen: but anyway before you dig yourself any deeper

Dylan: [replying to: tell him there's an . . .]

fucking rude

Gwen: you're both on a huge journey atm

Dylan: JOURNEY

Gwen: and you need to give yourselves time to settle in

Gwen: [replying to: JOURNEY]

yes you twat

Dylan stared down at her screen for so long it dimmed and she had to tap the corner to keep it active.

It was silly, really. She had spent the majority of their time in Australia sniping at him because he was completely absurd and uptight, but there were also moments that just had her second-guessing herself. Her ideas of him.

Before leaving for this trip, she would have bet her life on the fact that he was going to be a complete and total nightmare. There were definitely moments of that, but there were also . . . other moments. Moments where he felt like someone completely different to the stiff, frustrating man complaining about how she kept turning the air-con down to "unbearable levels."

With her lip between her teeth, Dylan replied.

Dylan: I did tell him about the abortion article though, so I
    guess it's not been ALL bad

Gwen: omg!!! And????

Gwen: if he was an arsehole about it, I'm booking the first
    flight to wherever you are so I can kill him

Dylan: lolol please do you think he'd still be living if he was an
    arsehole about it? I'd have fed him to a shark or a spider
    or something

Gwen: good to know Australia has so many body disposal
    options

Gwen: but seriously how did it go? Are you ok?

Dylan: it went really well actually

Dylan: I nearly cried in front of him when I started talking
    about how my parents can't wait until I'm burning in hell so
    that was embarrassing but his reaction was . . . really good

Dylan: all I could ask for really

It felt tragic when she worded it like that, like she was just hoping and praying for basic human decency. Which, to be fair, she supposed she was, but his reaction had been more than that. There'd been a fierceness in the way he'd responded that she hadn't expected, a determination to communicate that not only did he think everyone attacking her was wrong but he was personally angry about it.

She hadn't thought, prior to that conversation, that Jack ever got more than politely angry about anything. And for him to feel that way about her . . .

Well, that was a little too confusing to think about at the moment.

Gwen: see I knew there was more to him than trying to have
a go at you about bringing mugs out of your room

Dylan: aslkdjf I mean to be fair, there's a lot of that in
him too

Dylan: I guess it's just nice to know he's not a complete knob

Gwen: no yeah that's defo good

Gwen: wait omg I just realised what time it is there!!! Dylan!!!
Go to sleep! We'll talk tomorrow

Dylan: 😴 😴 😴

Dylan: but I miss talking to you

Gwen: I miss talking to you too but you need to sleep.
I'm sure you have a full day planned

Dylan: ugh fine. You're not wrong

Gwen: good night xx

Dylan: good afternoonnnnn xx

Dylan turned on DO NOT DISTURB and set her mobile on the bedside table.

She couldn't see Jack through the dark, but she also couldn't hear him rustling around beside her, so she assumed he must be asleep. If she really listened, she could hear his soft breath, and as her eyes adjusted to the pitch black, she could see the steady rise and fall of his chest.

She wouldn't say she was necessarily *worried* about Jack's apparent lack of interest in her. Gwen was right—they were still in this process of figuring each other out, and they were doing it in this incredibly bizarre way that took them away from everyone they knew. It was only natural that things were stiff and confusing between them.

But there were times where Jack looked at her and Dylan felt something of last March in his eyes. Where she felt that initial attraction was very much still there. And if that was true, she wondered why he was trying to keep a lid on it the rest of the time.

Dylan sucked in a deep breath and, determined to stop thinking herself in circles, snuggled her head into her pillow and closed her eyes.

When she woke up the next morning, there was one text from Gwen sitting in her notifications:

give him (and yourself) time—if it's meant to be, it'll be xx

CHAPTER 13

S o . . . what are we doing again?"

Jack was in front of the mirror doing up the last few buttons on his shirt. When Dylan saw his eyes shift to her in the background, she flicked her gaze up so she was no longer watching the swift, nimble movement of his fingers.

Dylan sighed and shook her head, though she had a smile curling at the corner of her lips. "Robot cabaret. I don't know what's not clicking for you."

Jack had asked her this half a dozen times since he'd read out the day's activities off the itinerary, and his confusion around their evening plans was delightful. He was either desperately trying to prepare himself or trying to will it out of being altogether. Either way, Dylan was going to have a fabulous time watching Jack process.

"It's the fact that 'robot' and 'cabaret' make no sense together." Jack fastened the last button and moved his gaze back to his reflection. He studied himself for a beat and, after adjusting his hair, turned around and looked at Dylan properly, his gaze sneaking down over the length of her before their eyes locked.

"You look lovely."

Dylan hadn't packed anything too nice, but she had thought to bring a few of her dresses along. The one this evening was really a pair of bright cobalt-blue separates. It hit just above the knee and had a twist in the center of the top that left a few inches of her midriff exposed, and while it didn't really go with the jacket she was going to have to pair with it, she loved the way this dress hugged her curves. And anyway, it wasn't the first time she'd had to deal with the cold if she wanted to look good.

Jack had been stealing glances at her as he'd been getting ready, too, and Dylan tried not to feel too self-satisfied about it.

"Thanks." She smiled before adjusting her hair in the mirror. "Oh, and"—she met his gaze again, her smile hitching up on the left side—"I guess you look nice, too."

He really did, despite the fact that he resembled every other rich arsehole on a night out. His white button-up was crisp (due to Jack's careful ironing earlier that evening, to which Dylan had spent a few good minutes taking the mick) and his black trousers fit him a little *too* well. His hair was standing up a bit and he had a shadow of stubble along his jaw. That, along with the amusement shining bright in his eyes, left Dylan feeling like she'd had the wind knocked out of her.

Jack laughed. "Cheers."

Their first day in Tokyo had been an easy slide into the city. They walked around Shinjuku, coffees in hand, before making their way toward the city center to tick off some of the touristy items on their list. The view from the top of the Skytree was even better than the view from Sydney Harbour Bridge had been, if only because Tokyo, compact as it was, gave her so much more to look at. Dylan took as many photos as she could to share with Jack—who, this time, had lingered in the center of the room rather than tempt his acrophobia—but they hadn't remembered to get a picture of them together until they were on the subway to Tsukiji Outer Market.

The photo they'd managed—the two of them standing in the center of the carriage, Dylan pressed back against his chest and Jack's camera arm wrapped loosely around her shoulders—was a surprisingly good one given the fact that they'd been swaying like trees in the wind the whole time. Though, if she was honest with herself, she was less worried about the picture and more focused on the way that she'd felt pressed up against him and the cool cedar scent of his deodorant.

She'd meant to send it to Mina—to have her post it on the station's Instagram and be done with it—but the more she looked at it, she hesitated. Dylan loved the flush on her cheeks, the bright look in her eyes, the way you could tell she'd been rushing around all morning. She didn't want to send a photo like that over to Radio 1. She wanted it for herself.

She and Jack took another picture when they got to the fish market—the pair of them underneath a large crab—and once she sent the new photo off to Mina, she posted the photo from the train onto her own Instagram, burying it in a swipe through of other photos of the trains rushing by. And it was the perfect opportunity to talk about the trains themselves, too. Her love for the Tokyo Metro was immediate and probably too intense for someone just visiting for a week, but the trains were clean and on time, people were polite, and it was nowhere *near* as unbearable as the Underground often was.

Jack found navigating the system and the sheer number of people (especially at Shinjuku station) deeply stressful, but Dylan was obsessed. She'd happily swap this for the tube any day.

That would have been the end of it, posting her little love letter to the Metro, but then Gwen texted her almost immediately—nice picture 😏. Dylan went to scroll back through the post and found a dozen or so comments that basically amounted to the same sentiment.

♥**@astronomicjuliana:** Ok like you guys are so cute???
I . . . ship it????

♥**@basicbytch:** wtf is going on @bbcr1 really matchmade you guys perfectly huh

♥**@too-turnt-tina:** ok but why are you two so fucking hot? where are you all from because I clearly need to move there immediately

Dylan had a few thousand followers, so seeing new usernames wasn't out of the ordinary, but there were far more on this picture than usual. Many of them, according to her notifications, had also gone on to follow her, but some didn't follow her at all. They must have just . . . seen the picture somewhere.

She was grateful for the engagement, but Dylan couldn't help the anxiety that twisted in her gut. She hadn't thought—and that was maybe her first mistake—about sharing the photo of them. Hadn't anticipated the response, but it was crystal clear to her now that she'd done it.

Of course people were lusting after them in her comments. *Of course* they were. Chantel had all but set this up like a couple's holiday, and though her articles so far had leaned away from that as much as possible, this picture had played perfectly into that narrative without Dylan even intending it to.

It had seemed fine then, just posting the picture on her account instead of sending it to Mina. Jack knew they had taken this photo with the express purpose of posting it publicly, but she felt weird about the decision to share it now. To put him in a different space than just the known radio account and to have everyone there drooling over them.

She needed to talk to him about it. Maybe tonight, when they were, hopefully, fresh off a good time.

The cabaret spot was a kilometer from their hotel, though they were keen to walk, even in the cold. Tokyo was unlike any city Dylan had ever visited—though, granted, before this year that list had only included London, Liverpool, and Cork. Every inch of space seemed to have someone in it, and somehow, despite how many people lived there, the city was probably the cleanest she'd ever seen. It didn't even have that city smell, the one that, in London, smelled like damp rubbish and exhaust.

The lights, though, were probably the biggest difference. Their hotel was surrounded by bland government buildings, but as they walked closer to Shinjuku station, screens and multicolored neon signs lit up the night.

But even with all the colorful buildings they passed, the Robot Restaurant stood out, sharp and blazing in its brilliance. From the rainbow letters across the whole of the building and the electronic marquees lining nearly every edge, to the backlit, light-lined photos of, presumably, the robots they were about to see, the Robot Restaurant was in a league all its own.

Jack turned to her. They'd been stood, frozen, on the pavement opposite just staring, and Dylan was sure the lights were permanently burning her retinas.

"I wonder what their electricity bill looks like."

Dylan laughed out loud. "I was literally just thinking that."

They walked down a narrow corridor lined with plastic duo-chrome panels and found themselves inside a lift covered in the same sheeting with glowing, rainbow lights inside. They had to wait in a reception area for half an hour before they were allowed into the actual restaurant, and everything in the waiting area appeared to be covered in mirrors and chrome, including the performers that sat at the piano in the corner, treating them to renditions of Japanese pop songs. Light reflected off nearly every surface of the room, and with the combination of colorful lights and white fluorescents lining every wall, Dylan felt more like she was inside a mirror ball than an actual room.

She sat in an armchair in the corner—it was shaped like one of those spiral shells and had probably the ugliest fabric she'd ever seen on the seat—while Jack made his way to the bar along the far wall. Dylan snapped a few photos of the place and managed to take a few halfway decent selfies before Jack returned, drinks in hand.

"I didn't know what you'd like, so the bartender suggested this." He held up a bright blue tin that appeared to have some kind of flower on the front. "Chuhai," he added, seeing her questioning look.

Their fingertips brushed, just a little, as he handed her the tin, and Dylan shrugged casually through the uptick in her heartbeat.

"If it's alcohol, I'll drink it." She could *not* continue to be sober in this place.

Jack dropped down into the seat beside her as she took a long pull of her drink. It was fizzy and fruity, the sharp grapefruit flavor just enough that she could distinguish it, and while she was sure it didn't have much alcohol, this would be a good starter at least. She took another sip, the bubbles sizzling against her tongue.

Give her a beach and a bit of sun, and she could drink a cool half dozen of these.

She set her drink on her knee to stop herself chugging it and nodded toward Jack's glass. "What did you get?"

He tilted it in the light. "Whiskey."

Dylan laughed. "Are you serious?"

Jack *would* travel to the opposite side of the world and get something he could just as easily have gotten back home.

He nodded and took a small, considered sip, his tongue sneaking out to swipe the last bit of amber liquid off his lip.

Dylan took another swift gulp of her drink.

CHAPTER 14

Dylan's excitement built with every step as they were finally ushered out of reception and into the performance space. They walked down what felt like a dozen flights of stairs to the show floor, passing walls painted with designs that reminded Dylan of the Ed Hardy T-shirts that had been popular a decade ago.

Every inch of the performance space was covered in LED screens flashing videos of robots while blasting music that reminded Dylan very intensely of knockoff Bon Jovi. There were three rows of stadium seating, and for every two seats, there was a narrow, silver tray table where they'd have dinner. It looked like a retro American diner shoved inside a spaceship. She instantly loved it.

Much to Dylan's delight, they were led to a table in the first row, more or less in the center of the room. Dylan turned, beaming brighter than all the lights combined, as she and Jack sat in their glittery red chairs.

"I can't believe we've got front row seats."

Jack raised his eyebrows in acknowledgment as he tucked his legs underneath the table. There wasn't a lot of legroom—even Dylan's legs were feeling cramped—and she felt a bit bad as Jack worked out that he was going to have to sit splayed if he had any hopes of containing his legs behind the divider.

"Just wondering," Jack said, checking his watch, "you've got paracetamol on you, right?"

Dylan laughed. Jack just stared at her.

"I'm not kidding."

They didn't chat much as the rest of the audience filed in, the sound in the room growing steadily louder. She could almost feel Jack's tension radiating off him. His hands were resting flat on the tabletop, his fingers spread like he was bracing himself for impact, and his shoulders looked so stiff Dylan was pretty sure you could have built a house on top of him and it would have remained steady.

She leaned over. "Are you okay?"

Jack turned his head slightly, not enough that they were too close, but enough that she could see his lips as he mouthed, *What?*

Dylan huffed a sigh and leaned closer. She could feel the distance between them as she leaned in, like the very air between them was vibrating. She was careful to speak loudly enough that he could hear her without her having to press herself right up against him, but that only made her that much more aware of herself. She drew in a soft breath and hoped he couldn't hear the way it shook.

"Are you okay?"

Jack hummed in acknowledgment and turned, his cheek bumping gently against hers, so that he could speak directly into her ear. She knew it was just so that she could hear him over the noise, but this close, she could feel the brush of his stubble against her skin and could barely focus.

"Yeah." And then she heard the smile in his voice. "Just wishing I'd grabbed another whiskey."

She laughed and then, realizing the action had made the end

of her nose graze along the side of his neck, immediately wished she hadn't.

"I think you can order one."

Jack let out a rumbling groan that she felt more than heard. "Thank god."

She could still feel the heat of his breath against her skin as he straightened up and looked around to try and flag down one of the servers.

Jack's whiskey had just been delivered when the lights in the room dimmed and the massive television screens filled with a series of rainbow starbursts. A line of Japanese appeared on the screens followed, underneath, by a line of English that they repeated over the speakers: "Welcome to Robot Restaurant! We hope you have a wonderful time!"

Dylan was practically jumping in her seat. She grabbed Jack's knee and shook it back and forth. "It's starting, it's starting!"

Jack lifted his whiskey to his lips and said, in an earth-shattering deadpan, "It's starting."

At that moment, a line of people in fully sequined outfits came dancing out of the wings to a house remix that Dylan was willing to bet they'd had on repeat in Ibiza last summer. The woman in the front was holding a microphone and had electric-yellow window-shade sunglasses on, and the two people behind her were wearing what looked like traffic signals on their heads. The leader began making a series of announcements in Japanese, their English trans-lations popping up on the screens, and then, in English, she shouted, "Now, repeat after me! Don't touch the robots!"

The first pass through the room was a little quiet, awkward as it always was when you asked a group of adults to yell something out in unison. The second time was louder, as those who hadn't spoken the first time found their voices. Dylan, for her part, shouted out into the room, but Jack just sat there silently drinking his whiskey. He glanced at her out of the corner of his eye, amusement clear in the arch of his eyebrow, as she cheered, "Don't! Touch! The! Robots!"

She should have expected, based on, well, everything she'd seen since walking through the doors upstairs, that even the safety briefing would be exciting, but Dylan couldn't have predicted the reality. The call-and-response was fun in and of itself, but then the traffic-light people did the absolute best thing they could've done.

They grabbed neon sharks. With meter-long light poles hanging off either end. And ran along the length of the audience.

Because they were in the first row, Dylan was treated to this up close and personal, the host running along in front of the shark telling them to "Lean back, lean back, lean back," and she was sure it was for their safety when the robots started coming out, but to Dylan, it felt more like a game, an interactive opening to what was sure to be a chaotic evening.

"Jesus Christ," Jack said, his voice tight as he leaned back just in time to avoid getting smacked with the light pole on the shark's second lap around the room. "This feels like a liability."

"Okay, Mr. Law Degree," Dylan said, patting him on the back of the hand, "simmer down."

There was, however, very little opportunity for him to simmer.

The performance was completely off the wall from the moment it started. A robot dragon emerged first, the base covered in flames that gave way to a circular metal frame that twisted ten feet up off the floor. The lights dimmed, leaving only a few orange spotlights to illuminate the space. The fiery haze revealed a person in a cat mask who promptly began hammering away on drums that twisted around the belly of the dragon. The music was so loud Dylan's ribs were vibrating, and as the robots continued rolling in through the flashing lights and explosions of holographic glitter, she felt the floor shaking right along with her.

There were sexy samurai dancing with fans, dozens of people in bright white plastic wolf masks playing the drums, ninja playing electric guitar, massive electric-pink prawn floats, and robot pirate ships chasing women (very slowly) across the floor.

It was easily the best show Dylan had ever seen. She could barely hold her chopsticks steady as she tried to eat her sushi. And she was sure the photos she took (when she remembered to take them) were all going to be blurry, but maybe that was the best way to represent the actual experience of sitting in a room that was like a barrel full of neon signs on the spin cycle.

Dylan half expected, especially once the drumming started, that Jack would have gotten up and demanded to be let out, but every time she looked over at him, he had his whiskey three-quarters of the way to his lips and an absolutely priceless look on his face. Through the flashing rainbow lights, she could see his wide-eyed, desperately confused expression, and the sight of it made her laugh out loud.

Two samurai had just had a sword fight/dance battle when she caught him staring again, his jaw hanging open. She laughed loudly enough that he could hear it over the dip in the music, and he turned to look at her, his eyes wide with shock.

He smiled when his gaze found hers, but it was less joyful and more wild amusement shot through with utter bewilderment, and then he reached over and took her hand. He didn't thread their fingers together like he had on the bridge, just looped his hand over hers, his palm grasping, like he was trying to tether himself to the earth.

Dylan very much knew the feeling, though truth be told, his holding her hand wasn't really helping her feel more grounded.

"I can't decide if I hate this or if I'm enjoying it."

She laughed, a bit breathless, and was grateful for the hurricane of sound that masked her pathetic response.

Dylan mustered what she could of her dignity and said, "If you're not enjoying it, then you must be desperately sad."

Jack laughed and gave her hand a delicious squeeze. "Who told you my deepest, darkest secret?"

She could still feel his laughter against her skin as he shot up, a moment later, to watch a giant panda warrior dance out onto the stage.

CHAPTER 15

By the time the show was over, Dylan felt like she'd lived a thousand lifetimes. Jack snorted when she told him as much as they stumbled out onto the pavement. He shook his head, the gesture looser for all the alcohol swirling through his veins.

"I can't believe we watched that." He sounded awed. "Like we sat there for ninety minutes and watched that."

"It was brilliant." She was aware of herself enough to realize she sounded tipsy, but was just tipsy enough not to care. She'd stolen Jack's whiskey off him after the giant panda had danced offstage, and between the two of them, they'd managed a few more glasses before the performance was up. "I'd go every night."

"I think your brain would melt if you went every night."

The night air was crisp, and the chill felt nice against Dylan's skin. Her blood was hot from the alcohol and her calves were burning after climbing all the stairs to get back to street level. She stripped her jacket off clumsily, tying it around her waist as they walked.

Jack frowned when he noticed her bare arms. "You'll catch cold."

"I'm boiling." Dylan slid her hand over her stomach, pulling the clingy fabric of her top up, just underneath the edge of her bra, so the air could circulate over more of her skin. "I need a minute to cool down."

The lights along the road were dazzling as they walked past Shinjuku station, but everything now seemed dull in comparison to what they'd just witnessed. Dylan couldn't help but rehash every single thing they'd seen—her favorite bits, the most confusing bits, the bits she wanted to watch again but this time in slow motion. She was talking at top speed, but even Jack matched Dylan's energy as they crossed the junction and started on the last half kilometer home.

She liked seeing him like this, his eyes bright, his smile easy. There was something electric about him, something that made her feel like she could sense the earth moving underneath her feet in the best way.

She couldn't help but notice, too, that Jack was walking closer to her than he normally would've done. And she could hear, if she really listened, the sound of their jackets brushing together as they walked, and then, *then*, she felt Jack's hand knock, ever so slightly, against hers.

It was embarrassing how that simple brush of his hand made her chest tighten. And the sensation of it—

It was too much for her to carry around. She felt it, heavy on her chest, thick in her throat, tingling in her hands so she felt restless, like she'd sooner crawl out of her own skin than carry on not touching him. It was a scary feeling, one that she wasn't sure what to do with.

A feeling that was made worse by the fact that several strangers had left her several comments that had really gotten into her head.

"Jack." Dylan wrapped her hands around Jack's upper arm. If he was shocked, he didn't show it. "Can I tell you something?"

Confusion creased his brows. "Everything okay?"

He was either a phenomenal drunk—like, really, class A, because he barely slurred—or he had a titanium liver. She wasn't sure which was true.

Or, at least, she wasn't until the toe of Jack's boot caught the tiniest crack in the pavement and he tripped, nearly bringing her down to the ground with him.

They burst into hysterical laughter, despite nearly concussing themselves. Dylan squeezed Jack's arm as he stood back up.

"You have to be careful," she said, brushing imaginary dust off his biceps and ignoring the slightly giddy feeling in her gut. "Big gangly thing like you."

Jack frowned, but the effect was ruined by the amused crinkles at the corners of his eyes. "I'm not gangly."

"Sorry, babe, you're definitely gangly."

Jack laughed and pulled his arm out of her grasp so he could wrap it around her shoulders. "*Babe.*"

Dylan wrapped her arm around his waist. "Shut up, I call everyone babe."

"You've never called me babe." He sounded so superior, she couldn't stand it. She wanted to shove him and run off, like she was a kid on the school playground.

Dylan made an imperious sort of face, her eyebrows rising in an attempt to smother her embarrassment. "I just did."

"Okay, but seriously." Jack's features were still lit up from their laughter, but there was an unmistakable curiosity in his eyes. "What are you on about?"

It took her a minute to remember. And even then, she decided to take the long way round.

Dylan started working the knot at her waist, but her fingers kept slipping. "Well, you know how we're sending those pictures to the station."

"Yeah?"

She was still fumbling with her jacket. Jack finally sighed and reached out, resting his hand tentatively on her elbow.

"Here." His voice was tender. "I can help." He flicked his gaze to hers, asking permission, and when Dylan nodded, he moved his hand tentatively to the knot sitting stubbornly in the center of her stomach. Jack slid his finger deftly between the two bits of fabric, but despite a lot of maneuvering, he barely managed to loosen the sleeves.

"Christ, were you a sailor in a past life?"

She laughed. "There are more interesting uses for knots than sailing."

Jack's cheeks blazed pink just as she'd hoped they would. It was probably a bit cruel, but teasing him like this was rapidly becoming one of her favorite hobbies.

Her sleeves finally came free and Jack held them carefully, moving the jacket so it wouldn't touch the ground. He handed it to her, still a bit pink in the cheeks, and Dylan grinned as she slid her arms inside.

"So the pictures." Jack sounded almost nonchalant, but not enough that he successfully managed the effect.

"Right. Well, it was just one, really." She grabbed the strap of her crossbody and hoisted her bag up to arm level. She had to open two of the pockets before she found it, but she eventually pulled her mobile from the depths.

"So I told you I'm writing these articles about our trip, but I decided to post some outtakes to Instagram. And, of course, I've been posting pictures, too."

"Okay." He dragged the last syllable out suspiciously and watched as she unlocked her phone and navigated to the app. There was tension in his expression, his shoulders pulled back like he was bracing for impact.

"Well, I included the picture we took on the train," Dylan said, handing her phone over. "I wanted to talk about the trains because we've been loving them, and it seemed like the perfect picture for that."

Jack stared down at her phone for a beat, his expression carefully blank, and Dylan hastened to add, "It's the last picture on the swipe."

Jack started swiping through the pictures, his gaze lingering on each one before moving on. He wasn't spending long on each picture—in reality it was only about five seconds—but it felt like minutes as Jack slowly made his way to the picture of the pair of them smiling up at the camera.

He definitely stared at that picture longer than the others.

"I thought you sent this to Mina."

"It— Well, I was going to, but I liked it. It's a nice picture." That was difficult enough to say, but this next bit was going to be near impossible. She swallowed hard. "The comments are what made me think I really needed to tell you. I don't have nearly as many followers as the station, but mine are more engaged. Sometimes they can be, uh, a bit much."

That was putting it lightly.

Jack stared at the photo for a second more before scrolling

through the comments. She was glad he wasn't shouting about violations of privacy right out of the gate, but if she was being honest, his silence was scarier to her than any amount of shouting would've been.

She was from a loud, shouty family. Shouting was in her blood. Silence wasn't something she was comfortable with.

"Apparently we're sexy," she said, laughing awkwardly.

Jack chuckled, the sound low in the back of his throat, and Dylan felt some of the anxiety in her stomach ease. "Well, that I agree with."

He laughed under his breath at a few of the comments, shook his head at a few others, but his face was completely inscrutable when he handed her mobile back.

"That was . . . interesting."

Dylan tried for a smile. "Picked the vaguest word you could think of, did you?"

He didn't sound angry, but she couldn't read his tone, either. It put her immediately on edge. She hated not being able to predict which way the dice were going to fall.

"I wish you'd asked me first," Jack said. "Just so I knew it was somewhere else on the internet."

Hot shame filled her belly.

"I'm sorry. I didn't think to mention it since we're already sharing some with Radio 1, but then I started getting those comments . . ." Dylan gestured helplessly toward her phone. "I know you're a private person and you don't need to explain why, it just started feeling weird not to tell you."

In part because many of those comments were definitely getting into her head.

He looked down at the pavement, and Dylan followed his gaze. She watched him trace half circles across the ground with the toe of his boot before, finally, Jack sighed.

"I appreciate you telling me." He swallowed, shaking his head, like he was trying to clear away a thought. "If you'd just asked, it would've been fine. It's really easy for things to spiral and I just . . ."

He drew in a deep breath, his eyes finding Dylan's again. "I took myself off social media years ago because of something that flew out of control, and by the time I found out, it was too late to do anything." He waved his hand in a loose circle, and as he did it, Dylan could practically feel the comments swirling in the air between them. "I'm just really cautious now."

Her curiosity was crushing her, but clearly Jack didn't want to go into it and there were better times for this conversation than when she was three-quarters drunk on some random corner.

Dylan's hand moved forward of its own accord, her fingers coming to rest gently at the back of his elbow. "I'm sorry that happened."

She left her hand there only for a beat, barely longer than a breath, but she could still feel the heat of him against her fingers as she pulled her hand away. "Obviously I'm writing these articles . . ." She didn't want to have to bring it back round to this, to make herself the center again. "How would you like me to handle it? Talking about you?"

Jack's eyes flicked to hers. "Have you been talking about me?"

"No." She shook her head so quickly, she thought it was going to rattle off her neck. "I've mentioned your name a few times because my editor's keen, but just small stuff, like how you chose the restaurant we ate at the last night in Australia. Nothing detailed."

She could feel herself starting to ramble and forced herself to stop, to give Jack space to react.

Part of her was tempted to pull all the threads apart on this right then, to tell him everything about how Chantel had framed the series and how she was desperately trying to reposition it in her actual writing, but if she *was* trying to keep people from falling in love with them (and she was), then she didn't know if it was even worth mentioning. If bringing up the idea that her boss was essentially waiting for them to have some kind of *encounter* would spoil the dynamic they'd built, she didn't want to risk sending them right back to the stiff, awkward Jack she'd started with.

Jack frowned down at his boots. "Okay, that's fine. Just . . . keep it brief. Or try to keep the focus off me if you can."

Dylan nodded, her throat thick so it was difficult to get the words out. "Yeah. 'Course."

CHAPTER 16

They started along the pavement again, though there was silence between them now. Fortunately, Tokyo more than compensated for their lack of conversation. Compared to how busy it had been that morning, the city was practically empty, but there was still steady traffic and a crowd of pedestrians.

Jack looked at her as they came to a stop at the junction across the street from their hotel, and there was something in his gaze. She wasn't sure what it was, but it was soft, warm, and she liked the look of it there on his face.

"I can't believe people think we're dating."

Dylan laughed in surprise. It was the absolute last thing she thought he'd say. "Because I'm terrible?"

"No, the, uh—" Jack scrubbed a hand along his jaw, and god help her. It was ridiculous. It was definitely the alcohol that was making something very like lust start curling in her belly. "Opposite, actually."

His tone was so earnest Dylan had no choice but to believe he meant it.

But if he did, then that opened up a whole new set of questions. If she was the opposite of terrible, then what was she? What did that mean about his feelings for her?

Was this, in fact, the exact kind of trip that Chantel wanted it to be all along?

"Oh."

He nodded, and Dylan watched as his tongue peeked out and traced his lower lip. His eyes flicked down to her mouth for one moment, two, before he met her gaze again. His eyes were dark, but there was the slightest lift to the left corner of his mouth as he spoke.

"You're always slagging me off for being posh. I didn't think I was your type."

Dylan smirked, some of the tension easing out of her. "A girl's got to rebel sometimes."

"And your preferred form of rebellion is—"

"Dating a posh bastard from, what, Chelsea?"

Jack looked anguished. "I'm originally from Kent."

Dylan barked a laugh. "Fucking Kent. You're unbelievable."

"Is it better or worse if I tell you I live in Bloomsbury now?"

Dylan shook her head as they walked through the automatic doors into their hotel.

"I mean," she said, walking backward so they could maintain eye contact, "it's better than, like, Kensington or something."

Jack's lips twitched with a smile. "If it makes you feel better, I never really liked Kent."

"Of course you didn't." Dylan leaned up against the wall, her shoulder sliding along the tile. "Who likes Kent?"

"My parents." The lift dinged and the doors slid open. "Though, I guess I liked Kent better than where they sent me off to school."

Dylan gaped at him. This just kept getting better. "You did *not* go to boarding school."

"From secondary school on. They didn't send Charlie or William, but they thought it would be a good idea to send me."

"Wait, you were the only one of your siblings?" Any interest she had in teasing him evaporated. "Why?"

Jack sighed, though it wasn't an annoyed sound. "I was a reserved kid. I think my parents thought it would push me to be more outgoing, but"—he gestured down at himself—"that clearly didn't work."

"That doesn't explain why they only sent you, though."

Jack shrugged, his lips pressed together in a resigned little line. "Well, William's a few years older than me, so he was already settled in secondary and they didn't want to transfer him."

Dylan's stomach started simmering with hot anger. "What the fuck."

"Yeah." He had the kind of calm in his voice that Dylan could never have achieved. The lift doors slid open and Jack lowered his voice as they started down the corridor. "They might've sent Charlie, as well, but it was clear from the time she was five that she's an absolute hell-raiser. They didn't want to tempt fate by letting her out of their sight. Like she wasn't going to do whatever she wanted either way."

His voice was thick with pride, and Dylan felt her heart clench. She could only imagine how much Charlie had to put up with from her parents, and Dylan loved that Jack, at least, was on her side.

"I really want to meet your sister."

Jack smiled. It was quiet, small, but full of a warmth that Dylan felt down to her toes. "She'd love you. She's always telling me I need to relax more, but I don't know. Middle child syndrome, I guess."

"I'm sorry your parents did that to you." It was all Dylan could think to say—or, well, all that felt appropriate to say, because she had several other comments that came to mind.

"Made me a middle child?"

"Sent you away."

Jack shrugged and fished the key out of his wallet. "It's okay."

"It's not." They walked inside and Dylan kicked her shoes off. "Your parents just, they didn't know how to take care of you so they just fucking . . . flung you away."

Even with everything going on with her family, Dylan was glad she'd never had to deal with anything like this growing up. There were times when, sure, she would've loved to have been as far from home as possible, but she couldn't imagine her parents actually sending her away.

And secondary school, Christ. Jack would have been so small, barely eleven, when they shipped him off.

"Anyway." Jack busied himself with straightening Dylan's shoes by the doorway before he toed his own off neatly to their right. "I think we've probably plumbed enough of my trauma for one evening."

"I'm going to fight your parents if I ever meet them," Dylan said. It wasn't her most mature response, but it was the best one she had with all the alcohol clogging her brain.

Jack's lips twitched. "Fair warning, though, my dad's pretty big, so he might be difficult to take down."

"I don't care," Dylan said. And she didn't. Even if she wasn't going to punch Jack's parents (probably wise), she would have words with them if they ever had the misfortune of coming face-to-face.

Jack swung his right hand forward so his fingers rested lightly on the back of Dylan's elbow. She felt a jolt spike through her at the contact.

He held her gaze for a long beat before he dropped his hand, grabbed the water glasses off the chest of drawers, and walked into the bathroom.

Dylan pretended she wasn't watching him go.

She slipped out of her jacket and chucked it onto the chair, before she walked over and dropped down onto the end of her bed. She should grab pajamas and get ready for bed, but now that she was sitting, all she wanted to do was let the momentum drag her down.

She fell back against the mattress and, with a bit of wiggling, managed to land on one of the pillows. She let her eyes fall closed for a second before Jack cleared his throat.

Jack held out one of the water glasses in his hands, and Dylan raised an eyebrow.

Jack tipped his head toward the glass. "That's for you."

"I don't feel like sitting up."

"You're going to get dehydrated."

"I'm comfortable."

"Too bad. I don't want to have to find a hospital and figure out how to tell them you need IV hydration."

"Ugh, you're so annoying."

Amusement sparked in Jack's eyes. "So I've been told."

Dylan awkwardly pushed herself to a seated position and held out her hand. Jack handed her the glass, the corners of his mouth twitching at her outsized annoyance. She downed the glass in two long pulls and set it harder than she intended on the bedside table.

"Careful," Jack said.

She scoffed and lifted her bum up off the duvet so she could slip under the blankets.

"I'm always careful."

Jack snorted through the drink of water he'd been taking and nearly choked. Dylan laughed as he wiped water off his chin, and though she expected him to frown at her, Jack was smiling.

"You are the exact opposite of careful," he said.

She touched a hand to her chest as she fell back onto the pillows. "That's incredibly hurtful."

"Somehow I think you'll survive it."

"Famous last words."

"Well, if you die an insult-related death in the night, I'll be sure to feel appropriately guilty."

"Good." Dylan grabbed her bag and fished out her mobile. She had a few messages—most were from Gwen, including a very cute picture of Cat Stevens, and Sean had sent her a TikTok *because APPARENTLY she never checked her TikTok anymore*. She answered them before she skimmed through her email and then stuck her phone on the charger.

"Oh, hey."

Jack was standing over by the chest of drawers now, and he looked up when Dylan spoke. "Yeah?"

"Can you go in the second drawer and toss me one of my T-shirts?"

"Any shirt in particular?"

"Nope."

He grabbed a shirt and, after he was sure she was looking, tossed it into her waiting hands.

"Cheers." She set it next to her before reaching underneath the duvet and sliding her skirt off her hips. She lifted up, trying her best to keep the blanket from slipping despite the fact that Jack was now very purposefully rummaging through his own drawer for pajamas. Jack had just turned around when Dylan pulled her skirt out from under the duvet and tossed it over the side of the bed.

Jack watched the trajectory of the fabric before he cleared his throat.

"I'm going to, uh . . ." He held up his clothes and gestured toward the bathroom.

Dylan nodded, reached underneath the back of her top, and undid the fastener on her bra.

Jack's eyes flicked down for a second, before he sucked in a breath and walked off to the bathroom. The bathroom door closed with a soft click and Dylan peeled her top off, tossing it and her bra off the side of the bed. She knew Jack hated when she threw her things around, but she always folded them in the morning, so who cared if things were a bit messy at night?

When Jack returned, she was tucked comfortably under the duvet, holding her phone directly overhead as she scrolled through the photographs she'd taken at dinner. She hadn't uploaded anything to Instagram yet, but Dylan wanted to find something to post before the night was out.

Dylan glanced over as Jack started tucking his dirty clothes neatly into his "to wash" bag.

"What do you think I should caption this?"

She held her phone out, though she knew he couldn't see the sequence of blurry photos she'd selected to showcase their night at the cabaret.

"Uh." He zipped his case shut and then turned. "'Still debating if this was worth the permanent damage to my retinas'?"

Dylan kicked her foot playfully in his direction. "Shut up, you had a great time."

"Did I?"

"Yes." She grinned at him. "I saw your face."

"That was horror, not enjoyment."

Jack switched off the light on the bedside table and Dylan fumbled her mobile in her hand, averting her face just in time so the phone smacked her neck instead.

"Ouch, fuck."

"You okay?" Jack sucked in a breath and she heard him pull back the duvet and slide into bed.

"You scared me."

"Sorry."

They were quiet for a minute, the only sound their soft breathing. She was about to turn over and close her eyes when Jack spoke.

"What's on the agenda for tomorrow?"

Dylan rolled her eyes. "You know I have no idea."

"Well, what do you want to do, then?"

"We're going to that owl café." They'd seen it yesterday on their walk around their neighborhood, and Dylan had been obsessed ever since.

Jack hummed. "I forgot about the owl café."

"As long as we see the owls, I guess I can forgive you."

"Oh, thank god." Jack's tone was intensely relieved, and she could see his smile reflecting back at her in the dark.

"But alright, so we're going to see the owls. And we can go to

Harajuku? See that, uh . . . I can't remember the name of that junction now, but that junction?"

Dylan yawned and covered her mouth with the back of her hand. She turned onto her side so she was facing him and curled her knees up into her chest.

"Yeah," she said. "That sounds good."

She was staring at Jack's profile now. He nodded slowly and she watched as he moved one of his arms up and put it behind his head.

"Okay." His voice was quiet, thoughtful, and there was something about it that twisted in Dylan's chest. Just days ago, they were at each other's throats, but now, all the teasing and taunting felt different.

She knew it had to be the alcohol talking. The alcohol, and his opening up to her, and the fact that he was sort of gorgeous.

But then Jack turned, and even though she couldn't make out the details of his expression, there was a tenderness to the way he was looking at her.

When he spoke, his voice was as soft as his expression. "Can I ask you a question?"

"Sure."

"How did you know you wanted to write for a living?"

She tried to ignore the disappointment at not having been asked a very different type of question.

"I've been writing forever," Dylan said. It felt like the answer every writer gave, but it was nonetheless true. "I've always loved it. I was always going to be writing no matter what."

"But how did you go from loving it to knowing you wanted to make a living at it?"

"It wasn't really an active choice. I mean, I guess it was, but, like, I didn't sit down and think about it like that, weighing up pros and cons. Though, to be fair, I'm not a pros-and-cons type person anyway, I prefer to just dive into things."

Jack muttered, "Isn't that the truth," and Dylan grinned.

"I just knew I loved it and I wanted to be happy," Dylan said. She was quiet for a beat, the years of her writing career passing in front of her eyes. That first impossible year of freelancing, the never-ending need to build her contact lists so her gigs could stabilize, the steady contract from *Buxom* that had promised a column which now was likely never going to materialize.

"I'm happier doing this than I would be doing something else."

"But what did your parents say when you told them you wanted to be a professional writer?"

"It wasn't a conversation. I just did it."

Jack exhaled heavily. "I can't imagine that."

She let that sit between them before she slid a little closer to the edge of her mattress. With so little distance between their beds, there was barely more than a foot separating them now. They could have been lying in the same bed for all the space between them.

"What would you have done if your parents hadn't pushed you into law?"

Jack was quiet for a long time, so long that Dylan started to think he'd gone to sleep or was ignoring the question in hopes she'd fall asleep herself. When he did speak, his voice was the softest she'd ever heard, a secret being whispered into the dark.

"I thought about doing photography when I was in school."

"Really?"

"I'd requested course packets from art schools and everything."

Dylan frowned. "Why didn't you go?"

"My parents weren't going to support me through a photography course. And they *hated* the idea of it, were always binning my course packets when they found them." He was quiet for a long beat, and when he spoke again, his voice cracked with emotion. "I just wanted them to be proud of me."

The hurt in his voice tore at Dylan's heart.

She reached over and, after a bit of feeling around on the mattress, took his hand, her fingers threading through his so easily she'd have thought they'd done it millions of times before. "I'm sorry they made you feel like you weren't worth supporting."

Jack shrugged, this one a little defensive. Like he was trying to convince her, or convince himself, that it was completely fine. "It's not like I suffered. They paid my uni fees, my housing, they paid for all of it."

"Them paying for things isn't the same as them supporting you. You deserved support." She hoped that she was imparting all the feeling she was intending to when he met her gaze. "You deserve that."

"No, I— Yeah. I know, I just— Who knows what my life might've looked like if I'd ended up going into photography. Maybe it's better this way."

"Maybe," Dylan said. "But you deserve a job that makes you happy."

Jack shifted his arm and Dylan thought he was going to let go of her hand, but instead he merely slid his hand forward into the gap between their beds so she didn't have to stretch as far.

He squeezed Dylan's hand and, very softly, said, "Maybe."

The alcohol was making her eyelids heavy, and without pulling her hand away, Dylan nuzzled her head into the pillow and finally let her eyes fall closed.

When Dylan woke up the next morning, her hands were snuggled under her duvet and Jack's fingertips were resting on her mattress like he'd been reaching for her all night.

CHAPTER 17

By the time she and Jack were packing their things to catch their flight to Bangkok, Dylan was surprisingly sad to be leaving Tokyo.

She watched the city roll by on their way to the airport, the bright lights and steel towers blending together, and hoped she would remember this place that had sparked something in her. Remember it for what it was, a seemingly limitless city full of energy and layers of history, so that everything, every moment in time, felt like it was all existing together at once.

She'd only scratched the surface here. And now they were on to the next leg of their journey, where they'd only start getting to know the city before they had to leave again.

Tokyo had opened an almost desperate curiosity in her, like she couldn't learn enough, couldn't see enough to ever feel satisfied. She felt it as she tried to write up everything she'd seen, but nothing came close to the way she'd felt in the city or, especially, the way that she felt seeing it all with Jack.

Though that, at least, she was trying to keep a lid on.

She could feel the connection between them in every sentence she wrote, could feel her interest in him blossoming with each passing day. She intentionally tried to edit it down, to write around him to respect his wishes, but even when she thought she managed it, her comments from Chantel were . . . less than stellar.

We need more Jack. One mention is not nearly enough.

She knew Chantel was right. Adding more Jack into her articles would definitely drive clicks (especially if the engagement on her Instagram was to be believed, people had started to become invested and backsearched her posts for evidence of him, commenting things like pretty sure that's his ear and has anyone found his ig yet????)—but she couldn't, in good conscience, talk about him as much as Chantel was asking her to.

Jack had asked her to be brief, to keep the focus off him, but Chantel wanted him in nearly every single line.

We're at deadline, so I'll approve this one, but be warned. You need to include the appropriate amount of detail in the next article or we're going to have to reassess whether or not we continue with this series.

Loathe though she was to admit it, the threats hung heavily over her head as she started making notes for her next article.

They only had one scheduled activity in Bangkok, a food tour on their second evening that promised an enormous amount of delicious food, but most of their time was unstructured. They spent hours wandering around the city—Dylan's favorite travel activity—but they'd also traveled out of the city center to a floating market Jack found online and passed an afternoon eating everything they set their sights on.

On their last night in Bangkok, they were headed to Khaosan Road, which, according to the internet, was one long road where backpackers from around the world wandered. Their hotel wasn't far away, but neither of them was feeling up to walking—it was unbearably hot, and even in her shortest shorts and crop top, Dylan was wearing far too much clothing. According to the receptionist at their hotel, though, this was nothing compared to the weather in the summer when it could be upwards of forty degrees Celsius.

Dylan couldn't even fathom that kind of temperature.

Though it was cooler out this evening than it had been that afternoon, it was still a little over thirty degrees and the air was thick with humidity. It wasn't long before Dylan's skin started to get slick, but luckily, they'd only walked a short way before catching a tuk tuk heading in the right direction.

"Thank you," Dylan said, smiling at the driver as she hoisted herself into the back. She slid along the vinyl seat and Jack dropped in beside her. She'd known the seats were small but was surprised at how tight it was now that they were crammed inside. Her and Jack's legs were pressed together from their knees all the way to their hips, and his arm kept brushing up against hers. It might have been easier to ignore had either of them been wearing longer layers of clothing, but as they were, she was hyperaware of every single spot his skin touched hers.

Having come from Tokyo a few days before, Dylan didn't find Khaosan Road to be the overwhelmingly bright, bustling place it seemed online. It was certainly electric—there were neon signs everywhere, the streets were packed—but the energy wasn't as overwhelming. Their driver dropped them at the bottom of the road and, smiling as Dylan swiftly counted out her bahts, wished them a good evening.

Dylan nodded her head in the driver's direction as she and Jack started wandering up the road. "Do you think they know we're about to get completely devvoed?"

Jack's eyebrows pinched with confusion. "What?"

"Drunk. Wasted. Hammered. Smashed. Tw—"

She could have kept going, but Jack held up a hand. "Are we?"

"Yeah." Dylan stepped in front of him, turning on her heel so she could face him. "Once we find those rum buckets."

She'd seen them when they'd been googling earlier, and apparently, they were a *thing*. It was a plastic toy bucket filled with a small bottle of rum, a can of Coke, and an energy drink. It sounded horrible and she needed to try one.

"You mean those?"

Jack pointed over her shoulder and Dylan whirled around. She spun faster than she meant to, so she wobbled a bit as she faced forward again, her arms going wide in an effort to catch herself. Jack laughed and grabbed her elbow, stabilizing her.

"If you're already falling down, we probably shouldn't tempt fate."

Dylan nudged him playfully before she walked through the crowd toward the stall Jack had indicated. It was right off the entrance to the road, and Dylan was sure they could find a cheaper price if they felt like looking for it, but then she spotted a bright purple bucket on the table, the only one there, and well, she couldn't leave it behind.

She quickened her pace, abandoning Jack, and grabbed the bucket, snatching it up like she thought someone else was going to try to take it. She nodded at the man behind the counter and he grinned.

"Three hundred."

Dylan felt Jack come up behind her as she counted out her money, and he started lifting the ingredients out of the bucket and setting them on the table. He was close enough that she could feel the space between them, but not so close that he was actually touching her.

If it weren't so hot out, she might have felt the heat of him, but everything here melted into the air around them.

"Thank you," Dylan said, smiling at the vendor as she handed over her bahts.

He returned her smile as he tucked the money away in a zippered pouch on his hip. "Have a good night."

"You, too." She turned to find Jack still staring down at the bottles in front of him.

"You weren't kidding about getting devvoed."

The word sounded funny in his accent, and she smiled.

"Nope." She unscrewed the top off the SangSom rum and dumped the entire bottle into the bucket.

They passed the bucket between them as they walked along the street, sliding in and out of the crowd. They didn't seem to be walking with any purpose in mind—Dylan certainly didn't have one and Jack was either following her or was similarly unconcerned.

It took them an almost embarrassingly short amount of time to finish their drink (something Dylan would attribute to the heat and the fact that it was surprisingly delicious) and the alcohol started hitting as one hour bled into two. Jack was carrying their empty bucket, and every so often, Dylan would catch him swinging it like a kid skipping off to the beach. It was moments like these that always made her pause, when Jack's stoic exterior peeled away just enough that she could get a glimpse at the man underneath. It happened more and more as the days passed—like the spark in his eyes when he teased her or the hilariously dry captions he kept suggesting for her Instagram pictures—she felt something like pride as she added these details to the list of things she now knew about him.

They dipped into a T-shirt shop at random, more to get a breather from the crowds and feel the brush of the shop's fan against their skin than to actually buy anything. Though Dylan was very good at spending her money when even mildly tempted.

"What if I bought that one?" She pointed at a white tank top on the wall that featured an impressive set of pecs and abs.

Jack snorted. "You'd actually wear that?" He was thumbing through the clothes rack on the other side, laughing to himself under his breath. She wanted to ask what he was looking at, but every time she went to, she got distracted by a new hilarious shirt and forgot.

"I would, though." She found the tank tops on the rack underneath, and after finding a size that was the perfect amount of oversized, she plucked it off the rack.

A few minutes later, Jack laughed again, this time louder than before. She looked up at the sound, but he immediately turned, hiding whatever it was behind his back.

"Do you remember when you said that I wasn't cool enough to wear snakeskin?"

Dylan made a face. "No?"

"When we met," Jack explained, an excited smile on his face, "you were wearing that top and you said you didn't think I could pull it off."

It took her a minute to remember what he was talking about, but eventually, she gasped. "I love that top."

It hadn't been much—a see-through long-sleeve snakeskin top with a very tiny bandeau underneath—but now, it was less the top that she remembered and more Jack's reaction to it. How she'd told him it was from Topshop, just to be an arsehole, and he'd written it in his phone like he was actually going to buy one.

It was that, really, that had drawn her to him. The way he so easily picked up her energy and ran with it.

"Me, too," Jack said. It was a simple admission, but it still made Dylan's cheeks heat. He was so endearing, it was actually heart-breaking.

"Glad we agree. Now what about it?"

"Well." Jack's smile widened as he pulled the shirt from behind his back. He laid it flat against his torso, the electric-green snakeskin fabric draping over his chest, and Dylan immediately burst out laughing.

"I think this proves you're wrong," Jack said. He was trying to be serious, but he was so clearly pleased with himself—his eyes were shining and the corner of his mouth kept twitching. It was addicting, that expression on him. She wanted to see it every single day. She wanted to be the one to cause it.

A realization that, had she been sober, would've scared the shit out of her.

"You're right." She ran her eyes over the length of him like she was assessing him. "You're really—I mean, straight off the runway."

"Milan," Jack agreed.

"You need to get that." She wasn't even remotely kidding.

"No." Jack laughed and turned to hang the shirt back up on the rack, but Dylan intercepted him.

"I'm buying it, then." And before he could stop her, she slid out of the aisle toward the woman working the front of the stall.

Jack gaped at her. "But it's not your size!"

Dylan grinned over her shoulder. "Good thing it's for you."

CHAPTER 18

Jack fell into step beside her as they made their way back onto the main road.

"I can't believe you bought that."

"I had to." She was swinging the plastic shopping bag, reminiscent of how Jack had been swinging the bucket earlier. He was merely holding it now, but the memory made her smile. "It's the first big step in your fashion journey."

"I'm only wearing it to sleep."

"No, come on!" Dylan grabbed his biceps with both her hands and shook him a little, accidentally pulling him closer so that her chest was brushing his arm. "The airport tomorrow! We'll both wear them. We'll be so cool."

"You can pull off a ridiculous shirt," Jack said. He turned to her, and though his eyes widened with surprise when he realized how close they were, he didn't move away.

She cocked her eyebrow. "I can pull off any kind of shirt given a little time."

Jack nudged her with the back of his hand, his knuckles bumping lightly against her hip. "You're too much."

"You love it."

"Yeah." He was smiling at her again, though there was something softer about his expression now, something a little more vulnerable.

"I don't know why you like me so much," Dylan said. She was touching one of her own nerves here, but she skirted around it enough to make the question seem as much a joke as it was completely serious. "I *constantly* take the mick."

"I like being kept on my toes."

Dylan hummed sagely. "I am an expert toe-keeper."

"And *where* do you keep your toes?"

"In a little bag. I take 'em with me everywhere." She dropped one of her hands from his arm so she could bring her crossbody around. "Want to see?"

Jack laughed and nudged her again. Dylan grabbed his hand as it fell back by his side, and Jack immediately wound his fingers through hers and started swinging their joined hands between them.

The swinging made it feel friendly, casual, the sort of hand-holding Dylan and Gwen had done a million times, but there was nothing friendly or casual about the thoughts swirling around Dylan's rum-logged brain.

"You do keep me on my toes," Jack said a few minutes later. Dylan turned to look at him, but Jack was looking down at their joined hands.

"I like that about you," he said. "Since the moment we met, I've just been waiting for what you're going to say next."

"It helped that I was drunk," Dylan said. "I'm funnier when I'm drunk. It's why I'm so funny tonight."

Jack gave her hand the slightest squeeze. "You're always funny. Though you are in exceptional form tonight."

Dylan snorted. "You're the only drunk person I've ever heard say 'exceptional.'" She slurred it a little, half on purpose, half because the "xc" sound was not working with her tongue at the moment.

"Well, I've got a reputation to uphold."

"What's that?"

"Being posh." He was looking at her like she was the densest person in the world.

"Hey! That's my joke."

"Yup."

"In my defense, you're less of a posh arsehole these days."

"Am I?"

She nodded, the gesture so loose she was surprised her head didn't wobble clean off. "Two weeks ago, I was ready to boot you straight to . . . wherever posh people go to die."

"Spain, I think."

Dylan frowned. "I was hoping for somewhere worse."

Jack breathed a laugh, but he sobered almost immediately. "I was a complete arsehole at the start of this trip, wasn't I?"

"Oh, don't forget my attempts at texting you before we left." She smiled up at him to soften the comment. "Those full stops were *outrageous*."

"What was wrong with the full stops?"

Dylan gaped at him. "Seriously?"

"Yeah."

She shook her head at him. "It's just, like . . . rude. No one uses full stops."

"Oh. I didn't mean to make you feel like that. I was just trying to, like, get down to brass tacks."

"You didn't seem *excited*." Dylan slid her gaze to one of the stalls across the road where a chef was slapping kebab after kebab onto the grill. "You sounded like they were going to kneecap you if you didn't agree to go."

"I'm sorry." The slightly anguished tone in his voice told Dylan he absolutely meant it. "That day had been shit and then they were calling me out of the blue . . . I'm not trying to make excuses, but if it helps—"

"It was the 'I had the restaurant picked out,'" Dylan said, facing him again. "I felt like you were trying to make me look like a hateful bitch."

"I—" Jack shook his head, a heavy exhale falling out of him. "I wasn't trying to make it seem like that, but I can see how it— I was trying to crack a bit of a joke."

"Well, maybe let me tell the jokes from now on, then, yeah? Yours are rubbish."

Jack breathed a laugh. "I really am sorry. I can't take it back, obviously, but I can imagine what you must have been feeling."

"Well, I'd pretty much written you off as a twat right away."

Jack reached up to scratch his temple, the bucket creaking ominously, like it was waiting for the first opportunity to whack him in the eye. "I deserved that."

"You did." Dylan let it sit there between them before she pulled the heat off him. "But you're not an arsehole. Well, you are sometimes, but that's one of the things I like about you."

Jack laughed again, louder this time, and his hand flexed in hers. "I'm glad you appreciate it."

"I do." Dylan turned so that she was standing in front of him. There was something different about facing him and holding his hand, something that felt a little more serious, but she was trying not to let herself think about it. "We're good friends, now. And, hey"—she smiled—"there's a reason I nearly snogged the life out of you, you know."

She thought she saw Jack's eyes darken, but it was hard to tell with only distant shop lighting to go by.

"You definitely snogged *something* out of me that night. I feel like I was out of my mind for, like, a few days after."

Dylan took the smallest step closer. "Really?"

"Really. My mates took the piss for a month, talking about how glassy-eyed I'd been when they found me." He was grinning, but there was something sheepish about it that made Dylan go soft.

"That's cute."

Jack's eyes dropped from hers and he scanned the small space between them. They weren't pressed together, not by a long shot, but they were close enough that the energy between them was starting to feel that much more like potential.

"I thought about that kiss, like, probably a weird amount," Jack admitted. His eyes flicked to hers and they were definitely darker now.

"Yeah?" Dylan wanted to step forward again, could feel the energy in her feet, there and ready, but she was determined to make Jack be the one to close the space between them.

"Yeah." Jack shifted his weight, but didn't move in just yet. "You completely knocked me on my arse."

"In a good way, I hope."

"In the best way."

He took a step forward, just a few small inches, but the difference was everything. The tension alone had her nearly grabbing him by the collar and pulling his lips to hers. Jack slid his hand forward, but with the bucket in his hand, he couldn't do more than rest his fingers awkwardly against her hip. The lip of the plastic bucket scratched against the outside of her thigh and she shifted her leg, testing it.

"Is this okay?"

"Mm-hmm."

Jack exhaled softly, the quietest sound vibrating from his throat, and it might have been that she was already so keyed up or it might have been the alcohol, but Dylan felt that bit of vibration everywhere.

Jack pressed his fingertips into the denim of her shorts, almost like he was trying to glue his hand to her hips. "Dylan, I . . ."

Maybe he was waiting for permission.

Dylan stepped forward, her hand moving up to rest on his forearm. She watched as she wrapped her hand around the muscle there, and her sweaty hand against his equally sweaty arm might, on another night, have been a bit revolting, but now, all it was making her think about was their skin, slick, sliding together and—

She flicked her gaze up and there must have been something in her expression because, finally, whatever it was holding Jack together snapped.

He leaned down, the movement so swift she nearly missed his moment of decision, and kissed her.

If she'd expected something slow or hesitant based on Jack's approach, she was wonderfully mistaken. She wouldn't call it fierce or frenzied, but there was an energy to this kiss, an undercurrent or muscle memory that had them skipping all the awkward bits of a first kiss. There was no tentativeness or the fumbling, just a focus on getting as close to each other as physically possible and socially acceptable in the middle of a public street.

Dylan squeezed his forearm, tugging him closer, and Jack smiled against her lips, one hand sliding across her jaw before threading through her hair.

She drew in a sharp breath, because hell this was going to her head, but as soon as she moved to kiss him again, a car behind them laid on their horn. Jack and Dylan both started, her nose knocking against his, and he immediately pulled back. Dylan thought he would have leaped a full two meters away if he could have managed it without throwing her to the ground.

"Fuck." Jack dropped his hand from her side, and after a beat, his other hand slid out of her hair. "Sorry—"

"No." She sounded like she'd run a bloody marathon. "I— It's fine."

"No, I'm sorry." Jack wasn't looking at her. "We're drunk and I shouldn't've—"

"We *both*—" Dylan said. "Jack."

She reached out and put her hand on his forearm. Jack let her hold him for a second, his eyes moving up to meet hers, but after a few moments, he sighed again and dropped his arm.

"Want to head back? We can find a tuk tuk . . . somehow." He looked around the end of the road, apparently not seeing the dozen tuk tuks just a few meters away from them.

While the prospect of getting back to their hotel—of getting back to air-conditioning—was too much to turn down, she was worried about leaving this spot, about the two of them never acknowledging this moment once they were both thinking clearly again.

Not that, god, she didn't want it to sound like they weren't thinking clearly, but she meant—

When they both weren't completely wasted, she didn't want this to be something they ignored.

Unless, maybe, this kind of feeling between them was something that only surfaced when they were both off their tits and so maybe she could spare her ego the conversation.

"Yeah." She swallowed and straightened up, determined to inject a bit of confidence into her posture. "Though I think I might end up caked in a frozen layer of sweat the minute we walk into the lobby."

Now *there* was a surefire way to distract him.

CHAPTER 19

They rode back to the hotel in absolute silence.

Thick, tense, horrible silence that made Dylan wish she'd walked back to the hotel rather than sat next to Jack for the ten-minute crawl through the busy streets.

There had been as much space between them as physically possible in the tuk tuk, and Jack's desire to avoid conversation was so palpable, Dylan would swear she could taste it.

Half of her wanted to force his hand, to tell him that he couldn't fucking kiss her, especially like that, and ignore her, but the other half . . . The other half was focused on sorting out her own feelings.

She knew she'd enjoyed the kiss, knew she would absolutely do it again in a heartbeat, but she also was growing increasingly aware that every time Jack had shown any significant interest in her, they'd been several sheets to the wind. It could be a confidence thing—maybe he felt more at ease showing his real feelings when he could reasonably pass it off as drunkenness if rejected—but it could also just as easily be, well . . . just drunken interest.

Which was fine, but with Jack, the thought made her feel a little sick.

She *liked* him. Liked him a lot more than she knew what to do with.

WhatsApp Chat with: Gwen

Dylan: so.....

Dylan: I might have.....kissed Jack a little

Gwen: !!!!!!!!

Gwen: WHAT DO YOU MEAN

Gwen: CALL ME RIGHT NOW

Dylan: asklj I can't he's literally in the bed next to me right now

Gwen: DID YOU HAVE SEX WITH HIM?????

Dylan: oh no I meant. Like the bed next to mine. It's the middle of the night here rn so he's sleeping

Gwen: ughhhhh

Gwen: BUT YOU KISSED HIM??? HOW WAS IT???

Dylan: well I thought it was good but then he like

Dylan: he kind of freaked out

Gwen: ......what do you mean

Dylan: he hasn't talked to me since

Dylan: like. Not a single word.

Gwen: what. The. Fuck.

Dylan: I know.

Gwen: are you ok

Dylan: I don't know

Dylan: I was just like...really starting to like him. Like actually like him

Dylan: maybe he doesn't like me and the alcohol just made him want to kiss someone and I happened to be there

Gwen: oh god you were drunk?

Dylan: yeah.... Not incredibly

Dylan: though I guess we'd had a bottle of rum between us
Gwen: JESUS CHRIST
Gwen: maybe talk to him in the morning. Or when
the hangover wears off
Gwen: it's probably not as bad as it seems right now

Dylan didn't reply, just turned the phone over in her hands. After a long moment, Gwen texted again, almost like she could feel Dylan's distress from thousands of miles away.

look at Cat Stevens—he keeps batting his springs under the
fridge and then doing this

Dylan laughed weakly at the picture—Cat Stevens's little paw was extended sadly, shoved under the fridge as far as it would go, his body flat on the ground as he peered desperately under the refrigerator. As amusing as it was, though, it was only enough to distract Dylan for about thirty seconds.

Jack carefully avoided Dylan as they moved around their hotel room the next morning packing their things, and didn't talk to her about anything other than the hotel's breakfast options and what time he thought they needed to leave for the airport (as always, far too early). Dylan had thought the walls between them had dropped, but all the casual touches from the last week stopped so abruptly that Dylan felt their absence viscerally. He practically tossed her coffee cup into her hand, and he leaned as far away as possible on

the plane; each new block he set up between them hit Dylan like a
punch to the gut.

It was very early morning in London and the plane's Wi-Fi was
spotty, so as much as she loved Gwen, Dylan knew sending a
ramble of text messages wasn't the best idea. She needed to sit
and sort through these feelings on her own first. There were a
million things mixed together—hurt and confusion and anger and
frustration—and so she did the only thing she could do when she
felt like someone had thrown her life into disarray and she needed
to start sorting out the pieces.

She wrote.

It's mad what a rum bucket and a hot, humid 35 degree
night can do, let me tell you.

First of all, it's important to acknowledge that my
Irish constitution was not at all prepared to endure these
sorts of temperatures. I was covered in a thick sheen of
sweat about five minutes in and practically begging for
death by minute ten. Luckily, the rum buckets they talk
about online are as good as they say and definitely took
some of the edge off.

She'd started off innocently enough. She described the feeling
of walking through the streets, the way the heat multiplied and
shifted as people moved. She talked about the tattoo she wished
she'd gotten and the absolutely brilliant muscle tee (*literally a
muscle tee*) she'd worn to the airport for their flight to Mumbai. But
the closer she got to The Kiss, the more her feelings started to find
their way into her words.

I'd known that, over the course of travelling together, Jack and I were going to get to know one another. That we were going to get closer, because how can you avoid it when you're thrown through a thousand time zones and into a thousand more airport security queues? But I hadn't ever expected to feel like I'd found someone I connected with. Someone I actually enjoyed spending time with and liked seeing these places alongside. Maybe even more than I would have liked seeing them on my own.

So I guess I shouldn't have been surprised how the night went. You know what they say about hot, sweaty evenings, after all.

Still all jumbled up after the hot and cold events of the past twenty-four hours, she sent the article off to Chantel without reading it back, slamming her laptop closed and diving straight into her Netflix queue to avoid thinking about everything she'd unloaded. It felt good, getting everything out, but when she checked her email again once they arrived at the hotel in Mumbai, she realized an emotional dumping might not have been the best idea. As soon as she read Chantel's enthusiastic acceptance— This is EXACTLY what I've been asking for! A few typos, but it'll be up tomorrow—anxiety started curling uncomfortably in her stomach.

And then she read the article back and knew she'd fucked up.

From: Dylan Coughlan (d.coughlan@buxom.co.uk)
To: Chantel Stainton (c.stainton@buxom.co.uk)
Subject: Bangkok Article [URGENT]

Hi Chantel,

   Can I make a few changes to the Bangkok article?
Upon reflection, I'd like to remove some things before it
goes live.
   Thanks,
   Dylan

It was a desperate attempt at clawing the article back, but Dylan hoped that Chantel would grant her a little grace. She should have known that it was a completely pointless spot of optimism, because Chantel was never kind to anyone unless she thought it might benefit her.

From: Chantel Stainton (c.stainton@buxom.co.uk)
To: Dylan Coughlan (d.coughlan@buxom.co.uk)
Subject: Re: Bangkok Article [URGENT]

   Article's already scheduled. No changes—it's going to
do numbers.
   CS

The dread Dylan felt reading that email was deep and immediate.

Jack had drawn very clear, very understandable lines around how much he wanted to be included, and in the midst of her trying to sort out her own feelings, she'd steamrolled right over his boundaries and then sent the evidence off to her editor for the world to see. She might've felt less anxious if no one had cared about her and Jack at all, but she was still getting comments on her Instagram about how "cute" they were, and this article was going to be a barrel of fuel straight into the flames.

Dylan was bracing herself for the worst, but even she wasn't prepared for the comments that started rolling in over their first few days in Mumbai.

♥@dotsby: did you two get together?? you're so cute!!

♥@clappart: @dotsby idk and they haven't talked about it but her Bangkok article makes pretty strong hints that SOMETHING went down and there were hints in her first article that now make SO much more sense

♥@dotsby: @clappart omg I didn't know she was writing about it. Can you link me???

♥@clappart: @dotsby here you go babe this is the first article, the whole series is there x bit.ly/555-jhk

♥@basicbytch: I went back and listened to the winning call because it's on @bbcr1's website and they met each other out one night, so 👀 👀 👀

They were literally crowdsourcing ways to torture her.

She could tell from the way things kicked off in the comments that this particular article had made its way to more corners of the internet than any of the others. Part of her was thrilled—this, finally, was the growth she needed—but the rest of her started seeing signs she remembered all too well from the last time she'd been this close to a viral piece.

♥ **@butchersbristols:** can't believe you got to do this after you literally promoted abortion last year

♥ **@user1489180:** fucking bitch

♥ **@ghostmario:** your going to hell

It was only a few comments at first, and she tried to course-correct on her Instagram posts, making a point of including nothing of Jack the rest of the time they were in Mumbai. If anything, though, that only fanned the flames of speculation. And nothing, apparently, was going to stop the trolls now that they remembered she existed.

♥ **@catfloof:** I bet she cut him out here because we were catching onto them and they weren't ready to go public

♥ **@superpare:** @catfloof cut him out like her helpless baby

♥ **@catfloof:** @superpare GET A FUCKING LIFE

♥ **@superpare:** @catfloof wish her baby could

Dylan was at a complete loss. On the one hand, she didn't think publicly talking about Jack more would settle things down in her comments, but it might calm the people who were now digging across every corner of the internet trying to find him. If she reined them in, that might mean her articles were splashed fewer places across the internet, that they weren't constantly sitting on *Buxom*'s home page, or (according to Gwen) all over her Twitter feed. On the other hand, talking about Jack would only open the door to further speculation, something that was particularly hard for her to do when there was literally nothing to be speculating about. Any attempt she made, even to tell the truth, would read as false, and that would only backfire and send people snooping that much more.

And then there was the fact that Jack had asked her, very plainly, to keep the focus off him. This decision to talk about him, to hint at everything that had happened between them was—there was no other word for it—a betrayal. She'd broken the trust between them so thoroughly that when he found out, she was sure he'd be livid. Sure he'd never look at her the same way again. She couldn't very well post about him now, even if it was the golden ticket to getting people to stop flooding her comments.

As she wrote her next article, the beauty of their destination faded into the background: Mumbai's sharp contrasts didn't feel real to her. She saw everything, took pictures of everything, and pretended she'd experienced everything, but there was an incessant, throbbing hum in the back of her mind and a tight, thick feeling in her chest that made sure nothing stuck.

Jack kept his distance those first few days after Bangkok—he was careful to avoid any suggestion, any contact, anything that might have been misconstrued. Each hesitant hand, each carefully constructed comment was a knife to her ego. But as reactions to the article started to heat up, she noticed Jack started easing himself closer to her again, softening up. They were being friendly again, with Jack having no clue what was spiraling online.

It made her sick, knowing what she'd done and seeing him try to get close to her again. She wanted to tell him, to shout out the story and take whatever reaction Jack was going to give her, but she was desperate to feel like her life wasn't three seconds away from imploding again. Every time she went online, she was immediately overwhelmed, and those moments with Jack—phone away, wandering through the city—were the only moments she had to pretend everything was alright.

And honestly, she'd missed the way that Jack was looking at her. Their days in Mumbai had eased things between them, and if she brought it up now, all this, all of *Jack*, would disappear all over again.

It wasn't much at first. A lingering glance as they got off the ferry at the Elephanta Caves their last day in Mumbai, a gentle hand hovering just north of the base of her spine as, exhausted, she wiped sweat from her brow. The gentle gestures increased when they landed in their next destination, Marrakech, and Dylan's guilt over saying nothing about the article only grew. As the comments snowballed, and Dylan withdrew more and more, Jack's attempts to draw her out became more obvious. The "spontaneous" dips into the markets and bakeshops when they arrived in Morocco, trips to the random places he found on Google, the way he carried the bulk of the conversation even though, really, he was mostly talking to himself. She appreciated each and every gesture.

But the internet was not interested in making Jack's job easier.

Jillybean ✔ @jillybean

this is literally so fucked up SHE'S JUST WRITING ABOUT HER HOLIDAY AND PEOPLE ARE STILL TRYING TO DOX HER OVER SOMETHING SHE WROTE A YEAR AGO

✉ **@spawner12491:** is her address still 97 Murray Grove N1 7QP

83 RETWEETS   54 QUOTE TWEETS   487 LIKES

As much as she appreciated jillybean's passion, Dylan really wished they wouldn't spread her old address around. It would only lead to the new people living there getting harassed . . . and the internet starting their desperate search for her new address.

WhatsApp chat with: Sean
Dylan: I may be on the road to getting doxxed again

She'd meant it as a joke, but as she typed it out, the anxiety started twisting in her gut, tying her up in knots. This wasn't as serious as last time, not yet, but it could be, and that reality . . .

Sean: are you serious
Sean: can I call?

And that.

Fucking hell, she was far too close to tears for someone standing in the middle of a hotel lobby.

"Are you okay?"

She looked up and found Jack staring at her, concern creasing his brows. His hand was halfway to touching her, like he'd thought about touching her forearm and then caught himself before he could finish the gesture.

"Yeah, 'course." She blinked and swallowed back the tears. Her hands were shaking and she quickly pressed her free hand against the outside of her thigh. "I just have to go real quick, my, uh"—she shook her mobile at him—"my brother needs to call me about something, I don't know."

And with that very ironclad excuse, she ran off to the lift. She barely caught Jack's "I'll wait here for you" as she jammed her finger into the button.

CHAPTER 20

The minute she was inside the lift she rang Sean. He answered immediately.

"Are you okay?"

At the concern in his voice, tears finally spilled down Dylan's cheeks.

"No." The lift stopped on the fourth floor, and Dylan started rummaging in her shorts pocket as she walked down the corridor. "I can't go through this again, Sean."

"What happened?"

Where to fucking begin?

Dylan fumbled with the key and, on the third attempt, managed to unlock the door. "So I wrote about Jack in my article about Bangkok and apparently these fucking people can't stop obsessing over who Jack is and now—"

"You're being threatened again."

The simplicity of Sean's statement made Dylan stumble to a stop. The hard slam of the door behind her was an annoyingly perfect echo of the feeling that punched her in the chest. She made a thick choking sound, the closest she'd get to words at the moment, and Sean continued.

"I saw it on Twitter." He sounded like he didn't want to admit it, but she was glad he had. The more she knew at this stage the better. "One of your stans who was desperately trying to figure out who 'sexy Jack' is linked it along with a thread of 'evidence,' and then half of the replies were . . . vile. I wanted to reach out, but I was hoping you hadn't seen."

"Oh my god." Dylan sat down hard on the bed. "Oh my fucking god."

"I've got to admit, I'm not liking the sound of this." Sean tried to say it casually, but Dylan could hear the worry in his voice. "Can you take a deep breath? I don't want you to have a panic attack on me."

"I—" She tried to take a deep breath, but it kept getting caught in her throat. "Sean, I can't."

"You *can*." His voice was deadly calm, like he was trying to coax a kitten out of a wood chipper. "Dylan, it's going to be okay."

She knew he meant well, but she also knew he was just trying to talk her back off the ledge. He wasn't very well going to sit there like, *Yeah, not gonna lie, love, this could all go to utter fucking shit again*, but it could, very easily, all go to fucking shit.

She and Gwen would have to move again. She'd be stuck at home, hiding under her duvet again. She knew Gwen would refuse to abandon her, that they'd find a place, and Chantel would, hopefully, let her keep her job. She had a safety net, but that didn't make plummeting to the earth any less terrifying, especially when said safety net could only cover so many parts of her life. It couldn't keep people from finding her. It couldn't keep someone from doing something horrible to her on the street.

"I know you feel like everything is out of your control, but it's important to remember that there are so many things you *do* control." Sean was quiet for a moment, probably listening to the desperate way Dylan was breathing. "You are nowhere near the people who are saying those things about you. The vast, *vast* majority of those people will never do anything about what they're saying online. They just want to chat a big game and look like Billy Big Bollocks—"

Dylan laughed. "Billy Big Bollocks? Do you say that to all your clients?"

"Only the ones I like." The smile in Sean's voice eased her anxiety a notch. He waited, and the longer he was quiet, the more Dylan felt her breathing start to regulate.

"I know it's horrible, seeing the things people are writing about you. But remember, almost none of them are ever going to do anything more than chat shit. The very rare few that *would* have no idea where you live and you were very, very careful about what you shared about your place since you moved."

He paused to let that sink in, and Dylan had to admit, he was right. Since she and Gwen had moved last summer, Dylan hadn't posted anything that could be used to identify her flat. No shots out the window, no pictures that matched up with rental advertisements, nothing.

"Have you let Gwen know?"

"Yeah." Dylan wiped underneath her eye and frowned at the mascara on her finger. "She said if anyone turned up at ours she'd make them regret it."

"I love her."

Dylan rolled her eyes. "Yeah, I know."

Sean laughed before he drew in a deep breath. "But, okay. Gwen knows, I'm assuming Chantel knows—"

"Yeah."

"Okay, good."

"I can't fucking stand reading it, though, Sean." All the worst comments flashed through her mind, a highlight reel of the most terrible things she'd ever read. "And I can't even fucking respond! Anything I say would just make it worse, but I hate that they can say whatever fucking horrible thing they like and I just have to take it like I'm not a human being with actual fucking feelings."

"You should delete social media off your phone again."

Dylan huffed a sigh. She'd assumed he would suggest it, but—

"I know you don't want to, but it really helped last time."

She hated when he was right about things. He was the younger one, he wasn't supposed to be right about things.

"I can't delete Instagram, I need it for work. It's—" The words got caught in her throat, and she swallowed hard to dislodge them. "It's helping grow the series. And I need that fucking column, Sean."

Sean was quiet, like he was trying to decide whether he should say what he clearly wanted to. Finally, after a moment, he exhaled. "Can they do *anything* at *Buxom* so you don't have to deal with this?"

"Short of shutting down all the comments on my articles, I don't think so," Dylan said. "And last time, that just drove people straight into my DMs, so . . ."

"Is . . ." Sean sounded like he was walking on incredibly thin ice. "Is getting a column worth putting up with all this?"

In the very back of her mind, a quiet voice whispered agreement. *Was* a column worth all this? Especially a column with Chantel at the helm?

"I can't let them bully me out of my fucking job, Sean." Dylan's throat tightened again and she consciously made herself breathe through it. "They almost managed it last time, and I'm not going to let them get that close ever again."

"Glad to see spite is still a big motivator for you."

"I'm motivated by nothing if not spite."

Sean chuckled and then was quiet for a long beat. "I'm really sorry that this is still happening to you."

It was such a small thing, the way he'd worded it. It wasn't *happening again*, it was *still* happening—things had quieted down, but they'd never really gone away, and she appreciated that he acknowledged that, even in this small way.

It would have been easy to regret writing about her abortion, to wish she could save herself all the trauma, but even knowing everything that had come after, Dylan didn't regret talking about it.

She didn't want to have to be traumatized to be "made stronger," but she didn't want to be silent to avoid people's negative reactions, either.

She drew in a deep, cleansing breath. "Thanks, Sean."

"Anytime. Though, actually"—there was his old Sean voice again—"don't take that as an invitation to start having panic attacks on me every day. That was a little too much last time."

A thick, watery laugh bubbled up out of her chest. "Yeah, I think I still owe you a few thousand quid, don't I?"

"And that's with the friends and family discount." He clicked his tongue. "I really should go into private practice, it's where all the money is."

Dylan laughed again, this one a little easier than the last. "Yeah, but then you'd never be able to live with yourself."

"I could wipe up my tears with piles of money. I'm sure I'd manage."

After ensuring that she was okay to go about her afternoon, Sean rang off and Dylan let the phone fall onto the duvet.

People were going to say whatever they were going to, and the only thing she could control was whether or not she read their comments. She wouldn't ask Chantel to turn them off, since that would really only hurt her in the long run, but she would stop reading them. She'd set up tougher filters on her email, block more words on Twitter, and change her permissions so people couldn't reply to her tweets for a while.

She sat on the end of the bed for the better part of twenty minutes, updating all of her social media settings because she knew that if she went downstairs, she'd never actually do it. Dylan was about to head out when her mobile lit up with a message. She thought it would be Sean checking in, but was shocked to see her mother's name there instead.

She stared down at the notification for so long that the screen went dark.

Part of her wanted to open the message now, to get it over with, but she was still feeling fragile and she wasn't sure if that was really the best course of action at the moment.

She only stared at it a second longer before she decided to just get on with it. Putting it off wasn't going to make it any easier to read.

Hi Dylan, hope you're enjoying your travels. Sean just rang to let us know what's been going on. Your da and I don't have Twitter, but Sean sent us some pictures of the things people have been saying to you. You know we'll never agree with what you did, but I hope you know that you don't deserve anyone saying those kinds of things to you. I know you said it's been like this all year and it's why you and your housemate had to move over the summer. I'm very sorry your da and I didn't support you through that—we couldn't see past what you'd done. I hope you know your da and I love you. Enjoy your holiday. Xx Mam

By the time she finished reading, Dylan was ugly sobbing at the bottom of the bed.

CHAPTER 21

Dylan didn't know how long she sat there. How long she cried. It came in waves, each time knocking her over and twisting her around until she didn't know which end was up.

She'd been sitting there awhile when she heard a few gentle taps on the door followed by the electronic click of the lock. She was fairly sure it was just Jack, but if it wasn't, well. She'd lived a good life. Or, at least, an interesting one.

"Dylan?" Jack sounded nervous, like he half expected she'd escaped out the window. She meant to reply, but all she could do was whimper into her hands in an attempt to control the tears.

The last thing she wanted was for Jack to find her like this.

But she also didn't want to keep sitting alone, either, feeling like everything was collapsing over and over again.

She counted Jack's soft footfalls as he walked into the room—one, two, three—before he drew in a sharp inhale.

"What's happened?"

Dylan buried her face in her hands and drew in a deep shuddering breath, tears soaking her palms.

"Oh, Dylan."

The edge of the bed dipped as Jack sat next to her, and Jack, for once, didn't hesitate as he wrapped his arm around her shoulders.

She didn't deserve this. She didn't deserve him comforting her.

She was in this mess because of something she'd said about him, something he still didn't know about.

"I am so, so sorry," he said. He didn't even know what for, but here he was saying it anyway. He could've demanded details, but he'd just accepted her situation without needing to know what caused it, and fucking hell, she hadn't known how much she needed that.

He slid closer, his hand cradling her bicep. He fitted himself to her, curving up against her as he moved his thumb in deep, soothing circles on her arm. That simple move—of his coming to her rather than dragging her to him—sank straight through Dylan's skin. He rested his free hand on the duvet, but Dylan reached out the moment she saw it and grasped it like it was the only thing tethering her to the bed.

It reminded her of the way he'd taken her hand back in Sydney, and the differences between the scenarios almost made her laugh out loud.

She should tell him everything now. While it was more or less out in the open. A selfish part of her thought it might be easier, too, to come clean while she sat there crying. He could be less likely to go off the rails about the very real part she'd played in all this. But it wouldn't be fair to tell him everything when he was inclined to excuse her, even if it would've made things simpler for her.

Or maybe that was just what she was telling herself. One more way to avoid a confrontation that she desperately didn't want to have.

"Everyone's okay," she said, though whether or not that was completely true, she wasn't sure. "It's just the stuff with my parents and everything on the internet is kicking off again and—"

Even trying to say it, she started sobbing again.

Jack made a few soothing sounds and rested his cheek on top of her head.

"It's okay. Whatever it is, it's nowhere near as big as it feels in your head."

"No, I know. I just—" She turned and buried her nose into his neck. It was the worst thing she could do, but the cool, cedar scent of his skin was soothing.

Jack turned and Dylan would have sworn, *sworn*, he'd pressed a kiss to her head. It felt like someone cracked a cold egg on top of her head, the way the sensation trickled down her spine.

They fell silent, Jack probably because he was waiting for Dylan to speak and Dylan because she wasn't sure what to say (or what she could say that would make sense and not end in her sobbing into Jack's lovely green T-shirt). She wasn't sure how long they sat there, but Jack didn't move, didn't so much as shift. He just held his arm around her, his thumb tracing along the side of her index finger.

She could get used to this. It was the wrong thing to think, all things considered, but she could sit here for the rest of the day. The rest of their time in Marrakech.

"We can stay here this afternoon," Jack said quietly. "We don't have to go anywhere, we can stay here and relax."

Dylan shook her head and slowly extricated herself. If Jack was surprised, he didn't say anything, just let his hands slide off her as easily as they'd moved around her.

"No, we should go out." Dylan brushed her hair back off her face before glancing at herself in the mirror. Her face was red and splotchy from crying and her mascara was streaked down her cheeks so she looked like a very pathetic Kiss reject.

"Just give me a second to wash my face."

She felt Jack's eyes follow her as she stood, so she tried to hide the way her legs shook beneath her. She couldn't tell where he was looking, but she could feel his eyes on her all the same. When she looked in the mirror, though, to try and figure it out, she found him looking directly at her, and she froze as their eyes caught.

He held her gaze for a beat, two, before he nodded gently.

"I'll wait here."

She should move. She knew she should move, but there was something magnetic about the way he was looking at her. She felt like her feet were glued to the spot, like she couldn't've moved even if she wanted to.

Finally, she blinked and drew in a deep breath. She traced it all the way down through her chest, her stomach expanding as it filled her.

"Thank you. For being here."

Jack half nodded, half smiled. "I'll always be here."

In any other circumstance, it would've been the absolute right thing to say. The words he would have said as the music swelled. She would have run, kissed him, breathed her heart into him until he was pressed back into the mattress, and even as she thought it, she could see it in her mind. Could feel the way his hands would rest on her hips, the tips of his fingers teasing the backs of her thighs, the way he'd exhale shakily against her lips as she pressed herself against him, the way he'd groan as she ran her fingers down the column of his throat.

Now, though, it made the guilt twist sharply in her stomach.

Jack swallowed. "What are you thinking about right now?"

Jack's fingers were knotted in the duvet and there was a rigidity to his posture, not like he was uncomfortable, but like he was a spring, coiled tight. His eyes, deep and dark as the ocean, were the only hint of the things swirling around inside him.

She would give almost anything to know what he was thinking just then. To thread her fingers through his and feel him against her again, to go back in time and stop herself from writing the article that made all of this a thousand times more complicated.

She should come clean, should tell him now, but she wanted to bottle this moment, and *god*, she just couldn't shatter his faith in her yet. Not while she was still on unstable ground.

Dylan exhaled. "Nothing." She swallowed down the guilt and flashed him the best smile she could muster. "But seriously . . . thank you."

She ran off before he could say anything else.

CHAPTER 22

In spite of her best efforts, Dylan still felt like she was flicking in and out of consciousness as they left Marrakech and made their way to Cape Town. She'd snap to and they'd be walking along the beach road, the azure water stretching out for ages on two sides, the white sand giving way to black rock the farther they walked. She'd have a slowly melting King Cone in her hands, a drop of vanilla trickling down her index finger, and the hit of sugar would be enough to keep her there for a minute, squinting through her sunglasses at the flash of the sun off the water.

This particular afternoon was like any of the others they'd had in South Africa—the heat of the day had ebbed and given way to a golden late afternoon—and Jack was chattering away about how excited he was for their dinner reservation while Dylan stared unseeingly out at the horizon.

Dylan was deeply amused by the role reversal.

"It's supposed to be one of the best restaurants in the city," he said. "It's family-run and everything is served buffet style—"

"Whoa." Dylan held up her hand. "You're excited about a *buffet*?"

"Yes. Apparently—"

She put on a mock-concerned tone. "Aren't you worried they'll revoke your posh card if you eat at a buffet?"

"They might bring me up in front of the tribunal," Jack said, his tone dry as ever, "but if the reviews are right, it'll be well worth it."

Dylan laughed out loud, and just for a second, nothing else mattered other than the two of them walking along the beach.

Cape Town was easily one of the most beautiful places she'd ever been. The steady warmth, the salt in the air, the way the city vibrated with life. But she felt almost like a ghost of herself or, no, like a marionette. Like she was remembering to lead herself through the usual things, but only because she wanted to maintain the impression that she wasn't three seconds away from crumbling to bits.

She couldn't decide who she was angrier at, herself, the internet, Chantel, her parents, or some combination, for the fact that she was only sticking her head up for air. That she was only experiencing pieces of this place that would have filled her heart if she'd been able to let it. It was outrageous that, once again, people were attacking her and ruining her life—or, at the very least, trying to—and she was sick of it.

It wasn't her fault. She wasn't responsible for the way people were treating her. For their unending harassment and attempts to drive her off the internet.

Because that was what they wanted, really.

They wanted to silence her.

And, well.

Fuck that.

On their last evening in Cape Town, Dylan and Jack were walking along the waterfront, desperately soaking up their last few hours in the city. Dylan was carving moments into her mind, stuffing them into her pockets, like at any second someone was going to drag her onto a plane and send her away.

She loved how the city and the beach bled together, how Cape Town was surrounded by sea but bracketed by gorgeous, foggy Table Mountain. Their dinner the night before had been, easily, one of the best Dylan had ever had, just as Jack predicted. The vibrant conversation, community, and warm food had wrapped themselves around Dylan's heart, filling her up in more ways than one. It felt like the whole world—or, at least, part of it—collapsed into miniature and brought to life by a steady breeze of warm, salty air.

The waterfront was bustling that evening, and as Dylan and Jack slid through the crowds, a thought suddenly struck her.

"Oh, hey." Dylan turned so she was walking ahead of him, an enticing smile on her face. "I want to take us somewhere."

"Okay? Is it nearby?"

"Sort of."

They walked to the very end of Beach Road, and instead of turning left toward the beaches, they snuck around, at Dylan's urging, the hotels that cluttered the inlet north of the docks.

"This can't be allowed," Jack said, frowning as they walked through a side gate surrounding one of the boat clubs at the edge of the marina.

"I'm sure it isn't," Dylan agreed. "But they haven't given us much choice."

Jack groaned softly and Dylan's smile flashed brighter as she took his hand.

"Just act like you're supposed to be here." Dylan moved her free hand to his bicep. "People won't question you if you don't look like you're out of place."

Jack glanced nervously at the guard outside the boathouse and leaned down to whisper in her ear as they walked past. "I feel like you have firsthand knowledge of that."

It took everything Dylan had to ignore the chill that trickled down her spine.

"You've got to live a little sometimes, Hunton."

Jack looked slightly sick, but he kept it together enough that no one bothered to talk to them as they passed through the boat club. It only took them a few minutes to make it through the gate and onto the cement barrier Dylan had seen earlier that afternoon on Google Maps. Jack glanced toward the end of the pavement and then raised an eyebrow at her.

"Are you walking us off into the sea?"

"Virginia Woolf style," she said, kicking a pebble at him and nodding toward his pockets. "Fill 'em up."

Jack's eyes went wide with alarm. "That's not funny."

"I'm obviously kidding."

Jack squeezed her hand. She'd long since dropped her hand from his bicep, but she hadn't been able to bring herself to pull her hand from his. His palm was warm, especially with the cool breeze blowing off the water, and she loved how connected to him she felt. How she could feel the subtle movements of his body as he walked, and how, every so often, his hand flexed against hers.

"I've actually been really worried about you these last few days," he said quietly. "You've been really withdrawn."

"I'm sure it didn't help finding me sobbing my eyes out the other day."

"No." Jack sounded like she'd stabbed him with a rusty knife and then twisted it. "That was one of the worst things I've ever seen."

He looked down and watched their hands swinging between them.

"You've been—" Jack swallowed. "I guess I haven't known you that long, but you weren't yourself and it was terrifying." He let that hang in the air for a second before he squeezed her hand. It wasn't accidental, but deep and purposeful, like he wanted her to really feel what he was saying.

"I'm not going to make you talk about it, but you know you can always talk to me? There's nothing you could say that would— I mean, I just—I want to support you. I don't want you to think you have to get to the point where you're broken down like that again."

Dylan turned so she was standing in front of him, their fingers still laced together. His expression was serious when he finally met her gaze, but there was a vulnerability there that made her heart contract.

"People've started leaving me comments again," she said finally. She might as well start there and work her way backward. "One of my articles went a bit viral, and it reminded people that I still exist."

Jack's brow furrowed. "What've they been saying?"

"I deserve to die, I'm a heartless bitch, they're going to find where I live and kill me." She said it casually, like it hadn't been destroying her. "The usual."

Jack stared at her, aghast. "What the fuck."

"It's nothing I haven't read before."

"That doesn't make it right for them to say it to you."

"No, I know." She tucked her hair behind her ear. "I've been in a weird place about it because I thought that I was past this. Like, they were finished sending me these things and I was finished taking them seriously." She smiled in sarcastic disbelief. "Guess I was wrong on both counts."

"You should take them seriously." He looked shaken. "No one should ever have to read that about themselves. They shouldn't be able to talk to you like that."

This was the most heated she'd ever seen him. She could feel the venom in his words seeping through her skin, and she had a flash of what it might feel like to have that kind of vitriol directed her way.

She shuddered and passed it off as a shrug. "I've blocked and reported most of them, but there's very little Twitter can do to keep them from making new accounts to harass me. Even with IP bans, the ones who know what they're doing can get around it pretty easily."

Jack shook his head. "That's— There has to be something they can do. They can't just let people get harassed."

"Well, they do," Dylan said. "Every day."

"How long has this been happening? This time around, I mean?"

She swallowed. If she was going to do it, now was the time to muster her courage.

"Since Mumbai. I—"

"Fuck." Jack practically spat the word out and looked toward the horizon. His face was creased with emotion, and his grip on Dylan's hand was firm. "I'm so sorry."

"No, Jack." She squeezed his hand, increasing the pressure when he didn't immediately look at her. "This isn't your fault."

This was all wrong. This was the last thing he should be saying to her right now.

"I should have been there for you. I just sat back and watched you curl in on yourself, like—"

"No." She encircled her fingers around his wrist. "I wasn't ready to talk about it. I would've shut you out if you'd made me and then we wouldn't've got anywhere."

It was true, even if Jack didn't want to believe it (and she could tell from his expression that he didn't). She needed him to understand this, to really believe her. She was probably using it as an excuse, something to talk about to avoid having to tell him the one thing she really needed to, but she couldn't let him think, even for one second, that he had any responsibility for this.

"I only talked to my brother and Gwen about it, like, a week ago." She flashed him a self-effacing smile. "I was very much determined to try and get myself through it before then."

Jack swallowed, his eyes sliding up to track something behind her head before he met her gaze again. "I'm glad you talked to them. I'm glad you're talking to me now."

She ran her thumb along his forearm, a silent agreement, before she let her hand fall back by her side.

She wanted to tell him about the article. She wanted to, she *needed* to, but she wanted to tell him about this, too. She wanted to let him in. To feel what it would be like to share this with him.

She could—she would—tell him. But if she was already being selfish, maybe she could do this first.

"The day you found me crying, my mam had texted and said that—" The words caught in her throat, and Dylan felt emotion start bubbling in her chest. "She said Sean had shown her some of the things people were saying to me. Apparently this was the first time it really sunk in for her that people were calling for my head on a fucking spike."

She laughed humorlessly.

"She fucking apologized for not being able to see beyond the fact that I'd had an abortion. For not being there for me when I needed her."

She hadn't meant for the words to sound so bitter, but there they were.

"I still haven't responded because I haven't figured out a nice way to say, 'Where the fuck was that support when I needed it, you can shove this up your arse.'"

Jack exhaled. "I'm not sure there *is* a nice way to say that."

"Probably not. I just—" She pressed her lips together to try to contain her anger, but the words soon got the better of her. "I don't think I was properly angry with them until I read that message. Like, she's seen everything people were saying to me, she *knew* Gwen and I moved because I'd been fucking doxxed, but instead of trying to have empathy and love for me, she dug her heels in because I wasn't the exact right version of myself that she wanted me to be. She pretended none of it was happening because if she'd acknowledged the way people were treating me, the people who agreed with her, by the way, then she would have to seriously think about the fact that she was on the same side as people who thought they could say the most horrific things to me on Twitter. They—I mean, they—"

The anger crested and crashed over her in the exact same moment, so that Dylan was, once again, fighting back tears.

"I don't know if I can ever forgive them for abandoning me like that."

Jack stepped forward, closing the distance between them. For a moment, Dylan thought he might kiss her, but instead, he pressed her to his chest. They were still holding hands, but he wrapped his free hand around her shoulder and held her against him, and the pressure of him—his hand on hers, his arm on her spine—made Dylan feel like she'd finally dropped back into her body. She relaxed against him, the tension in her shoulders easing for the first time in a fortnight as she slid her arm around his waist and laid her head on his chest.

"You don't have to if you don't want to," Jack said. His voice was right in her ear, and she would have sworn she could feel the brush of his lips. "But it's okay if you want to try and repair things, too. Whatever you want, it's okay."

"I don't know what I want."

"That's okay." Jack adjusted his hold on her, his hand moving up until she felt him playing with the ends of her hair.

In his arms, Dylan could almost tell herself that everything *was* okay. She listened to the steady thrumming of his heart, followed the soft touches of his fingertips against her back, and in that moment, she wasn't thinking about her mam or the arseholes on the internet or the fact that, very soon, she was pretty sure Jack was going to be blowing up at her for all the things she hadn't told him.

It was the last thing she wanted to think about, but she couldn't deny the truth of it.

After a few long moments, Jack pulled back, his hand sliding round to her waist. He smiled gently, warmly, like he wanted her to feel it against her skin.

"You don't have to mend any relationship you don't want to— even with your parents—but if you do, I promise you, there's a way back."

Dylan held his gaze, shivering as a chill ran up her spine with the most recent whisper of wind. It was hard thinking about his advice solely in the context he'd intended, hard not hearing the words as the signal of hope that, maybe, all wouldn't be lost when she finally told him what she'd written about Bangkok.

"Thanks." She drew in a slow, shaky breath and, with it, felt her lips hitch up into a smile. "Now, god, can we please move on, I feel like I'm going to implode if we keep excavating my feelings."

Jack laughed, a bright, hearty sound that Dylan felt right down to her toes. "Fine, fine." He turned so he was standing beside her again, his hand still in hers. "I'm curious what this mysterious destination of yours is."

"Ooh." Dylan grinned up at him and swung their hands. "You're going to love it."

"That makes me think I'm really not going to love it."

As they approached the end of the pavement, Dylan finally spotted what she'd been looking for.

"Okay." She tugged her phone out of her pocket and shoved it into Jack's hand before speed-walking to the end of the pavement.

Jack almost fumbled the phone in an attempt to get proper hold of it and match her pace. She jumped off the pavement onto one of the rocks in the water and Jack sucked in a sharp, shocked breath.

"What are you doing?"

"Take my picture." Dylan turned round and wobbled a little as the rock shifted under her weight. Jack made another sound, half shout, half groan, and Dylan rolled her eyes at him. "Relax, I'll be fine."

"I'll be sure to remember you said that when I'm dragging you out of the harbor to go to hospital."

"Aw, I love that you'd rescue me."

"On second thought, I might leave you here as punishment for giving me a heart attack."

Dylan laughed. "I guess I'd deserve that."

She picked her way through the rocks until she reached the wave breakers a few meters out. The nearest one had a flat piece sticking straight up that Dylan was pretty sure she could stand on. She boosted herself up and, after taking a second to steady herself, got to her feet and wiped the concrete dust off her hands onto her thighs.

She threw her hands straight up into the air and was absolutely sure that Jack had taken a whole burst of pictures.

"See?" She dropped her hands down onto her hips. "I told you I'd be fine."

"The real test'll be getting back."

She rolled her eyes. "Have you gotten any good ones yet?"

"Let's get a few more. Make you risking your life worth it."

Even with the worry lines creasing Jack's forehead, there was no mistaking his smile.

CHAPTER 23

It was just past four when they landed at Keflavík airport the next afternoon and by the time they boarded the shuttle that was going to take them to Reykjavík, the sun had started to dip below the horizon.

Dylan took a sip of the tea she'd bought in the terminal as she walked toward the back of the bus. The tea was too hot and far weaker than she would have liked, but it was caffeine and she would've put up with a lot worse for the promised energy hit. She spotted a sticker on the back of the seat in front of her as she dropped into her seat and gasped as Jack sat down on her right.

"Wi-Fi." She sounded lustful. "And a charging port. Can you hold this?"

She held out her tea and Jack took it, shaking his head. "You're ridiculous."

Dylan didn't look at him as she unzipped the inside pocket of her bag. "We've established."

She plugged in her phone and connected to the Wi-Fi before taking her tea back and watching the notifications over her email double.

"Fucking hell."

"What?"

Despite the fact that he'd been judging her, when Dylan looked over, he, too, had plugged his phone in. She raised an eyebrow at him, but otherwise decided not to comment.

"I just got a fuck ton of email," she said, bracing herself as she clicked into her inbox. "And I hope none of them are notes from my editor, because if it's anything more than, like, 'you spelled this word wrong,' I'm going to have a stroke."

She'd been really struggling to write about Cape Town. She had the right ending—sneaking through the boat club and standing out over the water, triumphant—but every time she read it back, there was far more Jack than she knew what to do with. Or how to remove.

She wasn't even trying to write about him. She was making a point to skate over things because she knew how easily people blew things out of proportion, but no matter how she wrote it, things always seemed to hover over him. Writing that first draft was useful in getting the feelings out (and, unlike her Bangkok article, wasn't going to be where she stopped), but no matter how much she tried to edit Jack out, she couldn't manage it.

He was inescapable.

She'd texted Gwen about it that morning, but Gwen had been fantastically unhelpful.

And downright rude, honestly.

Dylan: so I just word vomited a quick draft of this Cape Town article and I hate it

Dylan: [link] Cape Town Article—DRAFT

Gwen: let me read

Gwen: good god you're in love

Dylan: NO SHUT UP

Gwen: 'At one point, Jack looked up—we'd just finished licking our plates clean of all traces of umxhaxha—and our eyes caught. It felt so right, sitting there with him, listening to this family tell their stories, eating the most delicious food I've ever had.... I couldn't imagine having these experiences with anyone else, and in that moment, I felt like I knew it for the first time.'

Dylan: I. HATE. YOU.

Dylan: I KNOW YOU WENT INTO PREVIOUS VERSIONS TO GET THAT YOU MONSTER

Dylan: AS YOU CAN CLEARLY SEE, I DELETED IT SO IT'S NOT EVEN GOING TO BE IN WHAT I SEND TO CHANTEL. I HAD TO GET IT OUT OF MY SYSTEM SO I DIDN'T FUCK UP AGAIN

Gwen: lololololol

Gwen: you wrote that so you can't even be angry with me (even if you deleted it, you STILL WROTE IT)

Gwen: also 'get it out of my system' please be MORE obvious

Gwen: when are you going to tell him you're in love with him?

Dylan: piss off I'm not in love with him

Gwen: mmmmmhhhhhhmmmmmm

Gwen: please see above, you realising he's the only one you want to be travelling with

Dylan: oh no boarding now gotta go love you bye xx

Gwen: lol byeeee love you xx

But the more she tried to rework her article, the more she thought that maybe Gwen was right. Not about her being in love with him (because god, it wasn't that serious yet), but maybe she was fooling herself.

It wasn't that there was anything wrong with her having feelings for Jack, it was just . . .

Things were complicated at the moment.

She *really* needed to do something about that.

They had a six-hour drive to a glacier on Tuesday and she was planning to tell him then. Because if it couldn't get worked out after twelve hours locked in a car together . . .

Well, maybe they could sort it out at the Blue Lagoon on Wednesday. The waters were probably very soothing, and if it got to that point, she'd take all the help she could get.

It was still dark when they left Reykjavík at half eight on Tuesday, and they were quiet as they grabbed takeaway breakfast from the hotel restaurant on the way to the hire car. She'd come to appreciate this more and more, the seamless way they moved around each other—Jack's gentle hand at the base of her spine when he brought over cups of tea, the way he moved close to, but not directly up against, her every time he had to reach around her. Each move felt intimate, and the easy way they orbited each other made her whole body feel electric.

The sun came up as they drove, lightening the black sky by degrees. It was up fully, golden and warm, as they wove down the hill outside Vík, and even though she knew she should tell him about the article, about the conversation still spiraling out of control online, she couldn't bring herself to fracture these moments. To drive a wedge between them and explode what they'd built.

It was selfish, she knew, but she'd lost so much of this trip already and she wanted one more moment, one more hour, where she wasn't thinking about it.

Where, instead, she could focus on the glow of the sun through the windscreen, the gentle breeze ruffling Jack's hair when they stopped to take photos. She stared out at the landscape as they drove, her eyes tracing over the curves of hills and the wide, flat valleys where glaciers had been. There was a richness to the color here, even as the light seemed softer, more diffuse. There were few buildings, but even though it was far less populated than anywhere she'd ever been, there was a teeming, churning quality to Iceland that made it feel very much alive.

She wanted to file all these moments away in her memory—the brush of Jack's fingers against her shoulder as they posed in front of a distant waterfall, the smile on Jack's face as she tried and failed to sing along to "Með Þér," a song they played approximately every five minutes on the radio.

It was just past one in the afternoon when Jack flicked on his signal as they approached a small car park off the side of an otherwise nondescript road, and Dylan snuck a glance at the navigation. They were supposed to carry on another kilometer or so, and she could see the tents they were supposed to be heading toward across the bridge ahead of them.

"Is this it?" She glanced out the window again. "Is this the right spot?"

"No, but I did some googling before we left this morning, and thought we could take a brief detour."

She raised an eyebrow at him as he turned in to the small gravel car park. "*You* want to take a detour?"

Jack smirked as he cut the engine and undid his seat belt. "You've got to live a little sometimes, Coughlan."

Before Dylan could do more than smile, Jack opened his door and climbed out, his shoes crunching over the gravel before he shut the door.

Jack led them up the steep hill off the car park, laughing at Dylan's muttered curses as she slipped on the stones. When they reached the crest of the hill, Dylan realized that it was an equally steep walk down but—she felt her breath fall out of her as she took it all in—they'd be walking right up to the edge of the glacier.

Or rather, the lake.

The lake that had once been a solid glacier but was now a mass of water and ice chunks because, you know, the climate crisis.

It was—

She took another deep breath.

It was hauntingly beautiful.

And deeply, deeply sad.

Jack held out his hand.

Their hands stayed linked as they walked down the hill. Her shoes weren't the best for navigating the gravelly slope and she skidded a few times, but she wasn't the only one. Jack nearly slid down onto his arse more than once. The first time, Dylan caught her laugh before it fell out of her, but the second time, when Jack's free arm shot up into the air in a quick attempt to counterbalance himself, the reaction burst out of her before she could stop it. She squeezed Jack's hand hard and tugged upward in an attempt to keep him upright, her laughter ringing around them.

"I feel like a fawn," he said, straightening up. She was still laughing and Jack grinned down at her.

Only for the gravel to slide underneath him again.

"Fucking hell." She was gasping for breath, the cold air sharp against her throat. "Maybe this was a bad idea."

"This is what I get for trying to do something spontaneous." He grumbled the words out, but there was no mistaking the amusement in his eyes.

She expected Jack to let go of her hand when they got to the bottom, but he kept hold as they walked to the water's edge. He squeezed her hand as they came to a stop, a soft, gentle pressure she felt everywhere, and together, they looked out at the water.

The water seemed completely still, but as she watched, it became clear that the massive blocks of ice in the water were moving. They were shifting incredibly slowly and it took a great deal of her concentration, but once she noticed the subtle movement, she couldn't stop seeing it.

It was everywhere.

It was in the crisp chill in the air that was cold enough that you felt it, sharp against your skin, in the silence that made the sound of your own breath loud in your ears, and in the soft, cool colors that painted the entirety of the landscape.

Everything was slightly gray—the sky, the mountains in the distance, the reflection off the water—but the ice was highlighted by pops of blue that looked almost aquamarine in the afternoon light. Nothing was stark, and you might have considered the ice dull if everything else in the landscape hadn't been as softly painted. Everything was enormous—enormous in size, enormously old, an age she couldn't even comprehend because its life was hundreds, thousands of her own—and she felt like she was infringing upon something just by being there.

Dylan took another deep breath, the cold air scratching her throat, before she looked up at Jack, only to find him already looking at her.

"Dylan."

His voice was soft, the lightest brush of fingertips against skin, and she couldn't possibly avoid gazing at him when his voice sounded like that, when her name on his lips sounded almost reverent. It was too much, too intense, and it reminded her of the way he'd looked at her back in Bangkok. The plastic bucket pressing into her hip and the slight part in his lips, the way he was close to her, but nowhere near close enough. This was like that, but with the very real memory, now, of what it felt like to have his mouth on hers, what it felt like when her body pressed up against his.

And now that his eyes weren't clouded with alcohol, it was easy to pick out the depth in them, the feeling—there was a realness to the way he was looking at her, and even though she had the very same feelings coursing through her, there was a deep reticence in her chest that was impossible to ignore.

She couldn't kiss him after last time. After he'd apologized and not talked about it and in her frustration she had written about it for all the world to see.

And so even though she was still keenly aware of every spot where his body was touching hers—his hand in hers, his shoulder against hers—when Jack's eyes flicked down to her lips, Dylan stiffened.

Not much. But that slight tension was enough.

Jack froze, his eyes holding hers for a few seconds before he cleared his throat softly and dropped his gaze to stare blankly at the space between them.

He took a breath.

And then, when he looked back up at her, the heat that had been in his eyes had disappeared and Dylan wanted to take it all back.

"You ready to go?" he asked softly. "We don't want to miss the tour."

She nodded, swallowing against the pressure in her throat. They'd started up the hill toward the car when Dylan smirked.

"Be careful now."

Jack nudged her gently with his elbow, and then, almost immediately, he slipped on a loose patch of gravel.

CHAPTER 24

Jack connected his phone to the portable Wi-Fi when they got back to the car, and Dylan laughed as he brought the navigation up.

"Do you really need that?"

"I don't want to miss the turn."

"I think it would be impossible to miss. I can literally see it down the road."

"Oh, weird." Jack's brow furrowed. "My sister texted."

Dylan busied herself with buckling her seat belt. "Is everything okay?"

She should have known then that something was wrong. Looking back, she should have spotted how still Jack had gone, how every single emotion evaporated from his face until it was carefully blank.

In the moment, though, she didn't notice anything and instead pulled out her own phone and started choosing photos to post on Instagram.

Jack exhaled, the sound shallow, strangled.

"You wrote about what happened in Bangkok?"

Dylan's blood ran cold.

She wasn't sure what she was supposed to do—if she was supposed to start talking or if she was supposed to wait—but the longer he sat there staring at her, the more the tension and anxiety built in her gut and she felt like she had to say something. Something was better than nothing, wasn't it, but it was also quite possible she was just panicking?

"What?"

Great start.

"Charlie—she said I'm in an article?"

He turned his phone so she could see the screen.

> Charlie: ...this is you, isn't it? did you know about
> these?
> Charlie: also heads up mum has seen them on Facebook, so
> she might be texting you sorry

Underneath, there was a link, not to Dylan's article, but to a Twitter thread.

> **Jillybean** ✔ @jillybean
> By now we all know about the @bbcr1 @buxom drama, but
> people have gotten out of control with how they're talking
> about the author and her relationship with her travel
> partner and I have to talk about it 🧵

Oh god.

Her heart was beating so hard, she was going to pass out.

"I—"

"What did you write?" His tone was carefully measured, but there was no mistaking the anger. His expression was hard, and it tore at something inside her.

"Not a lot. And I didn't give details. You said to be brief and

I—I was. I tried to be. I didn't even say that we'd, you know . . ." She couldn't say "kissed." "People just assumed and . . ."

Jack's eyes were boring into her, and Dylan felt like she was grasping frantically along a cliff edge for any possible hold.

Her fingers trembled as she navigated to her browser. This could make things better or worse, but Jack seemed like the type of person who needed all the information before deciding how he felt about something.

She just really, really hoped that adding more information wasn't also adding fuel to the fire.

"I'll AirDrop you the article. You can read it. See what I said."

"I—" He pressed his lips together and his eyes fell closed. "I don't know if I want to read it."

"It might help," she insisted. His phone was there when she tapped SHARE, ready to accept, but she didn't click it right away. She looked over at him, thumb hovering over the button.

He didn't open his eyes, just silently pressed his fingertips to his forehead.

"Fine. Send it over. But, here—" He pushed open the door. "You drive. I don't want to be late."

Jack read silently as they drove. It was only a few minutes before Dylan was turning in to the car park, the car jostling over the dips in the gravel, but she felt every agonizing second. She chose a space away from everyone else—she didn't figure this was going to be pretty and didn't want an audience if she could avoid it—and cut the ignition, leaving a deadly silence behind.

She waited for a beat, two, and just when she was about to say something, anything, Jack spoke.

"So people read this and, what?"

His tone was flat, impossible to read, and her shoulders tensed, bracing against inevitable impact.

"They assumed something happened between us," Dylan admitted quietly. As much as she wanted to avoid the fallout, she knew that now she had no choice but to tell him everything.

She owed him that much.

"My boss has been framing this trip as some kind of couple's holiday since the beginning. I've been angling for my own column for a long time and this trip was just— It was the perfect opportunity for me to finally prove that I was worth it, and when she said this was a sexy, like, one-night-stands-reunited type thing, I just . . . I went with it. A little bit."

Jack's lips pressed so firmly together his mouth all but disappeared. "You pretended this was a romantic holiday? To draw readers?"

The careful control in his voice might have fooled someone else, but hearing just how desperately he was trying to conceal his feelings felt like a punch straight to the chest.

"Not on purpose. I mean—I guess, yeah, I wanted readers, but I wasn't thinking about intentionally making it seem like we were involved. Because we aren't—weren't. It was my boss's idea and I didn't try to play into it, but I didn't exactly . . . deny it, either."

"But *you* wrote this." Jack rapped his index finger against the screen. "You wrote about 'hot, sweaty evenings' and 'someone you connected with.' You *knew* what people would make of that. You *knew* it would draw them in."

"I—I mean, yes, that is what my boss wanted, but, Jack, I—I didn't want to be doing that. I didn't want to be twisting things around and making them sound like something they weren't. I didn't go into it with that intention, I was just confused."

She hated how desperate she sounded, but she needed him to know she hadn't done any of this on purpose, that she'd been spending the last fortnight trying and failing to get a handle on this thing that had so quickly spiraled out of her grasp.

"'Something they weren't.'" His voice was even flatter than before, and that made the anxiety ratchet up in her chest.

"I tried to cut you out of the articles—you can read them and see—but that just made people speculate more and all the comments on my Instagram have been people trying to find you in pictures, and then my trolls came back and started sending me death threats, which made other people feel like they needed to defend me, and then everything just got twisted together, and, I mean, I haven't read that thread"—she nodded toward the phone held limply in his hand—"but I'd bet that's what they're getting at. If I had to guess."

Jack let out a deep, heavy exhale, his lips pressed together like he was trying and failing to contain himself.

"Why didn't you tell me?"

"I wasn't thinking," she said immediately. "I—"

Jack locked his phone and dropped it into the cupholder between them. "Clearly."

Dylan reeled back in her seat. "Look, there's no need to—"

"No need to be like this?" Jack raised his voice a notch so he was speaking over her. His tone was sharp, and bloody hell, he sounded livid. "You didn't ask me before you wrote this." He tapped his index finger hard against the screen. "You wrote this and posted it, knowing thousands of people would read it. Tens of thousands, because it's all over Twitter."

Hearing him put it like that, Dylan felt the guilt twist tighter in her gut.

"Never mind the fact we were on your Instagram, we'd talked about that, I was fine with that." His tone was swift, like he couldn't get the words out fast enough, and it was such a drastic shift from the Jack she knew that she almost couldn't believe it. "But I don't understand why you wrote this. Why you apparently weren't bothered enough to tell me about it, and I had to hear it from my *sister*."

He let that hover there, his tone disbelieving and more than a little hurt. Dylan felt a million things settle onto her all at once, the memory of how hot and sticky her skin had been, the feeling of Jack's lips against hers and the thrill in her stomach, the pounding in her chest that gave way to her irritation over the ensuing days as he dodged every opportunity to talk about it, and, worst of all, deep shame at having done the one thing she definitely shouldn't've done.

She'd paid for that in more ways than one—she'd near had a fucking breakdown—but even knowing how severely the internet punished her didn't mean that Jack'd had the opportunity to process the way she'd violated him directly.

"I wasn't thinking," she said again, her tone soft, like she was begging him to understand. "And I'm sorry. It's just, you wouldn't talk to me, and—"

Jack scoffed. "Don't turn this around like I somehow made you."

"I'm trying to explain," she snapped.

Jack closed his eyes and pulled in a slow, steady breath through his nose. When he spoke again, he sounded like he'd managed to wrest some of his control back.

"Go on, then."

"I didn't do it out of vengeance. I was confused because we'd kissed"—she hoped Jack didn't hear the way her voice caught on the word—"and then you acted like it never happened."

Dylan wished there was more to pay attention to outside because it was easier talking when she was focused on something else. But the car park was basically empty, so all she could think about were the words coming out of her mouth.

"That hurt." Dylan shifted uncomfortably in her seat. "I needed some way of processing, and writing has always been the only way I know how to do that. I wrote this to get it out of my system and sent it to my editor without thinking and—I tried to get it back, to get her not to post it, but she refused and I didn't know what else to do besides pray people didn't think anything of it. But when they did and when they kept talking about it, I—Jack, I was a wreck." She stared at him, trying to impress upon him how much she meant it. "I already had the entire internet hating me, I didn't want you to hate me, too."

"I'm not going to excuse anything anyone said to you, because it's awful you have to go through that, but *please* don't try to use that as a reason I shouldn't be upset. You wrote this knowing I wouldn't be happy about it. You didn't even think to tell me about it. And," he said, raising his voice a little, because she'd opened her mouth to interject, "yes, I know your editor refused to withdraw it, but that doesn't excuse you sending it in the first place. Especially when you *knew* this would play right into her framing."

"I just—I ended up saying more than I meant to. I didn't see this as some grand reveal or—"

"But you'd already had people asking about our nonexistent relationship," Jack said. His voice was hard, cold, and "nonexistent" cut through her like a knife. "I know you're smart, Dylan, I know you could have put two and two together and figured out this was a likely possibility."

"I didn't do it intentionally—"

"I don't care if you did it intentionally!" His volume ticked up to match hers, and the last hints of control he had started slipping away. "Don't you remember what *you said*? Intent doesn't matter as much as impact!"

"No, I know, I just—I need you to know that I wasn't trying to hurt you. I was confused—"

"Well, how do you think I feel now?"

He hadn't shouted it, but for the effect that it had on Dylan, he might as well have.

"You could have talked to me," Jack continued. "But instead, you wrote about it online for everyone in the world to read—"

"I don't think everyone in the world reads my articles."

Jack's eyes cut across to her. "Hardly the time for jokes."

Dylan held his gaze, determined not to let herself be cowed by him. "It was fucked up that I wrote about you, and honestly, Jack, I'm sorry. I just didn't know what else to do when you wouldn't talk to me—"

"So your solution was to throw your feelings out onto the internet?"

Well, when he put it like that.

"No, but—"

"Exactly! You made all this public in exchange for a few clicks."

She scoffed. He wasn't wrong, but his wording *infuriated* her.

"Why are you so worked up about things being public? Are you that embarrassed to be seen knowing me?"

"You mean besides all the evidence from your experience alone that being online can have absolutely disastrous consequences?"

Dylan barked an affronted laugh. "So it's *my fault* for being a somewhat public figure that people are talking to me this way?"

"No." Jack started emphatically shaking his head. "I didn't say that. I'd *never* say that. It's not your fault people talk to you that way, but can you really blame me for wanting to keep my shit off the internet knowing how things can be?"

"I'm not saying I blame you, but—"

"When I was eighteen, someone who I assumed was my friend posted a whole Facebook album of terrible photos of me." He was still angry, she could hear it in the sharp edges of his voice, but there was a rawness to his words now that told her they were plumbing something deep here. "I didn't know they'd been taken and I didn't know he was going to post them, but one day, he posted sixty-three different photos of me in various states of distress and tagged me in each and every one."

Dylan's brows pinched. "What do you mean, 'various states of distress'?"

"Blackout drunk." He waved his hand, but Dylan could see how hurt he was, still, years later. "Awful things written on my face, gin bottles everywhere. My arse was out in one of them, with, as you can imagine, some very tasteful things written across my arse cheeks."

Dylan felt a breath fall out of her.

"I'd been doing a bit of work experience at the time with some firm led by someone my father was friends with—as posh kids do—and he called me into his office that Monday—I'll never forget it—and just said, 'Do you have anything to say for yourself?'"

He laughed, but there was no humor in the sound. "I had no idea what he was talking about, and when I told him as much, he turned his computer monitor around and then I was staring at a photo of my own arse on my boss's screen."

"Jack." The guilt twisted in her chest as she realized, finally, just how much what she'd done had hurt him. Unintentionally or not, writing about him, not telling him, all of it had brought this back up for him. She hadn't shamed him, hadn't actively tried to harm him by sharing the things she had, but she'd taken the choice away from him all the same and she knew, very intimately, how it felt to have things take on a life of their own online. "I'm sorry that happened."

"My parents were livid. A lot of 'We didn't send you off to this school so you could get drunk' and 'You've disappointed the entire family, Jack.' I was just a kid, but I was on my own and I was just trying to have a bit of fun, and then everything exploded in my face and I hadn't even known it happened until everyone else in the world knew.

"My parents thought I was going to be a failure after that. That I'd be laughed out of every law firm in Britain—or, at least, every posh corporate office in London, which, to them, were the only ones that mattered." He laughed bitterly and shook his head. "I worked nonstop in school to get top marks to get into a top university, I studied law even though I hated it because I wanted to show them I hadn't ruined my future, and then my father, deciding

I'd redeemed myself, got me a post in the busiest firm in London run by the most awful man he knew because then, I 'might finally learn some discipline.'"

The idea that Jack, someone so careful Dylan thought he might crack under the strain of holding himself together, needed to be taught discipline was laughable. "What the fuck."

Jack carried on like she hadn't spoken.

"And now, here I am. I can't wait to hear how I've confirmed my parents' worst fears, and that I am, in fact, their worst child."

"You didn't do anything wrong!"

"I quit my job to come on this trip!" He sounded anguished, livid, but clearly deeply, deeply upset, and it broke her heart. "I didn't tell my parents because I didn't feel like dealing with them, but I'm sure they know now, so, truly"—he touched a sarcastic hand to his chest—"thanks for that."

"Wait." She held her hand up in front of her. "You quit your job for this?"

"They weren't going to let me work remotely for two months while we, quote, 'gallivanted around,' and I hated it there anyway, so I told them that, starting in January, I no longer worked there."

"I—" She felt like his words were getting stuck in her brain and she couldn't process them quickly enough. "What have you been doing this whole time, then? On the planes and . . . ?"

She would have sworn he was working. He always looked like he was working.

"Fixing my CV and figuring out what I want to do with my life, because now I've thrown my corporate career in the toilet. I have no idea what I'm going to do, but I can't imagine thousands of people speculating about my sex life is going to help me when I have to start going to interviews."

And that, finally, knocked all the remaining fight out of Dylan.

It hadn't, until that moment, clicked that this could follow Jack back to his life in London. The implications for her own life were serious and she knew that they were real because she'd lived them before, but she hadn't thought about the fact that Jack, too, would have to deal with this when they got home. That something she wrote could have a lasting impact on him.

There were levels to this—like, yes, Jack wasn't having some of the most horrible things in the world said to him—but that didn't mean his frustration and anger with her were less valid. That his feelings of very obvious betrayal mattered less.

She exhaled, all the heat leaving her at once.

"Jack, honestly, I'm—" She moved her hand like she was going to put it on his leg but thought better of it at the last moment. "I'm so sorry. I wish I hadn't done it. If I could take it back—"

"Yeah," Jack said, and there was still anger there, but there was sadness there, as well. "I wish you hadn't, too."

And then Jack practically threw himself out of the car, and without waiting for Dylan, he stalked off toward the tent to check them in.

CHAPTER 25

Dylan thought she'd sat through awkward silences before, but they had nothing on the blistering silence that followed them on their glacier tour.

Jack sat as far from her as possible on the bench while their tour guide, Guðrún, helped fit ice grips on their boots. He was physically radiating negativity—even the tour guide barely spoke to him beyond making sure he had his gear—and he took himself to the very back of the safety rope when they queued up to strap in.

"We are not going anywhere very dangerous today," Guðrún told them as she ensured they were all securely tethered to the rope, "but it is important that we stay together. We'll have to work as a team, because it can be difficult to walk while tied together like this."

Dylan had a brief flashback to the last time she'd been tethered to a group of strangers. Sydney felt like a lifetime ago, and it wasn't only the bright Australian summer that played a sharp contrast to the gray Icelandic winter.

Though she had to admit, if there was one place to have this fight with Jack, it was this.

You couldn't get more poetic than a cold, barren landscape that was slowly melting due to global catastrophe.

Once they were all secured, Guðrún led them out of the base camp. There were peaks and valleys carved by the retreat of the ice over the years, but the surface itself was compacted dirt and loose rubble. She wasn't sure how long the glacier had been gone from this area, but it made her sad to think that all this had once been buried under a thick layer of ice and snow that now was some meters ahead of them.

Before they crossed the rope bridge onto the glacier itself, Guðrún gave them a quick overview of the ice picks they were taking with them and a last-minute warning.

"It may be tempting to come off the path, but remember, we are all tied together. What you do affects the rest of the team. There are many crevasses—most, we know about, but there is always the possibility we haven't identified one—and they are dangerous to fall into as they are typically very deep. Trust me, no one wants to fall here." Guðrún stared round at them all, like she was trying to impress this upon them. After a minute of firm staring, she cracked a smile and clapped her hands together. "Okay," she said, turning her ice pick around in her hands. "Let's go!"

It was a bit too chipper for someone who had just seriously warned them one false step could lead to their demise.

There was a thick layer of dirt tracked along the first few hundred feet of ice, a track that only darkened as they added fresh dirt from their boots. A few people were chattering away behind her, but all Dylan could think about was the sharp spike of her crampons in the ice and the slushy sound of the loose snow as they started up the hill.

It wasn't silent here, but Dylan felt the pressure on her eardrums all the same. Jack was all the way at the back, and his absence was like a hole in her chest. As they climbed their first hill, Dylan couldn't help but wonder what this might have been like if Charlie hadn't messaged, if Jack still didn't know, but she knew that Charlie wasn't the problem. Dylan knew this could've been avoided if she hadn't written about him as much. If she'd clarified what "brief" meant or if she'd brought up the full extent of the situation in Mumbai the moment everything started falling apart. If she'd just fucking *thought* before she'd hit SEND on that article in the first place.

They paused at the top of the hill, and once everyone fell quiet, Guðrún cleared her throat.

"The Vatnajökull ice cap covers about seventy-seven hundred square kilometers, about eight percent of Iceland's surface—it's still Europe's largest ice cap, though, over the last century, more than fifteen percent of it has melted."

Dylan's stomach twisted. She knew logically that this was happening, but this was the first time she'd ever been brought face-to-face with the reality of one of these places that was melting away. Though, really, she supposed she'd always been in one of these places without even realizing it. London, and Liverpool for that matter, were going to be casualties of flooding, and every single place they'd been to on this trip was likely to suffer in similar ways. Sydney and Cape Town and Mumbai were right on the water, Bangkok was set in a low-lying area that could very easily flood. Marrakech was safe from flooding, but the heat would rise, drought days would increase, and before too long, the land would be uninhabitable.

"This is one of the most sensitive glaciers to climate change," Guðrún continued. "Because it is a low-lying glacier, there is a lot of turnover in the glacier's mass each year, meaning that every summer, a large amount of melt occurs, and every winter, a high amount of snow falls, replacing the previous summer's melt. As temperatures rise and warmer periods last longer, the rate of melting will increase so the snowfall will not be able to replenish the glacier. We have already seen this at an alarming rate, but I urge you to keep this in mind as we walk across the glacier today. This ice"— Guðrún stomped her foot, ice chips flying to emphasize her point— "will very likely not be here in a few short years."

Dylan looked down at her boots and imagined herself sinking through thousands of years of snow and ice until she was standing on nothing but dirt.

She turned, pressing a little extra weight into her ice pick to serve as a counterweight, and craned her neck up until she could see Jack down at the far end.

She had to wait a second, two, but then he looked up and caught her eye.

He gave her one look, one firm stare, before he pressed his lips into a hard line and turned to look out over the ice.

They couldn't walk quickly, tethered together as they were, and though there were a few peaks and valleys in the ice, it wasn't a strenuous walk. It was the crampons on her feet that made it exhausting, the constant stabbing of her shoes into the ground for stability to then having to tug her leg free the next second to move forward. Each step required more energy, and she could feel the toll it was taking on her muscles.

Even as her body started to ache, Dylan didn't mind. The wide, flat stretches of snow and ice were astounding. She'd never looked across an entire landscape and seen only ice, and she couldn't imagine what it must have been like two hundred, five hundred years ago when it stretched farther still across the horizon.

In moments of rest, she took her phone out to take photos— her shoes in the ice, pick in the corner, the shock of the sunlight off the bright white ice, the peaks in the distance, a shock of black and gray against the sky—but she didn't feel like her heart was in it.

By the time they got back to the base camp a few hours later, Dylan's legs had turned to jelly. She lifted her right leg, intending to take off her crampon, but she'd grossly underestimated how tired her legs were. She wobbled on the spikes on her left foot, but before she could lose her balance, someone caught her elbow.

Even without looking, she knew it was Jack. She could feel the soft pressure of his fingers, especially now that she'd stripped off the hoodie she'd been wearing underneath her snow jacket. She looked at him and muttered, "Thanks," as she lifted her foot higher so she could reach it.

She unbuckled her crampon and let it fall to the ground. The moment she was stable, Jack let go of her elbow.

Dylan removed the rest of her gear, and after thanking Guðrún for the tour, she turned round to find Jack sitting on the bench outside the base tent. He'd already removed his helmet and his hair was unnaturally flat, but he was still working on his crampons. She found her gaze drawn to the movements of his fingers, the way they flexed and pinched in an attempt to undo the buckles that were, apparently, desperately clinging to his feet.

He looked up when he realized she was watching him. "You're driving back, right?"

She hadn't heard his voice in hours, and the shock of it physically jolted her.

"Uh, yeah." She pulled her beanie out of her pocket and slid it over her ears. "You drove here, so it's only fair."

Jack nodded once and then walked off to return his gear.

Dylan felt almost a little guilty as she watched him smile at their guide, the grin she already missed stretching over his lips. She was confident that, come what may, they'd manage to tolerate each other for the remaining two and a half weeks of their trip, but that—*tolerance*—felt like a knife to the gut when she compared it to where they were even five hours before.

Jack turned around and found her looking at him. The smile immediately fell off his face as he strode to the car.

Jack was in the car when Dylan arrived, passenger door open, legs stretched out into the car park. He shut the door as she settled in, and she noticed that he'd set the key fob and the phone charger in the cupholder ready for her to plug in.

She glanced over at him, but he busied himself with fastening his seat belt.

"Thanks," she said softly.

Dylan checked behind them before backing out and turning onto the main road. She didn't bother with the navigation—she wouldn't need to get off this road for hours—and, instead, set her phone in the cupholder and quietly switched on the radio.

They were playing "Með Þér" again and Dylan almost laughed out loud. They definitely wouldn't be singing on the way home.

Neither of them said anything as they drove. Jack looked either out the window or down at his phone, and Dylan stared through the windscreen and hummed along softly to the radio. Sometimes she was sure she could feel Jack's gaze on her or she thought, from the way he would suddenly draw breath, that he was going to say something, but every time she looked, he was looking away.

It had been twilight when they'd started off, and the sun continued to sink as they drove, so that by the time they were passing around the southern edge of Vatnajökull, it was dark. It was only half five, but between the darkness and the exhaustion in Dylan's bones, it could have been three in the morning. She was about to make a comment—*anything* to break the silence—when Jack spoke.

"Oh, fucking hell." Jack was staring down at his phone screen with an absolutely disgusted look on his face, an effect enhanced by the bright light shining up on his features. Dylan couldn't tell what had upset him, but when he pressed his phone to his ear, she assumed it was a phone call.

"Hello, Mum. To what do I owe the pleasure?"

Mum? Christ, this couldn't be good.

She could hear the sound of someone talking over the line, but other than picking up a vague impression of an accent (posher than the Queen herself), she couldn't hear what Jack's mum was saying. Which was probably for the best, because she was pretty sure Jack wouldn't want her listening in.

"Ah." Jack leaned back in his seat. "Charlie mentioned you'd seen."

Dylan felt her cheeks burn red and she focused that much harder on the road.

Jack's mum said something else, this time a bit louder.

"Well, to be honest, Mother, I didn't think that I needed to let you know I'd be leaving the country. . . . I— No, I didn't think you'd care."

Jack's mother said something that made Jack bite out a laugh. She hated the sound of it, hated how hard and grating it was compared to his usual chuckle.

"You spent the vast majority of my life not knowing exactly where I was, so I think we can drop the pretense." His voice was so thick with bitterness, with hurt, that it made Dylan's heart ache. She wanted to take his hand, run her fingers through his hair, do something, anything, to let him know he wasn't alone.

Jack scoffed softly at whatever his mother said in response.

"Fine. Is there anything else you'd like to berate me about while we're here?" Jack, to his credit, listened intently, though whatever he heard only irritated him further. "Yes, I quit. They weren't going to let me go— Well, yes, I thought traveling would be a better experience instead of working on pointless contracts. . . . No, Charlie didn't— *No*, I told her in confidence and asked her not to tell anyone, this isn't her fault." Jack rolled his eyes. "Dad can reach out all he likes, but even if they offer it to me, I won't take it back."

For the first time, Dylan heard Jack's mum clearly over the phone.

"You're being a *child*, Jack."

"I'm not." Jack shook his head, his voice hard. "I've hated that job from the moment I started, and I think it's about time I make my own decisions. . . . Please don't act like you haven't had a say, you've controlled everything since I was born." He laughed out loud, another sharp, sarcastic laugh. "Well, thank god for you, then. But, look, it's been an absolute pleasure, Mum, as always. Give my regards to Dad."

Jack rang off without waiting for a reply, and immediately opened his contacts and dialed someone else. He waited for a second, the light from the radio shining blue across his features, and started speaking the moment they picked up on the other end.

"I know it's not late there, Charlie, we're in the same time zone." Jack rolled his eyes, but there was affection there now. "Oh, 'after-work drinks,' so sorry. Well, I won't hold you up for long, okay?"

Dylan heard something that sounded like vague agreement over the line.

"Listen, I just talked to Mum— Yeah, she rang to have a go at me." Jack ran his hand through his hair. "She knows I quit and she thinks you had a hand in convincing me to leave. I made it clear that it was all me, but— Oh god, seriously? Okay, well, have fun."

Charlie made an angry sound, but that just made Jack laugh.

"Okay, love you, have an extra drink on me tonight, bye."

He rang off and then, after a few clicks, opened up his banking app. Dylan pointedly kept her eyes on the road as he navigated through his accounts, but she had to smile. She hadn't thought he literally meant *have a drink on me*, but it seemed Charlie was in for a few free drinks this evening.

Jack locked his phone with a heavy sigh and, after dropping it into his lap, set his elbow on the door and propped his forehead against his fist. Dylan wanted to ask, wanted to see if she could get him to talk to her, but she wasn't sure how to begin.

Finally, she glanced at him. "Everything okay?"

Jack exhaled again, this time even more exhausted than before. "Yeah, Dylan. Everything's fine."

CHAPTER 26

Despite Dylan's best efforts to let Jack thaw, things were frozen solid throughout their time in Iceland.

He never made a scene, never said anything angry, wasn't looking like he was imagining stabbing her with pins. He was just . . . silent. All of the time.

Honestly, she would have preferred having massive rows with him if only because then he would've been speaking to her.

They spent the whole of the next afternoon at the Blue Lagoon, and though Dylan had a nice time floating around wearing a face mask with a free drink in her hand, it would have been a lot better if she'd had someone to chat to while she'd been doing it. The place itself was astounding—the water was an unnatural shade of aqua and the heat of the water soothed every muscle—but she missed the commentary Jack would've made if they'd been going around together.

He would have pointed out, for example, the grown men in the corner doing cannonballs and disrupting half the pool. He would have carefully deliberated on which face mask to get before he slathered a thick layer of algae over his skin. She caught sight of him floating around sometimes, green smoothie in hand, olive mask splashed across his face, and it made her chest ache, seeing him without her.

She'd hoped that sitting next to each other for six hours on their flight to New York would have helped Jack soften up, but he didn't say anything to her beyond the absolutely necessary, and each time, Dylan felt the sadness settle heavier on her chest.

Gwen: honestly babe you did what you did and all you can do now is wait for him to forgive you or wait for the trip to be over

Dylan: wow thanks that's really helping me feel better

Gwen: ugh I'm sorry I knew that was harsh

Gwen: have you talked about it again?

Dylan: ...no. He won't even look at me

Gwen: maybe it's time to try again

Dylan: pretty sure he'd rather put a pen in his eye than talk to me

Gwen: what's your evidence?

Dylan: the fact that he hasn't talked to or looked at me in 3 days and we literally share a hotel room?

Gwen: ....

Gwen: fair enough

While she was pretty sure Jack would rather jump out of a moving car than have another conversation with her about the article, Dylan also knew there was absolutely no way she was going to ride out the last two weeks of this trip and hope she survived the awkwardness. Beyond saving herself another argument, there was no reason she should let it lie. She hadn't said everything she wanted to say or said it how she'd wanted to say it, and that was entirely because she'd done what she always did and gotten defensive.

Before she attempted to talk with him about it again, though, she knew there was one important thing she needed to do first.

Their plane landed in New York in the early evening, thanks to the time difference, only an hour later than the time it had been when they left Reykjavík. It had, as every film she'd ever seen about New York demonstrated, taken over an hour to get from JFK to their hotel in Manhattan. She could have been annoyed about the fact that it was more like sitting in a bloody car park than a motorway as the car crawled through the Queens–Midtown Tunnel, but when they finally emerged on the other side of the East River, and the lights from the city came into focus, Dylan would've happily sat through three more hours of traffic if it meant she got to glide slowly past the view.

Even living in London for years, Dylan had never seen a city as busy as New York. The first big junction they reached had four lanes of traffic going in one direction, buses and lorries and bright yellow taxis all rushing through the stop-and-go. Her only understanding of the city before arriving had been the television shows she'd watched as a teenager—*Gossip Girl*, mainly—and she found herself tracing bits of skyline to see if she recognized anything, although she was fairly sure she wasn't staying anywhere near the places those shows were set, and even if she was, they'd changed quite a bit in the years since filming had ended.

Suddenly, Jack gasped. "I'm pretty sure I just saw the Empire State Building."

They were the first voluntary words Jack had spoken to her in days, and despite the fact that Dylan nearly cried with relief, she tried to play it cool.

"Really?" She pressed her forehead against the window and contemplated sticking her whole head outside. "Where?"

It was just after eight by the time they finished checking in to their hotel, and though things definitely felt a little less awkward between them as they dragged their bags into the lift, they still didn't speak as they took their ride up to the fifteenth floor. Their room was small but beautiful, all exposed brick and crisp white duvets, though Dylan did little more than chuck her bags on her bed before running over and pressing her face to the windows.

The city was a collection of lights—traffic signals, taillights, office lights left on all across the skyline. She could just see the dark outlines of the buildings, but with how the windows ran together, it was impossible to tell where one building ended and the next began.

"Holy hell." She gestured vaguely toward the view without taking her eyes off it. "You have to see this."

Jack came to stand next to her, close enough that she could almost feel the heat of him in contrast to the cold window.

"Wow," he breathed. He sounded awed, as enchanted as Dylan was, and it was probably tragic, but she found herself clinging to the similarity.

She turned and looked up at him only to find him already looking at her.

He held her gaze for a beat before he sucked in a breath.

"I'm going to go get a shower."

Dylan swallowed. "Okay."

She faced the window as Jack walked away, though the whole of her focus was on the sounds behind her—the slash of a zipper, the rustling of fabric as he sorted out what he wanted to wear.

"Did you want to go out and get dinner? Or should we get a takeaway?"

She turned around slowly, afraid she'd scare him out of talking to her if she moved too quickly.

"I'm exhausted, but I say go out."

Getting out of the hotel would also afford her the perfect opportunity to get out of her head a bit. Stop her obsessing about what she was planning to do tomorrow morning.

"Okay, maybe we can get dinner nearby, then?" As he said it, he pulled a pair of jeans from his suitcase followed by a navy jumper. "Have an early night?"

"Okay." Dylan bit her lip to hide her smile when he tried to covertly add a pair of boxers to the bottom of the pile.

Jack nodded and then disappeared into the bathroom.

Dylan dressed quickly the next morning, intending to get out of the room before Jack woke up in hopes of sorting everything before he even realized she was gone. As she unzipped her bag to retrieve her laptop, though, he picked his head up off the pillow.

"What are you doing?"

His voice was thick with sleep, and when she glanced over at him, she saw that he barely had his eyes open.

She grabbed her laptop and, for good measure, her phone charger.

"I'm going to run downstairs to the business center," Dylan

said. She kept her voice soft in hopes he'd fall back to sleep after she left. "I've got to make a work call."

Jack groaned and rubbed his head into the pillow. His hair was going to be an absolute wreck today and she couldn't wait to see it. "Are you going to be long?"

"Should only be half an hour."

"Okay." He rolled onto his side, his eyes falling closed again as he tugged the duvet up underneath his chin. "I'll meet you downstairs for breakfast? Or are you coming back?"

Dylan grabbed her room key off the table inside the door. "I'm coming back."

The business center was about as depressing as Dylan could have imagined. It was little more than a pair of ancient desktop computers on small wooden desks, a few slightly worn armchairs, and a printer tucked away in the corner, but it was more than enough for Dylan to do what she needed to do.

She pulled her mobile out of her back pocket and sat down in one of the chairs, settling her laptop carefully on her lap as she opened up her contacts and started scrolling.

Dylan tapped Chantel's number and then waited, lip between her teeth, as the line rang. It rang twice and then went live.

"Chantel Stainton's office, this is Steph, how can I help?"

"Hey, Steph, it's Dylan," Dylan said, doing her best to keep her voice casual. "Is Chantel in? I wouldn't normally call, but I wanted to make sure I caught her with my time difference. I've got a question that's pretty time sensitive."

"Oh, uh . . ." Steph's voice stretched out awkwardly and Dylan would bet her laptop that she'd just leaned over to get Chantel's permission to patch the call through. "Yeah, let me check her calendar real quick, make sure she's not about to hop into another call."

Dylan knew that Steph knew Chantel's calendar inside and out, but she appreciated the rapid clicking in the background for the theater that it was.

"Okay," Steph said, her voice brighter, "right now is perfect, let me patch you through."

"Cheers, Steph."

Chantel answered a second later.

"Dylan." Week-old balloons had more levity than Chantel's voice. "How's New York?"

"It's lovely, Chantel, listen." Dylan drew in a deep breath, steeling herself. "I wanted to talk to you about the travel series."

Dylan heard the electronic beeping of a button being pressed, and the whirring of Chantel's treadmill in the background got louder. "What about it?"

"Well, two things. First, I'd like to stop writing about Jack completely."

The silence over the line was thick. Protracted.

"You'll see a significant decrease in engagement."

"I'm willing to accept that."

Chantel drew in a sharp breath through her nose and the sound alone was enough to communicate several levels of her annoyance. "Are you?"

Dylan nodded even though she knew Chantel couldn't see. "It's not fair to keep writing about him. He's explicitly asked me not to."

Chantel was quiet for a beat. Her silence always made Dylan feel itchy, and this time was no exception.

"You understand that you'd be giving up your chance at a column if you backed off the story now?"

Dylan frowned. "I could still get enough traffic to the articles. I wouldn't necessarily be forfeiting my column."

A heavy silence sat between them for a second before Chantel cleared her throat. When she spoke, her tone was final. Resigned. "Well, actually, that's something I wanted to talk to you about."

Dylan felt her blood run cold.

"After this recent bit of activity with the Bangkok article and people getting violent again, I've been thinking it's time to re-visit things." More treadmill beeping, now accented by aggressive typing. "I've spoken with legal and human resources, and they both agree we should refrain from drawing more attention to you for the time being."

She . . .

This couldn't be happening again.

After everything Dylan had been through, after she'd done everything Chantel had asked, here she was, right back where she started. Being sidelined again, silenced again, all because a few arse-holes on the internet wanted to send her death threats.

"Are you saying you wouldn't like me to finish writing the travel series?"

"It's not a matter of whether I'd like you to, Dylan. Of course I'd like you to. I just don't think it's a great idea at the moment."

Dylan did her best to keep her voice even. "I've been through this with legal before, though, and it didn't help, keeping me off of articles. If anything, people just used that as an excuse to reach out to me on my private social media."

"You can understand, however, why we wouldn't want *our* comments flooded with the kinds of messages you're receiving."

"I don't want my DMs flooded with them, either."

"I'm sure, so I can't imagine this will be an unwelcome change for you." She literally hadn't been listening to anything Dylan'd said. "You mentioned a second item?"

"Right." Dylan cleared her throat. She had an idea of how this was going to go now, but she couldn't leave it unsaid. "I want to post a public apology to Jack for writing about him. I've finished a draft of it and I'd like him to read it first, but I could have it ready today. It's the right thing to do."

"Oh, well." Chantel clicked her tongue. "That's an interesting idea, Dylan, but I don't think that'll work."

She'd expected as much, but she was still annoyed. "Is there any particular reason? I think it's important to take accountability—"

"No, I hear you. But, like I said, you want to lay low for a few months. Maybe then you can post something about the rest of the trip and include your apology there?"

Dylan was quiet for so long that Chantel must have assumed she agreed. "Okay, well, great talking to you, Dylan, I've actually got to hop on another call. I'll send through a few minor pieces you can get working on for the last fortnight of your trip and then we'll see you back in the office at the end of the month."

Dylan had barely said her goodbyes before Chantel rang off.

Part of her wanted to be surprised at how that conversation had gone, but that had burned off long ago where Chantel was concerned. Now, all that was left was simmering resentment, anger, and frustration.

She couldn't be back at square one again. She couldn't sit silently, name absent from everything she wrote, with her head in the sand and hope people forgot about her. She couldn't wait for Chantel to decide she was worth tempting with another column only to take it back at the last second and render everything Dylan had done completely and totally useless.

She knew what she had to do.

Dylan picked up her phone again and rang one more person. After a few rings, the line went live.

"Afua Addo."

It immediately made Dylan smile, hearing Afua's voice again. Dylan could almost see her sitting at their shared desk, her feet crossed underneath the table, everything perfectly organized. She was probably enjoying the peace and quiet without Dylan around.

"Afua, it's me." Dylan could barely get the words out through the emotions bubbling in her chest. "Do you have a second?"

"Holy fuck, Dylan? How are you? *Where* are you?"

Dylan felt her throat constrict at the genuine concern in Afua's voice. "I'm fine, yeah, we're in New York. Listen . . ." She explained the situation, and when she finished, Dylan felt Afua's stillness from all the way across the Atlantic.

"This is your moment, isn't it?"

Dylan swallowed. "Yeah. I wanted to give you a heads-up in case things started, uh, going down after what I'm about to do."

"What are you going to do?"

"Nothing that serious." Dylan was keen to keep as many of the details from Afua as possible. "I don't want you knowing too much in case Chantel asks."

"Okay . . ." Afua didn't sound convinced that keeping her in the dark was the best plan, but she seemed to accept that no amount of questioning was going to get it out of Dylan. "Well, can I help? Do you need me to do anything?"

"No, I have everything." She was pretty sure she still had the admin log-ins Byron in IT had sent her a few months ago when he'd been working on her laptop. Unless they'd changed, and she couldn't imagine they had, she had everything she needed. "Just keep an eye on the home page in a few hours and then probably, like, run away so you don't have to hear Chantel screaming."

Afua laughed nervously. "You're not making me feel better about this."

"It'll be great," Dylan said, more to reassure herself than Afua. "Or, well, it'll be the right thing to do."

"I never doubted that," Afua said. The confidence in her voice made Dylan's throat constrict.

"Thanks, Af. Have a good night."

"You, too," Afua said. "Give me a ring when you're back in London, yeah?"

"Will do, babe. Bye."

The connection cut and Dylan stared down at her screen, bracing herself for a second before she navigated to her email. She'd filed away IT Byron's email innocently enough when he'd first sent her the log-ins—his last-ditch attempt at fixing her access issues in the laziest way possible—though she hadn't once imagined using them until now. It was a fireable offense, of that she was sure, but she wasn't sure *Buxom* had been . . . well, the dream she'd always thought it would be.

It could've been—if she'd had a different editor or if she'd been a different writer, maybe she could have thrived here—but she didn't feel the need to make herself stay at this magazine anymore, even if it meant she had to go back to freelancing.

Part of her mind was screaming that she shouldn't take a step back, but, really, it was never a step back if you were betting on yourself. If you were valuing yourself above everything else.

Dylan pulled Byron's email up and then navigated to *Buxom*'s online posting platform. She normally only logged in here to post the articles Chantel had pushed through for approval; she'd never posted her own from scratch through the admin access screens. Luckily, the screens weren't significantly different, so it was only a few minutes before Dylan had her article pasted into the text box, "home page" ticked in the menu on the right side of the screen. Her heart was in her throat as she read it through, her eyes desperately scanning for typos, but once she finished making her final corrections, there was nothing else to do but to post it.

But before she did that, she needed to go get Jack.

CHAPTER 27

Jack was sitting on the end of his bed when Dylan walked through the door, enormous smile plastered on her face. She grabbed her coat off the hook with a flourish before setting her laptop on the desk. She probably seemed borderline unhinged.

"Ready to get breakfast?"

Jack raised an eyebrow as he got to his feet. "Are you okay?"

She barked a laugh that only served to make him that much more concerned. "I'm fabulous."

They filled up on bacon and eggs from the hotel buffet, though Dylan also grabbed a banana, a croissant, and a cup of tea on their way out into the chilly New York morning. It had been relatively quiet inside the hotel—just the buzz of conversation and cutlery against plates—but the moment they stepped out onto the street, they were hit with a wall of sound.

She didn't know if Seventh Avenue was a central route through Manhattan, but she assumed it must be because there were four lanes of traffic crawling past them. There was a crowd of people on the corner waiting for the signal to cross, though several of them were already standing in the street, trying to time their way across. She'd imagined New York would have been nothing more than a chorus of shouting and car horns, and while there was always a bit of shouting from somewhere and she could hear a few car horns, the city was more an amalgamation of things rather than any one sound. The rush of noise, the impatience of the cars and pedestrians, the way the buildings themselves crowded out the sky so you felt almost compressed—there was an unstoppable energy to this city, like it was going to keep going no matter what.

For a few seconds, she could only stand there, just staring out at the activity around her. Eventually, Jack cleared his throat.

"So, do you have a destination in mind?"

"Nope." Dylan grinned up at him before spinning on her heel and starting the walk up toward Thirty-First Street.

Dylan didn't know if it was the energy coursing through her or the fact that so many days of silence had stretched between them, but things between her and Jack finally felt less awkward. They still didn't talk much, but you couldn't have moved along the pavement, Dylan thought, if you weren't working as a team or, at the very least, paying attention to each other.

Out of a sense of obligation, they made their way to Times Square, its mass of neon and screens and pedestrians reminiscent of Tokyo in its energy. They posed for a photo down the center of Broadway to send off to Radio 1, and Dylan watched as Jack moved smoothly up and down the pavement taking pictures of his own. She found herself drawn back to him time and again, to the careful way he framed his shots and the crease in his brow right before he took a photo.

She could have been standing in the middle of the most vibrant place in the world and her eyes would always seek out Jack.

After ticking Times Square off their list, they started wandering down Broadway. The city shifted as they walked downtown—the steel skyscrapers were steadily replaced by shorter brick and stone buildings, there were more trees lining the pavements, and there were fewer cars and pedestrians on the roads. It was still busy, but the city hummed in a different way here, especially once they made it farther down. It was clear that people actually inhabited these spaces every day instead of flooding in, taking photographs, and leaving.

It was just gone noon by the time she and Jack found themselves in Greenwich Village, and after walking across what felt like the whole of Manhattan, hunger was now curling angrily in Dylan's stomach.

It was also probably about time that she get through this conversation she and Jack needed to have.

"Can we go grab some lunch? I, uh, wanted to show you something and I'll need Wi-Fi."

Jack's brows pinched. "Is everything okay?"

"Yeah." She tried to sound reassuring and less like she was about to be sick. "It's a good thing, I swear."

Jack looked like he wanted to press her, but then her stomach grumbled loudly and the corner of his lips twitched with a smile. "Alright, let's find some lunch, then."

They decided on a small Italian restaurant off Grove Street. Despite the cold, there were still tables lined up outside, and while Dylan was tempted to sit on the pavement and watch the traffic, the air was too biting to make it worth it. The specials were written in white paint on the front door in curly Italian script and again on one of the blackboards behind the bar when they walked in.

The restaurant itself was the perfect balance of rustic and modern—the exposed brick walls and original wood floors, especially when combined with the dark wood bar and dark, artfully chipped columns, retained some of the old charm, but it was brought to life by the bright white ceiling, the industrial rod lighting, and the eclectic mix of wooden tables and chairs.

The host led them to a two-seat table in the center of the restaurant just to the left of the bar. Dylan still caught Jack sometimes glancing at her with naked curiosity in his eyes, but neither of them addressed her more mysterious reason for wanting to grab lunch and, instead, focused on scanning the menus.

They put through their lunch orders, and once the waitress was gone, Dylan leaned her forearms on the table.

"I wanted to apologize to you," she began. At her words, Jack sat up a little straighter in his chair, his shoulders stiffening. "I know you probably don't want to hear any more about it, but I want you to know that I'm really, really sorry for how out of hand things got. And how I let them get that way by writing that article in the first place."

Jack nodded silently. Dylan swallowed, steeling her nerves.

"I think it's important that I apologize to you publicly, too. If that's something you'd be okay with."

She held his gaze for a second before, fingers fumbling, she pulled out her mobile. She still had the article open in her browser, and it made it easier for her to avoid any hesitation as she pushed the device across the table.

"You don't have to say yes," she said, watching as Jack slid the phone closer. "But I wanted you to read it because I think I said things better there than I ever managed to say when we were talking about it."

Jack held her gaze for a long moment, so long that Dylan almost thought he was going to refuse to read it. When her screen dimmed, though, Jack swiftly tapped it with his index finger so it lit up again.

"Okay." He lifted her phone gingerly and took it with him as he leaned back in his seat.

TO JACK: I'M SORRY

Full disclosure, I wanted to call this article "My Truth," but I figured I was already pushing the boat out by posting this and decided to cool it with the jokes. Just know that, in my heart of hearts, "My Truth" is painted across the top of this article in big, bold Futura. (I also could have made a Dear John joke, so, like, please appreciate the seriousness of the title.)

It feels a little cocky to say it, but I'm pretty confident that almost all of you reading this have already read most of the other articles in the series, especially the one I wrote about Bangkok a few weeks ago. That piece was difficult to write for a lot of reasons, but writing it had nothing on what was to come immediately after it was published. If you're reading this, you probably aren't a stranger to that, either, so I'll refrain from rehashing it here except to say that abortion is healthcare, I don't give a fuck about the knobheads in my mentions, and I hope that you enjoy your sad, lonely lives because I'm most certainly enjoying mine.

But I'm getting off track.

I should never have written that Bangkok article. I could sit here for thousands of words and give you a million reasons why I did it, but none of those reasons matter. What matters is I wrote it, I wrote about Jack, and

I did it without talking to him about it first, without confirming that what I'd written didn't cross a line.

I'm not saying anything groundbreaking when I say that was an incredibly fucked-up thing for me to do. You shouldn't post anything—a photo, an article, a tweet, nothing—without asking, and I did exactly that. And I did it knowing there was an audience anxiously awaiting the next bit of "news." I knew it would get traction and I posted it anyway. I posted this whole *series*—I gave in to my boss when she was asking me to tell a story about the romantic holiday I wasn't on. I never lied, but I blurred the lines in a way that, even now, makes me feel sick to my stomach. Because I let her manipulate my stories and I let myself manipulate you.

I don't expect Jack to forgive me, and honestly, I'm not sure that even writing this piece is the right move (two wrongs don't make a right, two public articles about a private matter don't make . . . a resolved private matter???) but it feels important to point out publicly that I was wrong for writing about him without asking. For assuming that, just because we'd been on my Instagram and we'd had one brief talk about boundaries one time, I had the right to air my private feelings when they very much concerned him. For assuming the things I wrote wouldn't have any kind of impact on him.

It should have been a conversation, and it wasn't, and I've already said this in person, but it needs to be said here, too. I did this publicly and it's important to take accountability publicly. And if you're reading this, just know that I gave Jack this letter before I posted it—he needed to hear these words before the rest of the world did—and the only reason you're reading it now is because he okayed it.

I'm sorry, Jack. Truly, from the bottom of my heart, I am so incredibly sorry. I know I violated the trust you put in me and I don't expect that trust back. I know I'll have to earn it and I can only show you, through my actions, that I mean it when I say I want to be someone that you can trust again.

I can't fix what I've already done, but I can change moving forward. Effective immediately, I've decided to leave my post at *Buxom*—I've nothing more to say other than it just wasn't the right place for me to continue my career. I am going to keep writing the rest of this series—I only have one destination left—but I'm not going to be talking about it here. You'll be able to find it over on my Instagram, @dylancoughlan. I won't be talking about Jack, but I will be writing obscenely long captions and sharing too many pictures of these gorgeous places, so honestly, I don't think you'll miss him (no offence, Jack).

If you want to hear more about brilliant sights, delicious food, and my tears as I think about going back to my post-travel life, we're going to have a lot of fun. If you were only here because you wanted to hear about my nonexistent relationship . . . well, thanks for being here, I hope you'll stick around, but I'll understand if you don't.

See you on the 'gram.

xx Dylan

His expression had been blank, guarded, when he'd first started reading, but as he continued on, Dylan watched his features soften. There were a few times, too, that Jack exhaled a gentle laugh, and each one sent a jolt of satisfaction through her chest.

When he finished, he looked up, and Dylan was immediately taken aback by the emotion playing plainly across his features.

She waited, hoping he would say something, but he was apparently of the mind that the look alone was sufficient. She sucked in a breath.

"What did you think?"

hank you." He said it immediately, like he was waiting for her to ask. "For apologizing. I—" His gaze slid down to the table for a second. "I really appreciate that you wrote it. I can't imagine that was easy."

She laughed a little, relief filling her. "It was easier than you'd think."

"Are you sure about leaving your job?" His brows pinched and Dylan knew that was only the barest hint at the thoughts likely swirling through him.

Dylan nodded. "I can't stay there. Especially because I'm not supposed to have the admin log-ins I used to get that post ready."

Jack's jaw actually dropped. "You *what*?"

Bless him, he was so innocent sometimes.

She waved her hand lightly. "The guy in IT sent them to me ages ago because he didn't feel like helping me fix an issue I was having. And Chantel wasn't going to let me post this, so if we want to post it, that's the way I'm going to do it."

"How do you know she isn't going to let you post it?"

"I called her this morning, but I barely got the words out when she told me there was no way it was going to happen. And even worse"—she laughed sardonically—"she also told me I should stop posting altogether. I'm drawing too much negative attention to them again."

Jack exhaled sharply. "That's bollocks."

She'd never heard him say that before and the way his accent twisted around the word, almost making it sound decent, made her grin.

"It's not like I haven't been here before," Dylan said. "That's how I got into this 'writing about your personal life' mess in the first place."

"So she told you you couldn't post this and you decided, 'Fuck it, I'll get the admin log-ins and do whatever I want'?"

She laughed. Leave it to Jack to summarize it that succinctly.

"Basically. If I had your approval."

Their waitress reappeared, food in hand, and they both leaned back in their seats to leave her enough room to drop off their plates.

The waitress smiled at them as she straightened up. "Can I get you anything else?"

"No." Dylan looked over at Jack to confirm and he shook his head. "This looks great, thank you."

The waitress nodded once before she walked off.

"What will you do if you quit?"

"Who knows." Dylan took a bite of her tortellini, groaning softly at the flavor of the roasted ricotta within.

Jack pressed his face into his hands. When he spoke, his voice was muffled by his palms. "We're both going to be out of work."

"Jack, honestly," Dylan said. She put her palm up on the table-top, an offering, and Jack looked up, his eyes finding hers. "We're going to be fine."

He put his hand on hers, and the heat of his palm seared through her skin. "How do you know? I don't even know what I want to do, let alone where I'm going to work."

"That's the beauty of it, though, isn't it?" She gave Jack's hand a gentle squeeze. "You have the time to figure it out."

Jack looked like he'd rather lie down in the middle of Seventh Avenue than have to figure anything out.

"Look," she said, trying to use her most pragmatic voice. The one she only got out for special occasions. "I have some money saved and I have dozens of contacts from when I freelanced. And, not to brag, but I think most of them will be begging to have me write for them again."

Jack laughed, but the sound caught in his throat so it sounded like he was drowning.

"I've been thinking about striking out on my own anyway." She hadn't been thinking about it until this very moment, but as she said it, the words felt true. "I've got a few thousand followers, I could grow that easily."

"And then what?"

"Sponsorships. Freelance." Dylan shrugged. "I don't honestly know all the ins and outs, but I've got the gist."

"How can you plan a future around *the gist*?"

"Sometimes you have to bet on yourself. And I've got support. Gwen and Sean aren't going to let me fall into ruin."

Jack stared at her, quiet intensity in his eyes. "I wouldn't let you, either."

Her heart gave a powerful squeeze.

"You'll figure it out, too. Really, you will," she said, laughing a little because Jack looked like he'd just swallowed a boulder. "Have you got anything saved?"

"Yes."

"And you've got law contacts if that's what you decide you want to do."

"Yes."

"Okay, so"—she smiled, trying to ease the anxiety written all over him—"what's stopping you?"

"If I don't go back into law, I have no idea what I'm going to do." The words rushed out like they were trying to escape before Jack could catch them back. "I have no other training, no other contacts, my parents will now absolutely let me hang out to dry and point and laugh and shout their 'I told you so's. I can try to ignore them, but I can't cope if I don't have a plan. If I don't at least know what I'm doing."

He sounded like he was begging her to tell him what the solution was.

"You have other skills, Jack," she said softly. She brushed her thumb along the back of his hand and he dropped his gaze to watch the progress of her finger across his skin. "You don't have to go back and sit in a stuffy office if you don't want to."

"I don't feel like I have any other skills that matter."

"Are you serious?" She actually laughed at that and Jack looked up at her, eyebrows raised. "You're a brilliant photographer. You're obsessively organized. I'm sure you're, like, an absolute genius when it comes to contracts."

Jack scoffed, though the sound was slightly garbled. "I don't think my contract knowledge will help me outside of law."

"I would've killed for that knowledge when I was first free-lancing. I could have avoided so many issues with companies trying to keep my money from me."

"You know what I mean, though," Jack said. He turned their hands over so he was more playing with her fingers instead of holding her hand. "I'm trained in law. I've only ever worked in law. If anyone outside of law looked at my CV, they'd think I was the least qualified person alive."

"It's about how you pitch it," Dylan said. "I've applied for a million gigs that I wasn't exactly qualified for on paper, but you pitch your skills slightly differently, and then, all of a sudden, you're the greatest find that company has ever had."

Jack exhaled heavily and Dylan gave him a beat to breathe before she added, "Honestly, I think you could pursue photography."

As easy as it was to imagine Jack sitting back in some office in London—a high floor in a glass building in Central that he rushed in and out of every day—she couldn't see him actually being happy there. It was the riskier of the options, delving out on his own, but the look in his eyes every time he was taking pictures, the care he had for his craft?

She wanted that for him. She wanted him to do something that filled him up.

Jack half shook his head, half shrugged, his eyes wide with something like panic. "I— How am I supposed to do that?"

"There are a million ways into it."

"But I don't know anyone in photography. I—"

"You're very good at finding problems, Jack, but we need to

start thinking of solutions." She said it with a wry smile on her lips to soften the comment, and Jack, luckily, exhaled and smiled back.

"All I did in law was find problems," he admitted. "I'm hard-wired to spot issues at this point."

She laughed. "Fair enough."

He brushed his index finger along the inside of her palm and the sensation—light and soft and barely there—made her shiver. Jack inhaled sharply and pulled his hand away, hastily grabbing his water glass.

Dylan traced the long lines of his throat as he drank before she swallowed and grabbed her phone.

"Here, let's make a list. Get your phone."

She opened her notes app and created a new note and invited Jack to collaborate.

He laughed. "'How to make Jack a photographer'?"

"Yes." She typed PROBLEM: no photography contacts at the top of the page. "We're coming up with solutions. How can we solve this contacts issue?"

She typed SOLUTION: underneath and looked at Jack expectantly.

"I guess I could talk to my sister? She might know some people who would be good to get in touch with."

Dylan typed it in and waited for Jack to add on. When he didn't, she leaned forward slightly, drawing his gaze to hers.

"I really think you should consider getting an Instagram. I know," she said, raising her voice a little because he was already making a face, "but I'm telling you from experience that it's one of the best ways to break in now."

"How is making an Instagram going to help?" She must have pulled some kind of expression, because Jack hastened to clarify. "I'm not . . . opposed to it. I just need you to explain why."

"It gives you a dedicated space to share your work," Dylan said. "You brand it, you maintain it, you control what goes out and how it's framed. When I was with *Buxom*, we found *loads* of photographers through their Instagram accounts, and a lot of the magazines I freelanced with did as well."

"So it's like a portfolio?"

"Exactly."

Jack hummed softly, his gaze sliding past Dylan's shoulder. His expression gave absolutely nothing away, and while Dylan was sure that was a key asset in law, it was making her sweat a little bit. After a beat, he looked down at his phone and started typing, the words appearing on Dylan's screen.

PROBLEM: no photography contacts
SOLUTION: talk to Charlie; make an Instagram account and start following other photographers and magazines I'd like to work for

"Yes!" Dylan grinned and Jack's own smile grew, his features relaxing. "Please follow me, I need your pictures."

"Mmm, I don't know if I'm going to follow *you*." Jack's expression was carefully neutral, though the brightness in his eyes gave him away. Weeks ago, she would have missed that, and seeing it now made her heart swell.

She kicked him under the table. "Arsehole."

He laughed and nudged her foot back.

"Stop kicking me, I'm brainstorming."

"Oh, so sorry." She set her phone down and grabbed her fork instead.

Jack nodded sagely before he gathered another bite of risotto on his spoon. "No apologies necessary."

They ate quietly, Jack interspersing his bites with bouts of typing. Dylan watched as Jack's words appeared on her own screen, smiling to herself as the solutions grew longer and longer the more he worked.

PROBLEM: I've only played around with Photoshop and Lightroom, I don't really know what I'm doing.
SOLUTION: find Photoshop and Lightroom master class (or a video online); practise editing some of the photos from this trip as it's more low-stakes

PROBLEM: I've never freelanced before
SOLUTION: Dylan has freelanced and she would definitely help me; there are a number of resources online I could refer to; I could reach out to photography contacts once I made them to talk about photography-specific issues; Charlie probably also knows freelancers I could talk to

PROBLEM: I don't know what standard freelance agreements look like
SOLUTION: I could look up references online; extensive knowledge of corporate contract and legal proceedings will undoubtedly be an asset; can look

up standard rates and agreement structures; may
also be able to reach out to legal contacts and see if
they have real agreements they can anonymise and
send as references

PROBLEM: I don't know if my pictures are good
enough
SOLUTION:

Jack stared down at that one for a long time before, finally,
he typed—**Ask Dylan to remind me that she likes my pictures; take more pictures and improve skill; remind myself
that I love my photos (most of the time).**

The idea that he was going to ask her—that she was the first
solution he thought of for his wavering confidence—made her heart
clench. She would tell him, she'd tell him a million times over, but
the fact that he knew it, and he knew to ask her for it when he
needed it, felt unreal.

"Okay." Jack's cursor disappeared from the note, though he
was still clicking around on his phone. "I think you're right and it
makes the most sense to at least set up an Instagram."

Dylan tried not to punch the air in her excitement. Instead,
she said very primly, "Of course I'm right."

Jack nudged her foot again. "Let me download it and then can
you help me, like, get a username? We can mess with the rest of it
later, but I want to do that before I lose momentum."

Once he had the app downloaded, he opened it up and sighed.

"What kind of username should I have?"

"It shouldn't be anything too complicated," Dylan said. "It should be clear from your handle what your account is going to be."

"So, like, Jack Hunton Photography."

"Yeah, exactly! Though you don't have to use your name if you don't want to, you could use a concept if you want to keep it more anonymous."

Jack thought about that for a second, his thumbs hovering over the screen.

"If I'm going to do it," he said slowly, testing the words as he said them, "it should be me. A concept is fine, but I don't even know what that would be and then I worry I'd hide behind it."

"Okay." Dylan nodded, a small smile at the corners of her lips. "I think that makes sense."

"Yeah." Jack seemed more to be talking to himself than to Dylan. "I want it to be me."

A minute later, Dylan got an Instagram notification.

♥jackhuntonphotography has followed you

Dylan immediately followed him back. He hadn't posted any pictures yet, but she couldn't wait to see the ones that would, very soon, grace this page.

"I still have no idea what I'm doing," Jack admitted. His voice was a little shaky and Dylan rested her hand on his.

"Don't worry, I'm an expert. I'll show you the ropes."

Jack gave her hand a deep, desperate squeeze, like he was dangling over the edge of a cliff and she was the only thing keeping him from the abyss. "Thank you."

Jack held her gaze for a beat, two, before he nodded down toward her phone. "So when are you planning on posting?"

"Uh." She set her fork down. "Now, I guess? If that's still okay with you?"

Jack nodded, and her fingers trembled as she opened her browser and logged into the admin portal. Dylan looked over the article once more before she hit SUBMIT and immediately navigated to *Buxom*'s home page. After an agonizing few seconds, her latest article popped up on-screen.

As soon as the article went live, she clicked swiftly into Instagram. She needed to adjust her bio and post the apology in case people missed it. She selected the most poignant paragraph and added the post to her link in bio. It took her a few seconds to decide which picture she should use—none of them screamed *apology*, but she wanted it to be . . . tasteful. Fitting.

After a bit of scrolling, she decided on a picture she'd taken just that morning, the bright blaze of the sun shot through the skyline. It took her a bit of fiddling to get her bio right—she removed "*Buxom* writer," but after that . . . well, she was stuck.

She really should have written this out beforehand.

After a long minute, Dylan made her final adjustments—she couldn't bear to look at it anymore and she could always fix it later. It wasn't the end of the world if it wasn't perfect right now.

Dylan Coughlan

that girl who travelled the world that one time

writer, bi as hell, freelance champion

pronouns she/her

linkin.bio/dylancoughlan

She locked her phone, looked up, and found Jack staring at her. "Done?"

She nodded. "Done."

She'd just finished eating her pasta when her screen lit up with a WhatsApp message from Afua.

> Oh my fucking god, it's a good thing you aren't here
> right now

Dylan wasn't altogether surprised, but she still felt a bit of anxiety curl in her stomach as she replied.

> Dylan: I'm guessing Chantel's seen
> Afua: Uh yeah
> Afua: I should have known that you would have made your moment as big and dramatic as possible, but I'm still impressed with how big you went

Dylan glanced quickly up at Jack as she typed out her reply. "Well, *Buxom* officially knows about it."

"That was quick."

> Dylan: thanks babe
> Dylan: it was an absolute pleasure working with you
> Afua: I know you don't think you're getting rid of me that easily
> Dylan: oh absolutely not
> Afua: Pretty sure Chantel is making wanted posters rn though

> Dylan: if you want to also throw a firebomb on your career, it
>   isn't too late. I doubt they've changed the admin log-ins
>   and I'm more than happy to send them to you
> Afua: HAHAHAHA I'm good thanks

Her phone started ringing then—a call from Chantel—but Dylan didn't feel the need to put herself through that conversation. Maybe it was cowardice, but as far as Dylan was concerned, she'd said everything she needed to. Chantel could send her an email. Dylan was finished letting her dictate her time.

"What's going on?"

"Nothing major." Dylan flipped over her phone, though she knew they'd both seen Chantel's name splashed across her screen. "My boss is just calling to fire me. She clearly didn't read the article and see that I'd already resigned."

A small sound escaped the back of Jack's throat and Dylan reached out to pat his hand again. "Breathe. It'll be fine."

And truly, she hadn't felt this free in years.

CHAPTER 29

"**F**ucking hell, why did I let you convince me to do this again?"

Dylan was bent over at the waist, clutching a horrible stitch in her side as her trainers slid on the narrow stairs lining the steep edge of the Pyramid of the Sun. The top of the pyramid was supposed to give beautiful views of Teotihuacán, but unfortunately for Dylan, she was going to die before she got to see anything.

Jack was red in the face and a little sweaty, but he sounded like he was breathing entirely normally. "*You* convinced *me*. I was perfectly happy to stay on the ground."

It hadn't taken a lot of convincing, actually. Jack had been keen to take photos from the top and *thought he'd be fine because it was just a glorified staircase.* She'd thought she'd won quite the victory at the time, but she knew now that she was an idiot.

"I regret it now." Her thighs were on fire. "I'm going to die."

Jack snorted and Dylan held her middle finger up at him as she pushed herself upright. "Stop laughing at me, you prick, I'm dying."

"You're not dying." He was still smiling, but he looked so sexy grinning at her like that she decided to let it go.

"I could be." She put her arms behind her head and leaned to the left, cringing as her muscles stretched through the pain in her side. She felt a little better as she dropped her arms, but was sure the pain would be back before long.

"You climbed the Sydney Harbour Bridge. You hiked a *glacier*. You can climb this pyramid."

"That bridge was ages ago and the glacier was basically flat. This is a fucking mountain."

Jack squeezed her hand. "Either way, you're going to kick its arse."

Dylan remained thoroughly unconvinced.

Mexico City was probably, when all was said and done, going to rank among her favorite legs of this journey. It was crowded, certainly, and anytime they so much as thought about getting into a car, there was traffic, but there was a vibrancy to this city that she loved. It was the layers of history, of histories, it was the murals and the art, it was people playing music on the streets—there was so much to this city she wanted to explore, and it seemed unfathomable that they only had five days to do it.

They'd woken early on their last full day in town and caught a taxi out to Teotihuacán. It was an hour northeast of Mexico City and the sun was just starting to come up over the trees by the time they arrived. Now, though, the sun was roasting the back of her neck, and she would have given anything to go lie in the shade of the trees surrounding the ancient city.

They'd been climbing the pyramid for nearly half an hour, though that time was largely spent waiting while Jack took pictures. Since setting up his Instagram, Jack's photographic efforts seemed to quadruple and he was taking pictures practically all the time. He'd spent half the flight from New York to Mexico City on Instagram, first following nearly every interesting photography account he could find and then fending off some very dedicated teasing from his sister before jumping in to edit some of his own photos to start posting. But no matter how long he spent in Instagram's editing feature, he never seemed ready to click POST, instead sneakily just saving to his drafts.

She couldn't tell what shots he was getting now, but there was an intensity to his focus and an energy in his movements that was addicting to watch. He looked how she felt when she was in a groove with her writing, like nothing in the world could stop her from doing it, like every possible thing was inspiration. It was astounding to her that he'd managed all those years sitting behind a desk pushing contracts when he was so obviously an artist.

They finally crested the pyramid nearly an hour after they'd started climbing, and Dylan tipped her head back in relief at being on flat ground again. "Thank god," she said, talking more to the clouds than to Jack. "My legs were about to give in."

Jack laughed softly, the sound carried away on the breeze. "I told you you could do it."

"Whatever." She rolled her eyes, ignoring the grin on his face, and turned to look out at the horizon.

She could see everything from up here, the dark green trees around the outside of the city, the Pyramid of the Moon off in the distance, and the smaller temples dotted throughout the plaza, and she couldn't believe people had built this. That they'd made something where you could see the world this way.

"This is brilliant," Dylan said. It wasn't enough, wasn't close enough to what she was actually thinking, but it was the only thing that came even remotely close to the awe she was feeling. "Are you okay?"

Jack was looking a little stiff now that they'd crested the top, and he took a few quick steps away from the edge. His eyes were a little wild, and Dylan reached out and touched his forearm.

"Do you want to head back down?"

Jack shook his head, though he didn't seem convinced. "I'm going to get some more photos first if that's okay?"

She nodded, and as soon as he stepped back, she sat down, crossing her legs and leaning her weight back onto her hands. The bricks were warm against the backs of her thighs and she could only imagine how hot they must get after a full day baking in the sun.

She was sure Jack was going to take ages, but she was in no rush. Her legs needed time to recover, and anyway, there were far too many things to see.

Sitting still, she felt like she was seeing the details—the grooves in the brick from years of rain and wind, the wear along the stairs from decades of tourists climbing up. Every now and then she saw a bird dart into the sky, sharp against the rolling green of the forest.

When Jack finally finished, he wandered back over to her. His eyes were bright, and Dylan's heart melted in her chest.

"You look like you took some good ones." She held her hand out. "Can I see?"

"Nope." He sat down carefully, so close she could feel the press of his leg against hers. "I'm not done yet."

They sat quietly for a while, listening to the sounds of the soft breeze.

So much had changed since their conversation in New York. With the burden of the series lifted from her shoulders, Dylan was brimming with creativity, and posting pictures and caption articles almost constantly. She still caught the occasional worried expression on Jack's face, but even those faded as he also relaxed into their time together.

They started finding more reasons to touch each other, too. That in itself wasn't different—he'd taken her hand before, had touched her before—but there was a new weight behind it now. A significance that, for Dylan at least, had always been hovering just underneath the surface.

They were engaging in what felt like an elaborate kind of dance. An, according to Gwen, *incredibly annoying game of will they/won't they except they obviously will and they need to just GET ON WITH IT ALREADY.*

She looked at him now. His cheeks were still flushed with exertion, and the time in the sun had sprinkled light freckles across his skin. He was staring out at the landscape, his eyes tracing over everything in front of them, and she loved the way he took the time to catalog the details. After a long minute, he sighed gently, and she felt her lips curve into a smile.

"What are you thinking?"

He met her gaze, his expression softening until he mirrored her own gentle smile. "I'm glad they pulled my name out of your phone."

"I'm glad they did, too."

"And not even just because of this." He waved his hand wide and Dylan looked out at the bright, cloudless sky. "It's— The whole trip has been great, but getting to do it with you . . . that's the best bit."

He sounded a little breathless, a little embarrassed, and god, Dylan could barely contain herself. He was gorgeous, heart-stoppingly so, and she'd never, in a million years, thought she'd be so lucky as to be on the top of a pyramid outside Mexico City with someone who looked at her like that. With someone who made her heart feel the way her heart was feeling right now.

Like it was absolutely fit to burst and she couldn't even hope to contain it.

"I think that's the best bit, too." Her voice was shaking a little from her rapidly failing effort to keep her head on. "I've loved all of it, but I don't think I could have asked for a better travel partner."

It reminded her of what she'd written ages ago, the throwaway line from her Cape Town draft Gwen had mocked her about, and it made Dylan's cheeks flush.

His eyes snapped to hers and he smiled that soft, easy smile she loved, and Dylan's breath caught.

"We make a good team."

"We do."

They were quiet for a beat before Dylan sighed and leaned over to rest her head on his shoulder. "It's beautiful up here," she said. "I'm not ready to go back down."

Jack wrapped his arm around her shoulders, tucking her into his side. "We don't have to go anywhere."

"Yeah, but"—she pointed toward the stream of people now walking up the stairs toward the platform where they were sitting—"we're about to get a lot of company."

"Still." He pressed a kiss to the top of her head, and Dylan felt her heart swell. "Let's enjoy this until they get here."

CHAPTER 30

It was late afternoon by the time they called a taxi back to Mexico City and, thanks to the traffic, an hour and a half before they were back outside their hotel. Jack took her hand as the taxi drove off.

"Are you hungry?"

Dylan pressed her free hand to her stomach which, at that moment, decided to rumble louder than the cars around them. "I don't know, probably."

The small taqueria down the road from their hotel had rapidly become a favorite. It didn't look like anything special—it was a dozen red tables packed into a space covered from floor to ceiling in white subway tiles—but Dylan would swear that the tacos she'd had there a few days ago had made her see god.

They grabbed the last free table in the corner and Dylan went up to the counter to put in their orders. Her Spanish was horrifically clumsy—she ended up speaking French more than Spanish—but she was better at it than Jack.

"You're so worried about getting it right that you don't actually end up saying anything," Dylan had said as they'd been leaving a bakery the morning before. "People aren't going to judge you for not speaking perfect Spanish. You're making an effort, that's what matters."

The teenager behind the counter remembered her from their

previous visits, so it was far easier to get through their order. Dylan took the plastic number the cashier had given her and made her way back across the restaurant, sliding past the small crowd of people waiting to order and muttering "Perdón" under her breath. Jack was sitting patiently at the table when she arrived, thumbing through something on his phone.

He smiled as she approached. "Ordered alright, then?"

"'Course. I'm basically a polyglot now."

"Good to know," he said with a snort.

"So I was editing my pictures from today," Jack said after a beat, his tone almost absent. "I think I got some decent shots."

Dylan sat up straighter in her chair. "Ooh, can I see?"

"Let me know what you think," Jack said, handing his phone over. "I have a few that I like, but I can't— I don't know. I don't know if they're good enough to post."

He trailed off as Dylan started looking through his camera roll. He'd never asked her to look at his pictures before—she'd seen them while casually scrolling through his phone, sure, but he was clearly asking her opinion on these. She could feel the anxiety rolling off him in waves as she studied each picture, but really, he needn't've worried.

Every single picture was gorgeous.

There were a few shots of the landscape—the smaller temple platforms in the foreground with the Pyramid of the Moon in the background, a shot down the Avenue of the Dead toward the Temple of Quetzalcóatl at the far end—but what really caught her were the others.

Detailed shots of the brickwork. Dylan's trainers, shot low to the ground, as she walked up the Stairs. The jagged lines of the ruins against the cerulean sky. Dylan, her full body this time, the sun shining in front of her so it gave her now tan skin a soft glow.

"These are beautiful," she said, handing his phone back. She sounded almost awed, but damn if she didn't mean every ounce of feeling. "You should absolutely post them."

She was a little jealous that he was going to get to post such gorgeous pictures of her onto his page, but she supposed she could let it slide.

"You think?"

"Yes." Dylan couldn't have said it more emphatically if she'd tried. "Jack, I'm serious. These are stunning."

Jack hummed thoughtfully and flicked through the photos again, the concerned wrinkle between his eyes softening as he looked at them once more. He tilted his head every so often, eyes squinting as he examined his work, but when his eyes found hers again, there was an unmistakable satisfaction there.

"I really do like them."

She laughed. "Of course you do. And"—because she needed to bring it back to the main point here—"I think anyone who sees these on Instagram will feel the same way."

Jack swallowed and looked back down at his phone, flicking through the pictures again. She watched him for a second, that crease growing between his eyebrows, before she drew in a soft breath.

"Why do you think you're so nervous about sharing them?"

When he'd decided to attach his name to his Instagram, she thought that something was changing for him, but facing the reality of being online was apparently still enough to deter him. Or at least make him feel more uncertain about what he'd previously seemed so sure of.

"I think I'm just worried because this seems . . . final, I guess. Like a step forward into something that I'm actually happy about, but . . ." He sighed and dropped his phone, reaching up to run his hand through his hair. "That sounds stupid."

"No, it doesn't." She slid her hand across the table and rested it on his. "You've been stuck on one path for the last, like, what? Decade? It's natural that you'd be nervous."

Jack's gaze tipped down to the table, a little sheepish. "Thanks. God, I don't know why I thought I could've done this when I was a kid. I wasn't made of strong enough stuff to hack it on my own."

"You just didn't believe in yourself," Dylan said softly. She paused for a beat, waiting for Jack to meet her eyes again before she continued. "It's hard to believe in yourself when no one else does."

Jack nodded slowly.

"But now you have me." Dylan squeezed his hand. "I believe in you so much, I'm going to be shouting it from the rooftops."

Jack laughed, his hand pulsing on hers. "That very much makes two of us."

"What?" Dylan quirked an eyebrow at him. "Believing in you?"

"No, believing in each other."

They sat there quietly for a moment, the sounds of conversation rising and falling around them, before Jack casually picked up his phone and turned it around in his hands.

"I guess I should just get it over with then, huh?"

Dylan nodded and Jack exhaled, his features relaxing, not naturally, but like he was consciously willing himself to settle.

"Okay." He seemed to be talking to himself as much as he was talking to Dylan. "I can do it."

Dylan had to physically bite back her smile as she watched. Jack was moving through steps Dylan herself had completed hundreds of times, but the care and the intensity with which he approached them was so far removed from her own feeling about Instagram that it was unbearably endearing. He made minor adjustments to the editing on every single photo, painstakingly tagged everything, and tried three, four, five times before he got a caption he liked, but when he was finished, there was a mix of pride and nervous excitement on his face that Dylan wanted a million snapshots of so she could stare at it every day.

Jack's smile grew across his face as his eyes found Dylan's. "They're out there."

Dylan grabbed his hand quickly, a short, excited gesture that made Jack's whole arm shake. "I'm so proud of you."

Jack laughed, "Thanks," but Dylan had already let go of his arm and started rapidly clicking into Instagram to see them for herself.

♥The most beautiful view ☀

There were a million things he could have said (Dylan was thinking of putting approximately thirty thousand of them in her own post later tonight), but this caption, so succinct and to the point, was perfectly Jack. The sentiment was clear, the connection to the pictures perfect.

She'd never liked a set of photos faster in her life.

She flicked to the full body shot and turned her phone around. "Can I share this on my Instagram story? You can say no."

Sharing his post to her story would immediately bring it in front of hundreds, if not thousands, of eyes, and when people put two and two together and realized just whose account she was sharing from, the people on Instagram desperately searching for Jack's account would finally have exactly what they'd been looking for.

Though, granted, they were probably looking for a personal account and not a photography account, but Dylan was fairly sure they would take what they could get at this point.

After a long beat, Jack nodded slowly. "Yeah, that would be okay."

"I don't want to share it if you don't want me to," Dylan said. She didn't want it to just be *okay*. She wanted him to want her to. "I know it immediately puts more eyes on you."

"I want you to," Jack said. His eyes stayed steady on hers, his expression even, and she knew he meant it. "I'm proud of those photos and I need to practice being okay with them, like, being out in the world."

Their gazes held for a long moment before Dylan finally smiled. "Okay. Thank you."

"For what?"

For trusting her with this?

"For taking some bomb photos of me."

Jack laughed and Dylan's smile widened as she tapped the SHARE button. She shared the post to her story with a little sun sticker spinning in the top corner and locked her phone before she got sucked into scrolling.

"I'm honestly so proud of you." With nothing else to occupy her hands, she grabbed her water bottle and took a long drink.

Jack pressed his lips together in an attempt to hide his smile. "Thanks. I still don't know what I want to do with it, but I guess I don't have to know yet."

Dylan beamed. A few weeks ago, she would never have expected anything like that to come out of Jack's mouth. "Exactly. And if your parents start pressuring you, you can just send them to me. I'll deal with them."

Jack exhaled a laugh. "I'm sure you would." He was quiet for a beat, his expression going contemplative. "Have you heard from *your* parents recently?"

Dylan snorted. "Absolutely not." She traced her index finger through the condensation on her water bottle. "I keep thinking about fixing things for some reason. Maybe I'm a masochist."

"You're allowed to want to fix things."

"I just don't know why I want to. We've been having the same conversations over and over because they just kept thinking about 'what I'd done' like it was the worst thing they'd ever heard."

"You deserve better than that."

"I know."

"But you can also tell them that. That you deserve better. You aren't betraying yourself by asking for what you deserve."

And that, right there.

He'd perfectly summed up every feeling she'd had for the last year.

She took a deep breath and met Jack's gaze again. "Maybe I should write to them. Get it all out at once."

Jack nodded encouragingly. "That's a good idea."

Before she could put it off, Dylan opened up a blank email. It took her a few attempts to get going—she kept stopping and starting, unsure of what to say—before Jack nudged his little finger against the back of her hand.

"Just write what comes to mind. You can always fix it later."

Something eased in her chest and her thumbs hovered over the keyboard for a few seconds before, finally, she started typing.

She started with the big things—the way her parents responded to her abortion, the expectation that she lived by their moral code rather than her own. The idea that they would want her to be forced to bring an unwanted child into the world had always felt sticky and horrible, as had the notion that she could do anything truly unforgivable. She wasn't a parent and never wanted to be, but she'd thought raising children meant loving and celebrating them, even when their life looked different than how you imagined.

Dylan had never, not once, felt like her parents supported her when she deviated from the path they'd set for her.

The more she wrote, other things started to unravel, too. She'd been scared of her parents' rejection for the vast majority of her life, a symptom of eldest daughter syndrome and being queer as hell, but she deserved more than tolerance or a lack of outright rejection. They should have loved her no matter what, been proud of her no matter what. They hadn't thrown her out when she came out to them, but she shouldn't be *grateful* they hadn't. That was the bare minimum, the very least she could have asked for. Especially when it came with strings and expectations and the feeling of constantly looking over her shoulder anytime she brought a girl home because there were still barbs, even if they were sometimes very cleverly disguised.

She meant to reread her email after she finished writing it, but as she set her phone down on the tabletop, she felt too raw to look at it again, like several layers of her skin had been peeled back.

She could feel Jack's eyes on her, and after a beat, she spoke.

"I think this is the most I've ever said to my parents."

"Did you say everything you wanted to?"

"Yeah."

"Good." Jack's voice was soft and Dylan looked up. "No matter what they say, you deserve the chance to say your piece."

Dylan exhaled heavily and looked back at her screen. Carefully, she tapped the TO box and added her mam's email. Luckily it was late back home, so they wouldn't see it until morning.

She could have sat there staring at the message all night, but there was no use pretending she wasn't going to send it. Her index finger hovered over the SEND button and she counted down from three in her head before she jabbed her finger into the screen and the email disappeared.

"Okay." She locked her phone and flipped it facedown onto the table. "I sent it."

Jack took her hands, his thumbs ghosting over her knuckles. "I'm proud of you."

The solidity and the heat of him in that moment was the only thing keeping her tethered to the ground. She squeezed his hands. "Thank you."

A server appeared by their table, his tray overloaded with food, and Jack and Dylan immediately moved their hands away.

"Hola," they said together.

The server smiled at them and said, "Hola," as he sat down their plates.

"Gracias," Dylan said, her thanks followed almost immediately by Jack's.

The server grinned at them and said, "De nada," before he tucked the serving tray under his arm and walked back through the restaurant.

Dylan grabbed her plate of tacos and the small bowl of limes. "We've really improved our Spanish since we've been here. That was basically an entire conversation."

Jack snorted. "Two words down, only a billion to go."

"I think we can count 'de nada'—I knew that one."

"Okay, three down, nine hundred ninety-nine million, nine hundred ninety-nine thousand, nine hundred ninety-nine to go."

She rolled her eyes at him and squeezed a lime over her taco. "You're obnoxious."

"Obnoxiously charming."

She snorted, "Sure," and took a bite of her taco. Although she knew exactly how it was going to taste (having literally had this exact thing barely twenty-four hours earlier), she still groaned with pleasure as the flavors hit her tongue. The sharp acid from the lime cut the silky flavor of the beef, the char on the meat brought a deep smokiness that perfectly complemented the coriander and the caramelized onions. Dylan could have cried right there if she wasn't worried about embarrassing herself in the middle of a restaurant.

Jack raised an eyebrow as he lifted his own taco to his lips. "Good?"

Dylan couldn't even say anything. She just took another bite and, her eyes rolling back into her head, gave him a thumbs-up.

CHAPTER 31

They were walking out of the restaurant when Dylan tore her phone out of her pocket again.

Jack froze at her sudden movement, mild alarm on his face. "Are you okay?"

"Yeah, I just—" She opened WhatsApp. "I realized I should probably warn my brother. I'd bet my entire flat my parents'll ring him the minute they read that email."

> fyi I wrote mam and da a very long email about ~feelings~
> so if they call you tell them not to talk to me until I get back to London

Sean read her message almost immediately and, a few moments after that, started typing.

> Sean: sus but ok
> Dylan: I'm not being sus!!!
> Dylan: I've just been doing some thinking
> Sean: the travel self-reflection curse gets another one
> Dylan: lol shut up

Sean: can't wait for your ~think piece~ about how travel is
        revolutionary and everyone should become jetsetters
Dylan: i literally fucking hate you

Dylan was about to lock her phone when Sean sent another
message.

tell your boyfriend i say hi btw—can't wait to meet him

She immediately felt her cheeks heat. "Oh my god."

Jack quirked an eyebrow. "What?"

Dylan turned the phone around so he could read Sean's last
message. His eyes scanned over the screen before he laughed and
his gaze flicked up to find hers.

"Boyfriend, huh?" He took her hand, his fingers winding
through hers.

"We don't have to talk about it now."

"Okay," Jack said, though he was smiling at her like he knew
something she didn't. "If you're sure."

She wasn't, but she also wasn't sure she'd be coherent if they
discussed it now, so she just nodded.

She clicked into Instagram while she had her phone open,
more out of habit than anything. She hadn't checked any of her
other notifications at the restaurant, and she was a little curious if
anything had happened since she'd shared Jack's post to her story.

Sure enough, there were a decent number of notifications
waiting for her.

"Holy hell."

"What?"

She just stared down at her phone, and Jack turned, concern creasing his features. "Is everything okay?"

"Eight hundred people have already seen my story."

Jack's concern morphed into confusion. "Is that a lot?"

She laughed, the sound breathless. "Yeah."

She immediately went to Jack's Instagram and laughed again. "Holy shit, Jack, you have, like, a few hundred followers now."

She half expected him to either (a) pull his phone out and check or (b) throw up with anxiety, but Jack took it in stride.

"I guess I'll have to keep posting, then."

"Uh, yeah," Dylan said, switching back to read through her own notifications, "you definitely will."

Most of them were for the pictures she'd posted of their tour the night before, and as she scrolled, she realized that Jack wasn't the only one with an uptick in Instagram activity. There were a few thousand likes on those pictures, masses of comments, but one in particular jumped out at her:

♥@cdmxtravel: gorgeous! love what you said here—we shared on our story, but mind if we repost? we'll DM you :)

She'd never clicked into her DMs so fast.

♥Hey, Dylan! We loved what you said in your post about Mexico City today. Would you mind if we reposted on our Instagram (along with your caption)? We'd, of course, credit you at the top of the caption and tag you in the photo (as well as adding a reposting bar at the bottom with your handle). We're the largest travel agency in

Mexico City, so we're more than happy to send you a
voucher so you can enjoy another one of our many
attractions while you're here! If you'd prefer email,
please reach out to our marketing coordinator, Juana,
at juana@cdmxtravel.com.mx. We look forward to
hearing from you!

They weren't verified, but a quick check of their profile (and
their forty-nine thousand followers) seemed legit, as did a quick
skim through their website. She googled them, too, and a number
of entries came up, including a few from some local newspapers
about travel recommendations. She bit her lip, excitement building
in her stomach, as she typed out her reply.

♥Thanks for contacting me! I'm so happy to hear you love
the post and thank you for sharing it on your story.
Unfortunately, this is our last night in Mexico City, but feel
free to repost my image and caption. Thank you for being
so clear with how you're going to tag the post. The next
time I'm in Mexico City, I'll be sure to ask for a list of
places we can't miss!

She read it over twice, both times catching minor spelling mistakes, before she held her breath and hit SEND. Once the message
had successfully found its way to their inbox, she shut Instagram
and hastily shoved her phone back into her pocket to keep from
staring at her screen, waiting for a notification.

Jack cleared his throat the moment her phone was safely
hidden away. "Anything good?"

"A travel agency reached out to me." Despite all her attempts to keep her voice light, it was still trembling. "They wanted to repost my post from last night and share my caption article."

Jack's grin was immediate. "That's amazing. What did you say?"

"I said they could absolutely repost, they have, like, fifty thousand followers."

Jack's jaw dropped. "Seriously?"

She nodded, eyebrows practically touching her hairline. "I don't know when they're going to do it, but, like . . . I'll probably get a few more followers from it."

Even as she said it, the wheels started turning. Based on one random photo dump and caption, this company had offered to send her activity vouchers, and not even for something she'd made directly for them, but things she'd made on her own. The sharing alone would grow her platform, but it was the promise of some kind of compensation for the work that really caught her attention.

She knew, vaguely, how influencers made an income, though no amount of "How I Make Money on YouTube" videos had ever satisfied her curiosity to the point where she felt like she completely understood every step of the process. It stood to reason, though, that if she continued growing her platform and kept finding ways to drive engagement, she could very easily start accepting sponsorships.

She didn't have the slightest idea how to do that, but she'd done enough freelancing to know the basics when it came to reaching out to strangers and chasing down payments.

Jack leaned over and pressed a soft kiss to the side of her head. "I'm really proud of you."

She turned, absolutely beaming, and met his gaze. "Thank you."

They'd seen a fair bit of Mexico City on their sightseeing tour the other night, but even still, Dylan felt like she was experiencing everything for the first time as she and Jack walked through the streets. The energy had been different every night they'd been here, like the people and the circumstances all played a role in making each night uniquely electric. Tonight, their last night, seemed particularly magical, though Dylan wasn't sure if it was the city or her own premature nostalgia that was tinting everything rose.

They walked down Calle Cacahuamilpa hand in hand, listening to the hum of traffic and conversation around them. One of her favorite things about this part of Mexico City was the way these five- and six-level steel-and-glass buildings sat next to two-level houses and painted concrete warehouses. There were gated courtyards tucked away in secret corners, pops of color and lush greenery. It was a study in contrasts, and Dylan couldn't get enough.

Their tour guide had told them that La Condesa was one of the most artistic areas of the city, and Dylan thought about that now as they walked. She could see the evidence of it everywhere—the architectural styles were varied, there were murals and graffiti painted on every free wall, and there were small art galleries everywhere you looked.

They paused at the end of the road while they waited for the traffic in the circle to pass before darting across the street into the Plaza Popocatépetl. There were tall trees planted around the perimeter, and the foliage somewhat deadened the sound of the traffic. The fountain in the center was a white, tiled Art Deco structure surrounded on all sides by water spouts. There were a few steps leading into the structure in the center, but Dylan was fairly sure you weren't supposed to run through the fountain (though she'd be lying if she said she wasn't tempted).

They walked slowly around the plaza before sitting down on one of the vacant benches. They sat close, their sides pressed together, and Jack wrapped his arm around Dylan's shoulders. Neither of them said anything for a few minutes, just sat and listened to the fountain and the swell of conversation on the surrounding streets. Dylan could have sat there the entire night and never once wanted to leave.

"I love it here," Dylan said eventually. "I see why so many people live here."

Jack hummed in agreement. "Do you think you'd ever live somewhere like this?"

"If I ever wanted to leave London, I think this is where I'd go."

"Really?"

She nodded. "I think I'd live most of the places we've been. Though here, Cape Town, and New York are my favorites."

"Oh, yeah," Jack agreed, "I think so, too. I loved Marrakech, but I think it's probably too hot for me."

She breathed a soft laugh and snuggled closer to him. "Yeah, it was. It was gorgeous, though."

"We really were lucky to get to do this. This is—" He shook his head and Dylan watched him trace his gaze over the scene. "This is more than I ever could've asked for in my life."

As he said it, she felt an unexpected surge of emotion in her chest.

She really did feel phenomenally lucky to be here. Even if she lived a full life, she probably never would've traveled to most of the places they'd been in the last few weeks. She might've made it to a few of them, especially the closer ones, but she never would've experienced these cities the way she had.

It felt silly, but she could feel the ways this had changed her. How it had opened her heart and her mind so that when she looked at the world, she was looking at everything with a completely new set of eyes. She was lucky to be here with Jack, too, with someone who was constantly pushing her, supporting her, making her laugh. . . . She'd said it a million times over, edited it out of so many articles, but she couldn't deny the truth of those feelings, not anymore.

She nodded gently and turned her head. She could have just gone ahead and kissed him, but she paused when she was only a breath away from his lips.

She could feel where his eyes caught, where they lingered—when he traced the long lines of her legs stretched out in front of them, the hollows of her collarbone, the curve of her lips.

And, god.

God.

She wanted his hands on her.

She wanted his hands skimming over every inch of her skin, weighing curves, pinching and coaxing and teasing and dipping between her thighs—

Jack raised his hand slowly and brushed his thumb over her lower lip, his eyes on hers, and even though it was the slightest touch, she felt it everywhere. His thumb traced down her chin as his fingers curled underneath her jaw and every brush of his skin against hers drew the threads in her stomach tighter.

"I'm going to kiss you," he said. His voice was barely louder than a whisper, certainly softer than the deep, ragged breath Dylan drew in immediately then tried to disguise as a laugh.

"Are you going to apologize after?"

"Absolutely not."

He barely had time to get the words out before Dylan leaned forward and kissed him.

It started off gentle at first, a way to communicate the depth of her feelings, but then Jack shifted on the bench so he was facing her more directly. His hand moved to cup her cheek and he tilted his head, running his tongue along Dylan's lower lip. She drew in a breath, her lips parting, and when Jack traced the tips of his fingers down the column of her throat, she gasped into his mouth.

He smiled against her lips, and in response, Dylan threaded her fingers through the hair at the base of his neck, using the leverage to angle his head backward. The groan that ripped through him shot straight through her.

She leaned forward and pressed a searing kiss to the underside of his jaw before she slid up so she could speak directly into his ear.

"I've been thinking about this for ages." She skirted her hand over his forearm and delighted in the way his fingertips trembled against her waist. "Every time I caught you looking at me, I imagined you putting your hands on me."

"I've thought about it, too," Jack said. His voice was thick, like he could barely get the words out, but he slid his hand up over the curve of her waist, his fingertips tracing the sides of her breasts.

"Have you?" She injected a bit of playful curiosity into her voice, but her movements were calculated. She trailed her fingers down his chest, their progress slowing as she neared the waistband of his jeans. When she spoke, she whispered directly into his ear and then ghosted her fingers along his zipper. "What did you imagine?"

Jack swallowed another moan, and Dylan ran her palm over his erection. She was probably getting too bold, too brazen, especially since they were still in public, but she couldn't seem to stop herself and Jack didn't seem to mind. There was no one near them anyway, and even if there was, they'd have to look pretty hard to see what they were doing in the dark.

She gave him a few seconds to say something, but when she kissed his neck again and he only bit back another groan, she assumed he didn't have the ability to say much at the moment.

She kissed her way along the column of his throat and hummed approvingly as he tilted his head to give her better access. "Should I tell you what I've been thinking about, then?"

He nodded jerkily and Dylan pressed her teeth into his neck.

"I thought about your fingers." As she said it, she traced the edge of his T-shirt, flirting with brushing against his skin. She circled one of her fingers over the button on his jeans. "About you slipping your hand in my jeans, and the way you'd moan when you realized how wet I was just thinking about you."

Jack groaned, a disjointed sound, and the thrill in her chest was almost too much.

"I thought about your mouth on my thighs." She pressed an open-mouthed kiss on his throat. "About you tracing your tongue over my clit."

She traced her tongue along his neck and Jack moaned softly.

"Fucking hell." Jack sounded like he was gasping for air and Dylan wanted to coat herself in the sound.

Her smile then was positively wicked, and she pressed it into his skin before grazing her teeth against his earlobe.

"Let's—" Jack moaned softly as she kissed his pulse point. "Let's go back to the hotel."

The tension compounded for the duration of their taxi ride to the hotel. They didn't speak, but she felt everything Jack wasn't saying in the dark, lingering looks he kept shooting her.

She could feel the particles vibrating with energy between them, feel the air against her skin, the barest echo of his body as he sat next to her in the car, stood next to her in the lift, walked beside her to their room. It was like there was a force field between them, an electricity, and the longer they went, the tighter it drew the threads in her chest so that, by the time she was outside their door, fumbling with her wallet to try to retrieve her hotel key, she was fairly sure she was going to die from lack of oxygen.

And as the door swung shut behind them, the thread immediately snapped.

CHAPTER 32

Jack's hand found her hip the moment they walked through the door, his other hand cradling her jaw as he leaned down and kissed her. There was heat to this kiss, but it contrasted sharply with the light, patient way he was running his hands over her. Dylan moaned softly as he brushed his thumb along her cheek, his fingers pressing into the back of her neck, and Dylan dropped her bag onto the floor to free up her hands.

She ran her hands over his stomach, pulling up the fabric of his T-shirt. She only looked for a moment—his smooth skin, the trail of soft brown hair that dipped into his jeans—before Jack grabbed the end of his T-shirt and pulled it over his head, dropping it somewhere behind them.

She spread her hands out over his chest. She half expected Jack would kiss her again, but he seemed content, in this moment, to watch her take him in. She'd seen him shirtless before, but seeing him in this context felt almost earth-shattering.

He had a light dusting of hair across his chest and an even lighter smattering of freckles across his shoulders, and the rush of feeling in her . . .

It was hot and bright and, alright, maybe a little desperate, but there was a softness to this feeling she hadn't expected. A warmth she felt across every inch of her skin.

She dragged her eyes up and she was sure she must have looked quite a state, because, good god, he was unbelievable, but all she cared about was how he was looking at her. The way he was looking at her like she was the only thing in the entire universe.

"You're amazing." She was fairly sure she was slurring.

Jack chuckled softly and Dylan's eyes immediately flicked down to watch the way it made his stomach move.

"You think so?"

She nodded, her eyes tracing a slow path over him again. "Pretty fucking amazing."

Jack stepped forward, his hands moving to her ribs.

"You're pretty fucking amazing, too." Jack's fingers slid underneath the hem of her top, his palms wrapping around the curve of her waist until his fingertips pressed into her back. She felt each and every fingerprint against her skin.

"Yeah. You're pretty lucky."

Jack laughed. "Oh, am I?"

She nodded, her hands moving to the waistband of her shorts. "Like you said, I'm pretty fucking amazing." She popped the button and Jack's hands pulsed before he moved one on top of her own.

"Can I do that?"

Dylan swallowed and, after sucking in a sharp breath, nodded.

If she thought his hands were moving slowly before, it was nothing to the way they were now. He slid his hands to her hips, completely ignoring the open button. He brushed his thumb over the bit of skin between her crop top and her shorts, and the contact was a shock to her system.

She exhaled sharply, and though she wanted to close her eyes, to let herself sink into this feeling, she couldn't bear to pull her eyes from his.

There was too much weight in them. Too much feeling. And she wanted to see it all, every last emotion, as it flitted across his face. She relished the way he was looking at her, everything plainly on his face, like she was the center of things, first, last, everything. And normally that would have scared her, but Jack . . .

There was something about Jack. There had always been something about Jack. Something that kept her coming back. Something that made her needy in this deep, almost spiritual sort of way, like she just needed him around. Needed his dry humor and his soft laugh and his stubborn energy.

She was waiting for him to take off her shorts, but he seemed content with leaving them unbuttoned for now. His hands moved, instead, to the buttons that ran down the length of her top. He traced his index finger over the bottom one and looked up at her underneath his lashes.

"Can I undo these?" He ran his finger over the buttons again, and Dylan felt the tiny tug of fabric over every single inch of her body.

She nodded jerkily and Jack smiled, that soft, secret little smile she loved, before he leaned down and pressed his lips to hers. It was light, barely there, but the soft pressure of his lips against hers stacked the tension so deep in her gut that, by the time he finally popped the first button on her top, Dylan was completely out of her mind for him.

He made his way down the column of buttons, popping them open at a painfully, deliciously slow pace, and when he'd finally unfastened all the buttons and her top fell open, he leaned back, his eyes dragging over her newly exposed skin.

"You're so beautiful." He traced one finger down the center of her chest, his fingertips brushing against her bra, before he slid off her top. The sound of her shirt hitting the floor compounded the anticipation that was making it harder and harder to breathe.

Jack pressed a kiss to her collarbone, another to the hollow of her throat, and Dylan tipped her head back, a soft groan falling from her lips. She felt Jack smile against her skin as he pressed another kiss to the side of her neck, one of his hands sliding to her back, his fingers deftly unfastening her bra.

As her bra fell to the floor, Jack stepped forward until their chests were pressed together. Dylan felt more than heard the groan that escaped him as he ran his hands up over her hips, one palm skimming the side of her breast before sliding around and pressing into her back, holding her against him. The feel of his skin against hers was intoxicating.

She threaded her hands through the hair at the base of his neck, pulled him down, and kissed him.

And though there was part of her that was aching to accelerate things—to strip off their clothes and just go for it—the way they were moving together now, with slow, measured strokes, was too delicious to give up.

Dylan traced her tongue along his lower lip and started leading them backward toward the bed before reaching between them and undoing the button on his jeans.

Jack hummed against her lips. "It's like you're reading my mind."

"That makes me sound like Edward Cullen," Dylan said, as Jack unzipped her shorts.

Jack gasped theatrically. "That explains the glittering skin."

"Arsehole."

Jack laughed, a deep, husky sound that started the heat pooling in her chest, and pressed a soft, lingering kiss to her lips.

He slid her shorts down over her hips, his thumbs catching on the waistband of her underwear.

"Can I take these off?" He traced his thumb underneath the band and Dylan sucked in a sharp breath.

"Yeah."

Jack grinned and pulled them down.

Jack's weren't far behind—Dylan laughed as he tried desperately to kick them off, but then Jack put his hands on her hips and muttered, "What are you laughing about, Coughlan?" before he kissed her—and now, naked, there was a new depth to this moment. A new intensity between them. Every cell in her body was vibrating, and she couldn't wait to get closer to him.

Dylan dropped to the bed, wrapping one hand around the back of Jack's neck and pulling him with her as she slid back across the duvet. He caught most of his weight on his hands, but Dylan still reveled in the press of Jack's body against hers as he settled between her thighs. Every time she inhaled, her breasts brushed against his chest, and his hands were curved over her hips and running across her stomach, like he couldn't decide where to touch her, so he tried for everywhere all at once.

Jack leaned down and pressed his forehead to hers. His eyes were closed at first, as they took one breath, two, their chests rising together, but then, as he skimmed his hand along the outside of her thigh, he opened his eyes and met her gaze.

"Hey."

She laughed, "Hey," and took his free hand. "You okay?"

She laced their fingers together and Jack gave her hand a firm squeeze.

"Just needed a minute," he said, and the corners of his lips twitched with a smile. "I'm a little overwhelmed."

He carried on holding her hand, but his free hand was tracing every bit of her he could reach, spiraling ever closer to the one spot she really wanted him.

"Overwhelmed in a good way, or . . . ?" She sounded breathless, out of her mind, but then, that was exactly how she felt at the moment.

"In the best way." He kissed the corner of her mouth, the underside of her jaw, and Dylan arched her neck to give him better access.

He squeezed her hand again and then his free hand dipped, finally, in between her thighs, and Dylan exhaled a moan.

Jack groaned softly and pressed a hot, open-mouthed kiss to her neck. "You're so wet," he murmured.

He swirled his fingers over her clit and Dylan moaned again, her fingers gripping his shoulder. Jack smiled against her neck before he kissed her again, his lips ghosting her skin, and the combination of it—his fingers brushing lightly against her and his lips barely touching her skin . . .

It made her feel like she was going to combust. It was unbearable, and *god*, she wanted to feel like this every single day.

He kissed along her jaw, the corner of her mouth, and then his lips were hovering over hers, their breath mingling, and she moaned again as he touched, *fuck*, just the right spot, and he inhaled sharply, like he was trying to breathe in the sound.

He met her gaze and she was surprised the heat in his eyes didn't send them melting straight through the mattress.

"Can I go down on you?"

"Mm-hmm." She sounded even less with it now. "Sure, sure, go ahead."

Jack raised an eyebrow and leaned down, kissing her cheek, the hinge of her jaw.

"Do you *want* me to go down on you?"

She groaned at the feeling of his breath against her neck and nodded, careful not to nod too enthusiastically because breaking his nose would probably have ruined the vibe.

"Yes," she said, her voice rough and definitely a little desperate. "Please, Jack, just—"

He swirled his fingers over her clit again and the rest of her sentence fell into a moan. Jack, though, didn't seem to mind that she hadn't finished her thought because he kissed her again, a quick, firm press of his lips against hers, before he started sliding down her body, pressing open-mouthed kisses across her chest, her stomach, her hip, before he settled between her thighs.

He kissed the inside of her left thigh as he took her right knee in his hand and slowly pushed her leg up the bed. The brush of the duvet against her burning skin, combined with the scratch of his stubble against her thighs, made the tension in her gut spike, but then he wrapped his arm around her hips, holding her down on the bed, and he leaned forward until she could feel his breath against her.

He tentatively traced his tongue up the length of her and she nearly burst out of her skin.

"Fuck." She fisted one of her hands in the duvet, her other hand moving down to brush through his hair—she had to actively remind herself, *soft, soft, soft*, because she was so keyed up she could accidentally start tearing at him otherwise—and Jack pressed a light kiss to the inside of her thigh before he centered himself again.

And this time, there was nothing tentative about the way he was moving his mouth over her.

He still took his time, but every movement was deliberate, a way to tease out what she liked and figure out how to give her just enough that she rocketed straight to the edge, but not enough that she fell over the cliff too early. And he was masterful, god, was he masterful, at figuring out what she liked, at working her to a peak and holding her there until every single cell in her body was shaking and her hands were scrabbling to hold on to something. And then he slid a pair of fingers into her and Dylan inhaled so sharply she was sure the rush of oxygen was going to make her pass out.

"Jack." Her fingers danced across her stomach before moving up and pinching one of her nipples. "Jack, I—"

He hummed in acknowledgment and the vibration made the threads in her stomach draw tighter. He curled his fingers inside her and flicked his tongue over her clit, and she moaned, the sound sharp and desperate and nearly there. She must have been chanting it—she felt like her lips were moving at any rate and Jack laughed again, another deep chuckle she felt more than heard—because he increased the speed a tick more.

She wasn't sure how much longer he kept at it, couldn't have distinguished the final move from any of the others. She only knew that he flicked his tongue over her again and the tension in her gut finally snapped.

He tightened his hold around her waist, his elbow pressing

down on her thigh to keep her from closing her legs around his head, but he didn't move from between her thighs as she rode the wave of her orgasm. He slowed, his tongue tracing lightly over her as he slackened his grip and began running his hands softly over her skin. The flurry of sensation as he teased her was enough to throw her over the edge again.

She grabbed him by the shoulders, pulled him up so she could kiss him. He just caught his weight on his hands, but she didn't care, wouldn't have minded if he'd crushed her, because she was buoyant and he was stunning and she was so damn full of him.

"Jack." She took his face in her hands and slid her palms over his stubble, delighting in the texture of it against her skin. "Please tell me you have a condom."

CHAPTER 33

I've got . . . one, I think."

"Jesus Christ, Jack, you better have or I swear to god."

Jack cast her a grin before he slid off the bed. "What are you going to do if I don't?"

"Die."

Jack laughed as he started rummaging through his suitcase. "You're not going to die— Aha!" He held up the small foil package and Dylan nearly lost it.

"Thank fucking god."

Jack climbed back onto the bed, dropping over her with an amused little smile. "Which god is the fucking god?"

She grinned, and though she replied, "Zeus, I think," she was more focused on his hands as he tore open the condom wrapper.

Jack snorted. "What?"

He started rolling the condom on, and with great effort, she pulled her eyes to his. "He fucked anything that breathed."

"Greek gods are weird foreplay."

She tried to frown, but her smile kept breaking through her façade. "Don't kink shame me."

"Sorry." He kissed her softly, contritely. "How can I be more supportive?"

Dylan grinned and wrapped her legs around his waist, pulling him to her. "Tell me I'm amazing again."

Jack laughed, his chest vibrating against hers, but still, as he slid into her, he leaned down and pressed a lingering kiss to her lips. "You," he said, "are so, so amazing."

She grinned against his lips and said, "I know," but the cheeky tone she was going for was ruined by the breathy moan that followed immediately afterward.

He moved slowly at first, so slowly she felt every single inch of him, and it was impossible to catch her breath. His hands were sliding over her skin, skimming her curves, and there was so much of him touching her and filling her heart and making it impossible to think.

He was everywhere. Absolutely everywhere.

Jack kissed her softly at first, in line with the rhythm of their hips, but then Dylan grazed her teeth along his bottom lip and he gasped into her mouth before he tilted his head and deepened the kiss.

And that, it seemed, was the trigger.

They became a mess of hands and scattered kisses wherever they could reach. Jack increased the tempo of his thrusts and Dylan held on to his forearm like it was the only thing tethering her to the ground and she could feel the tension in her gut starting to build again, and now that she'd acknowledged it, the fact that she was close, she was desperate again.

She reached down between them, rubbed her fingers against her clit, and the relief—

They both swore, and then she did it again.

"God." Jack leaned back a bit so he could look down and watch her hand between her thighs. "Dylan, you're so beautiful."

She drew a circle around her clit and moaned again, and Jack thrust harder at the sound.

"Fuck." Dylan arched herself closer to him. "Do that again."

"This?" He thrust again, this time a little harder than before, and it hit just the right spot inside her that Dylan felt herself creep all that much closer to the edge.

Dylan moaned again and pressed herself closer to him. "Yes. That."

Jack lifted her hips, his palm pressing into the small of her back, and the position had been good before, but it was dangerously good now, the sort of angle that left her feeling like she'd just run a bloody marathon.

Her fingers tripped over her clit, her movements becoming clumsy.

Jack ducked his head to look at her. "Are you close?"

She moaned again, higher this time, as she rubbed another circle across her clit and nodded. "Yeah, fucking—so close, Jack, I—"

He nodded jerkily and picked up the speed, not much, but god, it was enough, and she could feel the unbearable tension start peaking in her gut, and it was only a few more thrusts, only a few more passes of her fingers, before she was coming and god—

She wasn't alone, either, because Jack followed soon after. He slowed, his fingers pressing into her hips and his rhythm erratic as he fell apart. Dylan watched the orgasm blossom across his face—the flush on the high points of his cheeks, the way he tipped his head forward and his eyes fell closed—before he stilled. He took a breath before, still inside her, he lowered himself down onto his forearms and kissed her.

"You," he said between kisses, "are stunning."

She smiled up at him and reached up to brush the hair back off his forehead. "You're not so bad yourself."

He laughed softly before he kissed her again, his lips lingering despite the fact that he was simultaneously pulling away.

"I've got to get rid of this," he said. He kissed her again, his hand running up over her hip, settling in the curve of her waist, and Dylan smiled against his lips.

"Go." She put a hand on his chest and pushed him back onto his knees. "I'm not going anywhere."

Jack sighed and, after planting one more kiss onto her lips, slid back off the bed and went to the bathroom.

Dylan lay there for a beat before she sat up. She could just see herself in the mirror opposite the bed—she had a cartoonishly large grin on her face and she dropped her head into her hands at the sight. She breathed a soft laugh and pressed the heels of her hands into her forehead for a moment before she looked up and shook her head.

She couldn't believe they'd just—

She laughed again, this time pressing her fingers to her lips to stifle the sound.

Jack came out of the bathroom, eyebrow raised, cheeky smile curving across his lips. "What are you laughing about?"

"Nothing." Dylan hopped up, striding across the room toward him. "My turn."

Jack chuckled and pressed a soft kiss to her lips as she passed.

The bathroom was far colder than the bedroom, and Dylan felt goose pimples break out across her skin as she closed the door. She'd seen a bit of herself in the bedroom mirror, but the dazzling bathroom lights really emphasized her look at the moment. Her hair was all over the place, her mascara was smudged beyond belief, but she had this glow about her that hadn't been there before.

She made quick work of cleaning her face before she went to the bathroom and washed her hands. She was going to have to get a shower before they went to sleep, but she couldn't be arsed to do more than go back and lie in bed right now. She swiped a bit of moisturizer from the pot on the counter and dotted it across her face as she opened the door, and she was still rubbing it into her skin as she switched off the light with her elbow and walked back out into the room.

"Were you doing a full routine in there?"

Dylan held her fingers up at him before she ran her hands over her face one more time to make sure all the lotion was rubbed in.

"Moisturizing is very important."

"Is it?"

"Mm-hmm." Dylan sat down on the side of the bed. "Your skin needs moisture or you're going to get crusty when you're old."

Jack groaned and rolled over so he could drag her back down onto the bed. Dylan laughed as she lay down beside him, and Jack slid forward so he could press her back into his chest. "Don't say crusty."

"Why not? It's a fact of life, babe. You're gonna get crusty if—" Jack pressed his fingers into her ribs and Dylan shrieked and immediately tried to wriggle away from him.

"Oh, you're ticklish." Jack skated his fingers up her ribs, and though he wasn't tickling her, her entire body still stiffened as she barked out a laugh.

"Yes." She sucked in a huge breath in an attempt to steady herself. "And if you tickle me, I swear to god, I'm going to elbow you in the nose."

Jack traced his fingers lightly up her side before he laughed into her neck, flattened out his hands, and wrapped his arms more firmly around her waist.

"Don't worry." He brushed her hair aside and kissed her shoulder. "I'm not going to tickle you right now."

"You're not going to tickle me ever."

Jack snuggled her closer and dipped his head so she could feel his breath on the back of her neck. "Let's not get ahead of ourselves."

She snorted and moved her hands down to rest on his. Jack threaded his fingers up through hers and she felt him sigh contentedly into her skin.

And this.

His hands on her skin and his breath on her neck and the deep, warm feeling in her gut—she could feel this moment imprinting itself on her memory.

She almost wished she could live in this moment forever. Almost.

Because the thing was that she was deeply certain that this was only the beginning. That they were building something here. And god, it was terrifying, but she threw herself into every other terrifying thing, didn't she, so why should this be any different?

"What are you thinking about?"

Dylan stared out into the room, her eyes tracing over the curtains on the window opposite. "Me?"

Jack chuckled. "Who else?"

"I'm not thinking about anything."

"Don't lie. I can practically feel your brain working. You're getting hot like a laptop."

She turned in his arms and raised an eyebrow at him. "Careful with that kind of flattery. It might start to go to my head."

He breathed another laugh and ran his fingertips along her jaw. Dylan let her eyes fall closed as he brushed his thumb along the apple of her cheek and Jack sighed softly.

"You don't have to tell me," he said. "I was just curious."

She wanted to open her eyes to see his expression, but she wasn't sure she'd be able to handle looking him directly in the eyes at the moment.

"What are you thinking, then?" She knew it wasn't fair to ask if she wasn't sharing, but she needed a little courage.

Jack hummed, his fingers trailing down her neck, over the curve of her shoulder.

"I was thinking about you," he said.

Dylan laughed. "That's reassuring."

Jack didn't pick up the thread of her joke. "I was thinking about how soft you are. And how good you smell." He caught her hand, pressing her palm to his chest, right over his heart. They were quiet for a moment, just the sound of their breath between them and the feeling of his heartbeat ticking away under her fingertips.

"I missed this, I guess," Jack said finally, his voice softer than before, "but we've never—" He sighed. "This just feels good. Really good."

"You're getting really good at talking about your feelings," Dylan said. She was teasing him, and he chuckled accordingly.

"I'm trying. Now"—he slid his leg between hers—"your turn."

"I was thinking about you, too," she admitted, meeting his eyes again. "This feels . . . like the beginning of something."

He held her gaze for a beat before he leaned forward and pressed his lips to hers. There was nothing explosive about this kiss—it was soft, slow, barely there—but there was a depth to it that she could feel down to her toes. A steady warmth that floated out to the very tips of her.

"I couldn't agree more."

CHAPTER 34

When Dylan woke up the next morning, the last morning of their holiday, Jack was lying fully starfished across her. He had a hand resting on her stomach and a leg thrown over hers, and although she wasn't opposed to this position, she couldn't feel a single thing in her left leg. She shifted, the pins and needles sending a jolt up her spine.

Jack exhaled heavily and Dylan felt his fingers twitch as he rubbed his face into his pillow.

She should let him sleep, but honestly. Her fucking leg.

"Jack." He groaned, and Dylan bit her lip to hide her smile. "I need my leg."

Jack muttered something incomprehensible, but he lifted his leg and shifted on the mattress so he was closer to her. He slid his hand to her hip and used it as leverage to pull her into him. Dylan chuckled as she slid back into his chest and his arm tightened around her.

"What are you doing?"

Jack kissed the side of her neck before he buried his face in her hair. "Sleeping."

She grinned and ran her hand over the length of his forearm. "No, you're not."

"I'm snuggling you, then."

"Oh, well, snuggling me is alright."

"Just alright?"

She began absently playing with his fingers. "I can think of better things."

Jack's laugh was husky in her ear as he pressed her more firmly into his chest and kissed her shoulder.

"How'd you sleep?"

"Brilliantly."

"Mmm, good." Jack trailed his fingertips up the length of her spine and Dylan let her eyes flutter closed as she sank into the sensation.

"How did you sleep?"

"I had the most amazing dream."

"Oh, yeah?" She opened her eyes and Jack smiled at her before he pressed another kiss to her shoulder. "And what was this dream about?"

"Well." He shifted in the bed, hoisting himself up so he was almost hovering over her. He dropped a kiss to the base of her neck and Dylan shivered. "You were in it."

She tried to sound casual when she said, "What was I doing?" but she knew, from the breathy tone of her voice, that she failed miserably.

He kissed lower along her spine, and Dylan exhaled softly, barely suppressing a moan.

"It was a lot like this, actually," he said, kissing her again. "You, me, no clothes in sight . . ."

"Are you sure you dreamed that, or did you just have a long flashback to last night?"

Jack hummed and his chest vibrated softly against her spine as he pressed a kiss to the center of her back.

"Either way, I'm doing pretty well right now, aren't I?"

She loved the warmth of him against her, the heat of his mouth against her spine, and she arched back into him, desperate for even just a little bit more.

"Can you get a condom?"

He dropped another kiss to her lower back and pushed up off the bed.

They could have spent every last minute in Mexico City in the hotel room, but Dylan knew they'd regret it if they didn't spend as much time as they could out in the city. They didn't have long—only a few hours when they accounted for the time they'd need to check out—but neither of them wanted to waste a second.

They abandoned their bags at the front desk and went to a small café down the road for breakfast. It was nice, talking and laughing, taking pictures and drinking coffee, and the air was warm but not hot and the sun was shining, and god, it couldn't have been any better, this moment. It felt like their whole trip in miniature—a beautiful city, a colorful café, incredible coffee—but there was something familiar about it, too. Like they could have been in London, complaining about the Tories, eating pastries, and whiling the day away.

The café they'd chosen was a refurbished garage, and the massive steel door was rolled open so that the space was open-air. On the outside, the café was an explosion of color. Bold splashes of yellow, green, pink, and red framed the entrance, the color dragging over the edge and carrying on through the interior walls so you couldn't help but be drawn in. Dylan and Jack were seated in a pair of bright pink metal chairs at a tiny orange metal table, coffee in handcrafted mugs between them—it was the exact sort of place that, in January, Dylan would never have been able to imagine Jack visiting, let alone enjoying himself.

"I think this is the best café we've been to," Jack said. Despite ordering a very flaky dulce de leche croissant with his coffee, Jack didn't have a single crumb on him.

"It is." She popped the last bit of banana cake into her mouth and flicked a stray piece off her finger. "I'd come back just to go here again."

It wasn't impossible, coming back to this spot, but they'd never be able to come back to this moment again. These last golden minutes in the winter sun, her heart full as they flirted with the potential of what this could be.

Sean's joke about their relationship, and the words she and Jack exchanged last night, made her think, hope, that things were going in the right direction, but everything hinged on the shape their lives took once they actually got back to London.

Jack grinned. "Me, too." He held up his phone. "Want a few more pictures before we leave?"

Dylan beamed and immediately shifted into her first pose. "Obviously."

The airport was busy when they arrived, but they were both such seasoned pros by now that they were able to navigate easily through the crowds. It was eleven hours from Mexico City to their layover in Madrid, so it was half six the next morning when they got off the plane, exhausted and, in Dylan's case, mildly stumbling. Dylan almost laughed at the near perfect symmetry of this trip, though she wished that she could have bookended it with something other than "exhausted to the point of collapsing in public."

Their layover was brief, so after clearing passport control, they did little more than trudge to their next gate, grab coffee, and take turns in the bathroom. Jack had just popped to the toilet and Dylan, still fighting sleep, pulled her mobile out of her jacket pocket and connected to the airport Wi-Fi.

She hadn't bothered to check Instagram before leaving Mexico City, and now, there was a DM sitting in her inbox.

And unbelievably, a thousand new followers and hundreds of likes in her notifications.

She read the DM first—it was nothing much, just a quick thanks from the travel agency and a note that she should reach out if she ever found herself in Mexico City again. Dylan swiftly replied and went to check the comments on the post they'd shared.

There were thousands of likes on the picture, and she recognized some of the names in the comments from her list of new followers. She scrolled through slowly, reading each one, overwhelmed by the sheer positivity she found. Many of them were in Spanish, but the ones she could read nearly bowled her over—gorgeous pictures! and wow I can't wait to go back to cdmx and thank you for sharing her lovely pictures! going to follow. They were so different from the comments Dylan was used to that she nearly started crying.

Instead, she posted a quick comment herself—thank you so much for sharing! CDMX is one of the most beautiful places I've ever been. Can't wait to go back—before she decided to post something on her own Instagram to make the best use of this burst in following. She shared the agency's post to her story and then snapped a photo to hint at where she was now. It was just the coffee in her hand and the bags littered around her feet, but she liked the way the sunrise lit the shot. The sky was a rich orange and gold, and the blur of a luggage cart and their plane sitting at the gate in the background perfectly captured the feeling of the moment. She'd just finished posting the story when Jack appeared by her side.

"I think we're going to start boarding in a minute," he said. "We should probably get our things together."

Dylan rolled her eyes playfully at him and pressed a quick kiss to his lips. "We've got time."

The speakers crackled overhead, and after a few lines of rapid Spanish, the announcer repeated the message in English.

"Iberia flight 3179, nonstop service to London Heathrow, now boarding at S18."

Jack smirked. "You were saying?"

"Shut up."

At two and a half hours, the flight from Madrid to Heathrow was the shortest flight of their entire journey. She spent the first hour scrolling through Instagram (and nudging Jack every time she got a new comment), but eventually, even the coffee wasn't enough to keep her eyes open.

"You should close your eyes," Jack said softly.

Dylan lifted her head to look at him. It felt like someone had replaced her skull with a cement block.

"I can't sleep on planes."

"I know." Jack kissed her temple. "But you can at least close your eyes."

He patted his shoulder, an invitation, and Dylan gratefully accepted. She was awake for a little while longer—she could follow the conversations of the people around them, could hear the rustling of snack wrappers—but slowly, the whir of the engine started to drown everything out until, finally, it all faded away.

"Dylan." Jack ran a hand lightly over her forearm. "We're almost home."

She groaned and turned so her forehead was resting on his shoulder. Jack chuckled and kissed her head.

"Come on." His voice was slightly cajoling now. "I got you a snack."

She lifted her head. "What kind of snack?"

"A packet of lemon biscuits. I also got you some tea"—he pointed at the tray in front of him—"but it's probably cold now."

She looked at the seatback tray, and sure enough, there was a packet of biscuits and a small paper cup with a napkin over the lid.

Dylan felt the biggest rush of affection for him then. It was bright and warm in her chest and so big she didn't feel like she'd be able to hold it.

"Thank you." She pressed her lips lightly against his, smiling when Jack brought his hand up and brushed his fingers along her jaw.

"You're welcome." He pulled away slightly, enough that she could see him grinning at her, before he pulled back more fully and handed her her tea.

Jack held her hand the entire walk through Heathrow, only letting go to grab their bags off the carousel and when they boarded the escalator down into the tube station. He seemed alright, but the closer they got to leaving the airport, the more desperately he seemed to be holding her hand. She frowned at him as they came to a stop on the platform.

"Are you okay?"

Jack nodded loosely, but there was definitely panic in his eyes.

She let go of his hand, sliding her arm around his waist instead. She pulled him against her before pressing up onto her toes and kissing the corner of his mouth. "How are you feeling about being back home?"

It sounded like an innocent question in her head, but Jack sighed in response.

"Very worried about how little thinking I've done about my next steps."

Next steps. Sometimes it was like Jack was a walking board meeting.

"You have a whole note of next steps," she reminded him. "You've done loads of thinking."

"One note hardly counts as an entire career."

"You don't need an entire career. Not right now." He stared at her blankly, eyebrows pinched, and Dylan pressed her fingers into his hip. "You've just started out, Jack, give yourself a minute to figure out where you're going."

"I just—" He looked like she was asking him for the nuclear launch codes. "What if this is a mistake? What if me telling my boss to go to hell was the biggest—"

"Whoa, wait." She put her free hand on his forearm, her eyes wide. "You told him to go to hell?"

Jack's cheeks flushed. "Yeah."

Dylan laughed out loud, ignoring the stares from the other passengers. "That's brill."

"I would agree with you if I hadn't also completely tanked my prospects."

"Okay, Jane Austen." She rolled her eyes. "You'll be fine. You don't want to go back into law anyway, right?"

"Well, no."

"Then it wasn't a mistake," Dylan said. "You hated that job. And look at how well your Instagram's been doing in just a few days. You were excited about this—it's okay to be nervous, but don't talk yourself out of something that could be amazing. Think about what your life could look like if you stopped trying to fit yourself into the box your parents made for you."

His Instagram hadn't exactly exploded, but Jack had gone from single-digit followers to nearly a thousand, which was enormous growth in such a short space of time. Many people seemed to have migrated over from Dylan's Instagram story, and a few photographers had followed Jack back now that he'd posted some more content. Jack could build on that energy if he really wanted to and have his account rolling in no time.

Jack nodded slowly. "Yeah, I just . . . That's really scary to think about."

Dylan squeezed his hand until he looked at her, and when their eyes met, she smiled.

"I know it is. But I've got you. And you've got your solutions, remember?" The right corner of her mouth tugged up a bit higher, teasing now. "You can also plug your Instagram endlessly during the recap interview with Radio 1 tomorrow. Really grow that following."

He chuckled and leaned down to press a soft, lingering kiss to her lips. He pulled away just enough to rest his forehead on hers, and when he spoke, Dylan felt his words all the way down to her toes.

"Thank you."

Dylan dropped Jack's hand as the train pulled in, smiling at him as she stepped inside the empty carriage and grabbed one of the seats in the center. As the doors closed, Jack reached over and threaded his fingers through hers and rested their joined hands on his thigh.

"When do you get off?"

Dylan quirked an eyebrow at him and Jack nudged her lightly with his forearm. She laughed, which only made him shake his head at her. "You know what I mean."

"King's Cross," she said. "Then Northern line to Old Street."

Jack nodded and began absently running his thumb over the side of her hand, occasionally brushing lightly against the inside of her wrist.

"One stop after me, then."

"So we've got one more hour," she said. "How're we going to spend it?"

She watched his gaze flick down to her lips. His eyes had darkened when they met hers again—a bright, startling blue with a jet-black center—and he brought his free hand to her jaw.

She loved this, the way he held her and how he brushed his thumb along the apple of her cheek while his fingertips pressed into the back of her neck, angling her toward him.

He'd just touched his lips to hers when the train pulled into Terminal Two and Three, and Jack pulled away.

Dylan swore under her breath and Jack laughed, reaching up to tuck her hair behind her ear.

"Next time," he said softly.

She had half a mind to fight him on it, but then he squeezed her hand and leaned over to press a kiss to her temple and, well . . .

She supposed it was alright to just sit here and enjoy the ride.

CHAPTER 35

I'm home!"

Gwen was sitting on the sofa when Dylan walked in, watching what looked like an old *Dinner Date* rerun. She spun around at the sound of Dylan's voice, her face lighting up as she leaped to her feet.

"Welcome back!" Gwen didn't even bother walking around, just stumbled over the back of the sofa and threw herself into Dylan's arms.

Dylan laughed and, taking Gwen with her as she leaned over, set her bag down before she wrapped her arms around Gwen. "Hey, babe."

"I missed you." Gwen's voice was muffled by Dylan's hair. "You're never allowed to leave me again."

"I won't."

Cat Stevens, never one to be left out, leaped off his windowsill and, meowing, skittered across the floor so he could weave between their legs.

"How're you?" Dylan asked, giving Gwen one last squeeze before they stepped apart. Dylan grabbed her bag with a grunt and started making her way down the hall. "How's it been?"

"Quiet as hell," Gwen said. "You honestly haven't missed much."

"Uh, false. I missed you."

It smelled stale in Dylan's bedroom, and she supposed that made sense, but still. She needed to light a candle or something.

Gwen flopped down onto Dylan's bed, sliding her legs out of the way as Dylan swung her suitcase up beside her.

"Excited to be back?"

"Yeah. I've got no clue what I'm going to do with all my time, but . . ." She slashed open the zipper on her suitcase.

"Go on dates with your new boyfriend, I reckon," Gwen said, smirking. Dylan nudged the side of Gwen's foot with the back of her hand.

"Shut up, he's not my boyfriend."

Gwen snorted. "Please, sound more like you're thirteen. It's really convincing."

Dylan's scowl intensified. "Well, he isn't. Just because we had sex—"

Gwen had never shot up to a sitting position faster in her life. "What?!"

Dylan laughed and, to cover the flush on her cheeks, turned to put her clean socks away in her drawer. "The night before we left, yeah."

"Was it good?"

Dylan glanced back over her shoulder. "Yeah."

"And you're telling me you're not together?"

Dylan shrugged. "We didn't really talk about it."

She almost regretted now that they hadn't had an explicit conversation about it, especially when the opportunity had presented itself so plainly. Though, honestly, she didn't think that either of them could have meaningfully committed while they were still away on holiday. When the pressures of London were thousands of miles away.

"Hmm." Gwen raised an eyebrow, and though Dylan knew that look well enough to know they absolutely weren't finished talking about this, she was off the hook for now. "How does it feel, then, not going back to *Buxom*? Did you tell Chantel to spin on it?"

Dylan snorted. "I should have." She grabbed handfuls of clothes from her suitcase and started tossing them onto the floor behind her. "I think it's still just sinking in, if I'm honest."

"Are you going to start freelancing again?"

"Only on the side. I think I want to try being on Instagram. Writing there."

"Really?" Bless Gwen, she actually sounded excited at the prospect.

Dylan felt her smile widen. "Yeah. I was thinking about a blog because then I could write longer form stuff, but I don't know if people actually read blogs anymore?"

"I have no clue."

"Right, see, exactly, neither do I." Now out of clothes, Dylan started throwing her shoes in the vague direction of her wardrobe. "I like the idea of Instagram, though, and I honestly feel like it's been going well so far?"

"I've really liked reading your posts. They've felt . . . freer since you left *Buxom*. Like I can hear a lot more of your voice in your writing."

That was just about the best compliment she'd ever received.

"Thanks. I've been working really hard on them."

"I could tell." Gwen bumped her toe against Dylan's thigh.

"It'll be a matter of time before sponsors are practically banging down our door trying to give you money."

"As long as they're the only people banging down our door, I'll be okay."

Gwen's face pinched. "Are people still leaving comments?"

"They were batting around our old address, but they gave it up quickly enough when they realized we didn't live there. I've also gone on quite the blocking spree, which has helped."

"Okay." Gwen still sounded suspicious, and Dylan couldn't blame her. They'd been lulled into false senses of security before.

"If anyone starts kicking off in your comments, let me know." Gwen punched her fist into her hand. "I'll handle them."

Dylan barked a laugh. "Will do."

They ordered a takeaway curry and settled on the sofa, their feet on the coffee table and Cat Stevens meowing desperately between them. As much as she'd enjoyed traveling, she'd missed this. How calm and perfect it was sitting with her best friend, enjoying an amazing dinner, and watching a terrible TV program.

Dylan was able to sit up for a few more hours, but by about eight, she couldn't take it any longer. It was pathetic, getting into bed when it wasn't even nine o'clock, but jet lag was doing everything it could to destroy her and she'd stayed up late enough into the evening that she'd probably wake up at a semi-reasonable time the next morning.

Gwen offered to clean up, and Dylan kissed her gratefully on the cheek before trudging off to take a shower. She'd just unlocked her phone to queue up a YouTube video when she saw the small red *1* on her email app.

From: Chantel Stainton (c.stainton@buxom.co.uk)
To: Dylan Coughlan (d.coughlan@buxom.co.uk)
Subject: Clearing Your Desk

Please report to Buxom tomorrow morning at 9am
sharp to clear out your desk and complete your exit
interview.
CS

Dylan had half a mind to reply that Chantel had literally no business bossing her around anymore, but it wasn't worth the stress she'd just bring on her own head tomorrow. She deleted the email and tossed her mobile onto her bed before going to wash off the layers of airport grime.

She'd just finished getting her pajamas on when her mobile lit up again.

She grabbed it up off the duvet, assuming (or, rather, hoping) it was going to be Jack, and was surprised, instead, to see her mam's name. She stared at the screen for a beat, and when it became clear that she wasn't, in fact, seeing things, she accepted the call.

"Mam?"

"Hiya, Dylan."

Dylan immediately felt tears well up in her eyes at the sound of her mam's voice. She hadn't heard it in so long, had only read her bitter, angry words over text, but hearing it again, and hearing the warmth that had been missing for months, nearly brought Dylan to her knees.

Nearly.

She could still feel herself priming for a fight, waiting for that first jab to send her head spinning. It had to be coming because surely, by now, her mam had read her email and was calling to have it out with Dylan about how she hadn't bothered to ring them and had, instead, sent what she was sure her parents would classify as a "long, whingy note."

But rather than jump immediately down her mam's throat, Dylan decided to try to play it cool first. "Is everything okay?"

"Yeah, yeah." Dylan heard the squeak of springs over the line and knew her mam must have dropped down into her worn leather chair. "I, uh . . . got your email."

Dylan crossed one arm over her chest. "Okay."

"I—" It didn't seem like a good sign that her mam was already choking on her words. "I'm glad you wrote to us."

Dylan sank down into the chair at her desk, her arm falling by her side as she exhaled. She was getting ahead of herself—she was definitely getting ahead of herself—but the feeling of hearing her mother say those words . . .

Knowing everything she'd written in that email, all the feelings she'd kept bottled up for years splashed across the page, she'd never in a million years expected her mother would've been glad Dylan had written it.

"Really?"

"I won't pretend it was fun to read," her mam said, laughing a little in an attempt to smother the awkwardness in her tone, "but it was a lot of things you'd obviously been keeping in for a long time."

"Yeah, Mam." Dylan blinked rapidly to stop the tears falling. "A really, really long time."

"Look, I—" Her mam drew in a deep, shuddering breath. "I

have a lot of regrets about how your father and I treated you this past year. But, um . . . I didn't realize there were other things you were upset about."

That was probably the closest her mam had ever come to acknowledging that she'd done a fair few fucked-up things over the years. Dylan opened WhatsApp and sent Sean a quick message—mam may have just hinted she knows she was being homophobic and toxic prayers up—before pressing her phone back to her ear.

"Yeah, it— I mean, I knew you and Da weren't going to be supportive of my decision to have an abortion." Even hearing it now, her mam drew in a sharp breath. "But I'd at least hoped that you'd understand why I did it and know that it was the right choice for me. That you'd still love me—"

"We do love you."

"It didn't feel like it."

Neither of them spoke for a long minute, the weight of that admission sitting between them.

"Strangers were sending me death threats every day," Dylan said, her voice raw. "People figured out where I lived and started standing outside my house, screaming about how they were going to kill me if I came outside. They made my life hell, and those were the people you agreed with."

"We didn't—"

"You did! They were after me for having the audacity to make my own decisions, to do what I wanted with my own body, and so were you. You agreed with them that I was wrong, that I was a killer. You didn't stand outside my house, Mam, but you shouted your fair share of insults before you abandoned me."

Dylan was barely managing to keep her voice steady now. The

tears in her eyes were starting to stream down her face, but she needed to say this. Needed her mother to hear the words.

"I was afraid of your rejection my whole life. It was constant, from the moment I realized I fancied Olivia Costello in primary school and then when I came out, the way you clung so desperately to the fact that I could still fall in love with a man . . ." Dylan scoffed and shook her head. "It made me feel like I couldn't comfortably be who I am around you. Like you were always waiting for me to be someone different."

"Oh, Dylan, I—" Her mam sounded so deeply uncomfortable, and Dylan's first impulse was to retract everything she'd said, to let them move on from this mess of a conversation, but she stopped herself. Let her mam feel uncomfortable. She should feel uncomfortable, at the very least, for how she'd made Dylan feel for years.

"I'm sorry. I never meant for you to feel like that, I just —We just thought you were young, you know, that you didn't know yet—"

"And yet Sean wasn't too young when he was six and said he'd married some girl in his class."

"We didn't understand it," her mam admitted. "All we knew was that that was probably going to make your life harder and we didn't want that for you."

"My life isn't harder because I'm bisexual, Mam. It's harder because of biphobic arseholes. I'm not the problem."

"No, you're not," her mam said softly.

Dylan thought she might continue speaking, but her mam didn't say anything for a few long minutes.

"Okay, Mam, well—"

"I'm trying to see where you're coming from, Dylan." She

either hadn't heard Dylan trying to end the call or she'd decided to ignore it. "Not about being gay—or, uh, bisexual, but the . . . the abortion."

It seemed like progress that she'd said "abortion" and not "murder."

"I hate it, Dylan. I hate thinking about it."

Dylan couldn't keep the exasperation out of her voice now. "I know you do, Mam."

"But it's not—it's not just what you think. I hate thinking that you didn't trust us. That you didn't talk to us. I could've helped you."

"But I didn't want the help you would've offered me. It would have upended my life. And I know you're going to say I should have thought about that," Dylan said, raising her voice as her mam made an attempt to interrupt, "but it isn't my fault my birth control failed. I'm not going to pay for the rest of my life because of a torn piece of latex."

"No, no, I—" It sounded like there were tears in her mother's eyes. "When you explained that in your email, it . . . it finally started making sense to us, you know. I still don't agree with it, but I don't want this to, well—"

"Here's the thing, Mam." Her voice was hard, maybe too much so, but she was sick of having the same conversation and getting nowhere. "It doesn't ever have to be a choice you would have made. But it's the choice I made because it was best for me. You need to value me and my life and my humanity more than you value something that didn't even properly exist.

"I got my abortion eight years ago. I've never regretted it once, because my life would look nothing like it does now if I hadn't.

And I never want to be a mother . . . Kids deserve someone who wants them."

"I just wish that—"

"It doesn't matter what you wish. It was my choice to make, and I did. And I made it years ago. The moment that article came out, you turned your back on like you couldn't be arsed about the fact that my entire world was crashing down."

"Dylan, I—I'm sorry."

"Yeah"—she swiped the tears out of her eyes—"me, too."

The silence that fell then was heavy but weighted, for once not with things left unsaid but with the full reality of Dylan's feelings. Her mam could ring and apologize all she wanted, but the real test was what came after this moment. How she responded after Dylan laid out everything she'd been carrying around for years.

"Your father and I are going to be in London in a few weeks," her mam said finally. "He got us tickets to *Hairspray* and, well, anyway . . ." Dylan could practically hear her mother waving her hand. "'Dya like to meet us? I'd—we'd love to see you. Talk more."

Dylan's immediate impulse—her protective impulse—urged her to say no. To enforce the perimeter around her and keep her parents as far away as physically possible, because, yes, it hurt at a distance, but at least then she wasn't having to face their anger and disappointment up close. At least she was far enough outside the blast radius to avoid the inevitable fallout.

But she didn't want to think about the fallout as inevitable anymore.

Dylan drew in a deep, slow breath. "Yeah. I'd like that."

After they said their goodbyes, Dylan stared at her phone for a long moment. There were a million more things she was still going to have to say to her parents and she knew that one afternoon wasn't going to be enough to fix everything. It was going to take more than showing up once or twice, but it was the first step they'd taken in a long time, and this time, it felt like a step in the right direction.

Maybe she was getting ahead of herself, letting herself feel excited, but the promise of moving forward made her feel lighter than she had in ages.

She had half a mind to ring Jack to debrief from the entire conversation with her mother. It was feeling a bit raw, though, like it still needed time to sit before she dared touch it, so, in an uncharacteristic move, she decided to say nothing for the time being.

Dylan was just about to toss her phone onto her bed when her screen lit up with a notification, and god, she was already smiling, Jack's name was there on her screen.

> Jack the Posho: My flat's so........
> Jack the Posho: Quiet

She should probably change his contact to his actual name, but there was something deeply amusing about leaving it be. Her smile widened as she sat slowly onto her bed.

> Dylan: mine isn't, but I think I know what you mean
> Jack: Gwen's home?
> Dylan: yeah she was excited to see me. As was Cat Stevens
> Jack: ....What
> Dylan: omg did I not tell you

Jack: About Cat Stevens?! You absolutely did not

Dylan: [image]

Dylan: this is Gwen's cat

Dylan: Cat Stevens

Jack: Oh

Jack: Oh my god

Jack: I thought you meant.......

Dylan: omg I would never be that casual about the actual
   Cat Stevens

Jack: Good to know

Dylan looked down at her screen for a minute, unsure what to say next. It wasn't like this was some high-pressure situation, but now that she was in bed, she could feel sleep tempting her and she felt like she was trying to tread, mentally, through tar. Fortunately, Jack didn't wait for her brain to figure it out.

Jack: Is it sad if I say I'm excited to see you tomorrow?

Dylan: well if it is then I'm sad too

Jack: It's nice to be in good company then

Dylan: ditto

Dylan's fingers hovered over the screen. Finally, she muttered, "Fuck it," under her breath and sent the next message before she could talk herself out of it.

Dylan: I miss you

Luckily for Dylan's sanity, Jack's reply came almost instantly.

Jack: I miss you, too

Jack: I'll see you tomorrow xx

Dylan tapped out a quick reply (see you tomorrow xx) and stuck her mobile onto the charger. She was still smiling like an absolute fool as she slid under the blankets.

CHAPTER 36

While she was tempted to waltz into *Buxom* at half ten just to prove a point, Dylan was only fashionably late the next morning.

It felt almost like an out-of-body experience, being back in this office. She knew these corridors so intimately, had walked along them thousands of times, but today would be the last time she ever saw them. It was funny how something could go from being a massive part of your life to, well, absolutely nothing at all.

Afua jumped out of her chair the moment Dylan rounded the corner.

"Hey!" Afua ran around the desk and pulled Dylan into a hug. Dylan squeezed her tightly, fighting the sudden wave of emotion in her chest.

"I missed you," Dylan said. "How've things been?"

"Chaos," Afua said, lowering her voice. "Chantel might be on her way out."

"Fuck off, are you serious?"

Afua nodded. "I don't think it'll happen for a while, but there's been a lot of whispering about it."

"I never thought we'd see the day."

"I know. Do you think you'd come back if she left?"

Dylan didn't even have to think about it. "Honestly, no. Which feels wild to say," she said with a laugh, "but I think I was too restrained here. Even if I'd gotten that column, it would have been about what Chantel said I could write about, you know?"

Afua glanced covertly around them. "I think I might be right there with you."

"Holy shit," Dylan whispered. "Seriously?"

"Kelly McConville from *Bold* emailed me on Friday. We've got an interview set up tomorrow."

Dylan grabbed Afua's elbows. "That's amazing."

Afua's whole face lit up. "I know. And all the pieces they've been coming out with recently . . . it'd be a great fit."

"Hell yeah, it would."

"Dylan?"

Dylan turned and found Steph, Chantel's assistant, standing a few feet away.

"Hey, Steph." Dylan flashed her a bright smile that seemed to throw her off guard. "Chantel ready for me?"

Chantel was actually sitting behind her desk for once when Dylan walked into her office, her glasses hanging off the bridge of her nose and a stack of paper scattered in front of her. She looked up as the door opened and, when she spotted Dylan, immediately pushed her glasses up into her hair.

"Dylan." Her scary, carefully controlled voice. Okay then. "Take a seat."

Dylan sat, though she didn't get too comfortable.

"I have to say, I'm extremely disappointed in you."

Dylan almost laughed. "Okay."

Chantel seemed perplexed at Dylan's lack of argument, but pressed on. "You had the opportunity to finally get a column and—"

"No, I didn't."

"—you threw it away." Chantel's brows furrowed as she realized what Dylan said. "Yes, you did. We'd talked about it."

"And then you said it was too dangerous."

"We had to change tack, Dylan," Chantel said dismissively. "You were receiving threats."

"Don't pretend it was out of concern for me," Dylan said, rolling her eyes. "You knew that publicly silencing me was effectively shoving all the blame and trolls onto me and making everyone think you didn't support me."

"We're going to have to agree to disagree there."

Of course they were, because Dylan was right.

"I'm more concerned with your use of the administrative logins for your little stunt."

"It wasn't a stunt, it was an apology. And I've already resigned, so there's nothing you can really do about it."

Chantel stared at her for a long beat, her expression like daggers.

"We've discussed legal action."

Dylan actually laughed out loud this time. "There's nothing that says I can't use them, Chantel. There's nothing sensitive on the posting platform and those log-ins were given to me by a member of staff."

She pushed herself to her feet. As fun as it was trading insults, she didn't have time to play games anymore.

"I'm going to clean out my desk. Best of luck, Chantel."

Dylan was out of the office before Chantel could say another word.

One hour and two very full canvas bags later, Dylan was waiting outside Oxford Circus station so she and Jack could walk the short distance to the BBC. She'd been replying to Instagram comments when someone shouted her name from down the pavement and she looked up.

"Dylan!"

Jack waved as their eyes caught, and Dylan's smile took over her entire face.

She skipped over, bloody skipped, her bags clanging against her shoulder and everything, and kissed him hello. Jack grinned at her enthusiasm.

"Happy to see me, I assume."

She snorted. "That sounds like a chat-up line."

"Wasn't aware I still needed to be chatting you up."

"Were you ever?"

He laughed and wrapped an arm around her shoulders. "I was certainly trying."

"Well, that's awkward, isn't it?"

Jack pressed a kiss to her temple. "How was your day?"

He'd looked happy to see her when she'd first arrived, but there was something incandescent about the way he was looking at her then.

"You seem extra cheery today."

"Just glad to be here with you."

She nudged him gently in the ribs. "Melt."

"Whatever. I missed you."

He said it so plainly, like it was the most obvious thing in the world, and Dylan's heart swelled.

"I guess I missed you, too."

Jack laughed. "*You guess*. I think it's more than *you guess*."

"Hmm, I don't think so."

He quirked an eyebrow at her and moved like he was going to get his mobile out of his pocket. "Shall I get the evidence?"

She grabbed his arm, laughing as she tried to still him. "No, no, fine! I missed you, too."

Jack grinned, absolutely beamed, and caught her lips in a kiss.

"My day wasn't that exciting, to be fair," she said. "Just packed up my desk." She gestured to the bags hanging off her shoulder as evidence.

"Humor me anyway."

She gave him the overview—the look on Chantel's face as she walked out, Afua's news, the feeling of relief that she wasn't going back there.

Jack kissed her temple, his smile imprinting itself against her skin. "I'm so glad."

"Me, too. It was a welcome change from last night, I'll tell you."

He frowned. "What happened last night?"

"My mam rang." She tried to say it casually, but judging by the look on Jack's face, she hadn't managed the effect.

"What?"

"Yeah." Dylan swallowed. She was nervous now that she couldn't play it off like it meant nothing. "We had it out for a while, actually."

She recounted their conversation, just barely avoiding bursting into tears. Jack's expression became increasingly worried until his brows were so furrowed they were nearly a unibrow.

"She said that she and Da are going to be in town soon and wanted to meet," Dylan said. "To talk about everything."

"How do you feel about that?"

She let herself focus on the brush of his thumb against her skin for a moment. "I think it'll be hard, you know, but it'll be good. I hope it will be anyway. I'm sick of fighting with them. Honestly, even if we leave that conversation deciding we just can't make it work, it'll be better off."

"Yeah." When she turned, Jack was smiling at her, another one of those soft, bracing smiles she loved. "I think you're right."

"I was wondering if, uh . . ." She drew in a swift breath. "If maybe you wanted to go out after. Like, meet down the pub or something. To either celebrate or help me drown myself in gin."

She thought that he might laugh at her joke—she'd laughed—but Jack was completely earnest as he said, "Absolutely. We can get a trial run in tonight if you want—I told my parents this morning I needed to . . . not hear from them for a while."

"Really?! You spoke to them?"

Jack's cheeks flushed pink. "I texted. I didn't feel like arguing."

Dylan squeezed his hand. "You don't have to explain yourself to me." She waited until he looked at her before continuing. "I'm glad you stood up for yourself. No offense, but your parents sound like fucking arseholes."

He exhaled a laugh. "Yeah, well, they'd started breathing down my neck the minute we got off the plane. My dad had already emailed, like, five people begging them to employ me." Jack shook his head, and even though there was still frustration there, Dylan thought she saw pride, too.

"They've had more than their fair share of say in my life. I think it's time I actually sort things out for once."

Dylan wrapped her arms around his waist and actually gave him a shake. "Yes!"

Mina met them in reception outside the Radio 1 offices, her eyeliner electric pink today, just as cutting as Dylan remembered.

"We're going to have you on at the top of the hour," Mina said, leading them to the recording studio. "We have a nice long advert spot before, so there's plenty of prep time."

Dylan glanced at Jack. He seemed stiffer than he had a moment before, but the difference was subtle. There was a slight wrinkle across his forehead and his shoulders were pushed up toward his ears.

She touched her fingertips to his forearm, so lightly she worried Jack wouldn't feel it through his sleeve. When he looked at her, she raised her eyebrows and mouthed, *Are you okay?*

Jack nodded and took her hand, the tension easing out of his shoulders as he laced their fingers together.

"Dylan!" Scott beamed as they stepped into the studio and held out his hand for her to shake. "How're you?"

"I'm great, Scott, how're you? How's London been?"

"Lovely as always," Scott said, laughing. He turned to Jack. "And you must be Jack."

Jack shook his hand. "Nice to meet you."

"You as well. Now . . ." Scott clapped his hands together before he walked back around the desk. "You've only got one segment, so we aren't going to be here long. We'll be back on air in twenty." He pointed at two pairs of headphones on the desk. "Go ahead and pop those on."

Dylan and Jack were still adjusting their headphones when the introduction music started up.

"Welcome back to Radio 1. You just heard Mabel's 'Don't Call Me Up.' We'll be back to the music in a few minutes, but, first"— Scott caught Dylan's gaze—"I want to welcome our Around the World contest winners! Dylan and Jack, welcome back to Radio 1!"

They both leaned forward and said, "Thank you," into their microphones.

Scott smiled. "How was the holiday?"

"We had a great time," Dylan said, "but I don't think either of us is sad that we won't be in another airport for a while."

Jack laughed and Dylan looked up at him. He was grinning, his eyes bright in the dim studio, and he nudged his knee against hers under the table.

"Definitely not," he agreed. "We've spent more than enough time queuing at immigration this year."

Scott chuckled. "I'm glad you both had a good time, though, Dylan, your Instagram definitely gave me a bit of FOMO."

"Just the bit?" Dylan asked.

"Alright, more than a bit."

Dylan laughed. "Well, it's all because of you that we were able to go anyway, so you only have yourself to thank. And Jack's the photographer, so I can't take credit for that, either. His Instagram has even better pictures, you've got to see them—Jack Hunton Photography."

Scott turned to Jack. "Is that right?"

"Yeah, I, uh—" Jack scrubbed a hand through his hair. "I wasn't officially a photographer at the time, but I've decided to give freelance photography a more permanent go. So if you need someone—"

Jack exhaled shakily and rested his hand on Dylan's thigh. His smile softened as he turned to face her, his lips closer to her ear than the microphone. "Thanks for the push."

Dylan beamed. This was exactly what she'd been hoping for when she mentioned it.

She met his gaze, their faces only inches apart. "Anytime."

Something lit up in Scott's expression. "Ah. Seems like Jack's job isn't the only thing that's changed, then." When neither of them said anything, he elaborated. "You two seem fairly close?"

The implication in his question was clear, and though Dylan knew it wasn't going to make Scott any less suspicious, she couldn't help glancing at Jack again. Her stomach nearly bottomed out when she found him already looking at her.

"Yeah." Jack's smile widened, and Dylan watched curiously as he pulled his mobile out of his pocket and started typing. "We've bonded a bit."

The smile on Scott's face was clear in his voice when he spoke. "I'll say."

"Honestly, I—" Jack swallowed. "I'm really grateful you chose me out of her phone."

Jack slid his phone across the desk and Dylan saw he'd written something in his notes app.

It wasn't just a holiday thing for me. No pressure, but if you're ready for this, I'm yours xx

The words sank straight through her skin, twisting her up with excitement until she felt like she might burst with it.

"It was one of the best experiences I've ever had," Jack continued. He was very carefully not watching her read, as though he was worried about her reaction. As if he'd ever had anything to worry about. "Every city was beautiful but getting to see everything with someone as incredible as Dylan was life-changing."

She couldn't take it. Each word made her heart swell until the pressure against her ribs was so great she couldn't draw breath. Dylan grabbed Jack's hand underneath the table, desperate for some way to tell him how much this meant to her, how much he meant to her. His hand was trembling, but the moment she slid her fingers through his, he gave her hand a deep squeeze.

"I feel the same way," Dylan said. She could hear the emotion in her voice, but she couldn't be arsed to contain it. "I can't imagine having had these experiences with anyone else."

"The internet was wildly speculating about the two of you a few weeks ago." Scott's voice was careful, like he knew he was walking across very thin ice. "But you mentioned in your apology article, Dylan, that the relationship was nonexistent?"

Dylan glanced toward Jack once more, wanting his consent. He tipped his head slightly to the side, leaving it up to her, and Dylan grinned into the microphone.

"Well, it was then, but, uh, it's very much existent now."

Scott beamed at them and tapped a button on the switchboard that played simulated audience applause.

"Congratulations!"

Jack and Dylan both laughed and said, "Thanks," at the same time. They turned and looked at each other, mingled relief and amusement on their faces.

"When did this happen, if you don't mind my asking?"

Dylan flashed Jack an amused smile. "Very recently."

Jack's lips twitched. "She kept me on my toes until the last possible moment."

Dylan nudged him with her knee under the table and he laughed, his smile widening.

"And what are you planning on doing now that you're home?"

Scott asked. "How are you going to keep that spark alive now you're not traveling the world?"

Dylan had opened her mouth to respond—to say something about how happy she was they were home, how excited she was to see how they fitted together in London—when Jack replied.

"I'm just excited for all the normal stuff. Complaining about the tube, sorting out work plans—"

Dylan nodded. "We've got a row in Tescos on the schedule for next week."

She'd been going for a very serious effect, but Jack laughed out loud.

"I can't wait," he said.

Scott sighed. "Well, you two are adorable. I wish you both the best of luck, stay in touch with us, alright?"

They said, "Yeah," and, "Of course," in unison, and Scott smiled at them as he hit a few buttons on the keyboard in front of him. "Thanks again for coming on, guys, and thank you, Jack, for filling our Instagram with some really amazing photos over the last few weeks. Now, sit tight, I've got a few adverts for you, but we'll be back with rising star Holly Humberstone in ninety seconds."

Jack took her hand as they walked out of the station fifteen minutes later, and even though they were both wearing gloves, she felt a shock of electricity race up her arm.

"When I said it wasn't a holiday thing, I meant it," he said softly, his voice sliding like crushed velvet over her skin. "It's kind of scary how much I like you, honestly."

Even though her heart was soaring straight out of her chest, she couldn't help teasing him. "Why is it scary?"

"Because I don't know what to do now that you aren't around

all the time," he said. It was the kind of honesty she never would have gotten from him a few weeks ago. "It's not even been twenty-four hours, and I'm already so tragic."

"You were always tragic." Her words were practically trembling with excitement.

Jack frowned, and she laughed brightly before pressing a kiss to the edge of his mouth, smiling at the way he immediately softened.

"You know I only want you." She stayed close, and when he turned toward her, the tip of his nose brushed against hers. "No one else."

Jack hummed, the sound rumbling through his chest and straight into hers. His hand found her hip, his fingers pressing gently into her skin. He could have stopped walking, pulled their bodies together, and while part of her mind was now very busy thinking about how that might play out, the rest of her was very aware of the other people trying to walk along the pavement without being subjected to softcore porn.

"I only want you, too," he whispered, his lips brushing against hers. "No one else."

Her heart was so full she was sure she'd never be able to contain it. She kissed him again, the angle slightly awkward as they continued along the pavement, but the promise in it, the potential, made it one of the best kisses of her life.

"So, you're excited about the normal stuff, eh?" she said, squinting against the sun that had, miraculously, come out from behind the clouds. She wished she'd thought to stuff her sunglasses into her bag this morning, but her only pair was still buried in the detritus on her floor, possibly never to be seen again.

"Yeah," Jack said. "I loved traveling, but—maybe this is silly—I want to settle into this, you know? With you."

She did know. She knew exactly.

"You don't think it'll get boring? After running all over the world together?"

Jack laughed and shook his head, almost in disbelief. "I don't think anything could be boring with you around."

"True." He laughed at her immediate agreement. She squeezed his hand. "What kinds of normal things are you thinking?"

"Meeting up for dinner, complaining about our parents." He started swinging their hands between them and he was smiling at her and looked absolutely radiant in this light. "Staying over at each other's flats, getting groceries. Maybe having a nice picnic."

"I feel like I need to remind you that it's winter and the ground is going to be sopping wet until June."

He laughed and squeezed her hand again, tugging her into his side so he could kiss the side of her head. "Maybe we'll just go down the pub, then."

She felt like her cheeks were going to crack, but she couldn't stop smiling. The travel had been brilliant and life-changing and everything else, but this was where the real test would be. When they had to sink into the fabric of each other's actual lives and see how they fitted.

Dylan, for one, couldn't wait.

"I'm quite partial to my local if you think you can find your way to East London."

Jack laughed, and this time, he wrapped his arm around her shoulders. "I think I've already proven I'd follow you anywhere."

ACKNOWLEDGMENTS

This book would absolutely not have made it into the world without the support of so many wonderful people. Writing and publishing a book has been a dream of mine for as long as I can remember, and I am forever grateful to each and every person who helped make my dream come true.

A massive thank you to my wonderful agent, Jill Marr. From our very first call, I knew that you were the right champion for me and my globe-trotting book. Your joy and enthusiasm make me glad every single day that you connected with this story—I can't imagine venturing off into this with anyone else as my advocate. Thank you for putting up with my weird PowerPoint pitches, my too-long outlines, and the awful times I'm sure I email you given our time difference. I'm also so grateful for the entire team at Sandra Dijkstra Literary Agency—thank you, in particular, to Jennifer Kim and Andrea Cavallaro. I appreciate you and all your hard work behind the scenes.

Thank you to my brilliant editor, Gaby Mongelli—we had the most amazing mind meld from the moment we met, and it made working with you an absolute dream. Your love for this book and these characters infused every note and made this so easy. I cannot thank you enough for seeing the vision and knowing what this book could be, and for your guidance and ideas that always spark something in my head. I'm so glad we get to do this all over again with Book Two!

Everyone at Putnam was a true joy to work with. Thank you to Sanny Chiu, who designed a gorgeous cover that brought my book to life. Thank you to Leah Marsh, who made sure I didn't make silly mistakes (and for making me laugh when you pointed out my mistakes, because, wow, I made some silly ones). Thank you to Elke Sigal and Brittany Bergman for taking a Word document and transforming it into a book. Thank you to Sally Kim. Thank you to the wonderful marketing and publicity team: Molly Pieper, Nicole Biton, Ashley McClay, and Alexis Welby. You are a dream team, and I cannot have asked for a better group of people to work with. This book is what it is because of your hard work, and I appreciate each of you more than I can ever say.

Thank you, too, to my amazing UK editor, Hannah Smith. Bringing this book to our side of the pond with you has been the most amazing experience. I'm grateful to the entire team at Michael Joseph—thank you for making this book shine in the UK.

Enormous thank you to my Pitch Wars family! Jenny Howe and Courtney Kae, you were amazing mentors, and Dylan and Jack's story became what it is because of your feedback and never-ending support. I am so lucky that I now get to call you my friends, and I'm eternally grateful to Pitch Wars for bringing us together. Thank you to KT Hoffman, Alexandra Kiley, Jessica James, and all the wonderful 2021 mentees. You kept me laughing and were always so generous with your support and kindness. Thank you to Swati Hegde and Cassio, too, who were some of my first betas for *Wanderlust*—I can't believe you read that incredibly dodgy fourth draft, and I cannot thank you enough for the feedback that helped this book start growing into itself. Thank you to Sam and Marika for reading the (still dodgy) sixth draft—your excitement, encouragement, and feedback made this a better book. To the #2023debuts authors: I'm so honored to be part of your debut class. Without you, and without our incredibly detailed Slack full of resources and kind, supportive people, I'm not sure I would've known what to do this year.

I also have some silly but nonetheless important thank yous. Thank you to Friendly Space Ninja, lilsimsie, and Mike's Mic for creating content that helped me keep my head on when I was overwhelmed. You'll never read this (probably), but I need to put my thanks out into the universe anyway because I couldn't have gotten through revising this book without you and your creations. Thanks to TFL for providing the perfect (read: very loud) backdrop for my frantic after-school writing sessions, and thank you to Carly Rae Jepsen for always making music that speaks directly to my soul. I needed it more than once over the years I spent working on this project.

My biggest thank yous—my sappiest thank yous—to my amazing friends and family who tolerated me through the ups and downs that finally led to this book making its way into the world. To my dad, who has been excitedly asking about this book and everything happening with it since the moment I first told him Jill had offered to represent me, and for trying to strategize even when there was nothing to strategize about. You've told me time and time again how proud you are (and you keep trying to prove it by buying copies of this book), and I can't thank you enough for the reminder that I should be proud of myself and should celebrate these moments more before moving on to the next thing. To my sisters, Hannah and Megan, who I love and miss every day because I moved myself across the sea. Thanks for being as excited about this book as I am and for sending me SnapChats every minute of every day that make me feel like we aren't thousands of miles apart. I'm a little mortified at the idea of you actually reading this book, but I love you both endlessly (even if I prefer to make sarcastic jokes at your expense rather than tell you that). To my best friend, Eli, who has been listening to me blather on about nonsense for nine years and who is such a brilliant, supportive, hilarious person. Eli, you, Vanessa, Momo, and Biscuit are the best friends anyone could ask for and I love you. To the friends who bring a smile to my face every day: Mal, Ashley, Sarah, Sam, Beks, Serena, Eloise. To my fellow teachers who help me keep my head on straight, especially during full teaching days. To Muffin—I know you're a dog and, thus, can't read, but thank you for having the softest tummy fluff in the universe. Lying on the floor with you and avoiding my laptop at all costs was a very important part of the writing process and, without it, this book definitely wouldn't exist.

And, finally, thank you to Emmet, who, as a Leo, is probably very annoyed I've left him until last. I love you more than everything else in the world. Thank you for ignoring me while I sing TikTok sounds around the flat (and I'm sorry for "accidentally" getting said sounds stuck in your head) and for singing with so much enthusiasm whenever we start our near-daily Whitney Houston/Cher/ABBA singalongs. Thank you for listening to me exclaim how hilarious I am from the other room and for coming up with increasingly elaborate plans to market this book. I love your enthusiasm, but I don't think this book is appropriate for your school library. Thank you, too, for hiding my phone when I couldn't stop watching restocking TikToks. I definitely wouldn't've finished this book otherwise.

And I know I said finally, but thank you to you, too, for reading this book. I sincerely hope you enjoyed it and I cannot thank you enough for giving my words some of your time.

xx Elle

DISCUSSION GUIDE

1. If given the chance, would you enter a contest for an around-the-world trip? If so, who would you bring with you?

2. From the beginning, it's clear that Dylan and Jack are opposites. Why do you think they work well together? What is it about each of them that complements the other?

3. Dylan has always wanted to be a writer, but how does she find her voice throughout the course of the novel? Compare her work for *Buxom* with her personal posts. Where does she feel most herself in her work?

4. Whose travel style do you align with—Dylan's or Jack's?

5. Throughout the trip, Jack experiences a big transformation of his own. How do their adventures push him out of his comfort zone? Did your opinion of him change over the course of the novel?

6. As her article series takes off, Dylan starts to blur the boundaries of her and Jack's relationship in her writing. In what ways does Dylan cross the line? Do you think Jack's frustration with what she writes is justified?

7. Did you have a favorite location that Dylan and Jack visited? What was it about that city that appealed to you?

8. A big part of *Wanderlust* is the impact that the internet and social media can have on our personal lives. How much of one's life do you think should be broadcast online? What are some ways that social media can be rewarding? How can it be potentially harmful?

9. Dylan and Jack both have complicated relationships with their families. Discuss the ways in which they each either find support or strain in their connections to their parents and siblings. How do these support systems, or lack thereof, shape Dylan's and Jack's lives? How have their families impacted them by the novel's end?

10. What do you think is next for Dylan and Jack?

Author Photo Credit Solveig Settemsdal

Elle Everhart writes romantic comedies featuring the internet, sarcasm, and lots of queer characters. She is a secondary English teacher in East London, and when she's not writing or teaching, she's hanging out with her son and obsessing over the worst shows on television. *Wanderlust* is her debut novel.